Seduced by the Rebel

SUSAN STEPHENS
ANNE OLIVER
LINDSAY ARMSTRONG

D0522755

Published in Great Britain 2014
by Mills & Boon, an imprint of Harlequin (UK) Limited,
Eton House, 18-24 Paradise Road, Richmond, Surrey, TW9 1SR

SEDUCED BY THE REBEL © 2014 Harlequin Books S.A.

The Big Bad Boss, There's Something About a Rebel… and *The Socialite and the Cattle King* were first published in Great Britain by Harlequin (UK) Limited.

The Big Bad Boss © 2011 Susan Stephens
There's Something About a Rebel… © 2011 Anne Oliver
The Socialite and the Cattle King © 2010 Lindsay Armstrong

ISBN: 978-0-263-91195-4
eBook ISBN: 978-1-472-04490-7

05-0814

Harlequin (UK) Limited's policy is to use papers that are natural, renewable and recyclable products and made from wood grown in sustainable forests. The logging and manufacturing processes conform to the legal environmental regulations of the country of origin.

Printed and bound in Spain
by Blackprint CPI, Barcelona

THE BIG BAD BOSS

BY
SUSAN STEPHENS

Susan Stephens was a professional singer before meeting her husband on the tiny Mediterranean island of Malta. In true Modern™ romance style they met on Monday, became engaged on Friday, and were married three months after that. Almost thirty years and three children later, they are still in love. (Susan does not advise her children to return home one day with a similar story, as she may not take the news with the same fortitude as her own mother!)

Susan had written several non-fiction books when fate took a hand. At a charity costume ball there was an after-dinner auction. One of the lots, 'Spend a Day with an Author', had been donated by Mills & Boon® author Penny Jordan. Susan's husband bought this lot, and Penny was to become not just a great friend but a wonderful mentor, who encouraged Susan to write romance.

Susan loves her family, her pets, her friends and her writing. She enjoys entertaining, travel, and going to the theatre. She reads, cooks, and plays the piano to relax, and can occasionally be found throwing herself off mountains on a pair of skis or galloping through the countryside. Visit Susan's website: www.susanstephens.net—she loves to hear from her readers all around the world!

CHAPTER ONE

'*DAWN. and in front of us the idyllic English country scene. Smell that grass. Look at that thin stream of sunlight driving night-shadows down the velvet hills—*'

How long did he have to stay here?

With an exasperated roar, Heath flipped channels, silencing the farming programme. All he'd smelled so far was cow dung. And it was raining.

Resting his chin on one arm, he slammed his foot down on the accelerator. The Lamborghini roared drowning out the birdsong. Perfect. He missed the concrete jungle—no smells, no mud, no cranky plumbing. Why Uncle Harry had left him a run-down country estate remained a mystery. Heath was allergic to the country—to anything that didn't come with dot-com attached. His empire had been built in a bedroom. What did he need all this for?

And it was only after asking himself that question that he spotted the tent someone had erected on a mossy bank just inside the gates…spotted the small pink feet sticking out of the entrance. Forget hating the place. He felt proprietorial suddenly. What would he do if someone pitched a tent outside the front door of his London home?

Stopping the car, he climbed out. Striding up to the tent, he unzipped it.

A yelp of surprise ripped through the steady drum of falling rain. Standing back, he folded his arms, waiting for developments. He didn't have long to wait. A strident pixie crawled out, screaming at him that it was the middle of the night as she sprang to her feet. Red hair flying, she stood like an irate stick insect telling him what she thought of him in language as colourful as the clothes she was frantically tugging on—a camouflage top, and shot-off purple leggings that displayed her tiny feet. One furious glance at his car and he was responsible for everything from frightening the local wildlife to global warming, apparently, until finally, having got over the shock of being so rudely awakened, she gulped, took a breath, and exclaimed, 'Heath Stamp...' Clapping a hand to her chest, she stared at him as if she couldn't believe her eyes.

'Bronte Foster-Jenkins,' he murmured, taking her in.

'I've been expecting you—'

'So I see,' he said, glancing at the tent.

Expecting Heath to arrive? Yes, but not her reaction to it. He wasn't supposed to arrive at dawn, either. Around midday, the postmistress in the village had suggested. Heath Stamp, hip, slick, rugged, tough, and even better looking than his most recent images in the press suggested. This was a vastly improved version of someone she'd dreamed about for thirteen years, two months, six hours, and—

'You do know you're trespassing, Bronte?'

And as delightful as ever.

The years melted away. They were at loggerheads immediately. She had to remind herself Heath was no longer a wild youth who'd been locked up for bare-knuckle fighting, and who used to visit Hebers Ghyll on a release programme, but a successful Internet entrepreneur and the new owner of Hebers Ghyll, the country estate where Bronte had grown up, and where her mother had been the housekeeper and her father the gamekeeper. 'The estate has been deserted for weeks now—'

'And that's an excuse for breaking in?'

'The gates were open. Everything's gone to pot,' she told him angrily.

'And that's my fault?'

'You own it. You tell me.' Heath's inheritance had a special hold on her heart for all sorts of reasons, not least of which she considered the estate her second home.

While Heath had gained nothing in charm, Bronte registered as he turned his back, he clearly still couldn't care less what people thought of him. He never had.

He'd walked off to give them both space. Seeing Bronte again had floored him. Since the first time he had visited the estate—where ironically his real-life uncle Harry had used to run a rehabilitation centre for out-of-control youths—there had been something between him and Bronte, something that drew the good girl to the dark side. He'd tried to steer clear, not wanting to taint her. But he would think about her when he sat alone and stared at his bruised knuckles. She was light to his darkness. Back then Bronte had represented everything that was pure, fun and happy, while he was the youth from the gutter who met every challenge with his fists. He'd worshipped her from afar, had she only known it. That buzz between them surely should have died by now.

'That tree was struck by lightning, and no one's moved it,' she said, reclaiming his attention.

He hadn't even realised he'd been staring at the old tree, but now he remembered Uncle Harry telling him that it had stood on the estate for centuries.

'It'll stay there until it rots, I suppose,' she flared.

'I'll have it moved.' He shrugged. 'Maybe have something planted in its place.'

'It would mean more if you did it.'

He threw her a glance, warning her not to push it. But she would. She always had. Bronte loved a campaign whether it was free the chickens, or somewhere for the local youth to hang out.

'And just think of all the free firewood,' she said casually.

She was working on him. When hadn't she? And now it all came flooding back—what she'd done for him—and how he used to envy Bronte her simple life on the estate with her happy family. He'd felt a hungry desperation to share what they had but had never allowed them to draw him in, in case he spoiled it. He'd spoiled everything back then.

And now?

He was still hard and contained.

And Hebers Ghyll?

Was in the pending file.

And Bronte?

Heath raked his hair with impatience.

This was all happening too fast, way too fast. She hadn't expected to feel as shaken as this when she saw Heath again. Heading for the shelter of some trees where the thick green canopy acted like a giant umbrella, she sucked in some deep steadying breaths. She had to remind herself why she was here—to find out what

Heath's plans for the estate were. 'I heard the new owner was going to break up the estate—'

'And?'

'You can't.' Bronte's heart picked up pace as Heath came to join her beneath the branches. 'You don't know enough about the area as it is today. You don't know how desperate people are for jobs. You haven't been near the place for years—'

'And you have?'

Bronte's cheeks flared red. Yes, she'd been away, but her travels had been geared towards putting what she had learned at college into practice. As a child she had dogged Uncle Harry's footsteps, trying to be useful and asking him endless questions about Hebers Ghyll. He'd said she was a good lieutenant and might make a decent estate manager one day if she worked hard enough. When she left school Uncle Harry had paid for her to go to college to study estate management. 'I've been away recently,' she conceded, 'but apart from that I've lived on the estate all my life.'

'So, what are you saying, Bronte? You're the only one who cares about Hebers Ghyll?' Heath's chin dipped a warning.

'Well, do you care,' Bronte exclaimed with frustration, 'beyond its value?'

'I'd be foolish not to care about its value.'

'But there's so much more than money here.' And she had been prepared to camp out on the road leading up to the old house for as long as it took to prove that to him. 'Why else do you think I scrabbled round my parents' attic to find the old tent?' Heath's dark gaze flashed a warning, which she ignored. 'Do you think I like camping out in the rain?'

'I don't know what you like.'

The gulf between them yawned. It might have been easier to explain and convince Heath if she had seen him recently. The shock of seeing him again after all these years was something she hadn't anticipated. It wasn't how tall he was, or how good-looking—it was the aura of danger and unapologetic masculinity she found so unnerving.

'So, Bronte,' Heath observed in the laid-back husky voice that had always made her toes curl with excitement, 'what can I do for you?'

She exhaled, refusing to think about it. 'By the time I got back here, Heath, Uncle Harry was dead and everything was in a mess. No one on the estate or in the village had a clue what was going to happen—or whether they still had jobs—'

'And your parents?' Heath prompted.

She guessed Heath already knew the answer to that. The lawyers would have filled him in on what had happened to the staff at Hebers Ghyll. 'I can only think Uncle Harry must have realised he was gravely ill, because he gave my parents some money before he died. He told them to take a break—to fulfil their lifetime's ambition of travelling the world.' She was hugging herself for reassurance, Bronte realised, releasing her arms. It was hard to launch a cogent argument in defence of the estate while Heath was staring at her so intently. He knew her too well. Even after all this time he could sense what she wasn't saying. He could sense how she felt. They had always been uncannily connected, though when Heath had first arrived on the estate she'd been more concerned that the ruffian Uncle Harry was trying to tame would tear the head off her dolls. The feeling Heath inspired in her now was very different. 'I can't believe you're the Master of Hebers Ghyll,' she said, shaking her head.

'And you don't like the idea?'

'I didn't say that—'

'You didn't have to. Perhaps you think Uncle Harry should have left his estate to you—'

'No,' Bronte exclaimed indignantly. 'That never occurred to me. You're his nephew, Heath. I'm only the housekeeper's daughter—'

'Who walked in here and made herself at home.' He glanced at her tent.

'The gates were open. Ask your estate manager if you don't believe me.'

'That man was employed by Uncle Harry's executors and no longer works for me.'

'Well, whoever he was…' Bronte's voice faded when she realised Heath had only owned the estate five minutes and had already sacked one member of staff.

'He was a waste of space,' Heath rapped. 'And replaceable.'

Heath unnerved her. Was everyone replaceable in Heath's world?

'If there are so many people clamouring for jobs in the area,' he said, reclaiming her attention, 'it shouldn't take me long to find another man—'

'Or a woman.'

Heath huffed a humourless laugh. 'Still the same Bronte.'

The last time they'd had this sort of stand-off she'd been twelve and Heath fifteen, difficult ages for both of them, impossible to find common ground. Those years had changed nothing, Bronte registered, conscious of her furiously erect nipples beneath the flimsy top. She casually folded her arms across her chest. 'When can we meet for a proper talk?'

'When you approach me through the proper channels.'

'I tried to call you, but your PA wouldn't put me through. I'm only here now because I was determined to talk to you.'

'You? Determined, Bronte?' The first glint of humour broke through Heath's fierce façade.

'Someone had to find out what was going on.'

'And as usual that someone's you?'

'I offered to be a spokesperson.'

'You offered?' Heath pulled back his head to look at her through narrowed storm-grey eyes. 'What a surprise.'

'So, are you going to tell me what your plans are for the estate?' Why wouldn't her pulse slow down?

Because of that aura of bad-boy danger surrounding Heath, her inner voice supplied. The years hadn't changed it—and they certainly hadn't diminished it.

'I'll tell you what I'm going to do,' Heath said.

'Yes?' She held her ground tensely as he strolled towards her.

'This place is a mess,' he said, his gesture taking in broken fences, crumbling walls and overgrown hedgerows, 'and probate took time. But I'm here now. What happens next?' She swallowed deep as he looked down at her. 'I make an assessment.'

'That's it?' she whispered, hypnotised by his eyes.

'That's it,' Heath confirmed harshly, wheeling away. 'You haven't been inside the house yet, I take it?'

Bronte's brave front faltered. 'No. I came straight here.' Now her imagination had raced into overdrive. The estate comprised a hall and a broken-down castle as well as a great deal of land. Uncle Harry had lived at the hall, and had always kept it as well as he could afford to—which wasn't very well, but if anything was less than perfect it was only because Uncle Harry spent so much of his money helping others. The original stained-glass windows were beautiful, she remembered, and there was a wonderful wood-panelled library where the log fire was always burning, and a spotless, if anti-quated, kitchen, which had been her mother's domain. Was all that changed? 'What's happened, Heath?' she said anxiously. 'Can I help?'

'What can you do?' he said.

She was surprised he had to ask. And hurt that he had. It made her more determined than ever to find out what Heath's true intentions were. 'Rumours say you've already sold the Hebers Ghyll estate on—'

'Anything else?' Heath demanded, folding his power-ful arms across his chest.

His eyes were every bit as beautiful as she remem-bered and just as cold. She shook herself round. 'And bulldozers—I heard talk of bulldozers.' There was no point sugar-coating this. She might just as well confront him with the lot. 'One rumour said you were going to bring in a wrecking crew to knock everything down, and then you'd build a shopping centre—'

'And what if I did?'

Panic hit her at the thought that he might—that he could—that he had every right to. 'What about Uncle Harry?'

'Uncle Harry's dead.'

Heath might as well have stabbed a knife through her heart. Heath had always been closed off to feelings except on those rare occasions when he had lightened up in front of Bronte or Uncle Harry. Sometimes she won-dered if they were the only people he had ever opened up to. And that was a memory so faint she couldn't believe it had ever happened now. 'For goodness' sake, Heath, you're his nephew—don't you feel anything?' To hell with the job she had intended to apply for. 'Does Hebers Ghyll mean anything to you? Don't you remember what Uncle Harry used to do—?'

'For kids like me?' Heath interrupted her coldly. She'd taken him back to the past, and his father, Uncle Harry's wastrel brother—the poor relation with the taste for violence. Only at the court's insistence had his father agreed to a period of rehabilitation for Heath at Hebers Ghyll under Uncle Harry's direction. And how he'd fought it. Heath had thrown Uncle Harry's kindness back in his face. A fact he'd spent his adult life regretting.

'You know I didn't mean that,' Bronte assured him. 'Uncle Harry loved having you around. You must have known you were the son he never had?'

'Don't use those tactics on me, Bronte.'

'Tactics?' she exploded. 'I'm not using tactics. I'm telling you the truth. Don't pretend you don't care, Heath. I know you better than that—'

'You know me?' he snarled, dipping his chin.

'Yes. I know you,' she argued stubbornly, refusing to back down.

'You knew me then,' he said. And he didn't like reminders of then.

'I don't want to fight with you, Heath.'

Her voice had turned softer. Bronte backing down? That had to be a first. Had the years smoothed her out? Remembering her welcome, he guessed not. 'Apology accepted,' he said. But even as their eyes met and held he knew this small concession was the first step on the road to damnation, the first nod to his libido. Bronte was still as attractive as ever—more so, when she was all fired up.

'It's important Uncle Harry's work here continue,' she told him, her brow creasing with passion. 'And with you at the helm, Heath,' she added with less conviction.

His senses stirred. She was magnificent with those green eyes blazing and that dainty jaw jutting. She was unflinching. Boudicca of the Yorkshire moors. But she was also uneasy and unsure of him. She was unsure of what he'd do. Thinking back to what seemed like another life to him now, he couldn't blame her. 'You'll be the first to know when I make my decision. But know this: I don't do weekends. I don't do holidays. And I don't need a country house. You work it out.'

'I think that answers my question,' The green gaze remained steady on his face.

'If you care so much about Hebers Gyll, what are you going to do about it?' he said, turning the tables on her.

'I won't walk away without a fight.'

He didn't doubt it. 'And in practical terms?'

She tilted her chin at a determined angle. 'Whether or not you keep the estate, I'm going to apply for the job of estate manager.'

He laughed out loud. She really had surprised him now. 'Making jam tarts with your mother at the kitchen table hardly qualifies you for that.'

'You're not the only one to have made something of yourself, Heath,' she fired back. 'I have qualifications in estate management—and I've travelled the world, studying how vast tracts of land and properties like this can be managed successfully.'

Now she had his interest.

'It's only natural I want to know what your plans are,'

she insisted. 'I don't want to be wasting my pitch on the wrong man.' Out came the chin.

'My plans are no business of yours.' He stopped admiring her when it occurred to him that Bronte wanted something that belonged to him. Or at least, she wanted control of Hebers Ghyll, which amounted to the same thing. It was a challenge he couldn't ignore. A lot of water had passed under the bridge since he'd been a hard, fighting, rebellious youth and Bronte the housekeeper's prim little daughter sneaking out to see him, hiding in the shadows, thinking he didn't know she was there, but he hadn't changed when it came to protecting what was his. 'If you want me to make time to see you, clear up this mess and get off my property.' He pointed to the area around her tent, which, in fairness, was neat. Bronte had always respected the countryside.

'You promised we'd talk.'

'I'll make a start, shall I?' he said, losing patience.

She exclaimed with surprise when he swooped on a tent peg and jerked it out. 'What the hell do you think you're doing?' she demanded, launching herself at him.

'I wouldn't advise you do that again.' Seizing hold of her wrists, he held her in front of him. His gaze slipping to her parted lips. The urge to ravage them overwhelmed him.

'Let go of me, Heath,' she warned him. Her voice was shaking. Her eyes were dark. Her lips were parted—

Control kicked in. He lifted his hands away. 'Remove the tent,' he said.

'You don't frighten me,' she muttered, rubbing her wrists as she pulled away.

But he had frightened her. Bronte had feared her reaction to him. The snap of static between them had

surprised him. This was no ordinary reunion, he reflected as she began bringing her tent down. The redhead tomboy and the bad boy from the city had enjoyed
some high voltage scraps in the past, and it appeared
that passion hadn't abated. But it had changed, Heath
reflected. Bronte had felt slight and vulnerable beneath
his hands. She was all grown-up now, and her scent of
soap and damp grass had grazed his senses, leaving an
impression he would find hard to shake off.

CHAPTER TWO

HEATH STAMP was back. She kept repeating the mantra in her head as if that were going to make it easier for her to be close to him without quivering like a doe on heat. She had been expecting Heath, and had thought she was well prepared for this first encounter, but nothing could have prepared her for feeling so vulnerable, so aware and aroused.

'Get a move on, Bronte.'

'I'm moving as fast as I can.'

'Good, because some of us have work to do.'

'Yeah, me too,' Bronte muttered tensely. She had sorted herself out with a part-time office job in the area while she was still away on her travels—it was just sheer luck Heath had chosen to arrive at the weekend.

'Come on, come on,' he urged impatiently. 'I have to get back to London—'

'We all have things to do, Heath.'

The rain had stopped and Heath was pacing. He had always suffered energy overload and that force was pinging off him now. She wouldn't be taking so long if he didn't look so good. Fantasies she could handle, but this much reality was a problem. Heath's hair had always been thick and strong, but he'd grown it longer and it caressed his strong, tanned neck, curling over the collar of his shirt, and was every bit as wayward as she remembered. Waves caught on his sharply etched cheeks where his black stubble had won the razor war, and, though he might not have fought with his fists for many years, Heath was still built, still tanned, and, apart from the car, he didn't flash his wealth, which she liked. His clothes were designed for practicality rather than to impress—banged-up jeans worn thin and pale over the place where a nice girl shouldn't look, and boots comfortably worn in. Heath had sexy feet, she remembered from those times years back when she had spied on him swimming in the lake—

'Have you turned into a pillar of salt? Or is there a chance we might get out of here today, Bronte?'

'Are you still there?' she retorted, lavishing what Heath used to call her paint-stripping stare on him. The old banter starting up between them had stirred her fighting spirit—

Until Heath reminded her why she was here.

'Are you serious about trying out for the job of estate manager?'

'Of course I am.' She shot to her feet, realising how slender a thread her hopes were pinned on. 'And if you decide not to keep the property I hope you'll put in a good word for me with the new owner.'

'Why would I do that when I don't even know what you can do? Okay, I admit I'm intrigued by what you told me about your training and your travels. But what makes you think you're the right person for this job?'

'I know I am,' she said stubbornly. 'All I'm asking for is a fair hearing.'

'And if I give you one?'

'You can make up your mind then. Maybe give me a trial?' She knew she was pushing it, but what the hell?

Heath said nothing for a moment, and then his lips tugged in a faint, mocking smile. 'If I keep the estate I'll bear your offer in mind.'

It was enough—it was something. Heath never made an impulsive decision, Bronte remembered—that was her department.

'Go home now, Bronte. You've still got your parents' cottage to go to, I take it?'

'They wouldn't sell that.' There was an edge of defiance in her voice. 'Thank goodness they owned it—I heard you bought out all the tenancies.'

'Another of those rumours?' Heath's eyes turned black. 'It didn't occur to you people might want to sell to me? Or that this was their opportunity to do something new with their lives—like your parents?'

'And you wanted a fresh page?'

Heath didn't even try to put a gloss on what he'd done. 'No,' he argued. 'I wanted a clear field so there wouldn't be any complications if and when I choose to sell. What's the matter with you, Bronte?' His face had turned coolly assessing. 'Can't you bear to think of me living at the hall?'

'That's not it at all.'

'Then why don't you smile and be happy for me?'

'I am happy for you, Heath.'

'And you think we could work together?' he said with a mocking edge to his voice.

'I'd find a way.'

'That's big of you,' he said coolly.

Most people would be champing at the bit for a chance to work with Heath Stamp, Bronte realised, turning her back on him as she returned to her packing. She could only hazard a guess at the number of applications Heath would receive if he decided to keep the estate on and

threw a recruitment ad out there. Everyone loved a success story in the hope that some of the gold dust would
rub off on them—and Heath had gold dust to spare. His
story read like a film—the poor boy rejecting a hand
up from a well-meaning uncle who just happened to
be one of England's biggest landowners, only for the
boy to achieve success in his own right and then go on
to inherit the uncle's estate anyway. No wonder it had
made the headlines. But was she the only one out of step
here? Heath had always been open about his dislike of
the countryside—everything moved too slowly for him
and things took too long to grow, she remembered him
snarling at her when she had begged him to stay.

So, could she work with him?

Good question. The thought of seeing Heath on a
regular basis might send a warm dart of honey to her
core, but when her imagination supplied the fantasy
detail, which included a doting lover called Heath and
a compliant young girl called Bronte, she knew it was
never going to happen, so she just said coolly, 'I'll stay
in touch.'

Heath Stamp, Master of Hebers Ghyll? However much
Heath teased her with the prospect, she just couldn't see
it.

The years had moulded and enhanced Bronte—brought
her into clearer focus. She was still the same dreamer
who steadfastly refused to learn the meaning of the word
no. She was every bit as stubborn and determined as he
remembered—if not more so. Only Bronte could come
up with the crazy notion that by camping inside the
gates she could scope out the new owner of the estate—
potentially waylay the new owner, and then insist they
consider her for the job of estate manager. Nerve? Oh,

yes. Bronte had nerve—and she had never been short of ideas, or the brio to back them up.

'Go away, Heath,' she snapped when he went to give her a hand with the groundsheet. 'I can do this by myself.'

'I don't doubt it. I just want to make sure you don't leave anything behind.'

'So I have no excuse to come back?'

Looks clashed. Eyes darkened. Something else for him to think about. 'Just do it, will you?'

'Don't worry—I've got no reason to hang around here.' She threw him a disdainful look. 'Why on earth would I?'

A million and one reasons, Bronte thought, feeling all mixed up inside. She didn't want to go—she didn't want to stay. It didn't help she'd brought so much stuff and it was taking so long to fit it back in her rucksack. She could feel the heat of Heath's stare on her back. And low in her belly the dreamweaver was working—

'Come on. Get a move on, Bronte.'

'Yes, master—'

'Less of it—and more packing,' Heath snapped.

She was seething with frustration. Was this the same girl who had the right training for this job, as well as great qualifications? The girl who had worked her way round the world to make doubly sure she would be ready to apply for a job on the estate when she got back? And with the biggest job of all on offer, was she going to blow it now because she couldn't see further than Heath? Bite your lip, Bronte, was the best piece of advice to follow. There was too much at stake to do anything else. She should have rung the lawyers the moment she was back in the country and avoided this meeting. She should have approached things in the usual way.

*Could anything be usual where Heath was con-
cerned?*

If she had given him warning of her intentions, her
best guess was Heath wouldn't have turned up—or he'd
make sure to be permanently unavailable at his office.
But Hebers Ghyll needed him—needed Heath's golden
touch *and* his money. She had to put her personal feelings to one side and persuade him to keep the estate
together and not to sell or demolish any of the old buildings in the 'so called' name of progress.

'You won't be very comfortable without this,' he observed, toeing the edge of her groundsheet.

As she started to roll it up the scent of damp earth
stirred her memories. Her parents had met and fallen in
love at Hebers Ghyll, which gave it a sort of magic. The
freedom of the fields when she'd been a child—somewhere to curl up with a book and lose herself—all the
things that had made her feel safe and secure had gone,
because every last inch of this damp, sweet-smelling
ground belonged to Heath now, and there wasn't a thing
she could do about it.

'Why did you bring all this?' Heath had come to
stand very close.

She lifted her head and stared into the critical gaze,
wishing there were some warmth in it—some recognition that they had been friends once. 'I didn't know how
long I'd have to wait for you,' she said truthfully.

'You were only sure that you would,' Heath commented without expression.

'That's right,' she said, blazing defiance into his
eyes.

'Nothing changes, does it, Bronte?'

'Some things do,' she said. Let him know how she
felt. 'With the future of the village at stake I had no

alternative, Heath. No one sleeps on the ground out of choice.'

She could have bitten off her tongue. Heath's success had been forged out of a combustible mix of fiery determination and uncompromising poverty. He knew very well what it was like to sleep on the ground. Uncle Harry had told her once his parents used to lock him out when he was a child while they went to the pub, and if they were home late or not at all Heath had to do the best he could to find shelter. 'Heath, I'm sorry—'

With a shake of his head he closed the subject.

Sleeping on park benches to escape the violence at home had done nothing to soften him, Bronte reflected, returning to her packing. And that stint in jail must have knocked all human feeling out of him. Yes, and what would a man like that know or care about the countryside—or the legacy he had inherited? 'Heath,' she pleaded softly, sitting back on her haunches. 'You will give this place a chance, won't you?'

He surveyed her steadily through steel-grey eyes. 'I'm here to see what can be done, Bronte. And if I want to do it.'

'That's not enough.'

Heath huffed. 'It's all you're getting.'

'If you even think of turning your back on Hebers Ghyll I'll fight you every inch of the way.'

'Bare knuckle or Queensberry Rules?'

She stared at him intently for a moment. She hardly dared to hope that was a flicker of the old humour, but in the unlikely event that it was she wasn't going to cause a storm and blow it out.

'What about those cooking pots, Bronte?' Heath demanded. 'Am I supposed to clear them up? If you don't get a move on I'll fetch the tractor and shift them myself.'

'The tractor?' she repeated witheringly. 'Here is a man,' she informed the trees, 'whose knowledge of the countryside would fit comfortably on the head of a pin with room for angels to dance in a ring. Heath Stamp—' she introduced him with a theatrical gesture '—creator of imaginary worlds contained in neat square boxes— computers that can be conveniently switched off, and don't have to be milked twice a day.' She turned to Heath. 'What would you know about driving a tractor?'

'More than you know.'

'It would have to be more than I know—' But now Heath's hand was in the small of her back and every-thing dissolved in a flood of sensation. Jerking away, she bent down to pick up the overloaded pack.

'Let me help you—'

'Go away.'

'Bronte—'

Heath waited a moment and then he strode off.

She turned to watch him go, still heated and furious— desperate for him to go, and longing for him to stay. She couldn't believe how badly this much-longed-for reunion had gone. Heath, and that firm mouth—how she hated it. She hated the confident swagger of his walk, and those taut, powerful hips. She hated his manner, which was both cool and hot, and infinitely disturbing, as well as blatantly unavailable—at least, to her. Heath might have his own brand of rugged charm, but according to the press he attracted glamorous, elegant women—women who decorated Heath's life without ever becoming part of it—

She nearly jumped out of her skin when he reap-peared through the trees.

'Okay,' he said curtly, 'I can't abandon you here. Give me that pack.'

Heath didn't wait for her reply. Wrestling the pack from her shoulders, he stalked off with it, leaving her stunned by the brief and definitely unintentional brushing of their bodies. 'Hey—come back here,' she yelled, coming to as Heath and her backpack disappeared through the trees.

She might as well have been talking to herself. Grinding her jaw, she started after him. Heath had never been a man to mess about with, but she wasn't a girl to back down. Mud sucked at her trainers as she started to run. Wet leaves slapped at her face. Who could keep up with Heath? Bronte reasoned when she was forced to stop and catch her breath. Heath had always been a one-man powerhouse since the day he sewed the seeds of his empire on a computer he'd hidden in his bedroom, where damp dappled the walls and the only green Heath ever saw was the mould that flourished there. Bad start in life, maybe, but this city boy was fit—fitter than she was. Catching sight of Heath through the trees, she found a fresh burst of energy. He had always moved fast. The first time Heath had hit the headlines was because of the speed with which he had turned his old family home into an Internet café for the whole neighbourhood to use. The reporters had latched onto the fact that, far from turning his back on his miserable start in life, when Heath made money he celebrated his background, using his story to inspire others to follow his example and make the best of what they had. Leaning one hand against a tree trunk, she took another breather. So Heath Stamp was a saint, but right now that didn't make her like him any better.

But if he could be persuaded to do the same for Hebers Ghyll the estate might stand a chance...

With this thought propelling her forward she got a rush of energy—right up to the moment when Heath yelled, 'I'm dumping this pack on the road, Bronte. After that, you're on your own.'

So much charm in one man. Blowing out an angry breath, she wiped the mud off her face with the back of her hand and pushed on. When she finally caught up to him Heath was the epitome of cool. He hadn't even broken sweat.

'I'd give you a lift...' His sardonic gaze ran over her mud-blackened clothes.

'Save it, Heath. You wouldn't want to dirty your car.'

Heath threw her one of his looks. 'Your rucksack wouldn't fit in the boot.'

'Lucky you.' Heath's sexy mouth was mocking her. His eyes were too. Hefting the pack up, she turned her back on him and marched away.

CHAPTER THREE

HE COULDN'T believe how screwed up inside Bronte made him feel. And this didn't help. Heath was staring at the old hall, seeing it for the first time through adult eyes. He had thought he knew it well, and that he remembered every detail. But he hadn't bargained for the memories flooding in.

Thankfully, he was alone. There had been a moment just then when, despite priding himself on his fitness. It had felt as if his chest were in a vice. He could hear police sirens in his head. He could hear his mother screaming at his father not to hit her. He could see a small boy locked out of the house until his parents got home late at night, relieving himself against the back wall, the neighbours shouting at him. And he could feel the difference here at Hebers Ghyll all over again: the stability; the kindness shown to him; the patience that people had given a boy who believed he deserved none, the care he had so badly needed. He felt that same hunger again—not just the hunger for food, but the hunger for something different. He hadn't even known what was driving him back then. But he did know that here at Hebers Ghyll was where anger had started to grow like a weed twining round him as he turned from bewildered child into disaffected youth. The anger had been thick and fast and ugly, and he had expressed it with his fists.

If he stayed very still the echoes of those years were stronger—the first time he'd been to Hebers Ghyll he'd felt resentful and out of place. Seeing Bronte again had rubbed salt in that wound. The first time he'd seen her, his jaw had dropped to think such innocence existed—it was the first time he realised not every family was at war.

But however much Bronte wanted him to come back to Hebers Ghyll and work some sort of miracle—and she did—he couldn't shake off that old certainty that he didn't belong here. Who would want to be reminded of his past—of what he'd been—of what he could be? Back then there had only been one certainty—one overriding conviction. He could never be good enough for Bronte.

And now?

She had taught him to read, for God's sake.

Shame washed over him as he remembered. It made him want to jump in the car, drive home to London and never come back. Why shouldn't he do just that? He'd put this place on the market—leave the past where it belonged, buried deep in the countryside at Hebers Ghyll.

Decision made, he headed back to the car, but then a sound stopped him dead in his tracks. It jerked him back into the present even as it threw him into the past. He turned and stared at the old bell Uncle Harry had hung outside the front door so he could call the bad boys in for supper. Heath's mouth twisted as he shook his head. Whatever he thought about it, the past wasn't ready to let him go yet. Leaving the bell to its capricious dance, he jogged up the steps to the front door and let himself in.

He felt a sort of grief mixed up with guilt land heavily inside him as he stared around the entrance hall. How could this have happened so quickly?

What had he expected? A log fire blazing, the smell of freshly baked bread? There was no one living here— no one had been living here for months. The scent of pine and wood-smoke he remembered belonged to another, happier era. The air was stale now, and cold, and stank of damp. He walked around—touching, listening, remembering...

If there was one thing Uncle Harry had insisted on, it was that the log fire was kept burning so that visitors felt welcome. And the table where his uncle had taught him the fundamentals of chess before Heath crossed over to the dark side—where was that? Where was the board? Where were the chess pieces?

Melancholy washed over him and it was an emotion he had never thought to feel here. Bronte was right to think he had arrived with the sole intention of developing the property and selling it on to make a quick profit—until she had planted that seed of doubt in his head, reminding him of the old man who had done so much for both of them. Credit for his artistic flair and business savvy, Heath could claim, but the fuel that had fired his hunger to do better had been all Uncle Harry.

Raking his hair as he looked around, he thought the word dilapidation didn't even begin to cover this. Bottom line? He didn't have time for Hebers Ghyll. His life, his work—everything—was in London. His impressive-sounding inheritance was little more than a ruin—a hall, with a tumble-down castle in the grounds, whose foundations had been laid in Norman times, and whose structure had been added to over the years with a mixed degree of success.

Make that heavy on the failure, Heath thought as he leaned his shoulder against a wall and heard it grumble. He had to wonder what Uncle Harry had been thinking on the day the old man had written his will. It was common knowledge Heath hated the countryside. Even as a youth he'd scorned the idea that owning a castle was grand; it was just a larger acreage of slum to him—still was. There was nothing here but rotten wood and cracks and holes, and leaking radiators.

But at least he was no stranger to this sort of mess...

His talent was in inventing computer games and running a company soon to go global, but his hobby was working with his hands. It wouldn't be the first time he'd called a team together to work on the renovation of an ancient building.

Yes, but this was a huge project. He gave himself a reality check as he continued his inspection. Rubbing a pane of glass with his sleeve, he peered through an upstairs window...and thought about the dormitory Uncle Harry had set up in the barn for Heath and the other boys from the detention centre. They'd had fun—not that Heath would have admitted it at the time. They'd told ghost stories late into the night, trying to spook each other—and during the day they'd ridden bareback on the ponies, or risked their lives wrestling bullocks. The space and silence had got to him, but the village hadn't been without its attractions. A challenge from the leader of the country lads with their burnished skin and glossy hair had led to a fight and Heath had established quite a reputation for himself. When he returned to the city he took things one disastrous step further, fighting for cash in dank, dark cellars—until the authorities caught up with him. After a chase the police had arrested him here, of all places—at Hebers Ghyll. He'd returned like a homing pigeon, he realised now. He'd gone back to the detention centre for a longer stretch.

It was only in court that he discovered Uncle Harry had shopped him. To save him, the old man said. The memory of how he'd hated Uncle Harry for that betrayal came flooding back—as did the follow-up, which made him smile. The old man had sent him a computer— 'courtesy of his conscience', the greeting card had said. Heath had left it unpacked in his cell until one day curiosity got the better of him—and the rest was history.

His stint inside had left him wiser. He could make money, but not with his fists. Uncle Harry's computer was the answer. On his release he set up an office in his bedroom where no one could see him or judge him, and no one knew how young he was, or how poor. All he had to do was click a mouse and the world came to him. And the world liked his games.

Heath moved on as the wall he'd been leaning against shuddered a complaint. He was stronger than he knew— which was more than could be said for the fabric of this place. One good shove and the whole lot would come tumbling down. It would be easier to flatten it and start again—

Since when had he embraced easy?

His fingers were already caressing the speed dial on his phone to call his architect when thoughts of plump pink lips and lush pert breasts intruded. Another pause, another memory—the last time he'd seen Bronte at Hebers Ghyll she'd been trying to save him from the police. She'd overheard Uncle Harry on the phone, and had run down the drive to warn him they were coming. When that had failed, she'd kissed him goodbye. He shook his head as he tried to blank the kiss. He'd better check she'd reached home safely.

He found Bronte still at the side of the road where she was having a bit of a disaster. The strap on her rucksack had given way and she was kneeling on the rolled-up groundsheet, lashing it into submission with a yard of rope and a clutch of nifty knots. Drawing the car to a halt, he leapt out. 'Wouldn't a regular buckle make things easier for you?'

'The buckles broke in Kathmandu.'

He curbed a grin. 'Of course they did.'

'No, really, they did,' she insisted, lifting her head. Then, remembering they weren't quite friends, she lowered it again, by which time her cheeks were glowing red.

'Want some help?' he offered.

'I can manage, thank you.'

'Play me a different tune, Bronte.' Having nudged her out of the way, he attached the rolled groundsheet to the top of her knapsack and started carrying it towards the car.

'We already know it won't fit in that ridiculous boot,' she yelled after him.

'Then I'll carry it home for you.'

'There's no need.' Racing up to him, she tried to pull it out of his hands.

'Do you want that interview or not?' he demanded, lifting it out of her reach.

'Does this mean you're keeping Hebers Ghyll?' she demanded, staring up at him.

'We'll see,' he said.

'Give.' She growled.

His lips curved as he looked down at her. 'Is that pleasant tone of voice supposed to entice me to hand it over?'

'Give, please,' she said with a scowl.

'Okay.' He helped her to hoist the rucksack onto her back again, careful not to let his fingers do any more work than strictly necessary.

Hefting the pack into a more comfortable position, she wobbled a little as she grew accustomed to the weight and then tottered off in the direction of home. He stayed close to make sure she was safe.

'I'm fine, Heath,' she called back to him over her shoulder, breaking into an unsteady jog.

'Watch out—the ground slopes away there—'

Too late. As Bronte stumbled on the treacherous bank he dived to save her. Catching his foot under a tree root, he took her with him, tumbling down the slope bound together as closely as two people could be.

'Bloody idiot!' she raged with shock as they thundered to a halt.

'Thank you would do it for me,' he observed mildly, noting the jagged rock he'd saved them from as well as the comfortable tangle of limbs.

'Thank you,' she huffed, snapping her hips away from his. 'The townie who thinks he can run Hebers Ghyll can't even keep his footing on a mossy bank,' she observed with biting relish.

'Is that dialect for welcome?' he said mildly.

'More like shove off.'

But she was in no hurry to move away. Lust. The desire to have, to possess, to inhabit, to pleasure and be pleasured sprang between them like a bright, hot flame. Bronte was shocked by the intensity of it. Her eyes blazed emerald fire into his and her lips had never been more kissable. She was aroused. And so was he.

Closing her eyes briefly, Bronte ground out a growl of impatience. She could of course slip back into her fantasy world and stay here wrapped around Heath—or she could get real and go home. 'Excuse me, please,' she said as politely as she could.

Heath yanked her to her feet. No courtesy involved. She let go of his hands. Fast—but not fast enough. Her body sang from his touch in three part harmony with baroque flourishes. She didn't argue this time when he offered to walk her home.

'Something funny?' Heath demanded when she looked at him and shook her head.

'The way you look?'

'That good?' He curved a smile.

'If camouflage is fashionable this season, you look great.'

'I heard mud, leaves and twigs are huge this year.' He brushed himself down.

She laughed. She couldn't help herself—just as she couldn't stop herself following Heath's hands jealously with her eyes. They were almost communicating again, Bronte realised—and that was dangerous. This was getting too much like the old days when her heart had been full of Heath.

So she'd hide how she felt about him—what was so hard about that?

They walked along in silence until Heath lobbed a curving ball. 'If I decide to keep the estate and call interviews, are you ready?'

'If you're serious, Heath, I'm ready now,' she exclaimed. 'That is if the new estate manager isn't just part of some lick of paint project to tart the place up so you can maximise your profit and get rid of it faster,' she added as common sense kicked in.

'Since when has profit been a dirty word?' Heath demanded.

'People are more important.'

'Which is why I'm the businessman and you're the dreamer, Bronte. Without profit there can be no jobs—no people living in Hebers Ghyll. And I won't be rushed into this. I never make a decision until I know all the facts.'

'Then know this,' she said as their exchange heated up. 'You and I could never work in any sort of team.'

'No,' Heath agreed. 'I'd always be the boss.'

'You're unbelievable.'

'So they tell me.'

With an incredulous laugh Bronte tossed her burnished mane and quickened her step to get ahead of him. He kept up easily. 'If I do decide to do anything it won't be half-hearted. It will be all about renewal and regeneration.'

'Sounds impressive,' she said. 'Almost unbelievable.'

Bronte had always scored a gold star for sarcasm. She was paying him back for doubting her. And why was he even discussing something that was barely a glimmer of an idea? 'My hobby's building things—I've carried out restoration work in the past so I know what's involved.' And now defending it?

He got what he deserved.

'Get real, Heath,' Bronte flashed. 'This isn't cyber-space. You can't conjure up an idyllic country scene on your screen complete with a fully restored castle, click your mouse and wipe out years of under-investment.'

'No, but I can try. I might not be the countryside's biggest fan, but I'm not known for running out.'

'And neither am I,' she shot back.

'Are we agreed on something?'

She huffed.

'The only way Hebers Ghyll can survive is for people like you to get involved, Bronte.'

'Oh, I see,' she said. 'People like me do all the hard work while you direct us from your city desk? Unless you're going to live here, Heath, which I doubt.'

'Do you want Hebers Ghyll to have a future or not? Yes or no, Bronte? If you're serious about trying to get people to come back here there has to be something for them to come back to.'

'So now you're a visionary?'

'No. I'm a realist.' And he liked a challenge—especially when there was a woman involved.

'This is nothing like the city, Heath.'

'Isn't it?' he fired back. 'The air might be polluted with pollen instead of smoke, but, like you said, jobs are just as hard to find. So you go right ahead and walk away, Bronte. Let Hebers Ghyll slide into a hole. Or you can stay and fight.'

'With you? What changed your mind, Heath?'

Heath's face closed off. Why didn't she know when to keep quiet? She could only guess how he must have felt coming back here. She returned to the fray to divert him. 'You can't just plonk down a couple of computers in the village hall, maintain a cyber presence and think that's enough, Heath. People need proper work—and a proper leader on site to direct them.'

'Are you saying you wouldn't be up to that?'

'I'd do whatever was expected of me, and more, if I were lucky enough to get the job,' Bronte countered, rejoicing in Heath's attack. The way he was talking could only mean he was seriously interested in keeping the estate.

'Judging by your enthusiasm you'd work happily alongside anyone who does get the job?'

He'd got her. Damn it. Heath had always been a master tactician. She threw him a thunderous look.

He was all logic while Bronte was the flip side of the coin—all that passion with so little curb on it made it so easy to outmanoeuvre her, it was hardly fair. He hadn't made a final decision yet. The problems at Hebers Ghyll were nothing new for him. There had been no work in his old neighbourhood, but he had known that if there was enough money for tools and equipment there would be more than enough jobs for everyone. 'There's only one problem,' he said, reeling her in.

'Which is?' she demanded on cue.

'You.' He stared directly at her. 'You're the problem, Bronte. If I consider you for the job I have to bear in mind you took off once and went travelling. How do I know you won't do that again?'

'Because my travels had a purpose and now I'm home to put what I've learned into practice.'

'That's good,' he agreed, 'but if I take this on there will be nothing but hard work ahead, and a lot of difficult decisions to be made. I need to be sure that whoever I employ as estate manager has both the staying power and the backbone for what needs to be done.'

'What are you implying, Heath?'

He lifted the latch on the wooden gate that led through to her parents' garden. 'I'm saying I don't know you, Bronte. I only know what you're telling me. It's been a long time.'

'For both of us,' she reminded him tensely.

He propped her rucksack against the front door.

'Hey,' she said when he turned to leave. 'Where are you going? We're in the middle of a conversation.'

'We'll continue it another time. I have to get back now.'

'Can't we talk first? What's the hurry?'

Strangely, it pleased him that she wanted to keep him back. 'I have appointments I can't break. My work is in London, remember? It's where I make the money that might just keep this place alive.' He stopped at the gate and turned to face her. 'Just promise me one thing before I go.'

'What?'

'Parts of Hebers Ghyll aren't safe, Bronte, so please stay away.'

'The Great Hall's safe,' she insisted stubbornly. 'Uncle Harry was living there up to a few months ago.'

'And I'm telling you not to go near it until I get back.'

'So you are coming back?'

As her eyes fired he propped a hip against the garden wall. 'You'll be telling me how much you'll miss me next.'

'Ha! Don't hold your breath.'

'If you need me you've got my number.'

'What use is that when your PA won't put me through?'

'You give up too easily, Bronte.' Raising his hand in a farewell salute, he thought himself lucky to be out of range of any missiles she might have to hand.

CHAPTER FOUR

WHEN Heath left her Bronte was still high on adrenalin hours later. She needed action. Lots of it. She went back to Hebers Ghyll and broke in. Maybe this was the craziest idea she'd had yet, but she wasn't prepared to be run off a property she had always thought of as her second home. The moment Heath's car roared away she made some calls to girls in the village—girls who'd been friends for life. The chance to do a little exploring was right up their street.

How dangerous could the Great Hall be? It had only stood empty for a couple of months. She wouldn't take any chances, Bronte determined as she led her troops beneath a moody sky down the long overgrown drive. Everyone knew the castle was ready to fall down, but the hall where her mother had been housekeeper, and the rooms where Uncle Harry had used to live, they were safe. Heath was overreacting—or, more likely, trying to keep her away. She had explained to her friends, Maisie and Colleen, that there were no-go areas and that they mustn't go off exploring on their own.

'This is spooky,' Colleen said, echoing Bronte's thoughts as they all flashed an anxious glance into the impenetrable undergrowth.

They could speed-walk to international standards by

the time they reached the open space where a dried-up moat circled the ruined castle. The castle was a heap of blackened stone, lowering and forbidding beneath boiling storm clouds, and the ugly gash around it was full of brambles and leaves. 'Nice,' Colleen murmured.

It needed clearing—needed filling—needed ducks, Bronte thought. She wouldn't have trusted the drawbridge—most of the planks were missing, and a glance at the rusty portcullis hanging over it confirmed that Heath was right to warn her to stay away. But even the old castle could be transformed like one she'd seen in France. The fortress of Carcassonne had been faithfully restored and was now a World Heritage site. But that was for another day. 'We'll go straight to the Great Hall,' she told the girls, leading them swiftly past the danger zone.

Excitement started to bubble inside Bronte the moment she stood in front of the old hall. The sun had made a welcome return, burning through the clouds, and the warmth and light changed everything. It raised her spirits and softened the blackened stone, turning it rosy. This could all be so romantic, if it weren't so run-down. Her plan had been to bring the girls along to enthuse them, but she clearly had a long way to go. They had gone quiet, which was a bad sign. 'Come on,' she said in an attempt to lift their spirits. 'Let's see what we've got round the back.'

More decay. Dried-up fountains. Tangled weeds. Crumbling stone.

For a moment she felt overwhelmed, defeated, but then she determined that she would find a way. Scrambling through an upstairs window, she brushed herself down. The echoing landing smelled musty and dust hung like a curtain in the shadowy air. She could hardly expect

Heath to feel enthusiastic about this, Bronte mused as she walked slowly down the stairs, let alone spend his hard-earned money putting it right.

She could only hope the girls would stick with her, Bronte concluded as she picked her way across the broken floor tiles in the hall. How depressing to see how quickly everything had deteriorated. It didn't help to know she had only added to the destruction. She'd tried her mother's door key, only to discover that the one useful thing the previous estate manager had done before Heath sacked him was to change the locks. Adapting her plans accordingly, she had shinned up a drainpipe, forced a window and climbed in. And this was not the testimony to Uncle Harry's generosity that he deserved. Plants had withered and died, while chairs had mysteriously fallen over, and plaster was falling off the walls faster than the mice could eat it.

Shouldn't Heath be here doing something about this?

And why was she thinking about Heath when she could just as easily do something about it? She had already established that Heath's interest in his inheritance was mild at most. Heath only cared about the profit he could make when he sold it on. He'd made that clear enough. He could barely spare the time for this weekend's flying visit. Heath's life was all about making money in London now.

With a frustrated growl, she scraped her hair back into a band ready for work—only to be rewarded by an image of Heath in her mind, standing beneath the vaulted ceiling of the Great Hall looking like a conquering hero as he fixed her with his mocking stare.

Why did it always have to come back to Heath?

Because Heath was blessed with such an overdose of

darkly brooding charisma it was impossible not to think about him, Bronte concluded. But a man like Heath could hardly be expected to hang around when there were so many people waiting to admire him—and she was hardly the swooning type. So, who needed him? There was nothing here she couldn't handle.

Having convinced herself that she had ejected Heath from her thoughts, she now had to confront all the other impressions crowding in. 'I'm going to change this,' she murmured, staring round.

'Talking to yourself, Lady Muck?' Colleen called down to her from the upstairs landing.

Bronte's heart leapt. So the girls had decided to join her. 'You made it,' she called back. 'Come and join me. We've got the place to ourselves.'

'No boarders to repel?' Maisie demanded, sounding disappointed as she clattered down the stairs in a cloud of cheap scent and good humour. 'I thought there'd be at least one hunky ghost for me to deal with.'

Or Heath in full battle armour with a demolition ball at his command, Bronte mused—that was one boarder she wouldn't have minded repelling. Or, better still— half-naked Heath, muscles bulging, on his knees in front of her. Much better. She'd keep that one—as well as the quiver of awareness that accompanied it. Enough! she told herself firmly as a puff of plaster dust landed on her shoulder. Heath had gone back to London, and there was work to be done here. 'There should be life at Hebers Ghyll,' she announced to the girls. 'We can't let it crumble to dust and do nothing about it.'

'Aye aye, Captain.'

The girls delivered a mock-salute as Bronte warmed to her theme. 'There should be life and warmth and music—and there will be again.'

The girls whooped and cheered. 'How about we help you after work and at weekends?' Colleen suggested when they'd all calmed down.

Bronte was moved by the offer. 'I couldn't ask you to do that.'

'Why not?' Maisie demanded. 'It could be fun.'

'Spiders are fun?' Bronte seemed doubtful.

'Well, we can't leave you here on your own, can we?' Colleen pointed out. 'If you're going to be battling ghosts and spiders, we want to be part of it, don't we, Maisie?'

'I'll trade you my most excellent work with a broom and a ghost-busters kit, for a drink at the pub,' Maisie suggested. 'How about that?'

'Deal,' Bronte agreed. 'Let's get to it,' she announced, leading the way to the storeroom where the cleaning equipment was kept.

'Working party present and correct,' Colleen confirmed once they were armed with brushes and bin liners. 'Where would you like us to start?'

'Not with mouse droppings or spiders' webs,' Maisie protested, wielding her dustpan. 'The only thing I'm prepared to scream for is a man.'

I wish, Bronte thought, imagining she was in a clinch with Heath. 'The best I can offer you is a good scrumping in the apple orchard.'

'I think Maisie had something more hands on in mind than that,' Colleen suggested dryly.

'You do surprise me. Why don't we clear up as much as we can in here and then reward ourselves with a swim in the lake?'

'Skinny-dipping?' Her friends shrieked, hugging themselves in anticipation.

'Well, as we haven't moved in with our fourteen

wardrobes of clothes yet—seems skinny-dipping is our only option.'

'Could you arrange for the lake to be heated before we dive in?' Colleen demanded.

'You'll soon get warm,' Bronte promised as visions of childhood's endless summer days spent swimming or rowing on the lake filled her head with slightly rose-tinted images—swiftly followed by red-hot thoughts of Heath rising like a wet-shirted Mr Darcy dripping water from his muscular frame—

'Bronte?' the girls prompted.

'Sorry.' Tearing her thoughts away from Heath, Bronte focused on the here and now. It would be lonely at the hall without the girls and working together promised to be fun.

And if Heath never came back?

They'd get by somehow. But because she was stubborn she was going to make that call to London to check if he would be holding interviews for jobs at the hall.

'Daydreaming about Heath *again*?' Colleen teased her.

'I've got bigger things on my mind than Heath,' Bronte replied, trying to look serious.

'Bigger than Heath?' Colleen exclaimed, exchanging a knowing look with Maisie.

'You're disgusting.' Bronte smothered a smile.

The business trip he had left Hebers Ghyll to make had been a resounding success. He was back in town within the week, brooding in his office with Bronte on his mind. She was too inquisitive to quietly settle back into life at the cottage, which worried him. She wouldn't be able to resist taking another look round Hebers Ghyll, which was dangerous. She could be down there now with a bundle of energy and good intentions. He'd made sure everything was locked up securely before he left, but he didn't trust her—and good intentions wouldn't stop those walls falling on her head. He had no option. He had to go back.

He called Quentin from the car to make arrangements to cover his absence at the board meeting, and then he made a few more calls. There was no point in his going to Hebers Ghyll on a day trip—or just to yell at Bronte. He might as well start moving things forward. Whether or not he decided to keep the estate it could only benefit from a refit. And he could only benefit either way.

The two girls were as good as their word and came to the hall every night after work to help Bronte sort things out. One week of back-breaking work was nearly over and there was still no sign of Heath.

Still no answer on his phone either. Perhaps he'd given her the wrong number on purpose—or perhaps Heath's PA was even more efficient than she'd thought him, which was entirely possible. She couldn't pretend she wasn't disappointed that Heath had just disappeared again as if that visit had never happened, but she hid her feelings from the girls, and stubbornly refused to let it get her down. She distracted herself by working as hard as she could until all she could think about at night was a soft pillow and a long, dreamless sleep.

By the end of the week the three girls had systematically cleared, cleaned, and de-spidered the Great Hall, and had returned the kitchen to its former pristine state. They had weeded the formal gardens as well as the kitchen garden with its wealth of vegetables, and cheered when Bronte, whose hands and face seemed to be permanently covered in sticky black oil for most of the time, finally managed to get the sit-on lawnmower to work. Having tamed the grass and cleared the rubbish, a small part of the Hebers Ghyll estate, if not exactly restored to its former glory, was at least clean and tidy, and as a bonus they were all suntanned and healthy thanks to a timely Indian summer. And they were definitely well fed, thanks to Bronte's frequent raids on the vegetable patch. There was only one fly in this late-summer ointment as far as Bronte was concerned, and that was Heath. You'd think he'd want to know the place was still standing…

One hazy late afternoon when even the bees could hardly be bothered to hum, Bronte was down at the lakeside with Colleen and Maisie.

'What are you doing?' Colleen demanded grumpily when Bronte reached for her phone. 'You can't be ringing *him* again?'

'Yes, *him* again,' Bronte confirmed, firming her jaw. 'Heath gave me this number, and some time or other I'm bound to get through to him.'

'Dreamer,' Maisie commented.

'When he takes his phone off call divert,' Colleen added.

'Well, I'm not going to give up.'

'What a surprise,' Maisie murmured, brushing a harmless hover-fly away.

The phone droned. Bronte waited. And then sprang to attention. But it was only Heath's PA, who put her off in the same weary tone. Colleen and Maisie were right. Heath had no intention of speaking to her ever again.

'When are you going to get it through your head—' Colleen began as Bronte snapped the phone shut and tossed it on the ground.

'Don't,' she said. 'Just…don't.'

Bronte's friends fell silent as she flung herself down on the grass. Lying flat on her back, she gazed up through a lace of leaves to the hint of blue sky beyond. What if Heath sold the estate? What if he'd already sold it and they were all ejected? She should spare the girls that. They could be arrested. This was so unfair. They were seeing progress. They had a routine going. And a goal—Christmas in the Great Hall, recreating one of Uncle Harry's famous Christmas parties. Bronte imagined inviting everyone in the village. How could she disappoint Colleen and Maisie now when they'd worked so hard to achieve that?

What Heath might think about them planning a Christmas party without his say-so was something she would think about another day.

'The lake's too cold for swimming,' Colleen announced, distracting Bronte from her thoughts. 'I'm going home. Are you coming, Bronte?'

Maisie was on her feet too.

'No, you go on,' Bronte said. 'I'm going to have a quick swim.'

Pulling off her clothes as the girls disappeared through the trees, she stretched her naked body in the sun. Before she had chance to chicken out she scampered to the edge of the lake and plunged in. The shock of the icy water sucked all the breath out of her. She flailed around for a moment before steadying and starting to swim. Powering out to the centre of the lake with a relaxed, easy stroke, she turned on her back and floated blissfully in the silence…

Silence?

What silence?

Shooting up, she turned her head, trying to locate the source of a steady rumbling noise. It sounded like an armoured tank division coming down the drive. She swung around in the water, trying to work out how she could claim her clothes before anyone saw her—

Forget it, Bronte concluded as the rumbling grew louder. She'd never make it in time. She would just have to stay here, treading water...

Where was she? Heath frowned as he peered through the windscreen. Bronte was his first—his only thought as he drove up the drive. He'd called in at the cottage. She wasn't there. The old lady next door said Bronte would be up at Hebers Ghyll—as if it was a regular thing. He'd been angry since that moment—concerned and furious that Bronte had ignored everything he'd told her. But still, he'd hoped to see a flash of purple leggings—a glint of sun-kissed hair. Instead, all he could see were two other girls, sauntering out of the woods at the side of the lake as if they owned the place. So where the hell was she? And what the hell was going on?

Swinging down from the cab of his utility vehicle, he waited for the other men to assemble. Having issued preliminary instructions, he strode towards the girls. He wasn't interested in entering into conversation with them. He wanted the answer to one simple question: 'Where's Bronte?' he demanded, addressing the bleached blonde with a confident air.

'Heath Stamp,' she murmured. 'Is it really you?'

'I need to see her,' he said, ignoring the girl's attempt to distract him.

'I'm Colleen,' the girl persisted. 'Don't you remember me? And this is Maisie—'

'Where is she?' he cut across her in an ominous growl.

'A real charmer,' Colleen murmured.

'So what's changed?' Maisie agreed beneath her breath.

Both girls were staring at him warily now. So they remembered him. 'Are you going to tell me where she is?'

'I-in the lake,' Maisie stammered.

'In the lake?' he said, swinging round.

'Swimming,' Colleen hurried to explain.

As he turned to look he saw something that had him storming across the lawn, tugging off his clothes as he ran.

CHAPTER FIVE

SHE'D got trapped in the weeds. She'd been so trauma-
tised by the truck invasion she'd blundered about in the
water wondering what to do next and had got her leg
caught. Throwing her arms around as she struggled to
free herself, Bronte had attracted the very type of attention she had been trying to avoid. The long line of
wagons and builders' vans, led by a rugged Jeep with
blacked-out windows, had parked up in front of the hall.
Her heart jolted painfully to see Heath spring down
from the lead vehicle. Having spoken to the girls, he
turned to look at the lake at the precise moment she
started thrashing about. Impossibly bronzed and muscular, Heath, having tossed his shirt away as he ran,
was clearly intent on launching a one-man rescue. The
only option left to her was to swim as fast as she could
in the opposite direction.

Forget it, Bronte concluded, treading water. Her best
effort wasn't nearly good enough. Heath was streaking
towards her with a strong, fast stroke and had soon cut
off her escape route. Before she had chance to change
direction he gathered her up like a rugby ball and kicked
for shore.

'Put me down!' she shrieked the instant Heath found

his feet and started wading. 'I'm warning you, Heath—
let me go. There's no need for this.'

'There's every need for this.' Heath sounded less than
amused. Dumping her on her feet on the middle of the
lawn, he stood back.

She had never seen anyone quite so furious. She
hunched over, acutely conscious of her nakedness.

Heath seemed disappointingly unaware of it. 'What
did I tell you before I left?' he demanded.

Bronte's face flushed red. 'I haven't been near the
old buildings—'

'So you swim in the lake on your own? Brilliant.'

Heath's expression was thunderous. All male. All
disapproval. And the sight of his naked torso—powerful beyond belief, wet, tanned and gleaming in the
sun—was an unnerving distraction. She jumped alert
the moment she realised Heath's narrowed gaze was
roving freely over her naked body as if it were his to
inspect. 'Do you mind?' she flared, covering herself as
best she could.

'What the hell did you think you were doing in
the lake?' Heath snapped as if they were both fully
clothed.

'Swimming,' she said as if that were obvious. 'And
I know what I'm doing.'

Heath took one look at her. 'That would be a first.'

'Can't you turn your back or something?'

He ignored this remark. 'Never swim in the lake
again on your own. Do you understand me?'

'Perfectly.' She was trying to edge towards her
clothes, which wasn't easy with her legs crossed. At
last she managed to snag her leggings with the thong
still tangled inside them. Snatching them up with relief,
she held them in front of her. However ridiculous she

looked, it was some sort of shield. All she could do now was to start moving backwards, away from him.

She should have seen the tree root coming. She should have known that lightning did sometimes strike the same place twice. The breath flew from her lungs as Heath dived to save her—by some miracle he managed to swing her around before she hit the ground, cushioning her fall with his body. She was too shocked by the impact to do anything but yell, 'Get off me!' And scowl down.

Heath grinned up. 'I think you would have to get off me,' he pointed out.

Oh, great. She was straddling him, and Heath was clearly enjoying every moment of it—as well he might, with his great big hands firmly attached to her backside. 'Let me go,' she insisted, wriggling furiously. But the moment Heath lifted his hands away she missed them and wanted them back again. Fortunately for her, common sense kicked in.

'You don't really want to do that, do you, Bronte?'

She turned to look back over her shoulder at Heath.

'Seriously, it's not your best look,' he assured her as she continued to crawl away.

All she cared about was reaching a covey of trees over to her left where there were bushes to hide in while she sorted out her clothes. 'What do you think you're doing?' she shrieked with surprise.

Heath had grabbed her and trapped her beneath him on the ground. 'Preserving your dignity,' he said calmly, 'or what little remains of it.'

She followed his gaze. And groaned. Maisie, Colleen, and all of Heath's men had gathered at a safe distance to watch their little drama play out.

'Don't say it,' Heath warned her in a low growl. 'I can't bear to hear a woman swear.'

'Swear? I can barely draw enough breath to speak with you on top of me. Well—get up,' she insisted, only to be rewarded by a wolfish grin. 'Get off me, please,' she said reluctantly as their audience scattered. 'We weren't expecting visitors,' she said, acutely conscious of her naked body pressed into Heath's naked chest.

'Clearly,' he murmured, gazing down at her.

He seemed in no hurry to move away. 'Why didn't you warn me you were coming?' she said, thinking it best to make conversation in a position like this.

'Warn a squatter the owner's on his way?'

'I'm not a squatter,' Bronte argued. Her gaze slipped from Heath's mocking eyes to his sexy mouth, where it lingered. 'We're not even staying at the hall,' she protested faintly.

'And I should be grateful for that?'

She should be grateful for this, Bronte reflected, telling herself to relax and enjoy—would this moment ever come again?

'When will you get it through your head that Hebers Ghyll is not yours to do with as you like, Bronte?'

Nor was Heath's magnificent body, unfortunately. 'We were only trying to help.'

'Against my express instructions.'

'We stayed away from the castle.'

'Next time, do me the courtesy of asking if you can visit my property first. This obviously comes as a surprise to you, but this is my land, and safety is an overriding concern of mine.'

How could it be when Heath's chest hair was tormenting her nipples? The men she met on her travels were too busy fretting about their skin care regime or whether or not to wax their chest. Heath clearly suffered no such dilemmas.

'Well, this is nice,' he remarked, easing his position, which made her blink. 'I never took you for a nudist, Bronte.'

'And I never took you for Genghis Khan,' she fired back in an attempt to blank the sensation currently flooding her veins.

'Oh, yes, you did,' Heath growled softly.

Was it safer to stare into his eyes and see what he was thinking, or at Heath's firm mouth and long to kiss him? She was in trouble whatever she did, Bronte concluded, while Heath was hot-wired to all her erotic pressure points. She took the only option left open to her, and closed her eyes, shutting him out.

'Open your eyes, Bronte. This is no time to fall asleep.'

Or to experience that first seductive brush of Heath's lips, apparently. 'Oh, clear off,' she flared, trying to push him away. 'What are you made of?' she demanded when he didn't yield. 'Kryptonite?'

'Flesh and blood the same as you.'

'Not a bit like me,' Bronte argued primly.' I have manners.'

'And a naked bottom,' Heath commented mildly as she struggled to cover herself with an impossibly shrunken pair of leggings.

'You're such a barbarian.'

'Come on—get dressed.' As Heath sprang up he dragged her with him. 'This has gone on long enough, Bronte. You're still a trespasser with a lot of explaining to do.'

Snatching her hands free, she was crouched down in a ball again. 'Later,' she said. 'You can leave me now.'

'Oh, can I?' Heath demanded, planting his hands on his hips.

'Honestly,' she flared—though flaring was difficult from a crouching position. 'I really can't believe your ingratitude. We cleared *your* house—*your* grounds—'

'And if a wall had fallen on *your* head?'

'I already told you, we haven't been anywhere dangerous.'

'You've been back to the hall,' said Heath, who showed no sign of going anywhere.

'Do you seriously think I'd take the girls into a dangerous situation?'

'No, but you'd walk blindly in,' Heath argued. 'And you'd probably be hit by falling masonry before you got halfway through the door.'

'There's no need to sound quite so thrilled by the prospect.'

'Leaving me to clear up the mess,' he finished, talking over her. 'When I say don't do something, there's a very good reason for it.'

Oh, why wouldn't her clothes co-operate on damp skin? Her leggings had twisted round like a self-imposed chastity belt. All she could do was crunch over with her arms covering her chest as Heath threw her her top.

'When were you going to tell me about the window, Bronte?'

She froze mid-pulling it on.

'What?' Heath barked. 'You thought I wouldn't notice?'

She hadn't meant to do it and felt terrible. When she had forced the upstairs window to break into the hall the handle had come away in her hand. 'Oh, Heath, I'm really sorry—'

'Are you?' he said impassively. His hands on his hips, he confronted her with a stony gaze.

Displaying a truly magnificent chest, Bronte registered with a sharp intake of breath. She had forgotten how tall Heath was, how impossibly fit. And with nothing to cover those massive blacksmith's arms, or his powerful torso—

'Have you done staring?' he snapped.

'I'm going home,' Bronte announced in exasperation. 'I need to wash this mud off.'

'I'd say be my guest,' Heath observed sardonically, 'but as you have already made yourself at home.'

'I prefer to use my own shower, thank you,' she snapped back.

'As you wish.'

But now Heath stood in her way. Feinting past him, she snatched up the last of her clothes. 'I don't need anything from you, Heath.'

'Except a job, presumably?'

She froze.

'You're not going the right way about it, are you?' Heath pointed out. 'You broke into my house. You brought your friends along too.'

'This has nothing to do with Maisie or Colleen,' Bronte interrupted, rushing to her friends' defence. 'This is all my fault, Heath. Blame me, if you must. I was just trying to help. I thought that if we.'

'You didn't think,' Heath interrupted her sharply. 'You went straight into an old building without a safety review—just as you swam solo in the lake. I could forgive that, but you got your friends involved and that was irresponsible. Or had you conveniently forgotten that breaking and entering is a criminal offence? Go home, Bronte,' he rapped when she tried to defend her decision. 'I can't believe you're serious about applying for a job here. If that's still the case, you've made one hell of a start. I can't imagine how you're going to climb back from this.'

And neither could she. Heath's tone of voice made it clear that playtime was well and truly over.

She had alienated Heath. She had forfeited her chance of getting the job. She had lost the girls their promised pay-off—the Christmas party—which meant that all their hard work was wasted.

Things couldn't be worse, Bronte mused back at the cottage, where she was sitting on the sofa with her head buried in her hands.

So she'd just have to make it right, she determined, springing to her feet.

Heath couldn't possibly have appeared less thrilled when she turned up at the hall with Colleen and Maisie in tow.

'What do you want, Bronte?' he rapped, while she stood and stared. Heath in hard hat, steel-capped boots, and a high-vis' jacket, was a fantasy yet to be explored.

'We're here to help,' she said, conscious of Maisie and Colleen skulking behind her. The girls hadn't been exactly enthusiastic when she had sold them this idea over a drink at the pub.

'Help?' Heath demanded, narrowing his eyes suspiciously. 'We're on the roof, Bronte. How can you help?'

'Has the fresh air given you an appetite, possibly?' she enquired pleasantly.

'Why? Did you bring pizza?' Heath looked behind her to see if the girls were carrying anything.

'No.' Bronte shook her head. 'I'd only serve pizza if I'd made it myself. I was merely suggesting I could cook supper for you—but if you'd rather we left—'

'You cook?' Heath interrupted.

'Of course I cook. My mother was the housekeeper here,' she reminded him with a frown. 'And as you pointed out,' she added innocently, 'I have a great line in jam tarts. But don't stereotype me. I mend engines too.'

Heath hummed. 'I suppose the men will need feeding when they knock off, so if you're offering to cook supper for nine—'

'Twelve,' Bronte said, turning to look at the girls. 'I'll get started, shall I?'

With some reluctance, it seemed to Bronte, Heath stepped aside. The way to a man's heart would always be by the same route—something women knew and had used shamelessly across the ages. She was hardly a trailblazer in that regard, Bronte reflected as she led her troops towards the kitchen.

CHAPTER SIX

SUPPER was nearly ready. They just needed some fresh herbs for the soup, which Colleen and Maisie had offered to go and pick for her while Bronte kept an eye on things on the cooker. It was Colleen who drew Bronte's attention to the tableau being played out in the yard outside the kitchen window.

There was no harm in looking, was there? She joined her friends on the pretext of opening the window to let the steam out from her soup.

Heath, dressed just in jeans, was sluicing down in the yard.

Oh, yes, he was...

And very nice he looked too...

As he slowly tipped a bucket of water from the well over his head drops of water glittered in the last rays of the sun and flew from his hair as he raked it back with big, rough hands. She felt rather than heard him sigh with pleasure. And then those hands continued on as Heath slid the last of the water from his hard-muscled chest...

'Oh, my God—you could have an orgasm just watching him,' Colleen breathed, leaning over Bronte's shoulder.

'Shh! He'll hear us.' Bronte held her breath.

'I didn't even know men came built like that,' Maisie confided.

'They don't,' Colleen assured her. 'You want to get stuck in there, Bronte.'

'Me?' Bronte pretended innocence as she pressed a hand against her chest. 'Heath isn't interested in me.'

'Not much,' Colleen murmured, still avidly watching.

'Well, even if he was—'

'He is,' Colleen assured her with the resulting impact on Bronte's pulse.

'Well, let's get on,' she said, sounding rather like her mother, Bronte thought.

Inwardly, she was anything but. Her mother was calm and logical, while Bronte was a dreamer on a roller-coaster ride out of control. Her heart refused to stop thumping as Colleen and Maisie, having put Heath out of their minds, started laying up the long, scrubbed table. Then another horrible thought occurred—if her fantasies were an open book to her friends, they must be clear to Heath as well!

'Why wouldn't you be interested in a man like that?' Colleen demanded, doggedly returning to the subject as she came back for the spoons. 'You haven't been putting bromide in your tea, have you, Bronte?'

'Just sugar,' Bronte murmured distractedly, jumping back from the window too late to stop Heath seeing her.

Holding onto Bronte's shoulders so she could stare over them, Colleen observed, 'Licking that chunky-hunk is all the sugar I'd ever need.'

'Supper's in ten,' Bronte pointed out briskly, 'and I need those herbs before I serve up.'

'On it,' Colleen promised. Grabbing Maisie by

the wrist, she left Bronte to her own devices in the kitchen.

Heath came into the room moments later. He grunted. She grunted. She didn't trust herself to turn around. She could hear him moving around behind her—hanging up his jacket, putting his hard hat on the side, taking off his boots and leaving them on the mat by the door.

Had her senses ever been this keen before?

Warm man...a little ruffled, a little windswept, his hair a little damp—his jeans definitely wet, and clinging lovingly—

'Hey, what do you think you're doing?' she said, jumping with alarm as Heath brushed past her.

'Stealing soup,' he said. 'It smelled so good—'

'Hands off,' she said, smacking his hand away. 'And there's no need to sound so surprised.'

Heath's expression was deceptively sleepy, Bronte thought, with his face so close, and his eyes... 'Must you creep up on me?' Must you look so sexy? she thought, taking in the damply dangerous man who looked exactly like the answer to her every sex-starved dream.

'I didn't creep.' The sexy mouth tugged up in a grin. 'I think you'll find on closer acquaintance that I never creep.'

No, he never did, and that sluice-down in the yard had really intensified the scent of warm, clean man. And what did he mean by closer acquaintance? As she tried to work it out she dragged in greedy lungfuls of Heath's delicious scent when what she should be doing was watching the food on top of the cooker to make sure it didn't burn.

Her gaze started at ground level with Heath's sexy feet, and then rose steadily to take in the hard thighs stretching the seams on his damp jeans. She resolutely refused to notice the button open at the top of his zipper, or the belt hanging loose—and moved on swiftly to Heath's impressive chest, which was currently clad in the deep blue heavy-knit sweater he'd pulled on at the door—

She yelped with shock when he took hold of her elbows and lifted her aside. Heath shrugged. 'I'd hate you to burn that soup. And I owe it to the men to make sure you know what you're doing,' he added, stealing another spoonful. 'What?' he said, angling his chin as Bronte planted her hands on her hips. 'You didn't think I'd give you a completely free rein, did you?'

'You don't frighten me, Heath Stamp. Now, get out of my way—'

'Not before I've had another spoonful. This soup isn't bad,' Heath admitted. His amused glance made Bronte wonder if he was remembering her naked.

'If you want to catch your death in those wet jeans go right ahead,' she said.

'They're not drying as I'd hoped,' Heath said, his lips pressing down. 'Why don't you sling them over the Aga rail for me?'

'Like I want your wet clothes hanging in my kitchen? And don't even think of lounging round in your boxers while I'm making a meal.'

'You're making two assumptions there,' Heath told her, 'both of which are wrong.'

One: it wasn't her kitchen, it was Heath's.

And two?

Don't even go there, Bronte thought, noting the humour in Heath's eyes. 'I was merely suggesting you might want to change into some dry clothes before supper,' she told him primly.

'And if I had some dry clothes with me, I might do that.'

Heath had lightened up. Maybe breaks in the country were good for him, Bronte reasoned. Pity they weren't good for her composure.

And while she was musing on this Heath stole some more soup from the pot. 'There'll be none left,' she protested spreading out her arms to take command of the Aga. 'Here,' she said, opening the oven door. 'Why don't you stick your butt in there? You'll soon dry off.'

'That's a little drastic, isn't it?' Heath observed.

'It's an accepted method of warming up.'

'Really?' Heath said, making her wish she hadn't spoken. Folding her arms, she angled her chin as she waited for him to take her advice.

'Thank you, but no,' he said, allowing her a small mocking bow. 'I'm sure my body heat will take care of it.'

It was certainly taking care of her.

'Do I make you nervous, Bronte?'

'As if,' she scoffed. 'Though you do make me a bit nervous,' she said on reflection.

'Oh?' Heath's gaze flared with interest.

'You're eating all the soup,' she told him deadpan. 'Now clear off—'

She exhaled sharply as Heath caught hold of her arm as he brushed past. 'Why did you really come back to the hall, Bronte?'

'Why did you come back?' she said, feeling unusually flustered as she stared up at him.

'I asked you first.'

'I took pity on you—and, okay, I made a fuss about you doing something with your inheritance. I could hardly sit at home twiddling my thumbs after that.'

'To think, I almost drove you away,' Heath said, heaving a heavy sigh. 'Where did I go wrong?'

'I don't know, Heath.' She met the humorous gaze head on—and wished she hadn't. Hadn't she made enough mistakes for one day?

'Let me repeat myself,' Heath said, 'What are you really doing here, Bronte?'

'I couldn't stay away from you,' she said in her most mocking tone. 'Does that make you feel better?'

'At least you're being honest,' Heath said.

'You're so modest,' Bronte countered, stirring the soup as if her life depended on it. 'You know my only interest in being here is the future of Hebers Ghyll.'

'Liar,' Heath said softly.

'Could you put these bowls out for me, please?' She plonked them in his hands. Anything to keep Heath's hands occupied and give herself space to think.

'I have made you feel better, haven't I?' Heath sounded pleased with himself as he came back to prop a hip against the side.

'So good I hardly know what to do with myself,' Bronte agreed, sticking the salt pot and pepper grinder in his hands. 'Now move. You definitely can't stand this close to the heat without—'

'Without both of us getting burned?' Heath suggested.

'Without the soup getting burned,' she corrected him. 'Excuse me please...' Would her heart stop thundering? Hands on hips, she waited for Heath to move. Her only alternative was to stretch across him—and risk rubbing some already highly aroused and very sensitive part of her body against him? Not even remotely sensible to try.

'I'm still wondering what you came back for,' he said, 'and I mean the real reason.'

'Okay,' she said, staring him in the eyes. 'I'm serious about wanting the job and I thought if I came here and made myself useful—doing anything I could to help—you might remember me when it came to handing out interview times.'

Leaning back against the Aga rail, Heath crossed his arms and gave her one of his looks. 'So you're here so you can keep on reminding me how good you'd be?'

That wasn't quite the way she would have put it, but yes. 'I thought cooking supper for you would be a start.'

'And you're not a conniving woman?'

Heath's face was very close—close enough to see how thick his lashes were, and how firm his mouth. 'On the contrary,' Bronte argued, 'I am a conniving woman. And I know what I want.'

'And so do I,' Heath assured her as he straightened up.

'Well, seeing as you've shown willing.'

Heath laughed.

And now he was standing in her way again. 'Excuse me, please,' she said politely.

What was she supposed to do with a man who took up every inch of vital cooking space and who showed no sign of moving—a man who was staring down at her now with a look in his darkening eyes that suggested he would very much like a practical demonstration of just how badly she wanted to work for him? 'You're in my way, Heath.'

'Am I?'

He didn't move so she tried a firmer approach. 'If you want feeding you'd better get out of my way now.'

'I love it when you talk tough.'

She drew in a great, shuddering gust of relief when Heath finally straightened up and moved away. Fantasies were safe, warm things, but the reality of Heath's hard, virile body so close to hers was something else again. He hadn't even touched her yet and every part of her was glowing with lust—and she couldn't blame the Aga for that.

'Don't burn my supper,' Heath warned. 'If you do I shall have to punish you.'

Bronte drew in a sharp, shocked breath. The images that conjured up didn't even bear thinking about. Rallying, she turned to face Heath with her chin tilted at a combative angle, only to find a slow-burning smile playing around his lips. He was enjoying this. Heath was the master of verbal seduction and she was his willing partner in crime. Lucky for her, the girls chose that moment to return from the herb garden—if she counted luck in heated aches and screaming frustration, that was, Bronte mused, adopting an innocent expression by the cooker.

'Thyme?' Colleen held out a thick bunch of fragrant herbs.

'Bad time,' Heath commented dryly. Then pointing a finger at Bronte as if to say they had unfinished business, he left the kitchen to call the men.

She couldn't think of anything else all through supper. What had Heath meant by that pointing finger? If Heath meant what she thought he meant her fantasies were out of a job. Heath gave nothing away during the meal— he barely looked at her. She had cooked her heart out, silently thanking her mother for all those hours they'd spent together preparing food. She had everything she needed in the restored garden—and more eggs than she knew what to do with, thanks to the chickens being of too little value for Uncle Harry's executors to chase them down. Tonight's menu included minestrone soup, and a huge Spanish omelette, full of finely chopped seasonal vegetables and crispy potatoes, which she had browned beneath the grill until the cheese on top was crunchy. To complement this there was a bowl of crispy salad, along with some freshly baked bread and newly churned butter from a nearby farm. Then there was beer, wine and soft drinks from the local shop to satisfy twelve hungry mouths around the supper table. She loved doing this, Bronte reflected with her chin on the heel of her hand as the chatter continued abated—especially feeding Heath, who seemed to relish every mouthful.

'The country's not so bad, is it, Heath?' She couldn't resist saying when he dived in for second helpings.

'I'll freely admit it gives me a healthy appetite.'

And how was she supposed to take that? She drew a deep, steadying breath, but the tension between them remained electric. It was the same between Heath's men and Bronte's friends, she noticed. The village was severely depleted when it came to good-looking guys, as most had gone to work in the city, so this was an interesting occasion for everyone, to say the least.

'This is a real feast,' Colleen observed, passing the bread round.

Indeed it was, Bronte thought, glancing at Heath.

'Here's that cheese we bought to go with the bread,' he said, passing the cheese board round to an appreciative roar.

Bronte's glance yo-yoed between Colleen and Heath. They had walked to the farm together, which meant they must have talked. And Colleen was hardly noted for holding back. She must have said something about Bronte's feelings for Heath.

Well, it was too late to do anything about that now, Bronte thought, putting an Eton mess on the table for pudding—easy. fresh whipped and sweetened cream, thick Greek yoghurt, strawberries, raspberries, and crumbled chunks of home-made meringue. 'Please, tuck in,' she announced brightly, swallowing back her embarrassment at the thought that her feelings for Heath must have been aired extensively at some point today.

'This pudding is delicious,' Heath said, looking up.

His eyes held all sorts of thoughts that went beyond pudding—none of which Bronte trusted herself to examine too closely. How would Heath's energy translate if they were left alone together for any length of time? Perhaps he had better install a sprinkler system along with all his other DIY improvements.

'We're going to be here for the best part of six months according to the boss,' one of the men said, directing this comment at Bronte. 'I hope you'll be staying on?'

'She'll be here,' Heath confirmed.

'Oh, will I?' Bronte challenged.

'Where else would you go?' Heath demanded.

Everyone went silent and turned to look at them.

'We definitely can't let a cook as good as you go,' the first man said politely to break the standoff.

'We won't let her go,' Heath assured him while Bronte frowned. It wasn't just that she didn't like to be told what she was going to do—she was beginning to wonder if she had blown the bigger job. Not that she didn't enjoy cooking, but her mother was the one trained in household management, while Bronte's training had been geared towards managing the estate.

Don't make a fuss, her inner voice warned…*softly, softly catchee monkey*.

'I've really enjoyed cooking for you all,' she said honestly, thinking it best to leave it there.

'If you do stay on and work here,' Colleen piped up, 'I'm sure Heath will pay excellent wages.'

'We definitely need to talk terms,' Heath agreed above the laughter.

Great wages and impossible terms? Bronte smiled and kept on smiling as if she hadn't a care in the world. But when everyone started getting up from the table and she noticed Heath was looking at her, her senses sharpened. After what Heath had described as her less than promising start, she hoped she had gone some way to making amends tonight. But she still needed clarification about a formal interview—that was if Heath's offer still stood.

Her first thought was, what would the position be?
Missionary? Or up against a wall—
Stop! *Stop!*

Estate manager, or housekeeper, Bronte told herself firmly, wiping her overheated forehead on the back of her hand. She'd settle for either—though of course she would hand over the housekeeper's position to her mother, with Heath's agreement, the moment her parents returned from their trip.

She was so busy clearing the table and trying to see into the future that she managed to crash into Heath. 'Well?' he demanded, steadying her, his firm hands so warm and strong on her arms. 'I'm still waiting for your answer, Bronte.'

'Wages?'

'Terms,' he murmured.

'And is that look supposed to encourage me to accept?' His gaze was currently focused on her lips.

'I haven't offered you anything yet,' he pointed out. 'Is this a better look?'

His face was so close she could see the flecks of amber in his eyes. 'Barely,' she said.

Her body disagreed. Her body liked Heath's brooding look very much indeed. 'You can let me go now,' she said, staring pointedly at his hand on her arm.

Heath hummed as he lifted it away, leaving behind him an imprint of sensation that it would take more than a shower to wash off.

This was everything she'd ever dreamed of, Bronte reflected as she cleared the table—Heath back at Hebers Ghyll, picking up almost, but not quite, where they'd left off, flirting with him.

Flirting with Heath was a very bad idea indeed. It put her heart at risk, while his was in no danger at all. And she didn't kid herself where this was heading, if she let it. Heath had a healthy appetite, and it was up to her to decide yes or no and then take the consequences for her decision whatever it might be.

Everyone else had left the kitchen to return to work. No one stopped until a job was done now, Bronte had noticed, even thought it was quite late. Heath's influence, she supposed. He never seemed to tire. She had asked him to mend a fuse for her before he went back to join the others. 'Seems I can't get rid of you now,' she teased him as he straightened up.

'Isn't that what you want?' he said.

She was staring at his lips again, Bronte realised, shifting her gaze to Heath's work-stained top. 'Do you really think I find the scent of spark plugs and engine oil irresistible?'

'I think you love a bit of rough.'

'I—'

Before she had chance to deny it, Heath had dragged her into his arms.

'It might have escaped your notice,' she told him, coolly, 'but I'm in no danger of falling over at the moment.'

'You're right,' Heath agreed, lips pressing down. 'You're in no danger at all.' He lifted his hands away.

The master tactician was at it again, Bronte suspected, feeling the loss of him before Heath had even left the room. There was more to foreplay than she had ever realised. Turned out Heath was master of that too. Still, he'd gone now, which would give her chance to cool down. She'd clear up the kitchen—and then, as she'd announced over supper, she would paint the wall Heath had plastered. The plaster had dried out now, and she didn't feel like going down to the pub. Sometimes she liked to be alone with her thoughts—though where that would get her tonight was anyone's guess.

CHAPTER SEVEN

EVERYONE was going down to the pub in the village after work. Heath wasn't and neither was Bronte. She was still fixing up the kitchen. Having cooked and cleaned and cleared, she had declared her intention to paint the wall. He could hardly leave her to it.

Stubborn as ever, he thought, catching sight of her through the kitchen window. It looked cosy and welcoming inside with the lights casting a warm glow, and something Bronte had prepared for tomorrow bubbling away quietly on the Aga. She was up a ladder with her hair tied back beneath a bright emerald-green scarf—and she was wielding a roller—

God help them all. Cream paint extended down to her elbow, and there was a smudge of it on her nose. He'd better get in there before she painted herself to the wall.

'Knock it off now, Bronte,' he said as he walked into the room. 'It's almost nine o' clock.'

'Past your bedtime?' she teased him.

He wasn't even remotely tired.

Turning, she planted her hands on her hips, daubing her jeans with another generous lashing of paint.

'I hope that paint washes off.'

'You know something, Heath,' she said thoughtfully.

'You said I'd made a bad start. Well, now I'm wondering if I want a job here at all. The thought of you bossing me around all day and all night—'

'Is irresistible,' he said, easing onto one hip to stare up at her. 'You know you'd love it. Just think—you'd be able to argue with me non-stop.'

She sighed. 'Sadly, I don't have your stamina.'

Something he'd like to put to the test. But shouldn't. *Mustn't.* 'Now I know you're joking. I've seen that tongue of yours do the marathon. And, didn't I just tell you to stop?'

Her jaw dropped in mock shock. 'I obey you now?'

'Didn't I tell you that's part of the job description?' Cupping his chin, he pretended to think about it—and cursed himself for forgetting to shave. Barbarian? She was right.

She hummed. 'We may have a serious problem, in that case. Unless…'

'Unless?' he prompted.

'Unless you're offering to make me a drink?' she said perkily.

'Gin and tonic?'

'Coffee,' she said in a reproving tone.

Coffee won. Climbing down the ladder, she tried to muscle him out of the way when he took over the cooker. No contest. He was skipper of the Aga tonight. 'You can't stand the fact that I'm in charge,' he said as she bumped against him one last time and finally gave up. 'You've grown wild on your travels—uncontrollable—you've got no discipline—you're answerable to no one—'

'But you love me,' she said, adding quickly in her sensible voice to cover for her gaffe. 'I'm answerable to myself, Heath. And I learned a lot while I was away.'

He didn't doubt it, and while she took the pan off the cooker and washed out the paintbrushes he encouraged her to tell him something about her extended trip. So much of it turned out to be relevant to the job of estate manager at Hebers Ghyll, he couldn't help but put his baser instincts on the back burner as he listened. It was fascinating to hear how she'd gone from naïve, untried miss, to Capability Bronte, building fences, birthing animals, and helping to construct artesian wells along the way. He revised his opinion of her upwards another good few notches when she told him, 'Life's easy when there's no responsibility attached. I needed to get out there, Heath. I had to get away from this small village—not just to find out what I was missing, but to test myself and find out what I'm made of.'

'Sugar and spice and all things nice?'

'Now, you know that's not true,' she told him, smiling.

'So did you find the missing link?'

She thought about it for a moment. 'I discovered how much I love it here,' she said, biting the full swell of her bottom lip, as if lust for travel and the love of home were warring inside her.

'You love a lot,' he observed.

'How do you work that out?'

'You talk about love all the time, but love isn't a cure-all, Bronte.'

'Maybe not,' she said, 'but nothing much would get done without it.'

He held up his hands to that. 'Did you love teaching me to read?'

She held his gaze for a moment in silence as if she knew that everything that mattered to him would be contained in her answer. 'I loved being with you,' she said steadily. 'And you were a good student,' she added thoughtfully.

'And now?'

'I don't think I could teach you anything,' she said honestly.

'Well, thank you, ma'am.' He curved a grin. 'I can't believe you said that—'

'I can't believe it, either,' she agreed, and then they both laughed. And moved one step closer.

'I haven't had your education,' he admitted as she started clearing up.

'You've had plenty at the school of life,' she observed. And when she turned to him her face was serious. 'You had more schooling in that university than most people could deal with, Heath.'

They said nothing for a moment and then he curved a grin and let it go.

'This paint is supposed to wash off easily,' she grumbled from the sink, up to her elbows in soapy water.

'Am I allowed to smile?' he said.

'You do what you want from what I've seen.'

She turned back to vigorously washing her hands again, but not before he'd seen the blood rush to her cheeks. 'Towel?' he suggested.

'Please.'

He made coffee and passed her a mug. She hummed appreciatively and started sipping.

'Good?'

Emerald eyes found him over the rim of the mug. 'Very good—you're a man of many talents, Heath.'

'I'm a businessman. I do what I have to—as efficiently as I can.'

'But you are growing to love it here, aren't you?' she

asked him, unable to keep the anxiety out of her voice. 'Just a little bit, anyway?'

'Nothing would entice me to subscribe to your woolly view that love changes everything, Bronte. Do you seriously think love would be enough here?'

'Obviously, Hebers Ghyll needs a little more help than loving thoughts,' she conceded.

'Help from a jaded city type like me, possibly?'

'A man with enough money to make things happen? Yes, that should do it,' she agreed, brazen as you like.

A long-time fan of Bronte's directness, he wasn't fazed, and went in with a challenge of his own. 'And the sparring between us? Could we work round that?'

'I'd find a way to deal with it,' she said, frowning.

Was she thinking about the fun they could have making up?

'The only reason I'm here,' she assured him seriously, 'is to make sure you don't knock the place down when no one's looking.'

'And build a shopping centre?' He laughed. 'And, of course, that's the only reason you're here?'

'There's no other reason I can think of.'

Opening the fridge, he took out a beer, knocked the top off the bottle on the edge of the kitchen table, and chugged it down. 'I'm not a man who destroys things, Bronte—when will you get that through your head? I'm a builder by nature, and a games designer by trade. I see no conflict there. I create things. Cyber worlds, brick walls—they're all the same to me; it's what I do.'

'But your life is in the city, Heath. So you wouldn't stay here year round—and whoever makes a success of Hebers Ghyll would have to love it enough to live here.'

'Every second of every day?' He shrugged. 'I don't think so. That's what a good estate manager's for.'

Bronte fell silent as this sank in. Even if she won the job there would be no Heath.

'You can't run a place like Hebers Ghyll on good intentions, Bronte. Look at Uncle Harry—'

'Yes. Look at him,' she said fiercely.

And now they were both quiet.

She was moving their mugs to the sink one minute— the next she had grabbed the paintbrush, jabbed it in the paint-tray and come looking for him.

'You want a fight, do you?' he challenged, dodging out of her way.

So much, Bronte thought.

'You deserved that,' she told him, backing off having given Heath a stripe of paint across his arm.

'Did I?' He circled round her. 'The countryside is just a lot of empty space to me,' he taunted. 'Just think of all those potential building plots—'

'Stop it,' she warned him, making another lunge, which he just managed to evade.

'The noise and the rush of the city?' He backed her slowly towards the wall as he pretended to think about it. 'Or the silence and emptiness of the countryside? Hmm. Let me think…'

'Empty?' she exclaimed, making a double stab at him before slipping away under his arm. 'The countryside empty? You should open your eyes and look around, Heath.'

He wiped the paint off his cheek. 'My eyes are wide open, believe me,' he assured her, moving in for the kill.

'I don't know why you even came here,' she said as

he held her firmly with the brush dangling a tempting inch or two from her face.

'Profit, wasn't it?' he growled, easing her wrist so the brush laid a dainty paint trail across her cheek.

'Why, you—'

'Barbarian?' he suggested, directing the brush across her nose.

'I'll never forgive you for this.'

He wasn't concerned. Bronte's eyes told him something very different—and so did the swell of her mouth. He wouldn't leave a paint trail there, he decided, removing the paintbrush from her hand and putting it in the sink. That would definitely be against his best interests. 'I'm confiscating this,' he said, running water over the brush. Next, he dampened a cloth. 'And now I'm going to clean you up.' He raised a challenging brow when she threatened to resist him.

'I should go,' she said breathlessly, one step ahead of him as she stared at the door.

'No,' he argued softly, 'you should come.'

She drew in a sharp breath as she turned to look at him. 'Is everything a joke to you, Heath?'

'Is this a joke?' Wielding the warm, moist cloth with the utmost care, he swung an arm around her shoulder to draw her close and wiped the paint smears off her face. 'I've made a decision,' he murmured, noting the rapid rise and fall of her chest as her breathing speeded up.

'Have you?' There was only the smallest ring of vivid green around her pupils as she stared at him. 'This will all be worth it if I have persuaded you to keep Hebers Ghyll, Heath.'

He smiled into her eyes. 'Sorry to disappoint. The most I'm prepared to commit to at this moment in time is that I will keep the place alive and continue with the renovations. Don't look so surprised,' he teased. 'A demolition site is worth far less to me than a stately home.'

'I'll get the paint again,' she threatened him.

'Then I'd just have to wash you all over again…'

Her eyes widened. 'You wouldn't dare.'

'Are you sure of that?'

'What do I have to do to stop you?'

He didn't miss the note of pent-up excitement in her voice.

'Everything I tell you,' he murmured.

'What's the catch?' she said suspiciously.

'There is no catch.'

'Then tell me what I have to do—' She followed his gaze to the door. 'Heath, we can't—'

'Why not?' Angling his chin, he stared down at her.

'Because it's outrageous,' she whispered, her voice trembling with excitement.

'You don't do outrageous?' Dipping his head, he kissed her neck.

CHAPTER EIGHT

HEATH's hand cupped Bronte's chin. He made her look at him. She could see in his gaze what came next and how incredible it was going to be. His hand felt warm and gentle on her face. For such a big man, Heath could be incredibly sensitive—and intuitive. It was this mix of soothing balm and fiery passion she craved now. She was hungry for tenderness. Only-child syndrome, maybe, Bronte thought. With both her parents working there hadn't been much time to spare for cuddling. And though there had been other children visiting Hebers Ghyll she'd always felt on the outside looking in—except with Heath. They had both been different, she supposed—the dreamer and the wild boy from the city.

'Hey, come back to me,' Heath insisted.

She looked at him. They could both have used a hug back then. She had always been hungry for Heath. He had lit a fire no amount of common sense could hope to put out, and that fire had been smouldering for thirteen years. Could anything stand in its way now?

'This isn't so outrageous, is it?' Heath demanded, tightening his grip on her when she exhaled shakily.

'You're a very bad man indeed.'

Heath smiled, and then his lips brushed her cheek.

He was making her tremble. He was making the ache inside her turn into a primitive hunger that lacked every vestige of romance.

And then he brought her in front of him and Heath's steady gaze didn't leave her eyes as his hands moved slowly down her arms. He could read every thought and she felt violently exposed, yet glad that Heath could see her hunger for him. She exclaimed softly when his thumb pad caught the tip of her nipple—but it moved on. This was all intended. Heath had caught her in his erotic net. And she wasn't interested in escaping. She was only interested in what came next.

Heath's hand was moving lightly down her spine towards her buttocks. Her breathing sounded ragged as that experienced hand continued on, and when it reached the hollow in the small of her back it fitted so neatly, she relaxed, but when he moved on to map the swell of her bottom that was too much. With a shaking cry, she arched her back, offering herself for pleasure. Heath's hands maintained a detailed exploration—sensitively seeking, and yet never quite giving her the contact she craved. 'Oh, please—' She was shivering with anticipation, shameless in her need. 'Please don't tease me like this, Heath.'

Heath said nothing as he continued to stroke and prepare. Her breathing sounded noisy in the silence, and she knew he must feel her heat through the flimsy protection of her clothes. She was moist and swollen—ready for him, and the only thought in her head was, Don't stop.

'And if I stop now?' Heath said, pausing.

'Have you read my mind?' She heard the smile in his voice, and could picture the curve of Heath's lips, even with her face buried in the soft wool of his sweater. 'You can't stop now,' she said, gazing up at him, 'Because I can't stop now.'

'So, what's the answer?' he said, frowning.

'You have to kiss me.'

'Is that a command?' Heath's lips curved with amusement.

'Yes, please,' she said.

Maybe her memory of all those years back was faulty. Maybe one kiss would be the answer to resisting Heath—to resisting what her body begged her to do.

His mouth was so close her lips tingled. She sighed, climbing to the next level of arousal as Heath brushed his lips against hers. Reaching up, she laced her fingers through his hair, opening her body to a man more than capable of taking advantage of her. Her legs were trembling against his. She'd waited so long. Heath didn't disappoint. His kiss was firm and sure, and the touch of his hands on her body was indescribable. Heat ran through her like a torrent of molten lava, and when he teased her lips apart with his tongue she was glad of his arms supporting her. Hunger ruled her. She was captive to feelings so strong it was impossible to keep them in check. Breath shot from her lungs as Heath's grip tightened. She wanted him. She wanted to share his warmth and confidence. She wanted his body. She wanted Heath to take hold of her and position her as he pleasured her, and for him to go on pleasuring her until the world and all its uncertainties faded away.

There could be no more delays. She had no inhibitions left—no restraint. There was just an urgent need to feel Heath hot and hard inside her. She wanted him as a wild animal wanted its mate. There was nothing tender about this—no thought, no reason, just a glorious battle with one sure ending. Naked flesh on naked flesh, drugging and intoxicating—no kisses, no tender promises, only now.

She rejoiced in the rasp of Heath's chest hair against her pitifully sensitive nipples, and welcomed him, hard, hot and savage against her. She cried out with excitement when he brought her jeans down in one swift move and lifted her. 'Now,' she instructed him, crazy with need.

'Not so fast,' Heath murmured. His experienced hands had found her, checked that she was ready, and then he quickly protected them both.

She locked her legs around his waist. 'Oh, no…no…no,' she cried, shaking her head wildly from side to side as he started teasing her with just the tip.

'Oh, yes…yes,' Heath responded, taking her deep.

Her eyes widened. She gasped with astonishment at the size of him. She gripped his shoulder for support. Planting her hands flat against his chest, she braced herself—and when the pleasure became too great, she laced her fingers through his hair, threw her head back and rode the sensation. This was so much more than she had expected. She was lost in pleasure, lost to reason. Heath was every bit as intuitive as she'd known he would be, and infinitely sensitive to her needs. He must never stop, she thought wildly as he dealt her the deep rhythmical strokes. She wouldn't let him stop. She was floating on an erotic plane where she had nothing to do but accept pleasure while Heath, with one hand braced against the door, pounded into her.

'You're fantastic,' she screamed at the moment of release. As she collapsed against him she realised this was true. Heath was an extraordinary lover, and she was addicted to his very special brand of pleasure. She pressed her face against his chest, inhaling his warm, clean male scent. Heath was everything she had ever wanted in a man—everything she had ever dreamed he would be. He was so tender and careful as he lowered her to the floor. He didn't let go of her until he was sure she was steady on her feet; by that time her heart was full of him.

'Better?' he murmured, smiling against her hair.

'Transformed,' she told him. That was nothing more than the truth. She could hardly believe what had happened, and was so glad that it had.

'Until the next time?' Heath's voice was full of the affection she longed to hear as he nuzzled his face against her neck.

'We belong together, you and I, I've always known it,' she said, snuggling into him. Perhaps Heath did too. He'd said until the next time, which couldn't be long now, she thought, gazing up at him. She only needed a couple of minutes to recover, and then she'd be—

Something had changed, Bronte realised, feeling sick inside. She'd said too much as usual, and Heath had changed. She had frightened him off with her big emotions. She could feel the change in his body—in his stillness—in his drawing back. His hard frame was unyielding when seconds ago it had been hers. A chill ran through her at the thought that while she had been spinning like a dervish out of control, Heath had been quietly thinking.

But what they'd done wasn't wrong.

However many times she told herself this, it didn't change the way Heath had become. Hard flesh that had moulded her soft body was just hard flesh, and the sensitive hands that had catered to her every need while Heath held her safe had grown light and impersonal. 'Heath?'

He didn't move for a moment, as if he respected the

fact that they both needed a moment to come down and grow accustomed to this change between them. He might as well have left the room, Bronte thought.

'Okay?' he said at last, dropping a kiss on the top of her head.

'I'm fine,' she said as if she were reassuring him.

While she got herself sorted out she could hear Heath fastening his jeans and securing his belt. How quiet they were—how reserved…like two strangers. She didn't need anyone to tell her they'd got it wrong. The knowledge hung between them in the air. And into a mind that didn't want to accept the truth, she knew that sex—for that was all it had been with Heath—had been a terrible mistake, and that she must cut her feelings for him now before they swamped her. A relationship with a man like Heath was never going anywhere, so it was better to end it and show how sophisticated she could be before she ruined her chances of ever being taken seriously as a candidate for the job. She huffed lightly. 'To think I only asked for coffee.'

'I promised the lads I'd join them later,' Heath said, picking up on her change of mood. 'Are you sure you'll be okay if I go?'

As he spoke he reached out a hand, and she sensed Heath wanted to stroke her hair. She pulled back. There was nothing temperamental or dramatic about it, this was just a signal between friends that they understood each other. 'Of course I'll be okay,' she said. 'Why shouldn't I be? I'm just going to finish up in here, and then I'm going home for a long, hot bath and a lazy night in front of the TV.'

'If you're sure?' Heath looked puzzled.

'Are you sure you're all right?' she countered wryly. 'I can walk you to the pub, if you like?'

'I think I'll be safe,' Heath answered in the same ironic tone.

'Okay.' Angling her chin, she found a smile.

She waited until he left the room and then blew out a long, slow breath. Behave with dignity, she told herself firmly. She had wanted Heath—and had been determined to have him. And now she had, she must take the consequences.

So that was settled.

Good.

Hearing the outer door closing, she listened to Heath's footsteps crossing the yard. Even they were unbearably familiar, but gradually they faded. Bronte only hoped her feelings would do the same. Closing her eyes, she gave it a moment. No change. Still acting calmly, she was screaming in her head. There was no right way to handle this. Well, there was, as far as the outside world was concerned and Heath, but for her tonight was a memory to lock away, and to get out and examine whenever she needed to beat herself up.

But she couldn't stand here for ever feeling sorry for herself, Bronte concluded. Her feet might appear to be superglued to the floor, but even she couldn't live off emotion. It wouldn't decorate the kitchen any more than it would save Hebers Ghyll—both would need more direct action. And at least with decorating there was more certainty of success, she thought, picking up her brush. Men could punch the wall when things went wrong, but she'd settle for prising open a new can of cream paint. If she finished the wall tonight then at least something would have reached a satisfactory conclusion.

He didn't go to the pub or anywhere near it. He got straight in the car and drove back to the city. When he reached the open road he stamped his foot down on the accelerator. The hunger to put miles between him and Bronte was as fierce as the hunger that had flared between them. She was like a wild green shoot that couldn't survive his brand of tough. Beneath Bronte's fire there was tenderness and vulnerability. He'd always known it and couldn't forgive himself for what had happened. Bronte embraced life and all it had to offer, but her enthusiasm was coloured by the desperate hope that no one would hurt her—but they would. He would. And so he was leaving.

Heath grimaced as he roughly brushed a stubble-roughened chin against his arm. What the hell had he been thinking? Bronte was as innocent as she had ever been. And he had never been innocent. If he owed Uncle Harry anything, it was not to pursue this madness—this hunger—this…Bronte.

But even when he tried to clear his mind she was still in there—her fresh wildflower scent lingering, mingled with paint fumes. He could still see the humour in her eyes, and the determined jut of her chin…that stubborn mouth. That stubborn, kissable mouth—

He actually groaned out loud at this point. He should never have come to the country. He belonged in town. The only thing he could be thankful for right now was that his utility vehicle was eating up the narrow lanes with an appetite he shared. The sooner he replaced green fields and Bronte with a reassuring cityscape of concrete and uncomplicated women, the sooner he'd relax—

Was that right?

When Bronte had shaken him in so many ways? She'd touched on feelings he'd managed to successfully beat down for years. She'd left him questioning more than just his relationship with Uncle Harry and Hebers Ghyll.

She had reminded him of things he'd been ashamed of, and turned them into something to celebrate. She was the first woman to match his sexual appetite. The first woman to whom he had felt seriously attracted. The first woman he had ever come close to considering a friend—

Bronte's vulnerability stopped him dead in his tracks every time. Seeing that was the only warning he needed that this madness had to stop. They weren't meeting on an even playing field, or anything like. Bronte cared too much about everything—and she hadn't fooled him with her casual act. Bronte wore her heart on her sleeve—which was lovely, but not when he was involved. It would be too easy for him to trample her heart. And not intentionally. That was just the way he was. He had never made room in his life for emotion. He was stone to Bronte's soul. He had nothing to offer her. But he wouldn't break his promise. He had assumed responsibility for Hebers Ghyll, and that wouldn't change. And he would give her a shot at the job.

Dealing with Bronte on a professional basis would be different, Heath convinced himself as industrial units encroached on the fields, reminding him that his journey was coming to an end. He would be in control if and when she worked for him. Emotion had no part to play. Poverty had made him a stickler for control dating back to when he'd made his first big money and realised the changes he could make. He had controlled the spending to make sure not a penny of his hard-earned cash was wasted. He couldn't delegate. He had never learned to relax.

More reasons why he could never be the man Bronte wanted him to be. She wasn't even his type, Heath reasoned, stamping down on the accelerator as the lights changed. Her dress sense alone was bad enough—

To keep the thought of yanking Bronte's clothes off her at the forefront of his mind at all times.

He curved a smile—and then reminded himself about his good intentions. They were soon dispatched. But then there was The Temper. Wasn't that just what he needed? Why couldn't he meet some nice, compliant girl?

Because they bored him, Heath reasoned, swinging the wheel as he turned onto the six-lane highway leading into the city. That certainty only grew when he remembered the squads of eager candidates with their porcelain smiles and improbably inflated breasts. It made him smile to think those flutterbys had been effortlessly eclipsed by a tiny, passionate girl—so real, so true, he doubted he could ever go back to plastic.

She usually woke up and leapt out of bed at the cottage full of bounce because there was so much to do at Hebers Ghyll, and she so wanted to get there and do it—but not this morning. This morning she felt flat.

Because there was a whole world of beating herself up to do, Bronte realised as she crawled out of bed. She was still aching from Heath's spectacular attentions, and only wished she could feel differently about what had happened. But she couldn't. It still felt so right to her, though clearly Heath hadn't felt the same.

Heath was right. Get on with your life, Bronte reasoned as she walked down the now neatly manicured drive towards the hall. It was such a beautiful morning she wouldn't let anything get her down—

Where was Heath's truck?

Bronte's heart plummeted as she quickly raced

through all the possibilities, ending in the feeble: perhaps Heath had left early to get some supplies...

That wasn't the answer. She was just putting off the moment when she had to face the truth. Lifting her chin, she took a moment to steel herself before facing the others. She was her old self again by the time she let herself into the house—as far as anyone else could tell.

The kitchen was empty.

So empty.

With just a faint smell of non-smell paint. The first thing she did was open the window to let some fresh air in.

What had she expected, Bronte asked herself, gripping the edge of the table—Heath waiting with a bunch of flowers and a cheesy grin? Did that sound like Heath? He had never planned to stay long. And he had never misled her. If anything, she was surprised he had stayed in the countryside as long as he had. Heath ran a highly successful business in the city. Hebers Ghyll was just a hobby for him. He'd come down when he could spare the time, he'd said.

If all those elegant women queuing up to go to bed with him could spare him—

She mustn't think like that, Bronte scolded herself fiercely. What had happened last night was nothing more than the result of working in close proximity with a very attractive man. It was normal—natural. She was a free agent—she could do what she liked. And she liked what had happened last night. A lot. And what Heath chose to do in his own time was Heath's business. And—

And, damn it, she was crying.

CHAPTER NINE

DASHING her tears away impatiently, Bronte got the morning underway—putting the kettle on, slicing bread for toast. She had breakfast to cook, thank goodness. There was so much she had to do that would take her mind off Heath.

The laugh she gave now was poor competition for the whistling kettle. It was a horrid, weak, sniffly sort of laugh. She couldn't forget him. She couldn't let it lie here. As soon as everyone had finished breakfast she was going to ring Heath's PA and ask about the interviews. The job of estate manager at Hebers Ghyll was going begging, and no one else was going to muscle in while she was mooching around here feeling sorry for herself.

Bronte was stunned when Heath's PA rang her first. She was still tidying the kitchen, and had to sit down on a chair to take the call. Shocked? She was incredulous he'd even remembered her. Interviews for the post of estate manager had been arranged for the following week in their London offices, the posh guy called Quentin told her, and he was calling to make sure she was still interested.

'Absolutely,' she confirmed, branding the date and time of the interview on her mind.

Getting up, she paced the room. What did this mean? Did Heath miss her? Did he want her back?

Desperate twit, she thought, drawing to a halt to stare out of the window at the yard where Heath had put on his spectacular wet torso display. This wasn't about Bronte and Heath. This was about the job of estate manager. Heath had promised her this chance to attend a formal interview—why would he take that away? What would be the point? She was well qualified—a good contender; she had to hope the best. The fact that Heath had asked his PA to call her rather than doing it himself only proved that he wanted to keep things on a strictly business footing. It was the right thing to do. It was what she would have done had their roles been reversed, she told herself firmly. This was her chance to prove she was as professional as Heath—and a chance to tilt at a job she desperately wanted. If she was lucky enough to land the job it would be the best chance she ever got to take Uncle Harry's vision to the next level—and to prove she was more than Heath's latest sex-starved admirer.

She could do this.

She must do this, Bronte determined, firming her jaw.

'Did you call her?' Heath's tone was impatient. Almost as soon as he'd returned to London he'd had to fly to New York—one of his favourite cities, but waiting to get out of this meeting with his lawyers hadn't helped to soothe his frayed temper.

'Of course,' Quentin confirmed. 'I made it my first job—I even placed the call before I drank my coffee.'

'I appreciate the sacrifice,' Heath said dryly, but then the crease returned to his brow. 'What did she say?'

'She's coming.'

Heath relaxed back on the sofa overlooking Central Park. He hadn't shaved. He hadn't even showered yet. It felt like he hadn't slept for days. His emergency meeting had been called to sew up a deal that would take his company global. He'd texted Quentin to make the date with Bronte, thumbs racing beneath the table as he discussed figures the size of a roll-over lottery win at the same time. He had promised Bronte this chance, and he was a man of his word.

And that was the only reason he'd called her to interview, he'd told himself sternly when he stood to shake hands with the other men. It had absolutely nothing to do with the fact that all he'd thought of since leaving England, in those moments when the business relaxed its hold on him, was Bronte—Bronte's eyes, the swell of her mouth, the expression on her face, the sound of her voice when she was out of control with pleasure in his arms, or whispering to him in the aftermath. Most of all he wondered about the questions she never asked him, like, Why does it have to be like this, Heath? Why must the past always stand between us? Why can't you and I be together like any other couple? We enjoyed the sex—we're so good together, why can't it go on? And then the lies she would tell him if he let things run on. He could hear her saying, sex doesn't have to involve feelings, does it, Heath? Then she would look at him with those candid green eyes and they would both know she was lying. He couldn't hurt her like that. Sex had to involve feelings for Bronte. Everything had to involve feelings for Bronte.

When the lawyers from both sides shook hands and turned to congratulate him, he barely heard them. All he could think of was a long, reviving shower and the welcome journey home. For Bronte's sake, he'd shave.

Right now he looked more the barbarian than ever and he didn't want to frighten her when she interviewed for the job—he owed her that much. The interview was all she had ever asked of him, and he wouldn't let her down.

It was just her bad luck that Heath's office was located in the most fashionable part of the city, Bronte reflected, slipping on a robe after her shower at the cottage. And in a gleaming new building that had won style awards, for goodness' sake.

And look at me…

So she would just have to smarten herself up, Bronte told herself firmly. It might have been a while, but she could do it. Taking a deep breath, she stopped pacing her bedroom to open the robe and take a critical look at herself in the full-length mirror. The bits that showed outside her dungarees were tanned to a nice healthy shade, but the rest of her was pale and freckled.

And the tip of her nose was bright red.

Great.

Walking to the wardrobe, she opened the door and rooted inside. It wasn't that she didn't know how to dress or what would be expected of her at a high-powered interview. She hadn't dropped out of life completely, but she had gone country. There had been no reason to smarten up since she'd returned to Hebers Ghyll.

There wasn't time to buy a business suit, Bronte concluded, but appearances were everything if she wanted Heath to take her seriously. Appearances were important if she wanted to hold her head up high. Toe rings and braids she had down to a fine art, but a more sophisticated look might require a little help…

* * *

'You're going to Heath's office for an interview?' Colleen exclaimed, clearly impressed and excited for her. 'That's amazing. Heath must think a lot of you to invite you down to London.'

'That's where the interviews are being held,' Bronte explained. 'It's nothing special. And it was his PA who invited me, not Heath.'

'Whatever you say...'

They were clearing out the old stables when Bronte shared her news. Colleen had picked up on her tension, Bronte realised.

Leaning on her sweeping brush, Colleen stared directly at her equally dishevelled friend. 'So, tell me— what can I do?'

'I'm just worried that the job of estate manager suggests someone older than me—someone more staid.'

'I disagree,' Colleen said firmly. 'You're the new generation.'

'But what if Heath's PA doesn't see it that way? What if I don't get any further than him? He sounds so snooty, and appearances matter in the city. I don't think my muck-spreading look is going to cut it.'

'You might have a point,' Colleen agreed with a laugh as she took in the state of Bronte's dungarees. 'So you really think you've got a chance of landing the job? It would be wonderful if you did—it would give everyone such a lift.'

'Thanks,' Bronte said, smiling ruefully. 'I have to believe I stand a chance or I wouldn't go to London. I've got the right qualifications—and the right practical experience too. And I've got local knowledge, which hopefully will give me an edge. So, logically, I should be in the running...' Though whether Mr Logical would see it that way remained to be seen. 'But I must look as professional as I can, which is where you come in.'

'Whatever I can do,' Colleen offered.

'Well, I've been off the radar for a while—so I'll need a suit.'

'And there are so many shops round here,' Colleen said dryly.

'Exactly, and there's no time to visit the local town before my interview.'

'Well, you must look good for Heath.'

'This has nothing to do with Heath,' Bronte protested a little too hotly.

'Okay,' Colleen soothed, holding her hands up palms flat in surrender.

'Heath needs to come back to oversee this project,' Bronte said thoughtfully. 'An absentee landlord is no good to Hebers Ghyll.'

'And an absentee lover is even less use to you.'

'Colleen—'

'I'm just saying. If friends can't be honest with each other. Yes, of course I'll help,' Colleen confirmed when Bronte gave her a look. 'Do you really think you can persuade Heath to come back here?'

'He has to—look how much got done on his last visit. We have to be positive, Colleen. What?' she said when Colleen's gaze slid away.

'I just don't want to see you getting hurt, Bronte.'

'I'm not going to get hurt,' Bronte said firmly. 'I know what I'm doing. This is business. Let's get back to work, shall we? I can raid your wardrobe later.'

'You can take whatever you want,' Colleen assured her.

'Then that's settled,' Bronte said cheerfully, but her friend's concerned expression hadn't changed.

* * *

The trade journals had picked up on his coup and were going crazy. The office was going crazy—and more crazy was exactly what he didn't need. 'What do you mean, you can't cope?' Heath thundered to the only man who didn't quail when he let rip.

'If I didn't work with a bloody genius, you'd know,' Heath's harassed PA informed him testily. 'You think everyone can work at your speed, Heath—i.e. the speed of light. Well, I've got news for you—I've only got one pair of hands—'

'And if you spent less time slathering hand cream on them you'd have more time to spare for work.'

'Woo-hoo. *Bitchee*. Now who's suffering from a bad dose of Not Getting Any?'

'And since when is that your business?'

'I've made it my business. I have to suffer the back-lash every day.'

'If you weren't—'

'The only gay male friend you're ever likely to have?' Quentin interrupted smoothly.

'The only friend I'm likely to have,' Heath confessed ruefully.

Reaching up on tiptoe, Quentin threw a comforting arm around his boss's powerful shoulders. 'Take it from one who knows—you need to sort out that other problem first.'

'I'm working on it.'

'Good, then perhaps you'll calm down and stop carrying on like a bull with a sore head and we can get some work done around here.'

'Get some help.'

Quentin pouted. 'Now I'm offended.'

'I mean, go get someone in to handle the interviews if you can't cope.'

'Oh, I see.' Quentin smiled at the small victory as he examined his immaculately manicured nails. 'Maybe a temp to handle some of the run-of-the-mill work, while I supervise the interviews. What?' he protested. 'Did you seriously think I'd allow anyone but me to start the interview process for such a vital position on your lordship's new estate?'

'Firstly, I'm not a lord—and believe me,' Heath added dryly, 'Hebers Ghyll is not the dream property you seem to imagine, Quentin. I've seen better slums in my time.'

'And you've handled that sort of renovation perfectly. You'll handle this,' Quentin said, refusing to be dismayed.

'Maybe,' Heath growled. 'Well? What are you waiting for? Get on with it.'

Quentin gave him a mock bow. 'The master speaks and I obey.'

Heath cracked a smile. 'Now find me an estate manager who thinks the same way you do.'

Quentin pulled a hurt face. 'I can assure you, I am a one-off.'

'And I couldn't do without you,' Heath admitted.

'But I know what I'd do without you,' Quentin shot back.

'And what's that?'

'Save money at the salon—the stress lines I've developed since I started working for you—'

'And no, you can't charge your treatments to expenses.'

Quentin sulked for around a second. 'I'll get that temp in, then.'

'Yes, you do that,' Heath advised, returning to his screen.

* * *

She had never been put through such a gruelling grilling. Heath's PA, a man who went by the name of Quentin Carew, turned out to be the most formidable style maven Bronte had ever encountered, and he would be conducting the first screening process, Quentin had informed her.

Then she was out, Bronte thought. She didn't stand a chance. Quentin was infinitely better groomed than she would ever be, and Heath's offices far surpassed anything that even Bronte's lively imagination could have conjured up. A celebration of steel and glass, they were formidably smart, as was Quentin, whereas she—even with Colleen's best and kindest efforts—wasn't. But for some reason, Quentin seemed to like her. It was possible he could see right through her carefully subdued grooming and controlled manner to something quirky underneath. Perhaps it was the small heart tattoo on her wrist—something she had hoped her respectable shirt cuff would cover, but hadn't, and she had caught Quentin staring at it.

'I'm putting you through,' he announced.

'You are?' She couldn't have been more surprised, or more delighted. This was everything she had ever wanted—and was nothing at all to do with seeing Heath again, Bronte told her racing heart firmly.

'Heath could arrive at any time this afternoon,' Quentin explained, 'and as you probably know by now he can be a little…unpredictable? With a certain type of volatile…'

'Temperament?' Bronte supplied innocently.

'You might say that. I couldn't possibly comment,' Quentin remarked, picking imaginary lint off the lapels of his immaculate jacket.

The lengths some PAs will go to in order to protect

the boss, Bronte thought wryly. 'Thank you,' she said. 'And thank you for giving me this opportunity.'

'I don't know why you're thanking me,' Quentin exclaimed, confiding, 'Working here must have put at least ten years on me.'

'And you're looking great on it,' she said, smiling.

'Yes, well...' Quentin's beautifully etched lips tightened in a pout. 'That's no thanks to the man I work for.'

'Heath...' Bronte floated off into her favourite dream, and just as quickly dragged herself back again. She had to. There was a dangerous little capsule living in her mind that threatened to explode into infinite pieces of lust, self-reproach, and longing, given half a chance. And that would be too distracting when she wanted to concentrate on landing this job.

'Yes, Heath,' Quentin agreed, looking at Bronte closely. 'I should warn you that when he arrives it will be like a force ten storm hitting. You'd do well to be prepared.'

'I am prepared,' Bronte lied as her heart went crazy, knowing she could never be prepared to see Heath again.

'And you do understand that this is a high-powered office where we work at warp speed all the time?'

'I do,' Bronte confirmed, recalling the speed at which Heath could work.

'I doubt Heath will expect anything less of his staff in the country—and if he does, let me know,' Quentin added with an over-the-rim-of-his-glasses look. 'I might want to try out for a job there. I've always thought I'd look rather good in plus fours...'

'If I get the job I'll let you know,' Bronte promised as Quentin went off into his own private dreamworld.

Heath definitely hadn't let his PA into the full story at Hebers Ghyll. An outfit of plus fours—quaint knick-erbockers—teamed with a beautifully tailored tweed jacket and possibly a deerstalker hat was the clothing of choice for another type of country estate altogether—one where the visitors would expect everything to be sanitised and mud-free.

Shrewd blue eyes, enhanced by the most discreet hint of grey eyeshadow, switched channels to Bronte. 'From what I've seen of your CV you should be in with a serious chance for this job.' But now Quentin grew concerned. 'Are you sure that working for metrosaurus-man won't be too traumatic for you?'

'Absolutely not,' Bronte confirmed confidently. The work wouldn't be too much for her. *But Heath*…Heath was another story, and one that had forbidden written all over it.

'I wouldn't normally put someone as young as you through, but your CV is so strong,' Quentin observed.

'Thank you.' Why was Quentin looking at her like that? Bronte wondered, growing increasingly self-conscious. 'I normally wear jeans or dungarees,' she explained awkwardly, conscious that her borrowed outfit wasn't up to Quentin's standards.

'I don't doubt it,' Quentin said, confirming Bronte's suspicions. 'But Heath is all about the city. He's tuned into the pace of life here. Naturally, Heath can set his own standards, but he expects—no,' Quentin said frown-ing, 'Heath takes for granted the fact that his employees will dress a certain way. I'm only trying to help,' he de-fended when Bronte gave him a hard stare. 'I just think you'd stand a much better chance of getting this job if you conform to the sort of look Heath will be expecting. That's all I'm saying,' he said, raising his hands.

And she should be grateful someone as savvy as Quentin was giving her advice. She liked him. And now it was time to place her trust in him. 'I've never conformed,' she explained. 'So I'm not that sure how to do it—how to put a look together—if you know what I mean?' Quentin's interest sparked as she added, 'I don't suppose you could you help me...?'

Quentin's eyes narrowed speculatively as he looked her over. 'I could help,' he said thoughtfully, chin in hand. 'If you don't mind missing lunch...'

Bronte was round the desk in a flash. Anything to take her mind off meeting Heath.

'Heath has seen you in casual attire, I've no doubt,' Quentin pondered out loud as he walked round Bronte like a sergeant major on parade. 'It's time for him to see you dressed as a professional—sharp, contemporary, and of the moment.'

'Sounds interesting.'

'Sounds like a challenge,' Quentin argued.

'Well, if you're up for it, I am.'

'Budget?' Quentin enquired discreetly.

'Whatever it takes.' She would just have to use plastic and hope her card didn't self-combust.

'Excellent.' Quentin was already at the door. 'Well, come on—what are you waiting for, girlfriend? Let's go shopping.'

CHAPTER TEN

SOME hours later with her hair freshly shampooed at Quentin's preferred salon and left to curl in wild disarray almost to her waist, dressed in a short black skirt, black opaque tights and flat Mary Janes, with a tight little top that clung like sticking plaster to her breasts, Bronte wasn't totally convinced she looked like the archetypal interviewee for the post of estate manager at Hebers Ghyll, but more importantly Quentin was pleased with her appearance and declared her ready for her interview with Heath. 'Wouldn't I have been better buying a tweed jacket, or something?' she said, feeling increasingly anxious as the moment of truth approached. Craning her neck, she stared at her bottom, which was very tightly clad indeed.

'A tweed jacket?' Quentin demanded as if she had suggested wearing a homespun jerkin. 'Certainly not. Heath is not just the cutting edge, he is the leading edge—the spear, the arrow, the—'

'Okay, okay, I'm happy,' Bronte insisted, holding up her hands.

They returned to Heath's building where Quentin told her to wait in the anteroom to Heath's corner office.

She could do this, Bronte persuaded herself nervously, her knees jiggling up and down as she perched on the very edge of one of the smart black leather couches. Though why she was dressed as if to seduce the boss, when that was the last thing she wanted…

She was here to persuade Heath she could be a top drawer estate manager. She was not losing her nerve. She would not be fixated on how aroused she was at the thought of seeing him again. She would definitely not be scanning Heath's office for likely trysting opportunities. She would forget how she had felt after sex when Heath pulled away, and how deep the feeling was that what they'd done hadn't been wrong. She would be cool and professional. They had both moved to a new place. It was a good place. It was the right place for them to be—

And then the door swung open and the breath left her lungs in a rush. Had she really thought she was ready for this? Her heart was crashing against her ribs. Her awareness levels had soared beyond the possible. Heath stood framed in the doorway like a totem to all things sexual: a deity, a yoni god, a man with eyes of stone, wearing what, on the face of it, was a casual outfit— jeans and a top—but it was the kind of easy look that reeked of money and style.

For a moment her mind was wiped clean and her mouth refused absolutely to communicate with her brain. The last time she'd seen Heath he'd been groaning— She'd been screaming— They'd been—

Thankfully, she managed to summon up an autopilot voice—faint though it was. 'Hello, Heath.'

'Bronte,' he said briskly. All business. All coldly assessing as he took in her new look.

She wasn't sure whether to be glad of Quentin's assistance or not now. Something more low-key—something more mouse-like—might have bought her enough time to state her case clearly. Heath could convey more in one sharp stare than most men could hope to communicate in a lifetime, and that wasn't always a good thing. 'I'm your three o' clock,' she said, standing before she had too much time to analyse Heath's expression.

'I'm running late—so we'll have to make this quick.'

No, we won't, Bronte thought, frowning even as her heart beat the retreat. 'I've come all this way, Heath, and I know you're going to treat me with the same consideration you've treated all the other interviewees.'

Heath's expression didn't change. He wore a brooding look Bronte found impossible to interpret, other than to say it didn't fill her with confidence. 'I hope nothing's wrong?' she said pleasantly, determined not to be fazed. 'I guessed these interviews mean your attitude towards the country has mellowed—'

'Mellowed,' Heath cut across her, raising a brow.

'Okay, not mellowed,' Bronte conceded, but to hell with trying to phrase her words carefully. They'd known each other too long for that. She had to be candid even if their relationship had been somewhat turbulent lately. 'Finding time for Hebers Ghyll can't be easy for you, but I can take those concerns away—' The flexing of a muscle in Heath's cheek made her pause. His dangerous appeal was working its magic. Steeling herself, she pushed on. 'Give me a chance, Heath. Put everything else that's happened between us since I…since you—'

'Since we?' Heath angled his chin.

He wasn't going to make this easy for her. 'Since we had sex,' she said flatly, pressing her hands out to the side as if she were pushing the memory away. 'I'm the best person for this job. All I ask is the chance to prove that to you, Heath.'

'Go on, then, tell me why.' He leaned back against the door, drinking her in as she spoke about her experience and outlined her plans for Hebers Ghyll. She was even younger than he remembered and more innocent than he cared to think about. The fiery episode in the kitchen seemed all at odds with the girl standing in front of him now. Bronte had always led with her heart, but there was something different about her today.

He had felt energy blaze between them the moment he walked into the room, but Bronte was cool now. If anything, she was cooler than he'd ever seen her. She had moved to a new level, where ironically she was almost as unreachable as he was. She intrigued him even more. She presented more of a challenge. And she might well be the right candidate for the job. He'd made enquiries in advance of this interview—taking up her references at her old college, as well as talking to people she'd worked with. Bronte was outstanding, he'd been told. She was a terrific catch for any landowner, people in the know had assured him.

Catch was about right, he thought as he stared at her. They'd known each other for what felt like for ever—they knew each other intimately, yet they didn't know each other at all. She was certainly qualified, he just wished there had been more time to get to know what really made Bronte tick. He glanced at his wristwatch. There wasn't time. There was never time.

Then perhaps he should make time

Bronte took a breath and waited. She didn't know how long she could keep up this cool act with him towering over her like some feudal warlord—*and one who had pleasured her with the utmost skill.*

Forget that!

Forget that how? Heath's blatant masculinity blazed

in the frame of the intricate graphics framed in his office. He was both an artist and a warrior—and as hard as nails. She could forget those romantic notions she'd been nursing for the past thirteen years. Heath had no intention of softening towards her—towards anything.

'Is it that time already?' he said, glancing at his watch.

Her shoulders slumped. She'd barely been in his office ten minutes. Was that it?

'Shall we go?' he said, staring directly at her.

We? 'Go?' Bronte frowned. 'Go where, Heath?'

'As I told you, I'm running late, and I have an appointment I can't break. We can talk on the way.' He held the door for her.

She let out a tense breath. 'Of course.' It was an unusual interview, but it was an interview.

The Lamborghini was waiting at the steps of Heath's office building. They climbed in and shot away at speed. She couldn't pretend she didn't like Heath's decisive manner or that the electricity between them hadn't increased in the confines of his car. 'Where are we going? she said casually.

'To the launch of one of my games.'

'Great.' Hmm. Okay. Not an interview opportunity— perhaps that would come later, but interesting all the same.

The grand reveal took place in London's most prestigious store. People had been queuing round the block all night in the hope of securing the latest in the long line of hits, and now Heath had explained his premise to her Bronte could understand the enthusiasm that greeted this new game. The little guy putting one over on the bad guys would be a winner every time. And who knew better than Heath about the bad guys? Bronte mused as he escorted her inside the building with a light touch on her arm.

Heath and his team received ear-splitting applause when they took the rostrum. They looked more like a cool rock band than anything else in their motley tops and well worn jeans, fists raised to acknowledge their fans. Heath stayed on to give autographs until Bronte was sure his hand would seize up. He shot her a look halfway through that could be interpreted as: This is my home. This is where I belong—here in London with my team. It was a reminder that the only thing Heath was capable of feeling passion for was his business empire. Sex was a sporting activity like running, or sparring, or working out at the gym—something he enjoyed and was very good at, but realistically sex was only one more way to work off Heath's excess energy.

Which didn't prove to be nearly enough to wipe out how she felt about him.

When the signing was over they said brief goodbyes and Heath escorted her back to the car. She thought he might go back to the office, but their next stop was an upscale restaurant. Good venue to talk, she thought, initially approving Heath's choice. But seeing him again and spending time with him had shaken her up, and she wasn't sure she could relax in such refined surroundings. 'Must we?' She bit her lips, but it was too late.

'Aren't you hungry?' Heath asked. 'I know I am.'

Did Heath's stare have to be quite so direct? 'Well, yes, I am,' she said honestly, finding it impossible to think up an excuse while Heath was raiding her thoughts. She glanced up at the chi-chi sign. Heath had brought her to one of the most famous restaurants in London. 'I don't want you to think I don't appreciate this…'

'But?' he said, angling his chin.

'It's just a little stuffy. I don't know if I could be myself.' As she answered he hit the hazards and left the car. She watched him walk towards the restaurant. Not that Heath walked anywhere—he struts, he strolls, he strides, hummed through her head. Mostly, he moved as he was doing now with that confident, sexy swagger.

But it was a relief not to be entering the hallowed portals, Bronte reflected as Heath disappeared inside. Her emotions were red raw, and she didn't fancy putting them on show for the other diners. She sat forward as Heath breezed out. 'Well?' she demanded as he swung back into the car.

'I cancelled the table.'

'I'm sorry—I hope it wasn't a problem?' Nothing was a problem for Heath, she thought as the Lamborghini roared. 'So where to now?'

'Somewhere I hope you like better—somewhere fun, where you can relax and we can talk.'

'Sounds perfect.' They hadn't done enough of that. But would Heath relax? Glancing across at him, Bronte felt her cheeks burn when Heath caught her staring at him. She could tell he was still buzzing after the signing—still high on adrenalin. She wondered where he'd take her next, and decided to find out—the roundabout way. 'Am I dressed okay for wherever we're going?'

Heath glanced over. 'So long as you think you'll be warm enough.'

'We'll be outside?' She had hinted that she would like to eat somewhere less stuffy than the upmarket restaurant, and there were plenty of hot-dog stands and fast food stalls around London.

'We'll be outside,' Heath confirmed.

'Will I like it?'

'I know I will.'

Heath looked worryingly pleased with himself. She hazarded a guess. 'Why's that? Is there a pool table?'

'Better than that,' Heath said, stopping at the traffic lights.

Okay...

'I hope it isn't too noisy,' she said as the lights turned to green.

'Stop digging, Bronte. It's somewhere you will have to relax—and when you do, maybe we can get a serious discussion going.'

Fun and a serious discussion? How did that work? she wondered, falling silent.

'Still hungry?' Heath demanded, powering away from the traffic lights.

Sadly, for all Bronte's good intentions, she was starving—and not just for food.

CHAPTER ELEVEN

THE Lamborghini sliced through the congested traffic like a well-trained panther, sleek, fast-moving, and effortlessly responsive, while Heath's mind was full of Bronte—the taste of her, her scent, her heat, the way she cried out with pleasure at the moment she let go. It was hard to concentrate with all that running through his head. He made a conscious effort to slow the car, to drive responsibly, to think of Bronte in a purely non-sexual way. He couldn't remember anyone forcing him to look at things and people differently, but Bronte had. He should have known she would follow through with the job—and was glad she had. Bronte had turned out to be by far the best candidate with a wealth of experience, as well as local knowledge second to none. She was right about age having nothing to do with this. Had she been fifty years older he'd still have felt the same.

'Why are you laughing?' she said.

'Nothing,' he said, knowing Bronte had a definite advantage that had nothing to do with professionalism or age. He came up with a suitably distracting reply: 'I was just wondering how you're going to take it when I tell you it will take a while to get where we're going.'

'I think I can hang on,' she said dryly. 'I'm not a baby who needs feeding on the hour.'

'Or rocking to sleep?' he suggested, his mind taking her back to bed again.

'I prefer to keep my eyes open while you're around.'

She was sparking again. That was better. Banter between them was the best cure for tension he knew. Maybe it was time for him to wind down too.

'We'll get there,' she soothed when they got snarled up in a jam.

Driving was partly a distraction, but while they were stuck in traffic like this…

Resting his chin on the back of his hand, he brooded. He could spend the rest of his life living in the past, telling himself he wasn't worthy, but when they were sitting close like this—

'See, we're moving again,' she said just as his thoughts were heating up.

He should have laid everything on the line for her at Hebers Ghyll. He should have told Bronte the type of man he was—the type of man he couldn't be. He should have made that break nice and clean while he'd had the chance—

And then a vehicle swerved in front of them and Bronte exclaimed with fright. He'd avoided it, but it was close. 'You okay?' He reached over to reassure her.

She was staring at his hand on her knee. 'I think so,' she said.

He lifted his hand away. Touching her had fired him. He could only hope the inferno inside him hadn't engulfed the next seat. 'Who chose the outfit?' he said to distract them both.

'Quentin helped me pick it out.'

Traitor, he thought. Quentin was supposed to be his friend. 'You look good.' No harm in telling the truth—

though he put both hands firmly on the wheel. 'Have to say, I pity those sales assistants.'

'Quentin was very polite—and he knows all the best shops,' Bronte protested.

And she's loyal to a fault, he thought. 'I bet he does,' he murmured.

'Quentin was only trying to help, so don't go after him,' Bronte begged him.

'Am I such a monster?' He glanced her way. 'I'm just saying dungarees would have been a better choice for where I'm taking you.'

'I can hardly wait,' she said dryly.

Dipping his head, he scanned the traffic for the quickest way through, making Bronte exclaim a second time when he dropped a gear to overtake some slow-moving vehicles. 'I didn't mean to shake you up.'

'But you have,' she said, giving him the quake with fear routine. 'You're such a scary baddie in your powerful machine, and I'm such a little country innocent all alone in the big city.'

He couldn't have put it better himself.

'So, where are you taking me, Heath?' she probed.

'Like I told you, somewhere fun—somewhere they won't hear you scream when I really give you something to be scared about.'

'Sounds…interesting,' she said, pulling an uncertain face.

'It will be,' he promised.

She shrieked his eardrums out on the big dipper, buried her face in his jacket and clung to him with claws of iron on the Plunge of Doom. She couldn't have done that with anyone else, she assured him, after she'd made him queue for the ride a second time.

'I can't believe you don't know any other adrenalin junkies,' he said, wrapping her in his jacket when she shivered from a combination of freezing wind and her unbounded lust to ride the big wheel.

'I don't know anyone else who would brave my screams a second time,' she said, jumping up and down to keep warm.

The friction at such close range was…interesting. 'I don't mind you screaming, just so long as you don't do it in my ear. The big wheel?'

'Try and keep me off it.

'This was an inspired choice, Heath,' Bronte told him as she marched along, head down against the wind, 'if not exactly what I was expecting as part of my job interview.'

'Performance under stress? Surely, that's a normal part of any interview process?'

'Working for you, I'd say it's an essential part.'

'I aim to please.'

'So screaming might get me brownie points?'

'Screaming will get you all sorts of places, Bronte.' He had the satisfaction of seeing her cheeks glow red.

He gave her his jacket on the big wheel, wondering why he hadn't noticed before how slight she was and how quickly she took cold.

'Are you enjoying it?' she said as the wheel started turning.

'It's a little slow for me,' he admitted, 'though the view is good.' London was unfolding in front of them like one of his fantasy panoramas; a magic carpet in colours of umber and ash, bustling with moving lights beneath a rapidly darkening indigo sky.

'Can you see St Paul's from here?' she said, craning

her neck to look round as their seat reached the highest point.

'I don't know.' He was staring at Bronte when she asked the question.

'Yes,' she cried excitedly. 'Look, Heath—over there.'

Shimmering with light and unwritten stories, the sight of the city would have lifted anyone's mood and Bronte's excitement was infectious. 'I see it.' He sounded as excited as she was.

'This is such an amazing view, isn't it?'

'It's not bad,' he admitted wryly. Bronte's lips were red, her face was flushed and the tip of her pixie nose had turned crimson with cold.

'It's fun, Heath—admit it,' she threatened, doing what he called her bite smile—the big, touching one where the pearly teeth bit down on the full swell of her bottom lip. And this was certainly something. Fun in his world was exploring new markets for his games— checking balance sheets, checking the bank—but Bronte had jolted him out of that perfectly designed world into a realm full of crazy adventure and emotional overspill.

'So you see, you can spare the time,' she told him triumphantly, sitting back against the padded vinyl seat.

'Barely,' he murmured as the wheel began its painfully slow descent.

Bronte's eyes were half shut against the wind, and her face was all screwed up against the biting cold, but even so she was beautiful…and vulnerable, and deserving of someone who would cherish her and focus his whole attention on her—someone who would give Bronte more than he ever could. She shivered again and this time he resisted the temptation to pull her close. Once had been an impulse, twice would make it usual between them, as if they were boyfriend and girlfriend, which they were not.

'What shall we do now?' she said as the wheel stopped to let them get off.

He helped her out. 'What would you like to do?'

'I'll leave that to you—within reason,' she added quickly, shooting him a warning glance. 'And we haven't eaten yet,' she reminded him.

None of this had been planned. It had started out as one thing and ended up as something quite different— the need to talk, the need to get to know each other in the present and find out how they'd changed. The need to do something other than have sex and stalk round each other like two suspicious combatants in the ring. He didn't want to talk about Hebers Ghyll, or business, or Bronte's job. He wanted to do all the things they had never done together, things he'd dreamed about doing with Bronte all those years back—on the rare occasion when he had managed to lift his thoughts above his belt. This was a second chance—a voyage of discovery to find out whether his fantasies had legs.

Guys had fantasies?

Even tough guys like him had fantasies. You want to make something of it? he challenged his inner voice.

'Brrh, it's cold,' Bronte said, shrinking deeper into his giant-sized jacket.

'How about somewhere warm now?' he suggested.

'You read my mind.' She laughed up at him. 'Are you going to tell me where, or are you going to keep me hanging?'

'I'm going to take you to see a small corner of my world.'

'Will I need lifts in my shoes?'

He glanced down at her flats and laughed. 'I'll make sure no one treads on you.'

Bronte laughed. And now they were both laughing. And before he knew what he was doing he'd dragged her close.

She hugged him hard. They broke away as if they both knew it was wrong, and could only lead them down the same blind alley. There was a certain amount of awkwardness between them until he said, 'Can you dance?'

Her face lit up. 'What do you think, rubber legs? But I thought we were going somewhere to eat first.'

'We are. Come on,' he said, urging her towards the car.

'You're not taking me somewhere stuffy like that last place, are you?' she said, looking up at him.

He liked she'd got her confidence back. He was not quite so pleased when she raced ahead of him and started scampering backwards. He'd been down that road too many times. 'Wait and see,' he said, gathering her under his arm before they repeated their signature move.

'Okay,' she said, staring up at him as they strode along purposefully, side by side, keeping in step. 'This sounds mysterious. Are you going to give me any clues?'

'No.'

And with that she had to be content.

Why wouldn't Heath tell her where they were going? Another small corner of his world, he'd said. Today was turning out to be like a jigsaw someone had tossed up in the air. Find the right pieces and you might see the picture clearly. But she liked a mystery. And she liked what she'd seen so far.

Had she never dreamed that Heath was human?

Bronte wondered, snuggling deeper into his jacket while he drove them to another part of the city. Heath had shown another side of himself tonight, and it was a side that she liked—a side that tempted her to forget all her warnings to self about not getting in any deeper than she already had. She jerked alert and looked around as he pulled the Lamborghini off the road and killed the engine. 'You're kidding me?' she exclaimed softly as she peered out of the window. Of all the possible destinations, this was the very last place on earth she would have connected with the hard man at her side. A retro café complete with pink neon signs and garish orange paintwork. 'You're not short on surprises, Heath.'

'I have connections here,' he explained, only adding to the mystery. 'Maybe it's a little crazy.'

'Lucky for you,' Bronte admitted with a grin. 'I love crazy.'

Heath was one complex guy, Bronte thought as he opened the car door for her.

'I trust this fits your brief for something different?' Heath said, making her a mock bow as he helped her out of the car.

'I can't even imagine how you come to know about a place like this,' she said, staring wide-eyed at the clientele flooding in.

'My friend owns it,' Heath explained.

'Cool…I can't wait to see inside.' Though she was definitely underdressed for this gig. The girls she was following into the café were dressed in fifties outfits— high ponytails and bright red lipstick, their short flared skirts held out by yards of stiff net petticoats. They wore short white socks with high-heeled shoes, and wide, brightly coloured belts to emphasise their waists, while the men were boasting velvet-collared suits and winkle-picker shoes.

'You do jive, I take it?' Heath said dryly as he handed over the entrance fee for both of them.

She frowned—and, only half joking, asked, 'Is this part of my job interview?'

'You should know. You have to be quick on your feet on a farm.'

Bronte shook her head. 'I guess I jive, then.' She'd just have to get the hang of it in a hurry.

'Great—then, let's go,' Heath said, brandishing their tickets.

This certainly wasn't the man she thought she knew. Heath had more facets than a hard black diamond and kept most of them under wraps. She was surprised he was sharing this much with her.

Once bitten, Bronte reminded herself when she felt Heath's hand come to rest in the small of her back as he guided her safely through the crowd. That touch was a timely, if unwelcome reminder that having fun together was one thing, but having sex—well, that was a whole world of difference. Fun she could bank and smile about when she got back to work. Sex was something you didn't have with the boss—something that tore at your heart and left it in pieces.

So why melt? Why long? Why ache? Why do any of those things? Take the evening for what it was, and then get on with your life, Bronte told herself firmly, glancing around with interest and anticipation.

The beat was pounding inside an interior that faithfully recreated an authentic fifties coffee bar. There was a black and white tiled floor, Formica tables with lots of chrome around, and padded banquettes, covered in shiny red plastic that didn't even pretend to be leather, and the most fantastic burnished wood panelling. 'Carved by a regular customer,' Heath said, pointing it out. He went on to explain that the café had recently been made a listed building, which meant it was destined to be preserved just as it was. He'd barely had chance to give her this potted history when a good-looking man spotted him and came over. 'Heath—long time.'

As the two men shared a man hug Bronte wondered about the connection between them.

'Josh,' Heath said, introducing his friend to Bronte. 'Josh and I—we spent some time together when we were younger.'

No further explanations necessary, Bronte thought as Josh shook her hand. Josh was another bad boy made good.

'I haven't seen Heath for ages—you must be good for him,' Josh said, an attractive crease appearing in his face as he searched out a table for them.

'I think you'll like the food here,' Heath confided, dipping his head down to shout in Bronte's ear above the music. He was guiding her through the danger zone of spinning couples to take the booth Josh had indicated. 'It's all home-cooking. Josh's mother is in the kitchen making pasta, pies, bread pudding and custard, jam roly-poly—you name it.'

'Fattening?' she suggested wryly.

'Delicious,' Heath argued firmly with a smile that lit a bonfire in her heart.

It was a revelation to discover Heath's world wasn't the soulless vacuum of cyberspace she'd imagined, but something far more diverse and interesting. And he was loyal too—something she had already seen in his relationship with Quentin. So the lone wolf did have friends. It made her optimistic, somehow—

Irrelevant, Bronte told herself firmly as Heath sat down across the plastic table from her. This was a... business meeting? Heath's stare was disturbingly direct. What did he expect her to say or do? She felt uncertain suddenly.

And her heart?

Didn't stand a chance faced by this new understanding growing between them.

Friendship, Bronte thought as Heath handed her the menu. This was friendship growing between them, and that was...that was nice.

'Relax, Bronte—just choose something to eat and forget about everything else.'

Sure. She could do that. Wasn't living for the moment her speciality? Forget those thirteen years of longing, the trial relationships with other men—failures all of them, because all she had ever done was compare them with Heath, so every man had fallen short.

So here she was again, back on that same old roller coaster, Bronte reflected—all that was missing was a platter on which to serve herself up—

No. No! *No!* Being here with Heath didn't mean she was going to have sex with him. It wasn't compulsory. It didn't come with the bill. They were having a meal together. What was wrong with that?

She selected home-made cannelloni with spinach and ricotta and a tomato juice with the works to drink. Heath chose steak and chips, and a beer. 'Dance while we wait for the food?' he suggested with a glance at the whirling couples.

She drew a steadying breath before answering. Dancing was a kind of intimacy—there weren't too many things a man and woman could do together in rhythm—

Hey…lighten up, she told herself, glancing down at her flat shoes. 'Are you serious?' She wanted to dance, really. It would be fun. She couldn't jive, but what the heck?

'Those shoes are perfect,' Heath observed. 'Anyone would think you knew you were coming here. Think of the steps you can do in those.'

'I have thought,' she assured him dryly. 'And we both know my sense of balance isn't up to much.'

'It doesn't have to be,' Heath said, 'as I'm here to catch you.' Standing up, he made it hard for Bronte to refuse.

'I can't…I really can't,' she said, changing her mind. How could she when her heart was going wild at the thought of dancing with Heath?

'I'm not taking no for an answer,' he said. And when she still hung back, he grabbed her hand. 'I never took you for a chicken, Ms Foster-Jenkins.'

'Squawk squawk.'

'You can move your hips, can't you?'

Who knew that better than Heath? Standing hands on hips waiting for her to cave, Heath looked hot enough to fry a steak on. But this could end really badly, Bronte reasoned. Letting herself go with Heath was hardly sensible: hot, hectic movements—Heath's firm hands directing her—staring into each other's eyes— Hmm. When had she done that before?

And there was another issue. Most men couldn't dance. Could Heath dance? Or would she soon be running for the exit?

Heath could dance. Why was she surprised? Heath was so brazenly male, so relentlessly sexy, he could make any move look cool—something that wasn't lost on the women gathered round him. And he taught her to jive in the same effortless way in which he'd taught her to make love. And then the DJ changed the track and Heath's mouth curved in a challenging grin.

'Twist contest?' Bronte asked, eyes widening in trepidation.

'We have to,' he said, kicking off his loafers. 'And we have to do this right.'

She should have known Heath could out-dance a movie star and look hotter than hell. The crowd grew around him and somehow she forgot her good intentions again. Staring into Heath's eyes, she really went for it, while Heath's body brushed hers into a state of arousal.

Lucky for her, their food was delivered to the table or she'd have been right back where she started from, Bronte thought. Much safer to have Heath call it a day and escort her back to the table.

But with Heath's hand back home in the small of her back she couldn't help wondering who was kidding who here.

CHAPTER TWELVE

THE food was delicious and Bronte ate ravenously. It was easy to talk about Hebers Ghyll in such a relaxed setting, though she prickled all over when Heath admitted he still couldn't see how the inheritance would fit into his life. She could see the problem. Heath's life was cool and cutting edge. Hebers Ghyll was a lumbering great piece of real estate with thousands of acres of land attached. But it was somewhere she called home. She couldn't expect it to be more than another entry in Heath's property portfolio. She had to make him see it differently. If she could only persuade him to come back.

'Don't let your food get cold,' Heath advised when she started out down that route.

Heath would never be pushed. And she would not be moved. Things promised to get interesting. They already were; Heath was close enough for her body to warm at the memory of his touch—

'Penny for them?' he murmured.

Censored. 'Just thinking what a really great time I've had tonight.'

'I'll call for the bill.'

She dug out her purse.

'Put that away.'

Resolutions were easy to make, but the warmth and

strength of Heath's hand covering hers was too much. She snatched her hand away as if he'd burned it. 'I can't let you pay for me, Heath.'

'Then take it as wages. I must owe you something by now?'

'Yes, you do,' she said frankly, 'but this is different— separate.'

'Then you'll just have to repay me some other way.' Heath curved a smile. 'I'm sure I can find some filing for you at the office, if you're really desperate?'

'Temping for you?' she said. 'I don't think so.'

'You're probably right,' Heath agreed, 'I'd get no work done by the time you'd finished tempting—'

'Temping,' she corrected him. 'You mean when I've finished temping.'

'You say temping—I say tempting.' Heath's cheek creased in a grin.

Heath was enjoying himself. The revelation made her thrill inside. 'You're impossible,' she scolded him.

'I know,' he agreed, putting his hand up for the bill.

They went from the heat of the café into the cool of the night. Heath opened the passenger door of the Lamborghini and Bronte fed herself in.

'You're getting better at it,' he observed dryly.

'And you're not supposed to be looking.'

'I'll try to remember that.'

She doubted he would. And if it was possible to enter such a low-slung car without showing everything she was born with and a whole lot more, she hadn't got the knack of it yet.

'So where now?' she asked as Heath swung in beside her.

Self-doubt crowded in when Heath said nothing. Having sex with him would be spectacular—but wrong. It would be the perfect ending to the perfect night, but that didn't make it right. It was everything she had promised herself she wouldn't do. 'We'll find a hotel as we drive back to town—you can just drop me—'

'Let you loose on the unsuspecting?' Heath said, gunning the engine. 'I couldn't be so unfeeling towards my fellow man.'

'Look,' she said a few miles further down the road, 'that looks like a nice bed and breakfast. You can drop me here. It says vacancies—I'll be fine.'

More silence.

'Heath?' she prompted as he started to make a call. She couldn't risk everything she'd dreamed about and worked towards, sacrificed for a night that would leave her heart in pieces. 'Heath, what are you doing?' She felt the prickle of apprehension creep up her spine as Heath held up his hand to silence her, and as the conversation got under way she felt sick. The bottom dropped out of her world when she realised Heath was booking a double room at some swanky hotel in Knightsbridge. She was supposed to be grateful, Bronte guessed. And why should Heath think any differently of her? She'd had sex with him and enjoyed it—they'd both enjoyed it. She would be the first to admit she wanted him more than ever. But not like this.

'Yes,' Heath confirmed. 'An executive double for tonight.' He paused and flashed a glance at Bronte as the girl on the other end of the line obviously checked her reservation system. Once the booking was confirmed, he added, 'We'll be with you in around a quarter of an hour.'

'What are you doing?' Bronte whispered the moment

Heath cut the line. Had the wonderful time they had spent together been for this? Was the friendship she thought they had forged nothing more than an illusion?

'Lucky they had a room available.'

And she was available too? Bronte thought dully, turning to stare out of the window. This would ruin everything.

Her anxiety had reached epic proportions by the time Heath pulled into the approach of one of the most famous five-star hotels in London. She had to hand it to him, when it came to seduction Heath didn't stint.

'I know the staff here,' he explained as a uniformed valet approached the car and took his keys through the open window.

Of course he did. Where wouldn't Heath be known? Bronte wondered.

'They'll make you welcome, and you'll be safe here.'

Safe with Heath?

He was at her side of the car opening the door before the porter even had chance to react. 'Come on.' He held out his hand. 'I'll cover for you.'

He could still joke about this? She held back. Heath was waiting. The porter was staring. 'I don't have any luggage. What will people think?'

'Since when have you cared?' Heath lifted her out and deposited her on the pavement in front of him, holding her shoulders so he could stare into her eyes. 'I don't care what people think and neither should you. Where are you going now?' he said, catching hold of her wrist.

'I'll take a cab.'

'A cab where? Don't be ridiculous, Bronte.'

A well dressed couple made a point of skirting round them.

'It's only a bed for the night.'

'I don't know how you can say that.'

Heath thumbed his chin, and then he started to laugh.

'Did I say something funny?' Bronte snapped.

'What kind of man do you think I am, Bronte? Did you really think I'd let you take pot luck where you slept tonight?'

'I thought—'

'I know what you thought,' Heath said, losing the smile. 'I'm getting your signals loud and clear. Perhaps now is a good time to tell you that I've never had to engineer an opportunity for sex, and I'm sure as hell not starting now.'

'But you booked a double room,' Bronte challenged heatedly.

'Single rooms are too small—usually by the elevator, and always my last choice. I got you an executive double, the cost of which,' he assured her, 'I will knock off your wages. But as for sleeping with you, Bronte?' Turning, Heath pointed across the road. 'My house is right over there. Why would I want to stay with you?'

For no reason she could think of.

'You thought I'd booked a double room so we could have sex?' Heath's face was a mask of exasperation and disappointment.

'Well, excuse me for getting the wrong end of the stick,' Bronte fired back.

They were standing toe to toe when Heath shook his head and said icily, 'See you back at Hebers Ghyll?'

His meaning was clear. 'So for a misunderstanding I lose the job?' She was so far down the road she couldn't find her way back and was half out of her mind with panic and frustration.

'No,' Heath countered. 'For always thinking the worst of me you lose the job. How could you work for a boss you don't trust, Bronte? Well, could you?' And when she didn't answer, Heath raged, 'Do you know what?' His hair was sticking up in angry spikes where he'd raked it. 'I used to think I was the one stuck in the past, but now I see it's you, Bronte. You just can't let go of who I used to be. You've kept those thoughts alive for all these years—thinking tough is good and hard is sexy. Well, here's some news for you. I don't want to be that man—and I especially don't want to be that man with you.'

She looked at Heath open-mouthed. If only half what he said was true then she was bitterly ashamed. They changed each other, Bronte realised as she sucked in a shuddering breath. They brought out the best and the worst in each other. 'Heath—' she reached out to him '—please, I—'

Heath pulled away as if she had the plague. 'Stay or don't stay—I really don't care what you do. The room's paid for,' he rapped. 'Have it on me.' And with that he spun on his heel and strode away.

Wound up like a spring, she watched him, and stood rooted to that same spot until she heard the engine roar and saw the Lamborghini speed away.

It was a much subdued Bronte who followed the house-keeper to her room. In her current bewildered state it was much better to stay put, she had concluded. After all, she had nowhere else to go. Her guilt doubled and doubled again when she was shown into the most sump-tuous double room—*well away from the elevators.*

Sumptuously decorated in shades of aquamarine, ivory and coral, with ornate plasterwork on the ceiling playing host to a glittering chandelier, it was a mocking reminder that she wasn't always right, and that sometimes she was horribly wrong. She stood in the centre of the room when the housekeeper left her, inhaling the scent of fresh flowers from the market, beautifully arranged in a crystal bowl on the dressing table. If she had taken that bowl and smashed it she couldn't have done more harm tonight. She had taken something beautiful and twisted it with her suspicion. She had killed any hope of Heath being a friend, and a friend was something more than a lover—something less than both, but something precious all the same.

Lying on the bed fully clothed she ran through the evening in her head. What had Heath done wrong—other than his crazy driving and his insistence that she had to eat roly-poly pudding or he couldn't eat his?

Turning her face into the pillow, she was crying as she made an angry sound of frustration. She would go to any lengths not to hurt him—and had failed spectacularly. She had allowed her own insecurities to spill out in reproach and accusation. Why couldn't she just accept that Heath had wanted to do something nice for her? Was he always going to be the bad boy in her eyes? The fact he'd worked that out for himself made her clutch the pillow tighter. Heath had grown beyond his past, and he was right—she was the one who had refused to see it.

Rolling her head on the pillows, she refused to cry any more. She squeezed her eyes shut, welcoming the darkness. It was warm and soft, and short on condemnation, and with that and the lavender-scented pillows to lull her ragged senses she drifted off to sleep.

She woke up with a start an hour or so later. At first

she didn't know where she was—until she took in the huge bed, the crisp white linen and the rest of her surroundings, along with the fact that she was fully dressed. She was in a hotel—a very fancy hotel. Her room was sumptuous, but impersonal, as all such rooms were. The feeling that struck her next was loneliness. Hugging herself, she crossed to the window and stared out. Heath had said his house was just across the road…

Heath wouldn't be standing by his window staring out, Bronte reasoned turning away with a shrug. Heath would have more sense.

He was pacing. He couldn't stand inactivity and liked indecision even less. He hated the fact that the evening had ended on a row, and that the friction between them had increased, sending everything up in the air again, leaving everything unfinished. Before the row they had been drawing closer, getting to know each other all over again, but after it— He snapped a glance out of the window at the hotel where Bronte was staying. He had chosen a hotel most convenient to him—most convenient if things went well and if they went badly.

Bronte touched him in ways no one else had ever done, brought another side of him into existence—a side he had kept buried for most, if not all of his adult life. Emotions, inconvenient and dangerously distracting. He buried them. Bronte rooted them out, forcing him to confront his feelings and challenging his famous self-control.

And what had he done for Bronte?

He had made her face reality instead of blurring the lines between that and the fantasies she liked to weave.

So what was he saying? They completed each other?

He had thought the only thing that could touch him was business, but if those weren't feelings they'd been expressing tonight, he didn't know what they were. And if Bronte's face hadn't reflected her shock when she realised there was more to this association of theirs than pick-and-mix dreams, then that big dose of reality really had passed her by.

Turning back to his desk, he fingered the contract he'd had drawn up by his lawyers, itemizing the formal conditions for a six-month trial of the new estate manager at Hebers Ghyll. It was something he had intended to raise with Bronte, but they had both needed cooling-down time, and space from each other so they could rejig their thoughts. Bronte would leave London tomorrow. She was safer in the country—safe in the city too, so long as he stayed away. Tomorrow would be different. Tomorrow it would be all about business.

She took a long, warm bath, trying to convince herself that because this was such luxury it would somehow soothe her. It meant nothing. She would rather have slept on a park bench and remained friends with Heath than lie here in scented foam in the fabulous suite of rooms Heath had paid for because he wanted to keep her safe—because Heath had wanted to give her something nice, a treat, only for her to throw it back in his face. She'd get up early and go home, Bronte reflected as she climbed out and grabbed a towel. She could only wait and see if Heath's personal feelings would negate the grilling he'd managed to slip in while they were both relaxed enough to talk frankly to each other during their crazy fun day out.

'That was quite some interviewing technique, mister,'

she murmured wistfully, gazing at her shadowy reflection in the mirror on the wall. The suite was sumptuous, but the lights were cruel. Or maybe she had just aged. More likely, she'd had a shocking hold-the-mirror-up-to-yourself moment, and grown up.

All of the above, Bronte concluded.

She turned at a knock on the door.

Heath?

Heath was her first—her only thought.

Her heart was racing by the time she'd grabbed a robe and raced out of the bathroom, across the bedroom, to throw the lock, and opened the door.

On an empty corridor.

Glancing up and down, conscious she wasn't dressed for public display, she retreated quickly and pressed the door to again, locking it securely. It was only when she calmed down she saw the note on the floor. Express check-out details?

It had to be...

But they wouldn't call her Bronte, would they? The hotel wouldn't write that on the front of the envelope in bold script, using a fountain pen.

She ripped the envelope apart and let it fall to the floor. Unfolding the single sheet of high quality notepaper, she read the brief message. Heath would like to see her in the morning, before she returned to the country...9 a.m., his house.

She scanned the letter again. It was more of a note— no flourishes, no personal asides, just Heath's London address printed in raised script on the top right-hand corner. It was yet another kick-in-the-teeth reminder that Heath was in another place from the boy who had loved nothing more than a rough-house behind the stables with anyone foolish enough to take him on. Heath was a self-educated gentleman of culture and means these days, and it was Bronte who needed to get her head out of the sand.

CHAPTER THIRTEEN

THE outside of Heath's town house was a paean to elegance. Palladian pillars framed neatly trimmed bay trees either side of an imposing front door. The dark blue paintwork was so flawless it had the appearance of sapphire glass. The door knocker was a gleaming lion with bared teeth.

How appropriate, Bronte thought as her hand hovered over it. She was bang on time. She had made sure of it. As she waited on the neat, square mat she noticed the matching door knob was a smooth, tactile globe that would fit Heath's hand perfectly. Imagining his hand closed around it, she drew a sharp breath as he opened the door.

'Welcome to my home.' Heath, tall, dark and frighteningly charismatic, held the door open for her.

There was nothing to suggest he bore a grudge, or that last night had been the blitz of emotions she remembered. Heath was all business this morning. 'Thank you.' She stepped past his powerful presence into the hall.

Having left the crisp air of early morning behind only one thought hit her and that was, Wow. The warmth and luxury of Heath's home enveloped her immediately, as did the restrained décor in shades of cream, white, beige and ivory—the occasional blast of colour provided by vivid works of art hanging on flawless, chalky-white walls.

Everything was spotless, and in its place—but this wasn't just a showpiece, she realised, gazing around, this was a home. A bolt of longing grabbed her when she took in all the personal touches. They were in an imposing square hall tiled in black and white marble. The lofty ceiling was decorated with beautifully restored plasterwork, and the doors were heavy, polished wood. How had she missed so much about Heath? She must have been wearing blinkers. Yes, he was the same warrior, as evidenced by his business prowess now, but he was a protector too, as she knew from his care of her in London, and he was fun and sexy, clever—and could be a regular pain in the neck, when he put his mind to it, she thought, smiling to herself as Heath drew her deeper into the house. And the more she saw, the more she realised she had imagined many things over the years about Heath, but she had never pictured him as a homemaker. There was mail waiting to be posted on the antique console table with the gilt-framed mirror over it, as well as a couple of recently delivered yachting magazines, still in their cellophane wrappers. There was even a high-tech racing bike propped beside the front door—

'Bronte?' Heath prompted.

She was turning full circle like a tourist at the Louvre, Bronte realised—probably with her mouth wide open. How rude! Red-cheeked, she followed Heath down the hallway. She spied a litter of books scattered across a squashy sofa through one open door—his living room, she presumed. Classical music was playing softly in the background, and a log fire was murmuring in the hearth. He must have been relaxing there, waiting for her to arrive.

Nice to know someone could relax, she thought wryly as they passed another door. This opened onto a cloak-room with a boot rack stacked with an assortment of footwear and rugged jackets slung on antique hooks. It was all rather bloke-ish, and yet reassuringly normal for such a wealthy man.

And welcoming. That was her overriding impression, Bronte realised. Whether Heath knew it or not he had absorbed everything Uncle Harry had created at Hebers Ghyll. This was a real home, where the original features of the house had been retained and married with practi-cality and luxury, she thought as Heath showed her into his study. Understated and original were the keynotes that distinguished Heath's home—but then he was an artist too, she remembered. If Heath could be persuaded to work this type of magic on Hebers Ghyll, the estate really would live again.

And their friendship? What were the odds on that surviving? Bronte wondered as Heath invited her to take a seat on the opposite side of his desk. There was noth-ing intimate in his tone of voice. It was all business for him now.

'You know what this is?' he said, pushing a sheaf of documents towards her.

She looked at him—looked into Heath's deep, com-plex gaze. It sucked her in…and left her floundering. 'A contract?' she said, quickly gathering her scattered thoughts.

'It's a legal document setting out the terms for a six-month trial. Read it, and if you agree it, sign it.' Uncapping the same fountain pen with which he must have written the brief note inviting her to his London home, he handed it to her. 'I'll leave you while you read and consider—and you don't have to sign anything right away. You don't have to sign it at all.'

'But—' She stood, wanting to thank him. This was everything she had ever dreamed of. And how flat dreams could feel when they came true, she thought as Heath left the room.

But this wasn't just about her. There were others she had to think about. She sat down again and started to read, but all the time she was aware of the lovingly polished wood around her, and the warm, clean air, lightly fragranced with Heath's shower soap—

Heath...

She'd pushed him away, shaking her head as if that could rid it of him—and was left with a contract.

He'd had a breakfast meeting with the lawyers to get the contract finalised—except he hadn't eaten breakfast, and now he was hungry. He glanced at the cooker and the fridge—glanced at his wristwatch and thought of Bronte. He wanted her to be secure. He'd given her a cast-iron contract that protected her and gave her a pay-out if she changed her mind about working on the estate.

'I can't sign this, Heath.'

He turned to see her framed in the doorway. 'Can't or won't?' he said coolly.

'You know what's in here. It isn't fair.'

'No?' His lips pressed down in a rueful smile as she walked across the room. 'I thought it was very fair.'

'But there's nothing in it for you—no guarantees for you.'

'It's six months, Bronte.' He shrugged. 'You tell me how much I stand to lose.'

'You stand to lose a lot,' she insisted, coming close to make her point. 'You know you do, Heath.'

'Do I?' As Bronte's clean, wildflower scent invaded his senses he felt less than nothing about his losses—which was a first for him in business, he registered with wryly.

'Look at this clause, as an example,' she said, showing him the relevant passage. 'This is ridiculous—I don't need special treatment.'

'Do you find it patronising?' Heath asked as she turned her face up to him.

'Well, yes, I do, actually,' she said. 'Would anyone else get this sort of contract? I doubt it, Heath.'

'Does friendship count for nothing, Bronte?'

'Friendship…' She looked at him in something close to bewilderment.

Leaning back against the counter, he was acutely conscious of Bronte standing only inches away. 'Sign or don't sign,' he said, shifting position and moving away.

'I want to be the best person for the job, Heath.' She frowned. 'But you don't seem to care what I do, which doesn't fill me with confidence. I don't want any special favours. I want you to take me on because I'm the best.'

'You are the best candidate,' he said evenly, meeting her gaze.

'And the rest of it?' she said.

He stared away into his thoughts. 'I just want you to be happy, Bronte. It's all I've ever wanted.'

How could she be? Bronte wondered as her fingers closed around the contract. Heath was right, this contract had been her goal, but wanting Heath eclipsed everything, which meant this piece of paper with its more than generous terms fell so far short of what she had hoped for, she could hardly raise the energy to sign it.

'I'm not changing a word of it,' Heath told her. 'But I will give you a little more time to decide if you want to go ahead and sign it. In the meantime—' his lips tugged up in a faint smile '—have you eaten anything this morning?'

'No...have you?'

Their gazes held for a moment. If this was friendship—this feeling that survived everything—then she'd take it.

'Are you hungry, Bronte?'

Heath's question made her nose sting. 'I'm hungry,' she said.

'Then let's go into the kitchen and I'll make you something to eat.'

'You cook?'

'I cook,' Heath confirmed.

He led the way into a large, airy kitchen. With its glass roof, and fabulous state-of-the-art appliances, it had the spacious feel of an orangerie. 'Did you design it?' she said, looking around.

'I prepared the brief, did the drawings, and sourced the materials, so there could be no mistakes,' Heath explained, reaching for a pan and turning on the cooker.

'Did you do most of the work yourself?' she said, admiring the way the original ornate plasterwork had been incorporated into the modern design.

'Most of it—though I did allow the interior designers to plump the cushions when I'd finished.'

When Heath curved a smile it was like a light turning on, Bronte thought, but she mustn't be dazzled by it.

'Eggs Benedict?'

'Are you serious?'

'Absolutely. I like eating—so it's essential that I cook.'

She laughed, and finally relaxed.

He loved the sound of Bronte laughing. It was the only soundtrack he needed. He found a bowl and started whisking. 'Why don't you sit and read your contract? This will take a few minutes.'

As Heath got busy cracking eggs and reaching for the seasoning she laid the contract on the cool black granite, and signed it without another word.

Tipping buttery sauce onto the spinach, eggs and muffins, he came to sit next to her at the breakfast bar. 'You signed it,' he said, brow furrowing as he stared at the contract.

'And here's your copy,' she said, handing him half the papers. 'Eat. You must be hungry too. This is delicious, Heath,' she commented after the first mouthful.

Their arms were almost touching. This was the closest they had come to relaxing together since—since she didn't want to think about. She wanted to start over—this way—with a friendship between two adults—just see where it led. Nowhere, probably, but, hey—

'Now you're formally part of the team,' Heath said as he forked up egg, 'I'll tell you my thoughts about Hebers Ghyll.' Was that disappointment in Bronte's eyes? Wasn't this what she wanted? 'If there's something else you'd like to discuss first?'

'Nothing,' she protested, a little too vigorously, he thought. 'I'd like to hear your plans, Heath.'

'Okay.' As he talked he wondered if she was listening. She looked intent, but she was looking *at* him rather than listening to what he was telling her. It could wait, he thought, starting to collect the plates up.

'Is that it?' she said.

'For now.'

'So you started off thinking, "What do I need this for?" when you inherited,' she guessed, 'and then found me camped out on your latest acquisition and discovered a sense of ownership.'

A grin creased his face. 'That's pretty much the version I remember.'

'At least by camping out I got your interest.'

'You got something,' Heath agreed as they filled the dishwasher together, arms brushing, faces close. 'And your campaign won through,' he admitted tongue in cheek. 'I'm going to keep the place, aren't I?' he said, straightening up. 'And I want you to have the pleasure of telling everyone their jobs are safe.'

Her face brightened in a quick smile—a smile she found hard to sustain and so she turned away from him.

Everything would be all right now, Bronte told herself firmly. Heath would have to come down to visit. His visits would be formal affairs—but they'd be visits.

'I thought I might open part of the house and grounds to the public.'

She turned. 'But that's a wonderful idea.'

'It makes a certain amount of sense,' Heath agreed.

As always, he was the one under control. 'It makes more than sense,' she couldn't stop herself exclaiming. 'Uncle Harry would have loved that idea—'

'What you have to understand,' Heath interrupted, 'is that I own the estate now, Bronte.'

'Of course I realise that—I do,' she assured him, struggling to rein back her emotions. 'And anything you want me to do when I go back—just add it to the list.' She was ready to start work right away—this minute—but the look Heath was giving her was different from the way she felt inside. It was steadier—brooding, almost. 'What?' she said.

Heath's powerful shoulders eased in a shrug. 'I've been thinking that maybe I'll open an office there.'

Thank you, thank you...

Bronte's lips pressed down in a good imitation of, okay, then—no big deal. And then Heath got into practical matters—bricks and mortar, balance sheets, and making the place pay for itself, while she told him everything she could remember that made Hebers Ghyll so special to her. All the little things that had coloured her childhood, like the lush tang of newly mown meadow grass—eating hazelnuts straight from the bush, if the squirrels hadn't got to them first—blackthorn bushes heavy with purple sloe—

'Do you remember that sloe gin we made?' Heath interrupted.

'Do I remember it? I remember how sick we were after we drank it.'

'And then your mother threw it down the sink,' Heath said, laughing. 'She probably saved our lives.'

'Almost certainly...'

Bronte fell silent as a pang of regret swept over her. She missed her parents and wished she'd had the opportunity to tell them how much she loved them, and what a happy childhood they'd given her, before they left. She'd call them the first chance she got and make sure they knew. She had taken so much for granted, Bronte realised now this chance to see life through Heath's eyes reminded her that he had enjoyed none of her benefits, and yet had always looked to the future with optimism and confidence, while she had been restless and dissatisfied when she had so much. 'Your turn,' she said, prompting him. 'What else do you remember?' She grimaced as soon as the words left her mouth, thinking about Heath's difficult youth. 'Sorry—I didn't mean—'

'Hey—get over it. I have,' Heath said. 'Fun?' He thought about it for a moment. 'Sorting out this place.' He glanced around. 'It was a dump when I bought it. It was the only way I could afford something in central London—'

And then he started to tell her about the city he had grown to love with its galleries and museums, and the ancient buildings he loved to visit that had whetted his appetite for preservation and restoration. 'I enjoy the concerts too.'

'You like music?'

'Jazz, rock, classics—of course I like music. What?' he demanded when Bronte seemed surprised. 'Do you think I spend all my time working out and eating nails for breakfast?'

'Don't you?'

He laughed.

'And what about Hebers Ghyll, Heath? What good things do you remember about your visits?'

'Your mother's cooking,' he said immediately. 'Hot meals—Uncle Harry teaching me chess...' He fell silent.

'I'm sure Uncle Harry enjoyed those visits as much as you did.'

'We had a—' Heath pulled a face '—let's just call it a pretty explosive relationship, but chess was our meeting ground. The game was all about tactics, Uncle Harry said. He told me that whatever happened to me in my life, I would always need to use tactics—so I'd better get my head around them whether I liked chess or not.'

'That sounds like Uncle Harry,' Bronte said, smiling as she remembered. 'And did you?'

'Did I what?'

Heath was gazing at her lips. 'Did you like the game?' she said, wiping them surreptitiously in case some of their breakfast spinach was still hanging around.

'I like the game,' Heath said, transferring his level gaze to her eyes.

What were they talking about now? Tingles ran down her spine.

'Would you like me to complete the guided tour?' Heath suggested, stretching his powerful limbs as if the inactivity was starting to get to him.

'I'd like that very much,' she said.

CHAPTER FOURTEEN

THEY left the kitchen and walked deeper into the house, crossing wonderful rugs in shades of marmalade, clotted cream and russet that softened the marble hall and gave the space an inviting glow. Heath had created something wonderful and she guessed he must have dreamed of living in a house like this when he was a boy. Heath had not only fulfilled those dreams, but had done so with his own hands, which must have been doubly rewarding for him. There was a wood-panelled library where a worn leather chesterfield sat on a faded Persian rug and a log fire blazed in the hearth, as well as a high-tech studio where Heath could work. 'And below us in the basement I've got a cinema room, a home gym, and an indoor swimming pool,' he explained.

'Of course you have,' she teased him, but this was all seriously fabulous, even for such an upscale area of the city.

'Upstairs?' he suggested.

'Why not?' With this new understanding between them, why should there be any no-go areas?

They were easy together. They were going to have a good working relationship, Bronte thought as she followed Heath up the stairs. They'd had their explosion, their resolution, and now they were starting afresh.

Heath was so athletic she had to run to keep up with him, though he barely seemed to exert himself as he sprinted up the beautifully restored central staircase. 'The bathroom,' he said, opening one of the doors with a flourish.

She was still admiring the light-drenched landing. 'You are kidding me?' She stood on the threshold of the bathroom, staring in. 'This is fantastic, Heath.' The bathroom was clad in black marble and brightened with mirrors. There was a huge, walk-in drench shower, with a spa bath big enough to swim in. 'And I bet the floor is heated.' She kicked off her shoes. 'It is.'

'You don't exactly go down to the lake to freshen up.'

'Maybe not—but I know where to look when I need a refit.'

'It will cost you.'

She tore her gaze away when it held and locked with Heath's. Heath was at his most feral and the dream-weaver was back, and wouldn't take no for an answer, so when she should have left the room and allowed Heath to continue on with his tour she leaned back against the door, trapping them both on the bathroom side.

'Stop it,' Heath warned in an undertone, but then his lips tugged in a teasing smile. 'Don't you have a train to catch?'

'Yes,' she admitted. What was she thinking? She pulled away from the door, and Heath, ever the gentleman, leaned across to open it for her. Their bodies brushed. Electricity fired. This wasn't meant to happen—

'No,' he said, as if responding to her. 'No, Bronte,' he said more firmly.

Her eyes searched his.

'I'm no good for you,' he said.

She closed her eyes and inhaled sharply. 'And I'm stuck in the past? Stop it—stop it now, Heath.' Some primal instinct made her lift her arm and put her hand across his mouth. 'I don't want to hear that ever again,' she said.

Heath's eyes were laughing as his tongue went on the attack—tickling, and licking—

'Stop it,' she warned him, whipping her hand away.

'You stop it,' Heath said, laughing.

She exclaimed as he dragged her into his arms. 'What do you think you're doing?' she demanded as he swept her off her feet and headed for the drench shower. 'No!' she screamed when Heath's intention became clear.

'I need to cool you down,' he said. 'And if words won't do it—'

She watched him turn the shower to the coldest setting and screamed again, but it was pointless fighting Heath. And now he was under the water with her, holding her in place with embarrassing ease. 'Have you had enough yet?' he said, holding her in front of him.

They were both soaked through. 'What do you think?' She couldn't even pretend to be angry. Flicking her hair out of her eyes, she started laughing, and once she'd started she couldn't stop. Then Heath was holding her, and they were both laughing.

'Do you know what I think?' he said as she gasped for breath. Without waiting for her answer, he turned the shower off and, yanking her close, he kissed her—and this time there was no brushing, or teasing, or delay. They were hungry for each other and Heath kissed her in a way she had never been kissed before—in a way no one would ever kiss her again. He made her feel powerful and sexy and safe and more at risk than she had ever been in her life.

Life was a risk.

Love was a risk.

Was she going to spend all her life dreaming?

When Heath pulled back she waited. She was expecting the worst—planning for it—trying to work out how she could stalk out of his house with her head held high in soaking wet clothes. 'Not against the wall,' he murmured, his face creasing in a smile as he stared down at her.

'Been there—done that?' Bronte's brows rose.

She laughed softly against his face as Heath swung her into his arms, and then protested, 'We can't,' when Heath carried her straight out of the bathroom and into his bedroom.

'I can do what I like in my own house.'

'We'll make the bed wet.'

'You can count on it,' Heath promised as he stripped off his clothes.

'No,' he said when she started to do the same, 'that's my job.'

He undressed her slowly, kissing her naked flesh as he removed each garment with the utmost care. It was like the first time for her, Bronte thought as Heath stared down.

Bronte's naked body was a revelation to him—everything in miniature. It was the most beautiful thing he had ever seen—a work of art. She brought out the best in him. She made him draw on tenderness he hadn't known he possessed. He had always expressed physical emotions in a very different way. He embraced her gently, wanting nothing more than to protect her, and to forget all the reasons why he shouldn't be making love to her.

This was a moment out of time for both of them, a moment to give and receive pleasure, though she was so small against him—he couldn't believe what had happened in the kitchen at Hebers Ghyll. That had been a mindless frenzy, the result of years of pent-up need for both of them, but this was different…better. He could take his time and draw it out for both of them. And however fierce she was—and Bronte could be fierce—he would only use a fraction of his strength in response—and even the thought of that self-imposed curb aroused him.

'You're holding back,' she accused him, emerald fire blazing out of rapidly darkening eyes, 'and I want all your attention—'

'And you shall have it,' he promised, moving down the bed.

'I'm not complaining,' she hurried to assure him when he eased her legs over his shoulders. 'I'll never complain again.'

And as she groaned with pleasure he parted her lips and gave her his undivided attention for a considerable amount of time.

Her world exploded in a starburst of crystalline sensation, like firework night with constant repeats, Bronte thought as she heard herself exclaiming with guttural appreciation again and again. When she came to enough to take account of her surroundings and what she was doing, it was to find Heath cradling her in his arms. 'Oh…'

'Oh?' His lips tugged up as he dropped a kiss on her mouth. 'More?'

'What do you think?' she said, gasping as his hand found her.

'I think you've been missing this,' Heath said, easing her over the edge again with a few well-judged passes of his forefinger. 'That's it, baby…let yourself go,' he instructed, cupping her buttocks to hold her in place as she bucked and screamed for what seemed like for ever.

For two people who had decided absolutely that this must never happen, they were making a very good fist of it, Bronte thought wryly as Heath moved on top of her. 'You're so much bigger than me.'

'Somewhat,' Heath agreed wryly. 'I like that you sound so thankful.'

'Oh, believe me, I am…'

'Wider,' Heath murmured.

'Is that an instruction?' she challenged, giving Heath one of her looks as he pressed her knees back.

'What do you think?'

'I think I'm going to like this…'

'I think we both are.'

She cried out softly as he eased inside her. Filling her completely, he rested still for a moment, and when he began to move it was slow and deep, and all the while he was holding her in his arms and making love to her, Heath was kissing her, gently and tenderly, and with such a look in his eyes, Bronte wondered if anyone before them had known anything like this. She was so turned on by the extremes of pleasure it was almost inevitable her teeth would sink into him at some point.

'Wildcat,' Heath accused her, tumbling Bronte onto her back. And then they were rolling and tumbling and wrestling, until they managed to play-fight their way off the bed.

Lucky for them, there was a well-placed rug—lucky for Bronte when Heath cushioned her fall. 'This relationship relies far too much on my landing on you,' she said, pretending disapproval as she raised herself up on her forearms to stare down into his face.

'I just move faster than you do.' He grinned up.

'Your reflexes are perfectly tuned,' she agreed with satisfaction. 'I couldn't improve on them if I tried.' And with a contented sigh she nuzzled her face against his shoulder.

He caressed her, stroking her hair, knowing Bronte had a permanent place in his life even if it was impossible to see how those pieces could ever fit together. He would never mislead her. He would never promise Bronte anything he couldn't deliver.

'You feel so good,' she whispered, turning her head to kiss him gently on the chin. 'You're a marshmallow beneath all those beer cans and motorbike parts.'

'Don't break your teeth on this marshmallow,' he warned. 'I'm no Prince Charming, Bronte.'

'More Alaric the Visigoth? I love Visigoths,' she assured him, and then he was kissing her again, and she was kissing him back, and the future with all its complications faded away.

Heath's rough hands on her buttocks were so firm and thrilling, and yet they could turn so gentle when he was caressing her breasts. His fingers knew just how to torment her nipples and his hands were more than persuasive when he used them to cup her face to kiss her. She had never thought to be kissed like this—to be kissed by Heath like this. He made her feel as if anything were possible, as if she could feel this way for ever...

For ever starts tonight, Bronte thought, writhing in

ecstasy on the bed beneath Heath. And when he thrust one powerful thigh between her legs she refused to listen to the cynic inside her who insisted feelings as strong as this couldn't possibly last.

'Are you okay?' Heath murmured when she gasped as if in pain.

'Never better,' she said fiercely, and, staring into his eyes, she wrapped her legs even more tightly around his waist.

'Relax,' Heath soothed, pulling back.

Heath was so gentle with her it stoked her hunger until, refusing to suffer any more delay, she thrust her hips, claiming him, and only then did she see the slow smile on Heath's lips suggesting that was exactly what he had planned for her to do.

This slow, lazy way of making love was incredible. Breathing steadily instead of hectically, she was able to appreciate the sensation of being stretched and filled so completely, fully for the first time. She had always been in such a rush before.

'Are you okay?' Heath murmured when she thrashed her head on the pillow in extremes of pleasure.

'Your fault,' she gasped. 'You're so big.'

'Fault?' Heath queried, his lips curving with amusement. 'I've never heard it called that before.'

'I'm not complaining. I just have to get used to it each time,' she told him, lacing her fingers through his thick dark hair.

'I'm going to slow you down,' Heath told her when the urge became too great and she tried to hurry him.

'No,' she complained, increasing her grip on him, working muscles even she hadn't known she had.

'Yes,' Heath argued, and then he worked his hips— and not just back and forth with a compelling and irresistible rhythm, but from side to side, massaging persuasively until she screamed out her release in his arms.

'Better?' Heath murmured against her mouth.

'The best ever,' she groaned, still pulsing with pleasure and holding him in place.

That grip was all it took to make him hard again. They were good together. They were outstanding. He moved in response to Bronte's fierce instruction—hard—fast—deep. He could do that. With pleasure.

'Do you realise we've rocked the rug from one side of the room to the other?' he asked her some time later. 'I think it's time we took this to the bed.'

'You won't find any argument from me,' Bronte assured him, laughing against his mouth. Scooping her up, he carried her across the room.

'Do you think you'll ever get tired?' she said when he lowered her onto the sheets.

'I'll let you know,' he said. Slipping a pillow beneath her hips, he raised her up into an even more receptive position, and, taking his cue, she gripped the bed rail above her head.

'You're fantastic,' she cried out as another wave of pleasure hit her. Before she had time to recover, he turned her so she was kneeling in front of him with her hips held high. Holding her in place with one hand, he teased her into a frenzy of excitement with the other as he moved inside her to the rhythm he knew she liked best.

They must have fallen asleep with exhaustion, because she woke to find Heath watching her as she slept. 'What?' she whispered.

'You,' he murmured, barely moving his lips as he eased his head on the pillow.

'Me?'

'You…Bronte—'

'Don't say it,' she told him, putting her finger over his lips.

'I have to.'

'No, you don't. I know we live different lives. I know your life is here in London, Heath, and I'm glad I came down. I'll be able to picture you now.' She'd be able to hold it in her heart, Bronte thought. 'This was just one of those crazy episodes,' she said, 'for both of us.'

'And you're okay with that?' Heath said, frowning.

'I'm okay with that. We can still be friends. I mean—we're sophisticated adults, aren't we?'

Heath smiled his slow, sexy smile, but his gaze was somewhere else. 'We're adults,' he agreed.

'Okay,' she said softly, kissing his chest. 'So here's what we're going to do. No—this time, I'm setting the agenda, Heath,' Bronte insisted when Heath started to say something. 'You have to let me do this.' She waited a moment. 'You've got that copy of my contract. So—I'm going to take a shower now, and then I'm going to get dressed, call a cab—and go home.' There, she'd got it out. Her voice sounded a little wobbly, but still determined. Tilting her chin at the old defiant angle, she added, 'Anything else would be unbearable—so, please don't say anything. You're not allowed to speak.'

She slipped out of bed before Heath could argue. Dragging a cover around herself, she headed for the bathroom. It was over, this…little interlude. It was already in the memory box where the dreamweaver would take care of it.

She got the cab to drop her at the office first so she could pick up her things. She cried all the way. The cabby passed back a box of tissues without a word. No doubt he had seen this sort of thing before. She couldn't cry when she got back to Hebers Ghyll with the good news and spoil it for everyone. She couldn't cry at Heath's office in front of Quentin, who'd been so kind to her. And she definitely couldn't cry in front of Heath. 'Thank you,' she said, handing over a large tip when she got out of the cab.

'Look at it this way, love,' the cabbie advised. 'It can only get better from here.'

'Yeah—sure you're right,' she agreed, rustling up a smile. Thanking the cabbie and saying goodbye, she tipped her chin and put on her ready-to-see-Quentin face.

Quentin was subdued. Had Heath spoken to him already—asked him to have everything ready for her?

'Things didn't exactly go to plan, did they?' Quentin remarked.

'They went exactly to plan,' Bronte argued. 'I just left too much stuff out of the plan.'

'The devil's in the detail,' Quentin agreed.

'He certainly is. But, Quentin, the good news is, I got the job—thanks to you,' Bronte added, giving a surprised Quentin a hug. 'So I have to get back—there's a job waiting for me and people I want to share the good news with that Heath is keeping the estate.'

'Great,' Quentin drawled without much enthusiasm. 'Say hello to the country for me.'

'Why don't you come and say hello to it yourself?' Bronte suggested from the door.

Quentin grimaced. 'Like Heath, the thought of all that fresh air and organic food makes me wince.'

'I'm sure I could persuade you to change your mind.'

She refused to think about Heath. 'If you do decide to give it a try, you know where to find me.'

'Yes,' Quentin agreed witheringly, 'in a hay barn dressed in dungarees.'

'Not until next September. Until Harvest Home, then—'

'Harvest Home?' she heard Quentin scoff as she shut the door, but she could see him smiling through the glass.

CHAPTER FIFTEEN

CHRISTMAS came and went, and to everyone's disappointment the hall wasn't ready in time for the party. Bronte buried her disappointment in renewed effort. Not seeing Heath since she left him in London hurt most of all, but she remained in regular contact by phone and e-mail—and it was all very businesslike, which left her feeling hollow. Other than that, her efforts to bring the land back from the brink took up all her time, just the way she liked it. With the healthy proceeds from the fresh produce and the happy chickens she was able to take on more people from the village. Somehow she managed to find time to cook too. She considered that a pleasure—a reward for her hard-working team at the end of each back-breaking day. She had even been persuaded by the local authority to take on some disaffected youths on short-term contracts. With the proviso that they came with trained staff, how could she refuse, when each one that passed through the gates reminded her of the first time she'd met Heath?

Easter came and went and there was still no sign of Heath, though they exchanged e-mails and she delivered her report to him as agreed each Friday. But e-mails were cold, impersonal things, and she worried how easily they could be misunderstood. Their video conferences were almost as bad. Heath was always in such a hurry to get away.

'It's a compliment,' Colleen insisted. 'You're doing such a good job Heath doesn't need to interfere.'

Bronte laughed. 'Apart from his phone calls every day, twice a day, do you mean?'

'At least he calls,' Colleen pointed out. 'He must like speaking to you.'

'Heath wants to check up on progress,' Bronte argued as they cleared up after breakfast. 'I just wish—' She stopped herself just in time.

'You miss him,' Colleen supplied.

Bronte shrugged. 'This is Heath's property, not mine. I just think he should show more interest—do more than call.'

'Heath's a busy man, Bronte—and even if he does want to spend more time here, he'll have to plan for it—fit it in—and all that takes time.'

'It's been almost a year.'

'It's been nine months.'

'Okay,' Bronte conceded wryly. 'I could have had a baby in that time.'

'No way am I getting into that,' Colleen told her with a wave of her hand, heading out.

As summer ripened into its full splendour Bronte joined the workers in the fields. She came back most days exhausted, but content. Heath's team had worked wonders on the old buildings, and had even started work on the castle, while Bronte's team, which had expanded to include the local authority boys as well as some school leavers, had worked wonders with the harvest.

This was what Uncle Harry must have had in mind, Bronte reflected as she watched the last of the hay bales being dumped off the back of the harvester. The sky was a clear scrubbed blue with only a wisp of cloud, and the scent of fertile earth was unbelievably intoxicating. It was as if the summer sun had warmed the earth for just this moment, producing a scent Bronte only wished she could bottle and share.

She planned to give everyone a day off so they could sleep in tomorrow. Harvesting could be a tricky business if the weather was unpredictable, but it had been dry for days and promised to remain so—even so they'd worked like stink in case the weather changed. Their reward was plain to see. It wouldn't be every year that they would be able to contemplate a full hay barn as well as having spare stock to sell.

She looked like a regular land girl, Bronte mused as she strode back happily towards her cottage. Gone were the purple leggings and flimsy top, and in their place were the dungarees Quentin had mocked.

Quentin…Bronte smiled as she remembered Heath's PA, and then her thoughts turned inevitably to Heath. Why didn't he come? Why didn't the ache for him lessen? Some days she doubted it ever would. Instead of thinking about herself, she should be thinking about rewarding everyone for their hard work, Bronte reflected as she stood by the stile, dragging on the warm air and staring over the golden carpet of cut wheat. Heath wasn't here to do it, so she would do something special. They might have missed the Christmas party, but there was no reason why they couldn't have a party now. Why not have that Harvest Home she had teased Quentin about— invite everyone from the village? Invite Quentin—

And Heath?

And Heath.

She told her inner voice to be quiet now. That was

quite enough nonsense for one day and there was some important planning to be done.

Heath couldn't come. Why wasn't she surprised? But he'd send a representative, he promised Bronte during their regular Friday hook-up.

'Hi, doll—' Quentin appeared briefly at Heath's shoulder before hurrying away.

'Hi, Quentin.'

'Make it a good party,' Heath insisted, 'and don't forget to send me the bills.'

'I wi—' Was as far as she got before Heath cut the connection. 'And I'll be sure to attach some photographs to my next mail so you can see how much fun we had without you,' she assured the blank screen with a lump like a brick in her throat.

It was the perfect day for the perfect event. The sun had beaten down all week and the castle, with its newly renovated staterooms, would be open to the public for the first time. They had just managed to get the last bales of hay into the barn before everyone had to dash back home to get ready for the party. As well as dancing and a feast provided by Bronte, there was going to be a cake stall on the lawn leading down to the lake, as well as hoopla, a bran tub, and a bric-a-brac table. Colleen had gone the whole nine yards, dressing up as a fortune teller, complete with huge gold earrings and a headscarf, which she'd plucked from her normal accessory box, she told Bronte. And Bronte, feeling sick of the sight of the cakes she had been baking non-stop, had put herself in charge of the water-bomb stocks where the local head teacher had gamely offered to be pelted to raise money for charity. The bunting was flying, the band was tuning up, and the first of the guests were due to arrive within the hour. Bronte did her final check, wondering if she dared relax. Surely, nothing could go wrong now. Everything was ready for the party of the year, so now all she had to do was change her clothes.

He saw the red glow in the sky when they were still miles away.

'What's that?' Quentin said, peering out of the window. 'I thought you didn't get light pollution in the country?'

'You don't,' Heath said, stamping down on the gas.

The party was cancelled. Of course it was cancelled. Bronte was too busy forming everyone up in a line so they could pass buckets of water from the lake to the source of the fire to even remember she had once planned a party. If she'd had time to think about it she would have said she was numb, but right now she was all logic and fierce determination to save what she could.

The line of people stretched from the lake to the barn. She'd made the call to the local fire department and, with a heavy heart, to the police, and now all she could do was tag onto the line and help to pass the buckets until the fire service arrived.

The Lamborghini skidded to a halt. Throwing the door open, he ran. Wherever Bronte was, he was sure she'd be in the thick of it. Why the hell had he stayed away so long?

Because he never took holidays—because everything took time to arrange—

To hell with that—he should have been here sooner.

The smoke choked him as he grew closer to the fire.

His eyes stung, and fear clung to him with the same tenacity as the claggy filth of oily soot. He only realised now how fierce the fire was, and what a hold it had taken on the barn. Nothing could be saved, though a squadron of firefighters had high-powered hoses trained on it. He could feel Bronte's despair above the heat of burning hay and stink of choking smoke. He blamed himself for not following his instincts. Life, business, money, success, what did any of it mean without Bronte? The instant he'd been told what she'd done—starting slowly with some of the local, out-of-work youths, and then growing in confidence, until she was persuaded by the local authority to take on boys like him—boys like he'd been. If anyone knew what a mistake that was for a girl on her own, he did. The moment he'd heard where this new intake was coming from he'd dropped everything—but not soon enough. He knew what they were capable of, but Bronte steadfastly refused to see the harm in anyone. Glass half full, that was Bronte. But optimism and determination couldn't save her from this. He'd thought that by making a clean break it would give her space to fly, but she wouldn't fly far with her wings burned off.

He shielded his face against the heat. An officer told him to move back. He explained he was the owner of the estate and asked if anyone knew where his estate manager was. Bronte had called them, he was told, but no one had seen her since.

His darting gaze swept the crowd. Where was she? Then Colleen found him and told him about Bronte arranging the line of buckets while they waited for the engines to arrive. 'Have you seen her?' he demanded.

Colleen shook her head. 'Not since then.'

Colleen looked defeated. 'Go back to the kitchen,'

he ordered. 'Make tea—lots of it—strong and sweet. Everyone will need some.'

'I'll do that,' she said, looking grateful that he'd found her a task.

Bronte would get her water for the buckets from the lake, he reasoned, and the lake was at the back of the barn.

'You can't go there,' someone shouted at him.

He was conveniently deaf.

The best he expected to find was Bronte broken and sobbing on the ground. The worst he refused to think about.

As ever, she surprised him. He found her in the stable yard with her back braced against a stable door while the occupants she'd trapped inside were trying their best to kick it down. His relief at finding her unharmed was indescribable. His feelings at seeing her again were off the scale. 'What the hell are you doing?' Lifting her out of the way, he took her place. At the sound of his raised voice the kicking stopped abruptly.

'I saw them set fire to the barn,' she said, wiping a smoke-begrimed hand across her face. 'If I moved from here I thought there was a chance they could get out and get away—'

'They?'

'Two of them,' she explained.

'You imprisoned two grown men?' he exclaimed.

'They're just boys,' she said, flashing him a glance.

He swore viciously. 'This is my fault—I put this idea in your head. You should have waited for me to initiate a scheme like this.'

'What?' she fired back. 'Like wait for ever?'

He slammed his head back against the door in frustration. The sound echoed in the courtyard above the shouted instructions of the firefighters and the police. She was right. He should have been here sooner. This was his responsibility, not Bronte's. 'I'll call the police,' he said, bringing out his phone.

'Everything happened faster than the boys expected,' Bronte explained as he cut the line. 'The barn went up like a rocket, and there was no time for them to get away before the police arrived, and so they hid in here. I just dropped the latch.'

'You shouldn't have chased them.'

'What did you expect me to do? Stand around sulking because the party was cancelled?'

She was furious and he deserved it. Emotion welled inside him. 'I only care that you're safe,' he shouted, his voice hoarse with smoke and emotion.

They were silent for a moment, and then she said quietly, 'Hello, Heath.'

He shook his head, then held her gaze. 'Hello, Bronte...'

All the things he should have said to her long before now. All the things he should have done for her. His head was pressed against the door and as he turned to stare down at her he wondered what kind of fool he'd been. The door she'd been defending was one of the few yet to be replaced and the rotten wood was already splintering under the barrage of blows it had received. They could have killed her. 'Would you like to go and get changed for the party now? I'll deal with this.'

'The party's cancelled,' she said steadily, 'and I'm not leaving you.'

'I was hoping you'd say that.' He glanced at the petrol can lying discarded in the centre of the yard, and the box of matches Bronte had tightly clutched in her hand.

'It's all gone,' she whispered.

'Don't,' he said firmly. 'This isn't over yet. We'll build a new barn—we can buy in more hay—'

'But we didn't need to buy hay before this happened.'

'And now we do,' he told her calmly. 'All businesses have setbacks, Bronte. It's how you get over them that matters.' There were oily smudges on her face. Her eyes were red and wounded from the smoke, and from crying, he suspected—not that Bronte would show that sort of weakness in a crisis situation. 'You're quite a girl,' he murmured.

'And you're still an absentee landlord.' She scowled, rallying.

'Something I'll have to change.'

She didn't believe him. Why should she? Now wasn't the time, but it might be the only chance he got. 'I have a mature business, and when I realised what I was missing out on I think I finally learned to delegate. I've appointed a CEO, an operating officer, a financial controller, and a sales and marketing guy.'

'To do your one job,' she said. She didn't dare to hope that this might mean progress. 'No wonder you're such a pain in the ass, Heath.'

'They should be able to handle it,' he said wryly.

'While you take broader control of your business portfolio, which now includes a country estate?'

'I'm only sorry it's taken so long,' he said, 'but it takes time to find the right person.'

'And less than an hour to undo a full year's work,' Bronte remarked as she glanced over her shoulder to where the flames were still hungrily licking up the remains of the barn.

'We'll get over it,' Heath promised.

'We?'

'You and me. We'll get over this. I promise—'

'Together?'

He placed another call to the police. 'Go and hurry them along, will you, while I bring these lads out?'

'Don't take any unnecessary risks, Heath.'

'Thanks for the advice.' He flashed a rueful grin. 'I think I'll be okay. And if I'm not, I'll call for you.'

A faint smile touched Bronte's red-rimmed eyes. 'I'll be right back,' she said, starting to run.

He wanted a chance to speak to the boys without anyone being present. He wanted to see them punished and for them to make reparation for what they'd done, but he wanted them to know there was another way—if they chose to take it. He wanted them to spread the word when they went inside that there was someone who understood the poison that drove them and who had the antidote to it, and that this same individual would be running the boot camp at Hebers Ghyll.

CHAPTER SIXTEEN

HEATH worked like a Trojan alongside the officers to clear the debris and make everywhere safe, while the people who could stayed on to help. Bronte was touched to find Quentin in the kitchen making tea and sandwiches for everyone, and didn't even mind that he had taken command of her beloved Aga.

'I've never had such a huge piece of kit to play with before. Or so many interesting new friends in uniform.'

'Quentin,' Bronte scolded, knowing that if anyone could bring a smile to people's faces when they most needed it, it was this man.

'What's wrong?' Heath said, drawing Bronte aside discreetly. 'You've been so brave up to now. Don't crumple on me, Bronte.'

'I'm not crumpling,' she said, pushing him away. 'I'm just watching you and Quentin, and all the people milling round the kitchen, and wishing it could stay like this for ever. I know,' she said through gritted teeth before Heath had chance to speak. 'I know I'm dreaming again.'

He was too tired to argue. Everyone was tired and battle scarred, but he had to admit Quentin had come up trumps, making people laugh as he doled out mugs of tea and coffee, and the biggest, thickest sandwiches, which everyone professed to love. But it was to Bronte that most of the praise was due, Heath reflected as he watched her moving between people, offering her own brand of encouragement. She had worked tirelessly inside and outside the house, clearing up the mess, and offering words of reassurance, creating such a feeling of warmth and camaraderie that everyone wanted to stay on late to help out.

'You should try one of Quentin's sandwiches,' she said, distracting him by plonking a huge platter in front of his nose. 'They're really great.'

'And he's used to having them made for him,' Heath said, selecting one. 'Quentin's partner is a dab hand in the kitchen—with a penchant for gourmet food.'

'Lucky Quentin.'

'Lucky me,' he said.

They were too busy to speak after that. Bronte didn't go home with the rest of the crowd, but stayed on to help Quentin and Heath clean up the kitchen. It was like the day after a party when everything was set to rights... except there'd been no party. And now there was no barn, she thought wistfully, staring out of the window at the heap of jagged timbers and blackened ash.

'Don't go home tonight,' Heath murmured, coming up behind her.

She turned in his arms. I can't go through this again, she thought. The others had left the kitchen and all any of them were seeking tonight was comfort, but where would comfort lead with Heath? She wondered what to say to him, how to phrase what she had to say to him—to a man who had led so much of the salvage work today. I'm not in the mood, sounded ugly. I don't want to spend the night with you, would be a lie.

'I'm not going to let you go home to an empty cottage,' Heath said. 'I want you to stay here with me, Bronte.'

'I don't think that's a very good idea.'

Heath's smoke-blackened face creased in his trademark grin. 'I'll run you a bath—'

'Heath, I—'

'And I'll call you when it's ready.'

She could argue, or she could accept Heath's kindness for once. She could soak in soapy bubbles, which right now seemed an irresistible option.

She listened to Heath bounding up the stairs and marvelled at his energy. After everything they'd been through she couldn't have felt more exhausted. She supposed it was the knowledge that everything everyone had worked so hard to achieve had gone up in flames. What was the point—?

She was so wrong, Bronte thought as she caught sight of Quentin's neatly folded drying cloth hanging on the Aga rail. It was such a little thing amongst the monumental happenings of the night, but it showed Quentin cared. So many people had cared tonight, and if all that goodwill could be harvested there wasn't the slightest possibility that Herbers Ghyll would go to the wall.

Heath didn't call downstairs, he came downstairs to make sure she hadn't changed her mind. 'And I'm going to stand outside the door to make sure you're all right,' he said, 'and I won't take any argument. You just yell if you need me.'

'But you're tired too,' she said, gazing up at Heath's grimy face. 'You must be. You go and clean up—or aren't you planning to wash tonight?'

'It'll keep,' he said. 'When I know you're safely

tucked in bed I'll take a shower and clean this dirt off then.'

'Thank you,' she said softly, meeting Heath's gaze.

'There's no need to thank me,' he told her as he opened the bathroom door. 'And there's no hurry, either. You take your time.'

The hard man had laid out some towels for her, and also one of his robes and a T-shirt, both of which would drown her. She appreciated the gesture more than she could say. He'd even filled the bath with warm, soapy water. She climbed in and sank beneath the surface, wondering if she would ever be clean again.

She washed the filth from her hair and her face, and then took one last quick soak, conscious that Heath must be equally exhausted, however he appeared. Getting out of the bath, she dried herself, and put on the T-shirt and robe, wrapping her hair in a towel.

Heath was waiting as she came out of the bathroom, and, putting his arm around her shoulders, he led her into his bedroom. She was swallowed up in the huge double bed. The pillows were soft and the sheets held the faint scent of sunshine and lavender. He tucked the sheets up to her chin, and kissed her forehead. 'Sleep,' he murmured.

She didn't need any encouragement.

She woke in the night to find Heath lying beside her. *Wearing boxers.* She smiled. He was holding her in his arms. 'You cried out,' he said, stroking her hair back from her face.

'Sorry.'

'Don't be.' Kissing her again, he drew her close until she fell asleep wrapped in his arms.

Heath had gone by the time she woke up, leaving Bronte to wonder if she'd been dreaming. She'd certainly overslept, she realised, glancing groggily at the clock. And she had work to do.

Heaving herself out of bed, still half asleep, she staggered to the bathroom for a wake-up shower. She wasn't worried about where Heath was. He'd be here at Hebers Ghyll setting things right. There was nothing more certain in her mind.

When she came downstairs the yard was full of builders' vans and it seemed everyone from the village had come to help. And driving towards them was the biggest truck Bronte had ever seen, with huge prefabricated wooden sides and struts fixed onto the back of it with ropes. 'What's happening?' she exclaimed with excitement, bursting through the door.

'Come and see,' Colleen cried, grabbing hold of Bronte's arm and dragging her along.

Heath was standing on the girders putting a heavy beam into place with the boys who hadn't been involved in starting the fire helping him. Apparently oblivious to the cold, he was wearing his old worn ripped jeans and a tight-fitting top that could have been any colour it was so blackened by grime and dust, but he was setting a good example to the boys with his hard hat, work gloves, and steel-capped boots.

Bronte felt so proud as she stared up at him. Everything had come full circle to its rightful place. Everything they had ever talked about flashed through her head—everything they'd ever done together—everything they'd learned about each other. And while that circle had been turning and becoming whole again, she thought about the journey they'd travelled. And the fun they'd had—the rows too, not to mention the frantic, fabulous sex…as well as the slow, sensual love-making. Right up to last night when Heath had held her in his arms as she slept, and had just been there for her, watching over her, silent and protective.

As if he felt her staring up at him, Heath looked down. He hadn't shaved this morning. Heath was a man on a mission—a man in his most deliciously unreconstructed state. Their eyes met briefly. It was all Heath had time for before he hefted the beam into place.

'I'm going to go and get breakfast started,' Bronte told Colleen, who was a gem for bringing her clean clothes from the cottage.

'Lunch,' Colleen said with a laugh. 'It's almost noon.'

'Why didn't you wake me?'

'Heath said you should sleep—and everyone agreed. No one worked harder than you last night, Bronte—and no one blames you for sleeping in. No one lost more,' Colleen added when Bronte started to argue.

'Heath lost more. You lost more. I don't think I lost anything,' Bronte murmured as she turned to take one last look at Heath directing his team. 'We'll keep the excess hay,' she told Colleen as they walked back to the kitchen. 'We won't sell it as we'd planned to—instead we'll use it to restock the new barn.'

Heath was right, Bronte thought as she continued explaining her plans. All businesses suffered setbacks, but what had happened here, however dramatic and irreversible it had seemed at the time, was still something they could get round.

She was back, Heath thought, rejoicing as he towelled down roughly after his shower. Bronte was back, and firing on all cylinders. He'd seen it in her eyes when she came to watch the new barn being raised. She had recovered her fighting sprit. He'd felt it then, and he felt it now, that huge surge of something he now accepted was love. He'd fought it, ignored it, scorned it, and trampled it—whenever he'd got half a chance. But now he craved it. He wanted Bronte. He wanted Bronte to love him as he loved her, and he wanted to build a lot more than a barn with her.

The fire had been a terrible disaster, but out of it had come a reckoning of things that were important in life—things that could be rebuilt, regenerated, or reclaimed, and those that could never be. If Bronte had been harmed in any way he would never have forgiven himself. If the worst had happened, which he wouldn't even think about, no amount of determination in the world would bring her back to him. And now they had got to know each other all over again he doubted Bronte's nature could be ruined by anything—even him, because there was steel beneath that quirky daintiness, and fire beneath those caring, dreamy eyes.

He had even shaved. Leaning on the sink, he stared at himself in the mirror, wondering if this new fierce passion would be as easy to turn into victory as expressing powerful feelings with his fists had been. He thought not. Bronte was tricky. She could never be called predictable. But he was ready for her. Straightening up, he reached for a towel and patted his temporarily smooth cheeks. His thick hair refused to dry however much he towelled it. He slicked it back roughly with his hands. Time was a-wasting. He fastened his shirt as he headed downstairs, though, unusually, he paused to take a deep breath outside the kitchen door.

Blind to anything else in the room he only saw Bronte standing in front of the Aga. Apron tied round her waist and knotted in front, she was dressed in purple leggings and a flimsy top. The flip-flops and toe rings had been reinstated and her hair was hanging in crazy tangles to her waist. She had never looked lovelier—though that might have had something to do with the huge tray of delicious-looking food she was holding in hands—tiny hands—currently concealed beneath huge black oven mitts.

'I love you,' he announced, walking straight up to her.

Taking the gloves and the tray in one slick move, he put them aside. And then, because he was so tall and she was so tiny, he knelt at her feet holding both her tiny hands in his. 'I love you more than anything in the world.'

He only realised when he heard the raucous applause that they weren't alone, but nothing was going to distract him from his purpose. He waited for the noise to die down, and then he asked her clearly and steadily, 'Will you marry me, Bronte?' She hadn't said a word up to now, and he was in no way confident of the outcome.

Then she knelt too. Or maybe her legs gave way with shock.

'That wasn't supposed to happen,' he said, looking down. 'I'm supposed to be the supplicant here.'

'Better we face each other for this,' she said. 'I love you too,' she said simply. 'I've always loved you, Heath, and I always will.'

'But you haven't answered my question,' he pointed out.

'Patience,' she told him. 'I'm just getting to that.' Breathless silence surrounded them, which was released in a shiver of sighs when she added, 'Heath, that was the most romantic proposal any girl could receive.'

'And?' he demanded impatiently.

'Of course I'll marry you,' Bronte whispered as the kitchen exploded in a frenzy of cheers.

He wanted to give Bronte something very special to show how much he loved her—but what to give the girl who had everything? Bronte had nothing in a material sense, but she didn't want anything. Nothing he could buy her with money would mean a thing—she'd rather have a good load of quality manure to spread on her precious vegetable garden. He'd had to think laterally and go that extra mile…

And so he did. Swinging out of the Jeep just before Christmas, he dragged Bronte into his arms. They were getting married at the end of the week, so his timing had never been more important.

'Okay, Mr Mysterious,' she said, trying to peer inside the cab. 'What are you hiding in there?'

'Not what. Who…'

There was a pause, and then she said, 'Mum? Dad?'

He left them to it. He had been introduced to emotions, but they still weren't his best friend.

Bronte had her own way of thanking him. He was okay with that. Sunshine was streaming through the curtains by the time they could talk coherently. 'You're an excellent student,' he murmured as she dozed in his arms, 'if a little hasty sometimes.'

'Practice makes perfect—and seeing as I've got a lot more practice ahead of me…'

'Presents first,' he said, reminding her of their arrangement. 'You said you have something for me—and I've certainly got something for you.'

'You certainly have,' she said, punching him playfully.

She thought back to the youth Heath had been and the

man he had become, and just hoped she'd got it right. 'I hope you like it,' she said.

'I'm sure I will. Whatever you've chosen will be perfect—it had better be,' he teased her as she leaned out of bed to retrieve the tiny package she'd hidden away from him. 'Did you use a whole roll of sticky tape on this?' he said as he picked it open.

Freed from its wrappings, the small wooden chess piece lay in his palm. He stared at it for a long time.

'I do have the rest of them,' Bronte reassured him, 'and I found the board in the attic, as well as the table you used to play chess on with Uncle Harry. I had them renovated—they're downstairs. I would have given them to you—'

Heath stopped her with a kiss, and from his expression when he pulled away Bronte knew she'd got it very right indeed.

'That's the most thoughtful gift anyone's ever given me,' he admitted. 'And now I've got something for you…'

'What's this?' Bronte said, frowning when Heath handed over a large manila envelope. 'Is it another contract? A permanent one?'

'Why don't you open it and find out?' Heath suggested.

Tearing the envelope open, she started to read, and as she did her expression was slowly changing from interest into shock. 'Heath, you can't do this.'

'Why can't I?' Heath said. 'Hebers Ghyll is mine to do with as I like—so why can't I give half to you?'

'Be serious, Heath,' Bronte exclaimed, laughing as she shook her head, 'You can't just hand over half of an estate like Hebers Ghyll.'

'I expect you to take half the responsibility for it.'

'Of course, and I'd love to do that, but—'

'No buts,' he said. 'It's done.'

'Are you sure?' Bronte murmured, still not able to believe what Heath was giving her.

'Never more so,' he assured her. 'Oh—and there's something else. I've been carrying this around all evening.'

What a great sight, Bronte thought as Heath leaned out of bed to rumble in the pocket of his jeans. 'Just stay there,' she said. 'That's a good enough gift for me right there.'

'What?' Heath said as he swung back to join her. Narrowing his eyes, he gave Bronte a stern look. 'Were you staring at my butt?'

'As if I would.'

'I might have to punish you,' he warned.

'Please.'

'Okay, your punishment is to wear this on every occasion—even in the stables when you're mucking out.'

'What is it?'

'Guess,' Heath said dryly, handing over the small red velvet box.

It was one of those 'don't dare to hope moments', but she did dare. She had always dared, or she wouldn't be here, Bronte thought as Heath raised a brow.

'Maybe I'd better put some clothes on before you open it,' he said. 'I feel a little underdressed.'

'You'll do just as you are,' Bronte insisted. Opening the box, she gasped. 'I've changed my mind.'

'You have?'

'You're definitely underdressed. You should be wearing running gear—no way am I giving this back.' Removing a ruby the size of a plum surrounded with fabulous brilliant cut diamonds, she allowed Heath to place it on her wedding finger.

'Do you like it?' His eyes were dancing with laughter. 'I realise it's a little bold for someone who lifts hay bales for a living.'

'I'll get round it,' Bronte promised dryly. 'But, seriously, Heath, you didn't need to buy me anything—a piece of cord would do the job just as well.'

'Would you settle for a tent instead of Hebers Ghyll?'

Bronte laughed as Heath drew her into his arms. 'Don't you love it when a plan comes together?'

EPILOGUE

THE wedding was held in the newly renovated Great Hall at Hebers Ghyll a couple of days before Christmas. There was snow on the ground and a great spruce tree stood sentry outside the doors. Decorated with lights and stars and shimmering ribbons, it gave just a hint of the glorious scene inside. The log fire was blazing, and the hall was filled with workmates and friends, Bronte's family and just about everyone from the village. They turned expectantly as she reached the door, but all Bronte could see was Heath, looking like some latter-day Mr Darcy—though much better looking, she thought as the breath caught in her throat. There was a touch of Heathcliff about him too—all that darkly glittering glamour. Heath's hair was just as thick and black and as unruly as ever, though she knew he would have tried to tame it, just as he would have tried to shave so his face remained smooth for longer than five minutes. Both attempts had failed, she was pleased to see, though his tail suit was magnificent and skimmed his powerful frame with loving attention to detail. He must have gone to Quentin's tailor, she guessed as Heath's groomsmen took their place at Heath's side. Not even Quentin had dared to argue when Heath had named Quentin his best man.

The vast, welcoming space was decorated with Christmas flowers—spray roses, aptly named warm heart, crimson hypericum and frosted twigs, vivid gerberas and frowzy amaranthus, and the room was lit by candlelight, which gave the burnished wood panelling an umber glow. The scent of pine and wood smoke in the great stone hearth was such a wonderfully evocative smell, and as Bronte walked in on her father's arm and saw everyone who had helped to make this possible wishing them well she felt she were being carried along on a wave of goodwill.

She had found her dream wedding dress in the city—a simple fall of cream chiffon that floated as she walked, it was cut straight across her breasts and the delicate fabric was swathed and draped over a boned bodice. The gauzy skirt was drawn up on one side over a matt silk Dupion underskirt and had been formed into a delicate camellia on the hip.

Quentin, who had appointed himself wedding-advisor-in-chief, had all but swooned when Bronte had come out of the dressing room wearing this one. 'Perfect,' he'd said. 'We need look no further.' And then he had gusted with relief, because it had taken a solid week of looking for something that wouldn't be too grand, as Bronte put it, but wouldn't look as if she could cut it down to wear with flip-flops and toe rings either.

She had finally, after much argument, given way to Quentin over the veil. She hadn't wanted to wear one, but Quentin had insisted, and so she was wearing a floating three-tiered confection composed of creamy cobwebby net, dusted with the tiniest sparkling diamanté that fell into a long, floating train behind her. Even Bronte had been amazed at how feminine it made her look.

'Tiaras and tattoos?' she had said, laughing when Quentin had agreed she could wear one toe ring.

'Heath wouldn't want you completely changed,' Quentin observed, adding a discreet band of crystals to Bronte's hair while he distracted her.

'Quentin, you're wicked,' she had exclaimed.

'I had the best teacher,' Quentin had informed her and they both knew who he meant.

So now she was walking down the aisle towards the man she loved, dressed by royal appointment—as Quentin insisted she must think of it—in the stratospherically high heels Quentin had chosen for her. 'Heath is so much taller than you,' he had pointed out. 'And I refuse to listen if you start to argue with me.'

The one thing Bronte couldn't argue about was Heath's size. Heath was built on a heroic scale in every department, she thought happily, keeping those thoughts under wraps as she did her best to glide gracefully in front of her bridesmaids, Maisie and Colleen, both of whom were dressed in powder-pink Grecian-style gowns. She was trembling all over by the time she turned to pass her wedding bouquet to Colleen. Lush cream orchids with an intimate flash of purple at their core, the bouquet had been created to Heath's design, and when her father put her hand in Heath's Bronte was sure everyone must have heard her swift intake of breath. At this range he was even more devastating with his stubble-shaded face, and dark, slumberous eyes. The sweeping ebony brows and thick black hair curling rebelliously over the collar of his winged shirt gave him the appearance of some ruthless buccaneer who had sailed into this quiet harbour and taken it by storm—which was pretty much what had happened, Bronte reflected.

'Okay?' Heath whispered, heat and concern mingling in his eyes as he looked at her.

'I am now,' Bronte confirmed, meeting that fiery gaze. Now, if she could just concentrate on the ceremony and put the pleasures of their wedding night out of her mind, she might stand a chance of remembering what she was supposed to say and do.

And then Heath's lips brushed her ear. 'Good,' he murmured, 'because I've got plans for you...'

THERE'S SOMETHING
ABOUT A REBEL…

BY
ANNE OLIVER

Anne Oliver was born in Adelaide, South Australia, and with its beautiful hills, beaches and easy lifestyle, she's never left. An avid reader of romance, Anne began creating her own paranormal and time travel adventures in 1998 before turning to contemporary romance. Then it happened—she was accepted by Mills & Boon in December 2005. Almost as exciting: her first two published novels won the Romance Writers of Australia's Romantic Book of the Year for 2007 and 2008. So after nearly thirty years of yard duties and staff meetings, she gave up teaching to do what she loves most—writing full time.

Other interests include animal welfare and conservation, quilting, astronomy, all things Scottish, and eating anything she doesn't have to cook. She's traveled to Papua/New Guinea, the west coast of America, Hong Kong, Malaysia, the UK and Holland. Sharing her characters' journeys with readers all over the world is a privilege and a dream come true.

You can visit her website at www.anne-oliver.com.

To everyday heroes

CHAPTER ONE

IT WASN'T the rumble of approaching thunder that woke Lissa Sanderson some time after midnight. Nor was it Mooloolaba's tropical heat that had prompted her to leave the houseboat's windows open to catch whatever breeze was coming off the river. It wasn't even her seriously serious financial situation that had kept her tossing and turning for the past few weeks.

It was the sound of footsteps on her little jetty.

Unfamiliar footsteps. Not her brother's—Jared was overseas, and no one she knew would be calling in at this ridiculously unsociable hour. A shiver scuttled down her spine.

Lifting her head off the pillow, she heard the leafy palm fronds around the nearby pool clack together and the delicate tinkle of her wind chimes over the back door as the sound of approaching footsteps drew closer. Heavy and slow but with a sense of purpose.

Her thoughts flashed back nine months to Todd and ice slid through her veins. The Toad wouldn't be game to show his face in this part of the world again. Would he? No. He. Would. *Not.*

Swinging her legs over the side of her bed, she scanned the familiar gloom for her heavy-duty marine torch then remembered she'd used it to check the new leak in the ceiling and left it in the galley. *Damn it.*

The jetty belonged to the owners of the luxury riverside home that was rented to wealthy holiday-makers, but her lease on the private dock wasn't up for another two years. February was low season and the house had been vacant for the past couple of weeks. Maybe new tenants had arrived and were unaware that the jetty was off-limits?

That had to be it. 'Please let that be it,' she murmured.

The carport she used to gain access through the back yard and from there to her boat was security coded—who else could it be? She told herself not to overreact. Not to give in to the unease that had stalked her these past months. Both doors were secure, windows open but locked. Mobile phone beside her bed, both Jared and her sister, Crystal, on speed dial.

The footsteps stopped. A weighted thump vibrated through the floor, tilting it ever so slightly beneath her feet for a second or two. The resulting ripple of water lapped against the hull and the hairs on the back of her neck prickled.

Someone was on her deck. Right outside her door.

Okay, now she could be officially scared. She pushed up, grabbing her mobile and punching in numbers, then stared at the black screen. No charge. *Great. Just great.* Heart galloping, she darted to the bedroom doorway. From here she had a clear view down the length of the boat to the glass door where a light drizzle sheened the deck—and the stranger.

Tall. Male. His outline glistening with moisture.

Too broad-shouldered for Todd, thank God, but it could have been the hunchback of Notre Dame, his silhouette sharpening as silvery sheet lightning edged in bronze flickered behind him.

In the clammy air her skin chilled.

Then the hunch lifted away from his shoulders and she realised it was some kind of duffle bag. She pressed a fist to her mouth to stifle the hysteria rising up her throat. The bag or whatever-it-was hit the deck with a scuffed thud, then he straightened to a height and breadth rivalling her brother's and she drew back instinctively. The sound in her throat turned to a choked gasp.

She swallowed it down. Even as she told herself that it was probably a new arrival checking out the grounds, she was pulling on her dressing gown, yanking the sash tight. She pocketed the useless phone.

She could exit via the rear door near her bed, but to leave the boat she'd have to pass within a close couple of steps of him on the narrow jetty then make it past the pool to the carport, wait for the roller door to rise... Safer to remain where she was.

And if he wasn't a new arrival... *How had he managed to get past the security-coded roller door?*

Because he knew the code, right? Right. The thought was reassuring. Still, she had to force one foot in front of the other, her bare feet soundless over the linoleum as she skirted boxes and crates until she slipped on a pool of moisture that hadn't been there a couple of hours earlier. Arms flailing and swearing to herself, she came to a slippery stop in her tiny galley, gripped the edge of her equally tiny table and looked outside.

His sheer size swamped her deck. A flash of lightning revealed black clothing, bare forearms and uncompromising features. Alarmingly good-looking for a potential burglar. *Vaguely familiar.* Short black hair silvered with raindrops, dark stubbled square jaw. Big hands as he patted his chest then slid them down the front of his thighs as if he'd lost something.

Dangerous. The errant thought of those hands patting her own chest sent an unwelcome thrill rippling down her spine. Something shimmered at the edge of her earliest teenage memories. A guy. As out of reach and dangerous and darkly beguiling as this man...

She shook old images away. She'd been fooled by one too many tall-dark-and-handsomes to be fooled again. And this man was probably looking for his lock pick while she was standing here like a loon and letting him, when what she *should* have been doing was phoning the police. With her dead phone.

Her limbs went into lock-down while her slow-motion brain tried—and failed—to figure her next move. She could smell the calming scents of the jasmine candle she'd used earlier, the fresh basil she'd picked and put in a jar on the sink, the ever-present pervasive river.

Would they be her last memories before she died?

She watched, frozen, while he dug into a trouser pocket and pulled something out then stepped right up to the door.

Adrenaline spurted through her veins, propelling her into action. Reaching for the nearest object—a seashell the size of her fist—she curled stiff fingers between its reassuring spikes and stood as tall as her five feet three inches would allow.

'Go away. This is private pr—'

Her pitifully thin demand was gulped over a dry mouth when she heard the heart-stopping click of a *key* being turned in the lock. The door slid open and the stranger stepped inside, bumping into her brass wind chime on the way and bringing the fragrance of rain with him.

She yanked her phone from her pocket. 'No closer.' His silhouette loomed darkly as he moved and her nostrils flared at the potent smell of wet male. 'I've called the police.'

He came to an abrupt halt. She sensed surprise but no fear and she realised her voice had given her away. Female.

All-alone female.

She lunged forward, the makeshift weapon in her other hand aimed at his throat. She felt the pressure as the shell's prongs met flesh.

Before she could draw breath, his arm blocked hers. 'Easy. I'm not going to hurt you.' His deep voice accompanied the thunder that rolled across the ocean.

'I don't know that.' And she wasn't giving him the chance.

'You're on my boat. Leave. *Now.*' Tightening her fist on her shell, she jabbed at him again but his forearm blocked her. It was like pushing against steel.

He made some sound, like an almost bored sigh. 'You really don't want to do that, sweet cheeks,' he muttered, disarming her as easily as drawing breath. As if he fought off women for a living. Then his hand loosened, skated down her upraised arm from wrist to elbow and she didn't doubt that was exactly what he did—and on a daily basis.

The limb that no longer seemed to belong to her remained within the heat of his hand *of its own volition*, while hot and cold shivers chased over her skin. 'You're on my boat,' she repeated, but it came out like more of a whisper.

'Yet I have a key.'

Before she could analyse that dryly delivered fact or think of a response, he released her, stepped sideways and flipped on the light switch. Then he raised both hands to show her he meant no harm.

She blinked as her eyes adjusted to the sudden glare. As she noticed the red mark where the shell had grazed a bronzed neck. As her brain caught up with the fact that yes, absolutely, he had a key and he'd reached for the light switch with such easy familiarity...

Blake Everett.

She sagged against the table but her partial relief was quickly chased away by a different kind of tension. He wore faded black jeans and a black sweater washed almost transparent with age. The shrunken sleeves ended halfway down thick sinewy forearms sprinkled with dark masculine hair.

Jared's mate. Her first innocent crush when she'd been nine years of age and he'd been eighteen and joined the navy. Then when he'd come home on leave after his mother's death...oh, my... She'd been thirteen to his twenty-two but she'd looked at him as a woman would, dreamed of him as only a woman would and she'd kept the guilty pleasure a secret.

She doubted he'd ever looked at her other than the time she'd fallen off her skateboard trying to impress him and bloodied her nose, his whiter-than-white T-shirt and, most of all, her young pride.

Gossip had circulated. *Bad boy. Black sheep.* It hadn't changed the way she thought of him until eventually she heard the rumours that he'd got Janine Baker pregnant then skipped town to join the navy. In an odd way, she'd felt betrayed.

He had eyes that could turn from tropical-island blue to glacial in an instant and an intense brooding aloofness that had called to her feminine nurturing side even way back then. She'd spent a lot of time imagining what it would be like to be the focus of all that intensity.

And now…maybe now he was looking at her the way she'd always wanted him to…with a definite glint of heat in those summertime eyes. But where men were concerned, she wasn't as naïve now. And she wasn't looking back—not *that* way. Absolutely not. She wasn't thirteen any more and there was a major problem here.

'My name's Blake Everett,' he said into the silence broken only by an intermittent *plop* of water leaking from the roof into a plastic container on the floor. He remained where he was, hip propped easily against her counter top, his gaze skimming her too-slinky too-skimpy dressing gown and making her tingle from head to foot before meeting her eyes once more. 'I—'

'I know who you are.' Posture stiff, she resisted the urge to hug her arms across her braless breasts to hide her suddenly erect *traitorous* nipples. She concentrated on relaxing tense muscles. Shoulders, neck, hands. *Breathe.*

His gaze turned assessing, then stern, drawing her attention to the pallor beneath the tanned complexion, the heavy lines of fatigue around his eyes and mouth. But his lips… They were still the most sensual lips she'd ever laid eyes on—full, firm, luscious—

'You're one up on me, then.'

At his clipped reply, she dragged her wayward eyes up to his. He didn't recognise her. *Good.* 'So now we're even.'

He frowned. 'How do you figure that?'

She knew him? Ignoring the cramped muscles from the rain-lashed drive up from Surfers and the headache battering away inside his skull, Blake searched his memory while he studied her. No hardship there.

He hadn't been this close to a woman in a while, let alone one as attractive as this little redhead. After the navy's tes-tosterone-fuelled environment, she smelled like paradise. In the yellow light her hair shone brighter than a distress flare and her eyes were the clear translucent green of a tropical lagoon, but, just as the pristine-looking beaches he routinely assessed hid potential and possibly lethal dangers, there was a storm brewing behind that gaze.

And no wonder—the old man had obviously neglected to inform her that it wasn't his boat to rent out. Ten years ago when his mother had died, Blake had bought it from him to help get his father out of debt and to secure himself a quiet and solitary place to stay when he was on leave in Australia. He'd not been back since.

'I understand if you're renting. I've been overseas and my father—'

'I'm *not* renting. My brother bought this boat from your dad three years ago. It belongs to our family now. This is my home so…so you'll need to find somewhere else.'

'Your brother bought the boat…' He remembered the less-than-considered transaction and an ominous foreboding tracked up his spine. He should've known better than to trust a gambling addict—

'Jared Sanderson.'

Jared? The familiar name spoken in that stiletto-sharp voice sliced through his thoughts and he looked her over more thoroughly. The tousled bedroom hair, those aquamarine eyes and luxurious lips pulled down at the corners as she stared back at him. He'd lost contact with his long-time surfing buddy but he remembered the little sister…

'You're Melissa.' Still tiny in stature but all grown up and curvaceous and looking…different from the kid he remembered. Disturbingly so. Blood pumped a tad faster through his veins. *Don't go there.*

He flicked his eyes back to hers, catching a glimpse of generous breasts and smooth ivory décolletage on the way, before she jammed her arms in front of her. He didn't miss the remnant shadows in her gaze. 'I apologise for scaring you, Melissa. I should've knocked.'

'It's Lissa now. And yes, you should have.'

Her mouth pouted in that sulky way he remembered but tonight, rather than amused, he found himself oddly captivated. 'Lissa.'

She seemed to shake off the sulk. 'Okay, you just stripped five years off my life but apology accepted. And I didn't ring the police.' She lifted one delicate shoulder and gave a wry grimace. 'Phone's dead.' She blinked up at him, still wary. 'So what are you doing here?'

'A man can't come home after fourteen years?' He didn't elaborate. Now was not the time to ponder the demons that had sent him home to re-evaluate the universe and his place and purpose in it.

She shook her head. 'I mean what are you doing *here*, on the houseboat?'

'I thought I *owned* the houseboat.' Conned by his own father. He clenched his jaw. He should have made the effort to see his old man earlier today before driving up here but he hadn't needed the inevitable angst it would've entailed.

'No. You can't…' She frowned, confusion adding to the clouds in her eyes. 'I don't understand.'

'It's a long complicated story.' He rubbed absently at the tiny scratch beneath his chin.

'I'm sorry…about that.' She glanced at his throat and a pretty pink colour swam into her cheeks. 'I'll just get some—'

'Don't bother. I'm fine.'

But he didn't push the point as he watched her move to a cupboard and reach up…and up… Her shell-pink dressing gown grazed the tops of her thighs. Sleek, firm, creamy thighs that looked as if they'd been kissed by the sun.

Kissed. The word conjured a scenario he was better off not dwelling on but his lips tingled nonetheless. He ogled her spectacular rear without apology while she dragged out a box with assorted medication and pulled out a tube.

'This should…' She turned, catching him staring. He did not look away. It was the best view he'd seen in a long time. The colour in her cheeks intensified, bleeding into her throat. She thrust the tube at him, then, as if mortally afraid of skin contact, set it on the table beside them. 'There you go.'

'Thanks.'

She hesitated, as if finding the last minute or so discomforting in the extreme and determined to banish it from her mind, then said, 'Your long complicated story…I'm listening.'

He let out a slow breath, then said, 'Tomorrow I'll go back to Surfers, sort it out with Dad then discuss it with Jared. It'll be okay,' he assured her. He'd reimburse his old friend for the money he'd paid and help Melissa—Lissa—find alternative accommodation.

'It'll be okay, how? Jared purchased the boat when your father sold the home in Surfers and moved south. New South Wales, I think… No one knows exactly…'

It didn't come as a surprise. He acknowledged being left to discover the news about his father's apparent disappearance through another party with a shrug. 'I guess I already knew that.'

He'd paid his father cash for the boat the day he left

Australia, but he'd not actually signed anything…and the paperwork had never followed as promised.

When Blake had rung to query it, he discovered the phones had been disconnected and the emails began bouncing back… The old man hadn't been above using his son to suit his own purposes. Again, no surprise there.

'So…am I right then in assuming you own the house too?' She waved a hand towards the window. Outside, the predicted storm had set in. The rain had turned into a downpour, partially obscuring the view and pelting the roof and decking.

He nodded. He'd purchased what had been the family's luxury holiday house when he'd bought the houseboat. He'd gone through the bank to finance the deal and had the land title for that, at least, safely locked away.

'So why opt for the houseboat tonight when you have a more than adequate alternative?' she asked with a frown.

Despite having employed a service to stock the fridge and air the linen, he'd been unable to find the relaxation he needed to recuperate in the house. Too much space, too many rooms. Too many memories.

He'd lugged an old army bedroll he'd found in storage down to the waterfront hoping the familiar marine environment and solitude would help with the infernal headaches he'd suffered since the accident that had brought him back to Australia. Seemed he'd lucked out in both instances there too.

'I was hoping to catch up on some sleep.' He'd *not* expected to find a bed mate.

Her eyes widened, a hint of panic in their depths as they met his. 'But since I'm here already, you're going back up to the house, right?'

That had been his initial intention. Except…now his immediate plans for the night had been dashed he found he wasn't as tired as he'd thought and in no immediate hurry to bid the lovely Lissa Sanderson goodnight.

No, that wasn't quite correct, he decided. His *body* was

telling him to stay and get reacquainted, to absorb that feminine scent until his pores were saturated, to touch her arm again and feel that soft skin against his. His *body* had very definite ideas about where it wanted the evening to go.

His head was saying something else entirely.

His *head* didn't lead him astray. His diving team knew his reputation for remaining cool under pressure even in the most perilous situations.

Women were more likely to describe him as emotionally detached right before they slammed a door of some description in his face.

Either way, that was why he was good at his job and why he knew that Lissa Sanderson with her feminine curves and clear-eyed gaze that seemed to know exactly where his thoughts were going was trouble best avoided. For both parties.

Steeling himself for a restless night, he focused on that gaze. 'Okay, I'll leave you in peace. For now.'

'For *now*?' She stared at him, eyes huge and incredulous. 'This is *my* home.' Desperation scored her voice. 'You don't understand…I *need* this place.'

'Calm down, for heaven's sake.' Women. Always overreacting. 'We'll sort something out.' He glanced about him for the first time, remembering how the boat had looked years ago when his father had owned it. When Blake had lived on it.

Now a blue couch sagging beneath the weight of a jumble of boxes—some open, others taped shut—sat where there'd once been a leather lounge suite. Except for the addition of a microwave, the galley remained unchanged. If you didn't count the slather of paperwork on the bench. His gaze snagged on a final notice for payment for something or other attached to the fridge door with a magnet. *None of his business.*

Every square centimetre of the boat was crammed with stuff. Canvases against the wall beside an old tin of artists' brushes, another of charcoals and pencils. The bunk beds beyond were covered in swatches of fabric, colour palettes, magazines, wallpaper books. How did anyone live amidst such chaos?

Maybe it was the calming floral scents that pervaded the air or the potted herbs on a shelf near the window, but somewhere beneath the domestic carnage the place had a...comfortable cosiness. He'd not experienced anything like it since he'd been a youngster living with his mum, and wondered grimly if he could find sleep here after all.

He should leave the area entirely. Find somewhere else to rent along the coast somewhere while he was in Oz and forget he'd ever seen Melissa Sanderson. Solitude was what he wanted. What he craved until he felt halfway sane again.

A steady drip nearby diverted his attention, a silver teardrop followed quickly by another against the light, and he glanced up. Obviously the leak had been there for some time judging by the half-full container beneath it. He'd been too preoccupied with everything else to notice. Now he scanned other damp patches. 'How long's this been going on?'

She glanced up at the ceiling, then away. 'Not long. I can manage, it's nothing.' Instantly defensive.

Interesting. If he remembered correctly, the young Melissa had been anything but independent. Or so it had seemed. 'Nothing? Look up, sweet cheeks. If water gets into that light socket there we've got a problem.'

He saw her glance up, then frown. Clearly she hadn't noticed the extent of the damage. He looked at the puddle near her feet lapping around the base of the fridge. 'Don't you know electricity and water don't mix?'

'Of course I do,' she snapped. 'And it's *I've* got a problem, not *we.*'

He shook his head. 'Right now I don't care whose problem it is, the boat's unsafe—for any number of reasons.' Now he'd seen the potential disaster he couldn't in all good conscience just leave her here to fend for herself and go back to bed, could he?

As if to make a point, a flash sizzled the air, accompanied by one almighty crash of thunder that reverberated between his ears in time with his throbbing head.

'That's it.' He rapped impatient knuckles on the table. 'Two minutes to grab what you need. You're sleeping in the house.'

CHAPTER TWO

'I BEG your pardon?' Lissa glared at him. It was hard to glare when faced with such gorgeousness, but she was through taking orders. From anyone. Ever again. 'I'm no—'

'Your choice, Lissa. You can come as you are if you prefer, it's irrelevant to me.' His super-cool gaze cruised down her body making her hot in all the wrong places. 'Just thought you might want a change of clothes.'

Then he stepped closer and she flinched involuntarily as memories of another man crowded in on her. Big, intimidating. Abusive. She'd thought she loved him once.

Shoving the sharp spasm away, she pushed at his chest. 'Personal space, *if* you don't mind.' He was warm, hard. Tempting to forget past fears and let her hand wander…to feel the beat of his heart against her palm. Heat shimmied up her arm and her own heart skipped a beat. She dropped her hand immediately, lifted her chin. 'I'm staying right here. On this boat,' she clarified quickly since they were still standing way too close. 'I should be here…in case something happens.'

'Something's going to happen all right if you don't get your butt into gear and move.'

She bristled at the commanding tone but he backed off. Still, she knew without a doubt, he meant what he said. And she hated to admit that he was right; what *would* she do if water started leaking through the light socket? Or worse. She'd never known such a downpour. The situation was much more dangerous than when she'd gone to bed. More dignified to acquiesce with whatever grace she could summon up.

'Fine, then,' she said crisply, over her shoulder as she turned and walked to her bedroom. '*You* stay here and keep an eye on things.'

'I intend to.' His voice boomed down the narrow passage.

Oh. Really? Obviously this superhero was immune to the dangers he'd so helpfully pointed out. Well, that suited her fine. She had enough problems without adding gorgeous male to the list.

She plucked the jeans and the T-shirt she'd worn today from the bottom of the bed, considered changing but decided against it. Stripping now with him only a few steps away would put her in a vulnerable situation, and she knew all too much about vulnerable situations.

'So, what, storms bounce off you, then?' she tossed back, grabbing basic toiletries and shoving them in a carry-all.

No reply from the other end of the boat but she could almost hear him: *I can look after myself.*

And she couldn't? She hurried back to the kitchen with her gear and came to a breathless stop a few steps away from him. Breathless because the impact of seeing him standing in her small living space all distant dark protector sucked her breath clean away. No, not all dark, she noted, because his eyes were cool, cool blue.

But they were still barriers. And he was still the intense brooding Blake she remembered from all those years ago. 'I'm not that helpless little thirteen-year-old any more.' Her cheeks stung with embarrassment. She hadn't meant to remind him.

A muscle tightened in his jaw and his gaze flickered over her, the merest glint of heat in the cool. 'I'm better off alone. That way I don't have to worry about you slipping and breaking a leg and drowning in the process.'

'I *do* know how to swim.' She thought vaguely that she'd like to sketch him now, with the lines of maturity settled around his mouth, around his eyes. Those sharp planes and angles of cheekbones and jaw—

He shook his head. 'You may not be helpless but I'm betting you're as stubborn as ever,' he muttered.

Stubborn? 'How would you know *how* I was?' She could do cool too. Iceberg-cool. 'I didn't exist to you.' She stepped away. Turned to the bunk beds against the wall. 'But yes, I'm very stubborn where my work's concerned. I have merchandise here I need to protect from the weather...should anything happen.'

'I'll take care of it.'

'Nice offer, but I don't want it to get wet.' She dragged a couple of plastic storage containers from beneath the lower bunk. 'If you really insist on this...evacuation...all of this has to be stored and brought to the house.'

'All?' He sounded doubtful. 'Do you really need it *all*?'

'Every last fabric swatch. My work depends on it. I'm an interior designer.' Unemployed interior designer at present, but he didn't need to know that.

'Come on, then, let me give you a hand.'

'Fine,' she clipped, packing the containers swiftly, anxious not to have him too close. His proximity was unnerving her; his musky warm scent was making her itch. 'If you could get those sketch pads.' She waved him away. 'There are plastic bags...'

It took them a few minutes to pack everything up.

'I'll bring the rest up to the house after we've got you settled.' He had to raise his voice above the rain drumming overhead.

Settled? Hardly. She straightened, a container beneath one arm, her carry-all over a shoulder. If he wanted to play Mr

Protector, so long as her stuff was safe from rain, she'd put up with it.

'Thanks.' Said grudgingly. She really did *not* want his assistance. Slipping into her rubber thong sandals by the back door, she slid the glass open and stepped onto the deck. A torrent of water slammed into her where it should be dry and she glanced up at the flapping canvas. She might not want his help, but she was forced to admit she needed it.

She stepped onto the jetty, Blake following behind her with a load of plastic-protected work. Her thongs slapped wetly as she made her way past the sapphire pool edged with moss-covered boulders, the palm-fringed undercover entertainment area to the wide glassed door.

Over the past couple of years she'd watched the beautiful house and its parade of beautiful people come and go. Now it was her turn to get a good look inside. It wouldn't be so bad to sleep in such luxury for a change, would it? And from a designer's point of view she couldn't wait to see the décor.

Didn't mean she had to like the arrangement but at least it was dry. She waited for him to come up alongside her and unlock the door, then followed him inside. He flicked a switch and light flooded the magnificent home.

She gazed up at the bright source of illumination. A myriad of tiny crystal spheres exploded from a central orb, splattering rainbows across the room.

Open-plan living gave it an airy atmosphere. The honeyed wood-panelled ceiling slanted high over two storeys, with a staircase against a feature wall in the same treacle tones leading to the upper rooms. White-tiled flooring merged with the white walls giving the impression of space. A black leather lounge with cushions in lime and tangerine tones was positioned against the exterior slate wall. The minimal furniture was teak and glass.

Stunning. But impersonal and maybe a little dated. It had been rented out for years to wealthy international jet-setters and lacked that lived-in ambience. A tingle of excitement lifted her. Maybe she'd ask if he wanted to redecorate…

They offloaded the stuff in one corner.

'I'll go back for the rest in a moment,' he said, already walking towards the stairs.

As he led her to the mezzanine floor she admired a wall of rich wooden patchwork. She did *not* admire the shape of his taut backside encased in those hip-hugging black jeans—she imagined a painting or feature of some sort in soothing blues on the wall instead.

She thought of all the times she'd looked at the house and never known Blake owned it. In fact, she hadn't thought about Blake in a while. But now…now it was as if those intervening years had never happened. Her feelings were as bright and strong as they'd been back then. And just as futile. But they zinged through her body and settled low in her abdomen at the prospect of dreaming about him again. They'd always been such…interesting dreams.

He indicated an expansive room with thick cream carpet and a mountain of quilt in striped olive green and black. The glossy black furniture was devoid of the usual knick-knacks. The window looked out onto the house next door and a view of the river. But not the houseboat.

Perhaps he'd chosen it intentionally, she thought as she walked past him and set her bag and clothing on a silk-covered boutique chair next to a chest of drawers. No way to spy on him. No way to drool over him and think lustful thoughts while she watched him work. Bare-chested, his skin gleaming, those rippling muscles—

'Shower's through there.' He spoke behind her. 'I haven't looked yet but I'm informed the pantry's been filled today so help yourself to breakfast in the morning.'

Breakfast. A sudden tension gripped her. She hoped Blake didn't decide to look in her pantry or her fridge because she hadn't stocked up for a week. She'd been skimping on meals, counting her last dollars. Breakfast was a luxury she'd managed without. And she *loved* breakfast.

Blake looked like a man with a large appetite. A breakfast-with-the-lot kind of appetite. In fact the way he was watching her, eyes kind of slumberous, lips slightly parted, he looked hungry right now.

Hungry enough to take a bite out of her... No. *Bad thought.* Her stomach turned an instant somersault and she licked suddenly dry lips before she realised she'd drawn his attention to them.

'I don't normally eat breakfast,' she lied. 'My cupboards are a bit Mother Hubbard at the moment.' *So don't bother looking.* 'Why don't you join me here in the morning?' *Why don't you stop staring and say something?*

'I was planning to walk into town and grab something there.'

Okay, so he didn't want to be anywhere near her. Humiliation vied with embarrassment and she was that attention-seeking thirteen-year old again. 'Suit yourself.' She huffed silently. Now she even sounded like a thirteen-year-old, all wounded pride and disgruntlement. She'd always acted differently around him. Why hadn't that changed?

To her chagrin, after all these years she was still allowing him to affect her. Helpless to stop all those teenage emotions exploding into her mind like big red paint splotches on a blank wall. As if time had wound backwards. As if he'd never left.

Disgusted with herself, she was already turning away when he touched her shoulder. A feather-light touch, barely there. So gentle. *So sensual.* She imagined suddenly, and with devastating clarity, how it might feel if her shoulder were bare and it were his lips rather than his hand. Heat blossomed where his palm rested and she jerked to a startled stop.

'But since we've a few matters to discuss...' he began in a neutral tone that belied the fact that his fingers sculpted over her shoulder were pressing ever so slightly into her flesh or that his thumb was creating tiny circles of friction on the back of her neck '...breakfast might be a good place to start.'

And for a few unguarded seconds she found herself relaxing into the sensations he was creating. The fresh scent of the soap he'd used to wash his hands. The shimmer of heat down her back from his body— *No.* She pulled away. 'All right.' Spoken coolly as she swung to face him. His hand slipped off her shoulder and she almost sighed at the loss. 'How do you like your eggs?'

'You're going to cook?'

He looked so surprised, she had to grin. 'I do know how these days.' And she had every intention of being up and dressed and *prepared* before he arrived.

He nodded without a glimmer of humour. 'Shall we say oh six hundred?'

'Make it seven.' She needed time to acquaint herself with the kitchen.

'Seven, then. I'll rescue the rest of your gear then take a look at the boat. Do you have anything I can use for repairs?'

'Try on the deck by the door. Under the tarp.'

He nodded. 'Goodnight, then.'

'Goodnight. And be careful.'

'I'm always careful.'

She watched him turn and walk away. Was he? *What about Janine Baker?* a little voice whispered. Janine had left town too and Lissa had never heard, nor asked, what had happened to her or her baby.

She was still watching when he turned back. 'And the eggs...? I like them hard.'

'That makes it easy, so do I.'

She had the distinct feeling neither of them were talking about eggs.

As soon as she heard the front door close she headed for a better view of the river. And Blake. She found it in the master bedroom. With the living-room lighting spilling onto the rain-swept patio, she watched him stride swiftly down the path. Past the pool. Along the jetty. A tall, impressive masculine figure, an image no less powerful than when he'd been standing outside her door as a possible intruder. And no less unsettling.

When he'd disappeared onto the deck, she turned and gazed at the room. The light from the hallway slanted onto the rumpled king-sized bed, the upper sheet twisted and hanging off one side. The imprint of his head on the pillow had her stomach fluttering with the kind of nervous excitement he'd always instilled in her whenever she'd thought of him.

She crushed a hand against her middle and ordered herself to settle down. He'd been sleeping in here. Or trying to. What had made him up and leave such comfort and seek out the houseboat in the middle of the night? Bad dreams? Or physical pain—she'd seen it behind his eyes, hard and brittle as if he'd been fighting it a while.

Or was he missing a special woman that he'd left behind in some foreign country?

She looked about for some hint. His open bag lay on the floor against a wall, clothes neatly stacked inside. A pile of sail-boat brochures were stacked on the dresser along with his passport and some loose change. She was so tempted to look at his passport and see where he'd been, but she couldn't bring herself to invade his privacy.

Instead, hardly aware of what she was doing, she moved to the bed and picked up his pillow, closed her eyes and breathed in. It smelled of sunshine with a subtle whiff of masculine scent that she'd come into close proximity with earlier. It had been a long time, but she remembered that smell. Blake. A moan started low in her stomach and rose up her throat—

'Everything okay here?'

Oh, God. Her heart jumped into her mouth. Oh, *no*. Her knees almost buckled from under her and her eyes snapped open though she'd rather they'd stayed shut. Then she could have imagined herself invisible instead of seeing Blake standing in the doorway, one arm on the doorjamb, head cocked to one side. His dark figure blocked the light from the hall. She had no idea what his expression was, or what he must be thinking, but it couldn't be good.

'Yep. Everything's fine.' Forcing a smile, she stepped away from the bed. 'I…ah…wanted to check the boat was still afloat.' She laughed; too bright, too high. 'Silly, I know…' *But you already have that opinion about me.* 'I'm…just grabbing an extra pillow on the way if that's okay… Was there something you wanted?'

And how dumb was she, how *reckless*, standing next to his bed in the semi-darkness in her mini nightgown and asking that question? Not that he noticed…or did he? He wore a bemused expression and she pressed her lips together before she got herself into even more trouble.

'My phone.' He turned on the light, regarded her a moment longer then switched his attention to the empty night stand and frowned. 'You haven't seen it, have you? I'm sure I left it here somewhere.'

She shook her head. 'Perhaps you knocked it onto the floor.'

'Or perhaps you did,' he pointed out. Faintly accusing.

Anxious to move this beyond-embarrassing situation right along and leave, she dropped the pillow on the bed and sank gratefully to her knees to hide her flaming cheeks.

'Is it there?'

'Um…'

'Do you need a hand?'

Oh, *yes, please.* The impact of those somewhat ambiguous words spoken in that low sexy drawl invoked an image she was better off not thinking about. 'Ah…' Her fingers closed over smooth plastic. 'Found it.'

Blake heard her muffled reply as he watched her silk-draped bottom wriggle backwards. She had it all right: the perfect backside. He tried, he really did, but he couldn't tear his eyes away. It had been a long time since he'd seen anything so...spectacular.

The last time he'd seen her she'd been a skinny thirteen and a blusher. Still was apparently. Her curtain of auburn hair obscured her face but he knew without a doubt that her cheeks matched it. She could be telling him the truth about the pillow and the boat but he seriously doubted it.

She was attracted to him.

Jared's little sister. Jared's very attractive, very sexy little sister.

She pushed up, held his phone at one end as if it were red hot.

'Thank you.'

'Sure.'

If she felt that zing when his fingers came into contact with hers, she didn't show it. She smoothed her hair behind her ears, straightened and met his gaze almost defiantly. Pink-cheeked and pretty.

Not words that normally came to his mind, but they suited Lissa. His chest cramped in an odd way. Sitting too long in the one position, he assured himself.

A scowl tightened his facial muscles and he studied his phone, pressed a couple of buttons. He didn't do pink and pretty and its association with hearts and flowers and ever afters. It wasn't for guys like him, always on the move. What was more, he didn't need it. *Way* too problematic.

Hot and fast and uncomplicated—*that* was what he needed. And by crikey, he thought, his lower body suddenly hard as rock, he needed it soon.

'Got someone special waiting for you to ring, huh?'

His head jerked up. 'You always did get straight to the point, didn't you? I need to make a few calls.' A plumber and an electrician for starters. But it could wait till morning.

'Your tools are worse than useless. I've secured the tarp over the main leak for now. Are you even aware of the state of the roofing?'

She looked away. 'I was going to get around to it.'

Yeah? When? 'I'll organise something for tomorrow.' He turned and walked to the door. A thought occurred to him and he turned back…and his mind went blank.

She was holding his pillow by one corner and staring at him. He imagined himself walking over there and taking it from her hands, leaning close and breathing in the scent of her neck. Feeling the silky heat of her flesh against his knuckles as he untied her sash and slid the dressing gown from her shoulders before laying her down and letting her help him forget why he'd come home.

But pink and pretty didn't deserve to be used in that way. *She* didn't deserve to be used in that way.

She arched a brow, waiting, and he realised that he'd been about to ask a question before he'd been blindsided. 'Are you working tomorrow?'

She hesitated, looking uncertain. 'No. Not tomorrow.'

She also sounded vague. 'Are you sure?' he prompted. 'You're not thinking of playing hooky, are you? Because—'

'Because you're here to take care of everything and not to worry my pretty little head over it?'

Right. He wouldn't have said it in quite that way but, yep, that pretty much summed it up.

She made a dismissive snort and didn't look the least bit impressed. She had that sulky pout going on again.

He didn't see the problem. Protection came naturally to him. Other women would be grateful for his assistance. And only too willing to show that gratitude. In any number of ways.

Not Melissa Sanderson apparently.

'Okay. Fine.' *Whatever you say.*

But there was something she *wasn't* saying, he could see

it in the way she evaded his eyes. He also remembered the almost hunted gaze from earlier and the way she'd pushed at him. 'I'll say goodnight, then,' he clipped. 'Oh, and if you're looking for a spare pillow, there are three other bedrooms to choose from.'

As he walked out into the stormy night he wondered whether she had, in fact, planned to sleep in his bed. The thought of that soft satiny skin on his sheets and that alluring feminine scent on his pillow smouldered through his bloodstream. Lengthening his stride, he distanced himself as quickly as possible.

CHAPTER THREE

BLAKE carried the rest of her decorating gear up to the house, then returned to see what he could do about the mess. He swapped the small container beneath the now free-flowing drip for a bucket and snatched up a newspaper from beside the couch to absorb the water on the floor.

As he spread it out he noticed an ad for a retail assistant's job in a beachwear shop circled in a red felt-tipped pen then crossed out with 'TOO LATE' scrawled beneath it and a sad face. Hadn't Lissa said she was an interior designer?

Was that why she wasn't working tomorrow? Because she didn't have a job? He glanced over to the final notice on the fridge door. Obviously she was in financial difficulty and just as obviously she hadn't told Jared because if he knew his old mate, no way would he have let this situation arise. No job and inadequate accommodation. *Dangerously* inadequate accommodation.

Bloody hell.

Blake had inherited a duty of care here. Not only because it came naturally to him but because Jared had been his closest mate, the brother he'd never had. As a young teenager, when neither of his parents cared whether he even came home at night, Jared had been there. Until his friend had taken on the heavy responsibility of parenting. It was no wonder he'd done such a good job with his sisters.

The rain continued to pelt down while he surveyed the

deck once more. Nope. Useless to try doing anything more until the storm blew out to sea. He went inside to ensure all the windows were closed, located the fuse box and turned the power off.

Then he stood on deck a moment, glaring at the house while water sluiced down his face and soaked down to his skin. He needed the chill factor. The fire in his groin, which had been smouldering since he'd first laid eyes on Lissa, had morphed into a raging inferno the instant he'd seen her nose buried in his pillow.

Hell, he needed more than wind and water to douse the flames. He needed a woman.

And now he was going to have to try and sleep up there after all, knowing one very attractive, very sexy woman was a few quick steps away down the hall.

The strip of golden sand was strewn with shells, driftwood and dead palm leaves where the rainforest met the sea. An azure sky, the air laden with the pungent smells of lush vegetation and decaying marine life. It should have been a tourist paradise.

Even in sleep, Blake knew it wasn't. Because the heavy pounding at the back of his skull was gunfire.

He'd been one of five clearance divers on the beach that day. It had been a routine training exercise. Until the jungle had exploded. Exposed and caught unprepared, they'd returned fire and made a run for it. But the newest member of the unit, Torque, had frozen.

No time to think. Blake dodging bullets as he retraced his steps. Grabbing and dragging the quivering kid back across the beach with him. Then more shots, searing the air and zinging past his head. Torque's last agonised cry as he fell against Blake, knocking him off balance. Rocks coming up to meet Blake as he fell. Then blackness…

* * *

Blake woke dry-mouthed, shaking, his heart hammering against his ribs. He was chilled to the bone, lathered in sweat, his skull reverberating as if he'd been struck from behind by Big Ben. It took a moment to draw breath, fight off the sheet, which had twisted around his legs.

He reached for the heavy-duty painkillers on the bedside table, swallowed them dry. The hospital doctor had ordered Blake to take them for at least another week. But he'd refused the sleeping pills even though he never slept more than a couple of hours at a time. If only the doc could prescribe him some magic potion to take away the nightmares.

He pushed upright and stared out of the window where the pre-dawn revealed a star-studded charcoal sky swept clear of last night's storm. Torque had been just a kid, full of fresh-faced ideals and too damn young to die.

Blake had been that young idealist too, once.

Unwilling to subject himself to further night horrors, he rose, pulled on a pair of shorts. He almost forgot about the boat—he glanced out of the window again to make sure the thing was still afloat, then headed downstairs. Past the bedroom where Lissa dreamed untroubled dreams.

Stopping in front of the living room's glass door, he slid it open to let the damp breeze cool his face. He could almost smell the nightmare's beach and the decaying marine life. The hot scent of freshly spilled blood.

He heard a shuffling noise behind him. His military-honed senses always on alert, he swung around, one fist partially raised.

Lissa. In the shadows. Eyes wide. Looking as fragile as glass in that tiny excuse for a nightdress. And shrinking away from him. Perfect. He'd terrified the life out of her twice in one night.

A wave of self-loathing washed over him. Gritting his teeth, he turned back to the window. 'What are you doing here?'

'I heard a cr— I heard a noise.'

He could hear the soft sound of bare feet as she crossed the floor and groaned inwardly, imagining those feet entwined with his.

'What are *you* doing here?'

He didn't answer. Just closed his eyes as the scent of her wafted towards him. Fresh, fragrant and untainted. She knew nothing of the atrocities committed beyond her protected little world. And he wanted to keep her that way. Safe.

Safe from him.

'Are you okay?' Quiet concern with a tinge of anxiety.

'Yes. Go on back to bed.'

'But you…'

Her hair, a drift of scent and silk, brushed his chin as she stepped in front of him. The feather touch of one small hand on his bare arm. 'I thought I heard… Are you sure you're okay?'

His eyes slid open. Wide eyes blinked up at him in the dimness. And those luscious lips… He could all but taste their sweetness on his own. She barely reached his shoulder. So tiny. His hands rose to hold her. To keep her away. To keep her safe. He could feel the firm muscles of her upper arms move beneath warm flesh.

Then he was sliding his hands up and over her shoulders, his thumbs grazing the petal-soft indentations just above her collarbones. He'd forgotten how smooth and silky a woman's skin felt. How different from his own.

His whole body flexed and burned and throbbed. So easy to lean down, seal his lips to hers and take and take and take until he forgot.

But he'd never forget. He could never be that casual young guy she remembered. The remnants of his dream still clung to him like a shroud. Contaminating her. Dropping his hands, he turned away from those beguiling eyes. 'Go away, Lissa, I don't want you here.'

He barely heard her leave and when he glanced over his

shoulder a moment later she was gone. Without another word. Relief mingled with bitter frustration. Damn it all, he didn't want to offend her. He waited a few moments then went back to his room and pulled on his joggers. A two hour run might rid himself of some of his tension.

The street lights still cast their pools of yellow, and after last night's turbulence the air's stillness seemed amplified as his feet pounded the pavement.

Lissa tossed and turned for the next couple of hours as the room slowly lightened. She'd left Blake's pillow right alone and taken a spare from another bedroom as he'd suggested. To prove that her story that she needed an extra wasn't a lie to get her out of an embarrassing situation. Not that he'd believed her for a second and she cringed at the memory. Why the heck had she bothered? Her pillow worries wouldn't even register on his horizon—not after seeing him downstairs in the darkness.

Hurting and alone and determined to stay that way. She'd heard him cry out. And for a moment she'd thought maybe she'd helped a little until he'd dropped his hands from her shoulders as if the touch of her skin had burned him. His curt dismissal had stung, especially when for a heart-trembling moment earlier she'd thought he was going to kiss her.

Which only proved she *still* had zero understanding when it came to men.

She would *not* take it personally. If she remembered anything about Blake at all, he'd have refused anyone's help. Except she hated seeing anyone hurting like that.

As soon as the boat was repaired she could be out of his house. Right away from him. Away from temptation.

Except for his claim that he owned the boat...

That wasn't a problem she could sort on her own so there was no use dwelling on it now. She threw back the sheet and rose. The storm had passed, leaving the sky a glorious violet-smeared orange. She opened the window to enjoy the bird's dawn chorus and early humidity.

Leaning on the sill, she looked out over the palatial homes and their moored million-dollar yachts and reflections on the river. A private helicopter circled further up the river then landed on its helipad.

She could hear a steady splash beyond the high concrete fence. Their next-door neighbour, Gilda, whom Lissa had met and spoken to a few times, was taking her regular early-morning dip in the pool.

Gilda Dimitriou was a well-known socialite, heavily involved in charitable works. Her husband, Stefan, was some bigwig in finance and they frequently entertained. Lissa was probably the only person within a hundred-kilometre radius without a high-flying job and a bulging bank account.

A fact that Blake Everett did not need to know. No one knew about her financial situation. Not even her family. Especially not Jared. She didn't want or need his help. Hadn't she spent the past year and a half proving that she could manage just fine in Mooloolaba on her own? Mostly.

Except that the interior design shop she'd worked for had gone out of business due to a dodgy accountant, leaving her with no income apart from a casual three-hour-per-week stint cleaning a couple of local offices. She'd had to put off the repairs out of financial necessity.

She'd hit a little bump in the road, that was all. She collected the clothes she'd brought with her. Determined not to see Blake until she'd showered and tamed her hair, no matter what dire circumstances and humiliations she was about to face, she headed for the en-suite.

And what an en-suite. It was as big as her entire houseboat. White tiles, gold taps, thick fluffy towels in marine colours of aqua and ultramarine. She breathed in their new and freshly laundered scent and switched on the shower.

After the boat's mere trickle, the water pressure was an

absolute luxury and she took her time, pondering her bump in the road. She still wanted to start her own business. It had been a bitter source of tension between her and Jared which had led to her moving here. She so badly wanted to prove she was capable.

Mooloolaba was a wealthy man's town on Queensland's Sunshine Coast. Plenty of people here would think nothing of paying exorbitant prices for a home makeover. She just needed to find them and convince them they needed her services.

Somehow.

For months now she'd taken cleaning jobs while scouring the papers and searching the Internet for the kind of work she wanted. Nothing. She'd had no response to her ads in the paper and on the net. The locals went for the services of the big, well-known, well-respected names. Lissa needed to come up with something different, something unique, get out there and make herself known.

Yes, she could drop Jared's name. His reputation for building refurbishments was well known around these parts. She wrenched off the taps and swiped the towel off the rail. No way. Absolutely out of the question. Because that would be admitting to Jared that he'd been right, that she couldn't do it on her own. And after walking out the way she had, she was too…ashamed.

So she'd have to settle for second best for a while longer. Which meant finding a full-time job—of any description. Which were few and far between. Back to square one.

And right now she had to face breakfast with a man she didn't know how to react to this morning.

CHAPTER FOUR

SHE had the toast buttered, coffee freshly brewed when Blake appeared in the kitchen on the stroke of seven. She just knew he'd be one of those super-punctual people. Always on time. Ruthlessly organised. Socks always paired and rolled together. How did he live with himself?

The only reason she was ahead this morning was because she'd been too wound up after their recent rendezvous in the living room to relax. She'd spent the time familiarising herself with the spectacular wood-panelled kitchen and every modern appliance known to man.

She'd psyched herself up for seeing him but the first glimpse still packed a punch as he walked to the kitchen table, leaving her breathless and feeling as if she'd run a cross-country marathon. He'd changed into a khaki T-shirt with some sort of blood and tar design all over the front but he still wore the same kind of snug-fitting jeans he'd had on last night.

He seemed more relaxed. His eyes weren't the haunted ones she'd glimpsed last night, even though they were still somewhat aloof, but, hey, this *was* Blake Everett and aloof was his trademark. Whatever his demons last night, he'd apparently shrugged them off. He'd showered and smelled as fresh as the new day.

Yes, a new day, she thought. Best to pretend last night never happened…

'Good morning.' Her smile was automatic, unlike his stern expression, as she lifted the coffee plunger and concentrated on pouring a mug without spilling it all over her hand. 'Coffee?'

He set a couple of those sailing brochures she'd seen on the table. 'Never touch the stuff. But thanks,' he added in what sounded like an afterthought.

His gravelly morning voice did strange things to her insides as he moved to the cupboard, pulled out an unopened box of Earl Grey tea. Real leaves, not the tea-bag kind. She watched him reach for a teapot on the bench, dump in a large fistful of leaves.

'Kettle's just boiled,' she said, wanting to be helpful and desperate to break the awkward silence that seemed to crowd in on them. She should have stayed right away last night. Stuck her head under the pillow or something.

'Not a morning person?' she said, briskly. He shot her a glance as he poured water into the pot. 'That's okay, I am. So that kind of balances it out, wouldn't you agree?'

He lifted a brow. 'I'm up at five a.m., rain or shine, how about you?'

Oh. She stared at him a moment. 'I've been known to drift home around that time.'

That earned her a look and she wished she'd kept her mouth shut. 'On weekends. Some weekends. As a matter of fact, if you're free, there's a party tonight down on the beach...' She trailed off as his jaw tightened. 'Maybe not.'

And not for her either. She studied him as she sipped her coffee. No, she wouldn't imagine he'd fit in with the party scene. She needed to forget her teenage crush, pull herself together and remember that he *wanted her boat*. 'How does the damage look this morning?'

'Haven't checked it out yet.' He poured his tea, already thick and black as molasses, and added two sugars, then took a seat opposite her at the table. 'After a closer inspection last night, I turned off the electricity, locked up and came back here.'

'Oh,' she murmured. 'I did wonder what you were doing in the liv—' Then bit her lip, wishing she'd never mentioned it.

'It needs major work,' he said, not looking up as he flicked through his brochures. 'Could take a while.'

She stifled a retort. It wasn't that bad, surely. It was just a ploy to keep her away and it wasn't going to work. After breakfast she was going to take a look for herself. She'd not gone down earlier because she'd thought he was there and didn't want the awkwardness of catching him asleep. After all, what if he slept naked?

She quashed the warmth that spun low in her belly and joined him at the table, pushing the plate of toast to the centre. 'You must have left eggs off your shopping list.'

'Toast's fine.' He reached for a slice, bit in with a crunch.

'You planning on going sailing while you're here?' she said, eyeing his reading material.

He didn't look up. 'Could be I'm planning on purchasing one.'

'But aren't you…in the navy?'

'Not any more.' He glanced up a moment, his eyes focused on middle distance. 'What do you reckon—sailing solo down the coast, stopping anywhere that takes your fancy. No time-tables, no schedules, no demands. Just you, drifting with the tides.'

'Sounds…' *lonely* '…magic. Is that what you're planning?'

'Could be.' He popped the rest of his toast in his mouth.

'You've given up navy life, then?'

'Reckon so.' He folded a corner of a page to mark it, then flipped the brochure shut, picked up his mug and leaned back. 'I'll ring a plumber this morning. And an electrician. Do you use anyone in particular?'

Obviously he didn't want to discuss the navy or his reasons

for leaving. 'Up till now, I've not needed anyone.' She nibbled the edge of her toast. 'Jared would know someone, but he's away.'

At the mention of her brother's name, Blake's demeanour brightened. 'So what's Jared doing these days?'

'He has his own refurbishing business in Surfers. He's on holiday overseas at the moment, with his family. They've been gone nearly two months.'

'Jared's married now?'

'Yes. He and Sophie have a three-year-old son. Isaac.'

'Good for him.'

His lips curved in one of those rare smiles she hadn't had the pleasure of looking at in ten years and her pulse skipped a few beats. At this rate she was going to need to see a cardiologist.

'You see them often?' he asked.

She refreshed her coffee, then nodded. 'Every couple of weeks and that's not counting birthdays and celebrations. I drive down to Surfers, though. A houseboat's no place for kids, it's too cramped and too dangerous and Crystal has two now.' She didn't tell him that after she'd walked away from her home, Jared made a point of not coming to Mooloolaba to see her unless specifically invited.

He regarded her a moment while he blew on his tea. 'When's he due back?'

'A couple of weeks.'

'I'll need his phone number. I'd like to catch up after all this time and I need to contact him about the boat.'

The boat. The way he said it. As if he'd retaken ownership already. 'No.' Her fingers tightened around her mug. 'You can't tell Jared about the boat.'

His brows rose. 'Why not? You pay rent.' He studied her coolly through those assessing blue eyes. 'Don't you?'

'Of course.' Except she'd missed last month's payment.

She'd assured Jared she'd have it by the end of the week. Stalling. Hoping another job would come up.

He'd be furious she'd not called him about the leak earlier but she'd been anxious to show him she was capable of organising things like repairs herself. And worse, Blake was going to tell him the boat was his, she just *knew* it. She had no idea who stood where legally but she couldn't let Blake take it from her. Wherever would she be then?

'Lissa.'

He brought her attention back to him, set his mug on the table. He met her eyes and she felt herself start to quiver. The soft way he'd just said her name... Oh, he made her weak. He'd always made her weak.

More like weak and stupid.

'What?' she demanded, knowing he wasn't going to say something she wanted to hear and determined not to fall for his husky low voice. His husky, low, *cajoling* voice.

'Forget about the boat and Jared for a moment. Tell me about you. Your place of employment, for instance.' The last words were silver-edged sharp as his gaze held hers.

She shrank back from the almost physical touch. Uh-oh, not cajoling, but worse. Much worse... 'I already told you. I'm an interior designer.'

'But you don't have a job at present, do you?'

Her stomach muscles clenched. She wanted to look away. Sweet heaven, she wanted to look away. Away from the man who'd starred in so many dreams for so many years. But these weren't the lover's eyes she remembered from those dreams. They were the eyes of a teacher demanding to see her homework and knowing she hadn't done it. No point denying it.

She placed her palms firmly on the table. 'Look, I'm having a few problems right now. Not that it's any of your business.'

'Make it my business, then,' he said, unoffended. 'I might be able to help.'

Help? Of all the people in the world, she didn't want Blake's help. She wanted him to go away and not ask difficult and embarrassing questions. But that wasn't going to happen. She smiled tightly. 'You know of a short-staffed interior design business round these parts?'

'Is that what you really want?'

Did he think her lazy? She'd been accused of burning the candle at both ends in the past and drew herself up straighter. 'Absolutely it is. I studied hard, have my diploma to show for it and I don't want to do anything else.'

He watched his mug as he twirled it on the table between them, then looked at her once more. 'So are you after employment or are you looking to branch out on your own?'

She took a deep, resigned breath. In a way it was a relief to talk to someone about it and he wasn't going to be around for long. He was nothing to her, she told herself. Nothing.

'Okay.' She studied her hands on the table to avoid looking at him. 'I haven't been able to get employment in any of the interior design shops here since the business I worked for went bust. So I have a low-paying part-time cleaning job, which doesn't allow for me to save anything like the money I'd need to start my own business.'

'Jared can't loan you the money?'

'I don't want Jared's help. Jared and I...we had a disagreement of sorts. I moved up here because I needed some space.'

'Space?'

'Space. Independence.' She lifted a shoulder. 'After I qualified, I worked at a design shop in Surfers for two years but I *know* I can do better than work for someone else. Jared told me not to rush it. We argued. I left. He didn't take it well.'

Blake studied her a moment; the intensity was unnerving. 'I'm sorry to hear that.'

She heard genuine regret in his voice and tried to shrug it off. 'We still get on okay.' Mostly. Except now she realised

Jared was right. She'd been in too much of a damn hurry. 'So I want to maybe freelance for a bit,' she continued, 'but people round here don't want to take a chance on a nobody.'

'You're not a nobody unless you think that way. Trust me, I know.'

Trust him? She met his eyes across the table—cool and calm and blue as a summer lake. Ah, so not only was he super-efficient and a protector hero, he was one of those super-positive, role-model motivational types as well.

But it was the underlying flame in those cool depths that turned her inside out and had her gripping the edge of the table and reminding her she was nowhere near ready to trust a man again. Not even Blake Everett. To have another man in her life, even as a friend, was a leap she wasn't sure she could make.

'I'll be fine. Something'll turn up.' Did she really believe that? Or did she just not want this man in particular to see her fail? 'How long are you here for?'

'I haven't decided yet. A few weeks, a couple months…'

Watching the play of emotions cross her gaze as she spoke it was obvious to Blake that she wanted him gone, as far away and as quickly as possible. But at the same time he saw the attraction shine out of those eyes and felt its burn all the way down his body.

He wasn't the only one confused, then. *Stick with what you know and leave the emotional minefield well alone.*

But emotion and attraction aside, it was obvious she needed some sort of financial assistance to get her up and running. It was just as obvious, a matter of pride for her, that she didn't want her brother's support. Which left Blake. And he owed Jared.

He guessed he wasn't going anywhere until something was sorted.

'Do you have a vision for this business, Lissa, should you set one up?'

'Do I ever.' She leaned forward, eyes alive with enthusiasm. 'In a nutshell: Beauty, Functionality and Innovation through Experience and Knowledge.'

She smiled with such glowing satisfaction that he just bet she'd been itching to give her spiel to anyone who'd listen.

More than a few thoughts flashed through his mind, none of them business, but he wiped out all distraction and focused on the here and now. His socialite mother's death had left him a wealthy man. He also owned investment properties here in his own right. Right now he was jaded and disillusioned. He needed a challenge, a distraction. Something new to light a fire in his belly.

Lissa Sanderson's vision promised all those things. He wanted to help her, not only because she was Jared's sister, but because she was young and vivacious and fuelled with the same energy he'd had at her age. At a fit and healthy thirty-two he was hardly an old man but he wanted that energy that had been lacking lately, that zest, back in his own life.

'Oh, and it must be eco-friendly,' she went on, 'working with rather than against the environment. And colour. Lots of colour. Bold...' She trailed off as she caught his eye and her cheeks grew rosy. 'I'm getting carried away.'

So was he. With her ideas, the way her voice and its passion for her work flowed over him. But more so with the woman. Her eyes. Her emotions clearly visible with that hint of the sea in their colour. Her hair, its vibrant auburn tint catching the morning sun, her creamy skin. He fisted his hands and rubbed his knuckles to try and curb the impulse to reach out.

He mentally shook his head, assured himself it was *purely sexual*. It was the perfectly natural response of a horny man to feminine sexuality. And far more comfortable than the alternative.

But she drew him in ways he couldn't explain. And he'd not felt that intriguing pull of desire for a woman in a long while.

He didn't *want* the alternative. Didn't want the complications that came with it. He didn't want to hurt her because of it. So…he'd need to make sure this…sexual tug…didn't clash with a possible temporary working relationship.

'I'm looking for somewhere to invest some money,' he said carefully. 'A business, perhaps.'

She went very still. He saw a tiny crease in her brow appear as she absorbed his suggestion. Her eyes took on a different shade. The way light changed when one moved from sandy shallows on some tropical shore to the deepest ocean dive.

'If you're thinking what I think you're thinking, forget it.' Her tone was cool. Very cool. Then she rose, took a few steps away. Distancing herself. 'I don't want or need your charity.'

'I'm not suggesting a handout,' he said, mildly. 'Charity was my mother's forte. I'm suggesting a partnership. I'll provide the start-up capital but you'll be the one slaving your guts out and responsible for the day-to-day running of the business.'

She turned. Her shoulders square, looking taller than her small stature, she hesitated before saying slowly, 'You mean you'd be…like a silent partner?'

'Exactly.'

'Why?'

'Because everyone deserves a chance and I like what I've seen so far.'

With a scowl, she crossed her arms, drawing his attention to the deep cleavage at the top of her emerald T-shirt. 'What do you mean—what you've seen?'

Uh-oh. Right word choice, wrong place to look while saying it. He lifted his eyes. 'I have to admit I flipped through some of your work last night before I brought the rest of your gear over.'

Lissa watched him from across the room, her sudden exuberance quickly dissipating. What would he know about interior design? He'd just eyed off her cleavage, what did that tell her? That he'd finance her business in return for sex?

No. She'd never stoop to that. Not to get herself out of difficulties, not for a chance at success. Not even for the chance of sleeping with Blake Everett. Rubbing her upper arms, she looked away. 'I'll find my own business partner, thanks.'

'It could take a while to find the right person and you don't have the luxury of time. Meanwhile you're not bringing in a reliable income and you're living on that pathetic excuse for a boat.'

He made sense. Damn it, why did he have to make so much sense?

'So how about taking me on until you find someone else?' he suggested. 'That special someone with financial backing *and* a flair for interior design who wants to take a more active role. When you find that suitable person we'll renegotiate.'

Little bubbles of cautious excitement fluttered as she leaned against the sink and studied the black slate floor. It would solve her immediate problems. She'd be able to afford the boat's repairs, pay off her debts, and maybe, just maybe, she could give herself a real chance at the career she so desperately wanted—

'There's one condition,' he said slowly.

The Catch, she thought, her heart sinking as she looked up and met his gaze. Wasn't there always a Catch?

Blake studied the wary eyes, the slight lift of her upper lip, the flared nostrils. Damned if she didn't expect him to suggest a wild, no-strings affair. And damned if he wasn't tempted. But this was his money he was putting on the line.

'I want to see how you work, so I'd like you to redecorate the living room here. It's been more than ten years and it's looking tired. I'll pay you, of course.'

Her posture straightened and a renewed spark lit her eyes. 'You'd let me have free rein?'

'Absolutely. And if we're both happy with how things progress—'

'But hang on, you said you're here temporarily.'

'Not a problem these days with email and the Internet.'

'So apart from the financial end, you'll keep out of it?'

'Unless you ask for my help, which I'm more than happy to give. Ah. One proviso, party girl. The business comes first. No coming home at dawn.' *Unless I'm coming home with you.* The thought popped into his head and he frowned. Where the hell had that come from?

She turned, reciprocated his frown with one of her own. 'Just because I was the Gold Coast's number one party fan, doesn't mean the legend continues here. I'm not eighteen any more, I've more important things on my mind. So I go to the occasional party—doesn't everyone?' Still watching him, she shook her head. 'No, I guess they don't.'

Damn right, they didn't. 'Say the word and I can have the money in an account this afternoon.'

She leaned back against the sink, fingers tense on the edge, and nodded slowly. Cautiously. 'Okay. But I don't want Jared to know. Not yet, anyway.'

'So we'll keep it between the two of us.' A sudden awareness—or was it wariness?—crept into her gaze and he knew she was thinking of the way he'd linked the two of them. 'It's just a business arrangement, Lissa. A temporary one until you find someone else.'

She nodded, blew out a breath. 'Okay, we have a deal.'

CHAPTER FIVE

'Oh…wow!' Lissa's whole being seemed to light up.

'We'll need it in writing,' Blake said, sharper than he intended, remembering the boat fiasco, which still needed discussing. After his father's betrayal, never again would he trust another as easily. No matter who it was. No matter how attracted he was.

'Of course.' Linking her fingers above her head, she laughed with surprising abandon, spinning a circle in the middle of the kitchen. 'I'll get right on it.'

She all but danced across the kitchen, reached up on tiptoe and flung her arms around his neck. 'Thank you.' Her breasts, firm and full and not constrained by a bra, grazed his torso, sending a spurt of lust straight to his groin.

Before he could respond in any way, she came to an abrupt halt. Her eyes widened, her cheeks coloured and she backed away fast. 'I…I'm going to go take a look at the room now and write up some ideas before you change your mind.' Then she turned and hurried from the room.

Lissa clutched her neck with both hands and willed the hot rush of heat to subside as she raced upstairs to her room. She'd got carried away and practically climbed up his chest. *Oh, God.* And he'd looked positively shocked. She went straight to the en-suite, splashed herself with cool water. She did *not* look at her reflection.

Sucking in calming breaths, she sat on her bed and took a few minutes to take stock and absorb the conversation. His generous offer. The offer that was conditional on whether or not he liked her work.

When she could breathe normally again, she walked downstairs to the living room and straight to her supplies stacked against one wall. To her relief, Blake was nowhere around.

She flipped her sketch pad open to a new page and sketched the room's layout. This was a tropical coastal town, so a beach or watery theme. Elegance. Simplicity. The furniture had to go. She glanced up. The exploding crystal orb of light stayed.

'Ideas?'

She heard Blake behind her but didn't turn. *No distractions.* 'Blues. Ocean theme. I'm thinking dull turquoise. It has both warm and cool undertones so it's compatible with almost any colour. It works well with charcoal—that slate wall's ideal. A lift with lime green or even red. Or if we go with a darker version of the turquoise, gold can look very dramatic, which could lend itself well to the honeyed wood...' She pulled out her big blue paint samples, chose two. She glanced over to him. 'Can you visualise your walls this shade, or is it too dark for you?'

'I'm leaving it up to your professional judgement.'

'But can you live with that colour?' She walked to the wall and held both samples up high, against the slate.

'I won't be here.'

Blake wasn't looking at the samples. He was looking at the strip of enticing flesh between her jeans and T-shirt. And all he could think of was how she'd felt pressed against him for those few seconds in the kitchen.

All he knew was he wanted that feeling again. He found himself standing behind her, breathing in the fragrance of her hair. His pulse drummed in his ears. 'The darker one. More full-toned.'

He heard her surprised intake of breath as he studied her

neat little fingernails against the colour card. When she didn't pull away, his hands closed around her waist, his fingers straddling the ridge between her T-shirt and smooth warm skin.

Her hands drifted down the wall; the colour cards fluttered to the floor. He turned her around slowly, looked down at her. 'I'm going to kiss you. God knows I shouldn't. You're Jared's little sister.'

Her eyes grew huge and glassy; her pupils seemed to swallow the green. 'I won't tell him if you don't,' she whispered.

He leaned nearer, felt her breath against his face. Felt the heat of her body against his chest. He pulled her closer. 'Ah, but I'm not going to lie to him, he's my mate. It's a matter of honour. But then I'm not feeling particularly honourable right now.' He dipped his head.

'After all this time...' she murmured against his mouth.

'After all this time...what?'

'Never mind.'

The breathless sound spilling from those luscious-looking lips, her fragrance shimmering on her skin, the sensation of two tight nipples pushing against the middle of his chest... No, he agreed silently, never mind...whatever it was.

His erection surged hotly against his jeans. Barely smothering an involuntary groan, he slid one hand to the small of her back and encouraged her body into closer alignment to ease the pressure down there.

It didn't. It only made him hotter and harder. And a whole lot hornier.

Denim shifted against denim as her legs moved against his. She stilled momentarily as the front of his jeans came into contact with her belly. Her eyes locked on his. Knowing, but not quite acknowledging. Not yet.

Then her fingertips crept up his chest, her arms slid around his neck. 'Unbelievable,' she murmured.

'Believe it,' he murmured back.

Lissa looked up into those liquid blue eyes framed with

thick dark lashes and wanted to drown there. She slid her fingers into his short military haircut and released a sigh that seemed to come from the depths of her soul.

Then, in a flash like a remnant of lightning from last night's storm, she hesitated. Did he *know* how she'd always felt about him? Was he about to take full advantage of that knowledge?

His erection butted against her as if in answer and, oh, how long had she wanted that? But, 'Wait…' She relinquished her hold and pushed at his chest. Reluctantly but firmly.

His brows lowered, his gaze turned bemused, those perfect, *ready* lips turned down at the corners, but he didn't quite let her go. His hands still rested on her waist. 'You okay?'

'I…yes.' Of course he didn't know.

But how well did she really know Blake? Did she believe the old gossip about him? She didn't know—she'd never had any personal contact with him beyond the casual 'hi and bye'.

She'd thought she'd known Todd. She'd trusted him with her heart, and with her body, and he'd abused that trust. In so many ways. The niggle turned to panic and flared bright and urgent within her. She started to pull out of his hold.

'Hang on, where are you going?' He tugged her back, his arms slid around her, steel bands holding her prisoner.

She fought down a sudden feeling of claustrophobia. 'I just remembered I need to…be somewhere.'

'No.' He released one arm to lift her chin with a finger so that she was looking up, up into his eyes. 'No,' he said again, softer this time, but no less demanding as he gripped her chin and dropped his mouth to hers.

Futile to fight it. The old thought flashed through her mind and hot panic geysered up her throat but as his lips moved over hers the bad drained away as quickly as it came.

She'd fought Todd when he'd made the same move on her over and over while she'd struggled and died inside, but here, beneath the heat of Blake's mouth, even within his uncompromising hold there was a whole world of difference.

Because she knew instinctively that she could pull away at any time.

Masculine dominance. Strength. Control. She'd come to fear them, but with Blake, here, now, it faded away like mist beneath a tropical sun. She felt none of that familiar trepidation, only a willingness to meet him equally, man to woman, and an urgent desire for more.

His stubble grazed her chin. Her legs trembled and she clutched at his T-shirt to keep from sliding to a puddle at his feet. She could feel the hard wall of his chest, leashed power humming just beneath his skin, the heavy thump of his heart against her fists.

This was nothing like a simple meeting of mouths. Nothing like it had been with any other man. Here, as his lips moved over hers, there was fire. The same fire, the same hot desire that burned brightly within her.

Until Todd had left her feeling inadequate as a lover, she'd never been a woman to shrink from her own desires, from taking what she needed from a man and giving in return. Celebrating her sexuality, absorbing her own pleasure, while ensuring she reciprocated in full measure. But she'd never felt the overwhelming emotional connection that suffused her whole being now, with Blake.

Her mouth parted only too willingly as he sought entry, his tongue dancing lightly over hers at first, then deeper, bolder, exploring the inside of her cheeks, her teeth. So easy to let emotion take command of her body as she absorbed the rich dark flavours he brought, the low growl she could hear deep in his throat, the feel of his fingers beneath her chin, against her neck. So simple to forget everything but this urgent, raw desire sweeping through her and give herself up to it.

Blake had never known that passion could be laced in such delicacy. His hands were unsteady as he tilted her head for better access to more of her sweetness, lifting them so he could glide his fingers through her silky hair and hold her close, where he wanted her. Where he needed her.

With her pale skin and clear translucent eyes she reminded him of a miniature porcelain doll. Easily broken. So he was careful to keep the fire that roared like an inferno through his blood contained.

Something had spooked her a moment ago, but now…now she clung to him, all lithe limbs and soft feminine curves. Her body melted against his, fitted with his as if she'd been made expressly for that purpose.

A rumble rose up his throat as he cruised his hands up over her shoulder blades, taking it slow, testing her response, testing his own. Then down her spine, all the way down so that he could tuck that spectacular bottom even closer against him.

But when his erection ground against her belly and she let out a sexy turned-on moan, all reason, all thought fled except the overwhelming desire to have her. His greedy hands raced up to skim the outer edges of her full round breasts. Taking their weight in his palms, he indulged in her warm, womanly shape.

Hunger. An insatiable hunger that demanded to be appeased. And need. Hot, acute, devastating need that rushed in with a torpedo's force to fill the void he'd learned to live with.

Dipping his head, he nuzzled a breast until he found its pebble-hard nipple. Heard her murmur, 'Oh…yes…'

He drew it into his mouth and suckled her through the soft jersey while his hands slipped beneath the hem of her T-shirt to feel her silky smooth belly against his palms. When he nipped at the erect little peak with his teeth, she gasped and arched against his mouth.

As if from a distance he heard a muffled sob as she cried out his name, sending white-hot shards arrowing straight to his throbbing groin. He shifted his attention to her other breast while he eased the T-shirt up over her ribcage, his thumbs already grazing the undersides of those perfect globes.

Then her hands pushed at his chest and through the roaring in his ears he heard the words, 'Blake...stop...'

Stop? It was enough to shake off the sexual fog that enshrouded them. He looked into those wide, passion-drenched eyes and knew she wanted it as bad as he. 'Okay, we'll take this somewhere more comfortable,' he murmured.

But when he ran a finger over the neck of her T-shirt, skirting the swell of her breast, she wrapped a restraining hand around his. 'No sexual favours...'

He frowned. 'Is that what you think this is? Repayment for my assistance?'

'I don't know, I...'

She thought so little of him? And suddenly he knew why. She believed the gossip. A bitter taste lodged in his throat. 'This is called sealing the deal with a kiss,' he muttered harshly, 'and you were enjoying it as much as me.'

'It wasn't *just* a kiss.'

Then his brain caught up with the rest of him. Her wavering, the hesitation. Her incredulous, 'After all this time.' Her reluctance to explain. Ah, hell.

She was a virgin.

And here he'd been well on the way to spreading those lovely tanned legs wide and taking her against the slate wall. For God's sake. She *should* think so little of him.

Gritting his teeth against his throbbing erection, he backed off. Carefully. Her virginal dreams no doubt included love and commitment. *Not* being taken against a damn wall. No way...

Lissa dragged in some much-needed air. Needed because he'd just kissed her as if the world were coming to an end and sucked her oxygen clean away. She felt as if she were waking from a dream just when it was getting to the interesting part.

Her sensitised nipples were begging for more of that attention he'd been paying them. Why had she stopped him? Calling a halt to the most exciting sexual experience of her life *and* with the man she'd most wanted to experience it with?

Because at this point in time she needed something more.

She didn't know Blake well enough for this *intensity*. But she knew of his reputation…

'This is going way too fast,' she said, still struggling to catch her breath. 'Right now I'm more interested in an income than…anything else. I can't risk any distractions getting in the way of that. So priority one: I need to focus on this room makeover. Okay?'

He didn't return her smile, possibly because she wasn't even sure she *had* smiled. Her tingling lips felt as if they belonged to someone else.

'Understood.' He shoved his hands in his jeans pockets. 'I'll organise for the arrangements to be detailed in writing immediately.' He spoke as though he were chewing on scrap metal and his brows lowered over eyes carefully blanked of all that emotion she'd seen only seconds ago. He backed away as if he couldn't wait to be gone.

'Great. The sooner, the better.' Her hand itched to reach out and touch his morning-stubbled jaw and tell him…what? That she'd changed her mind and wanted him to finish what he'd started and to hell with everything else?

'I know a solicitor.' His voice was as stiff as the painful looking bulge in his pants. 'I'll check whether she's still in the area and give her a call now.'

Chewing on her still-throbbing lips, she looked away quickly down to her hands in front of her. 'Right. Okay.'

He turned on his heel and left the room.

Lissa watched him go, her pulse still galloping from here

to eternity. She touched her mouth, still damp from Blake's. With him she was still that naïve girl who didn't know any better and who hadn't learned that she didn't choose wisely when it came to men.

Right now her career future was more important than getting intimately involved. If it went wrong between them she could lose this chance to makeover his room and any future financial backing.

And yet…he'd not taken her without care. He'd stopped when she'd asked. He'd considered Jared and spoken of honour. How many men spoke of honour, for goodness' sake? He was a decent guy. Those rumours had to be *wrong*.

Todd was the reason she didn't trust men's motives. His dark good looks had hidden an even darker side. The Toad had lied to her about his past and manipulated her feelings for him. A man of deceit and no morals. The opposite of Blake in every way that counted.

But she wouldn't think about how right and perfect Blake's body had felt against hers or the taste of his kiss…oh, no, she would *not*. That road led to certain heartbreak. Because he could be gone at any time.

She picked up her dropped paint samples. She was counting on Blake not telling Jared about the boat's problems or their agreed partnership until she gave the nod. She'd concentrate on his generous offer, pay for the repairs from the income she made and work her backside off to show she was worthy. To show him, and herself, and then her family that she could be the successful career woman she wanted to be.

First up, she'd impress him with her transformation of his living room. With renewed enthusiasm, she shimmied towards the wall with her paint samples and a swatch of gold-coloured fabrics.

Blake poked his head through the doorway catching her mid-shimmy.

'Can you be ready to leave in thirty minutes?' His gaze

drifted from her hips to linger on her breasts where her T-shirt still bore the damp circles from his mouth.

A flush crept up her neck. 'I'll be ready.'

Her reply finally drew his attention to her face. 'Great,' he said, and disappeared again.

Lissa glanced at her tell-all top and jeans. But not in these clothes.

Blake returned to the study, pleased with the ease with which he'd been able to organise the solicitor. Deanna Mayfield was an old school friend from Surfers who practised law in Mooloolaba. She was twice divorced and had been delighted to hear from him. She'd even juggled appointments to fit them in.

Next, he arranged for a plumber and an electrician to come in the afternoon, then searched the local area for men's clothing stores on his laptop.

It kept his mind occupied and therefore off Lissa and what had happened in the living room. That had been his intention, except that he could still taste her, could still smell her scent on his clothes.

He'd made her a business offer in one instant and kissed her to kingdom come in the next. Only he hadn't stopped at a kiss. He'd been so blind-sided it hadn't registered that she might be a virgin. How many twenty-three-year-old virgins were there these days?

Was she keeping it for Mr Right? Or was it because she hadn't she found a guy with enough power and vigour to light her fire? He preferred the latter. He was no woman's Mr Right and he'd already glimpsed the smouldering evidence in her eyes.

He drummed restless fingers on the desk. Trouble with virgins was they attached too much emotion to the sexual act and the last thing he needed was an emotional female who expected more. He had a gut feeling Lissa would be a woman who expected that 'more'.

She was Jared's sister. Getting physical with a mate's sister was one thing, but when said sister was a virgin? No way. No how. Out of bounds.

He needed to remember their agreement and maintain his focus on the goals they'd set and his hands off her body.

Her vivacious, voluptuous, *virginal* body.

His gaze flicked to the Titian-haired reclining nude in a Pre-Raphaelite original painting, titled 'Chastity', on the wall and wondered vaguely why his father hadn't tried to sell it. Had to be worth a quid.

Disturbed by the maidenly beauty and its similarity to a certain redhead, he averted his eyes and glared at the computer screen. Perhaps he and Deanna could have a drink later, catch up on old times.

He thought about the six-foot-tall blonde who'd won the Miss Sunshine Contest at seventeen when he'd been a gangly star-struck sixteen. Maybe he could suggest they…what?

On an oath, he shut down his computer. The thing was… the *mystery* was…he had a churn-in-the-gut feeling that no woman was going to take the edge off his need unless that woman was Lissa. The sooner he had the business plans drawn up and boat repaired, the better off it would—

Lissa's ear-piercing shriek from out back had him shoving out of his chair and bounding for the door.

Lissa stared in numb disbelief at the empty space where the houseboat had been only moments ago. 'Oh, my God, oh, my God.' She'd yelled until her vocal cords had given out and now she couldn't seem to raise her voice above a murmur. Her legs felt like spaghetti and every vital organ within her body was twisting and churning.

This was a mistake. A dream—a *nightmare*.

She heard the back door slide open. Heard a muttered series

of harsh four-letter expletives, then Blake's heavy footsteps sprinting along the path.

The steps slowed, stopped behind her. She didn't turn around. Her eyes were riveted on the swirling water, a gurgling liquidy sound and the rectangular shape disappearing beneath the surface. 'No!'

'Lissa.' Firm hands gripped her shoulders. 'It's going to be okay.'

She watched bubbles stream to the surface as her home sank deeper and blurred and felt herself start to shake uncontrollably. '*Going to be okay?* Going to be okay? My boat, my home, my whole life. Gone. And you're telling me it's *okay*?' Her hands flew to her face. 'Why didn't you tell me how bad it was? Why didn't you *insist* I pack up everything last night?'

She hated being told what to do so *why was she blaming another person for her mistakes?*

'We saved your all-important samples, that's—'

'My clothes!' she shrieked again. 'I've lost all my clothes!' Then they both stared in silence as a pale amorphous shape drifted up from the murky depths. Two small mounds popped onto the surface like mini desert islands.

'Well, maybe not all,' he murmured, and dropped to his knees, leaned down and plucked her buttercup bra out of the water.

'Oh…shut up! I hate you!' Vaguely, her mind registered that under normal circumstances the sight of his tanned long fingers on her most intimate of garments would have thrilled her, but right now all she felt was the burn of humiliation.

She snatched it out of his grasp. She couldn't look at him. Her eyes were stinging and deep inside she was very afraid she was coming apart and was disgusted with herself for that weakness. Why, of all people, did it have to be this particular man witnessing her defeat?

'Hey. I shouldn't have said that.' He turned her in his arms and held on tight. 'The Lissa I know is strong and resilient, she'll get through this.'

'How would you know *how* I am?' Her presence had barely registered on his personal radar. 'I was just a kid and you *didn't* know me.'

'Ah, but I did know you. You were one very determined, very single-minded kid.'

'Yeah, right.' He *meant* stubborn and spoiled. Indulged and irresponsible. Didn't this prove it? It had been her duty to look after Jared's boat and now...

But his reassurance was gruff against her ear when he said, 'The most important thing is you're safe.'

Safe? How was she safe when she had nowhere to live? Why hadn't she packed an overnighter, at least? She'd let him tell her what to do and now...now look at the mess she was in. She fought against him but it was like fighting against a warm rip tide.

'They're just things, Lissa. Everything can be replaced.'

'But they were *my* things,' she said, a single tear spilling down her cheek. 'Every stick of furniture, every knick-knack. My mother's bluebird of happiness brooch. They might mean nothing to anyone else but they meant something to me. I worked my backside off for it all, right down to the last scented candle. And before you ask, no, I don't have contents insurance.' Because she'd let it lapse two months ago due to lack of funds.

She felt him draw a deep breath but he didn't nag her. Instead, he held her against him and muttered soothing noises against her hair.

'You know something,' he said a moment later, 'I could fit all my worldly possessions in the back of a station wagon and I do okay.'

She looked up to see if he was joking. How did a person cram their life into the back of a car? Unbelievable. It wasn't normal. She let her forehead fall back onto his chest. 'You have this house. This *mansion*.'

'True.'

Closing her damp eyes, she gave up the fight and leaned into his musky warmth. And all she could think was if he hadn't been here, if he hadn't insisted she sleep in the house despite her vigorous objections, she might be at the bottom of the river now.

He drew back, still holding her upper arms. 'Guess we won't need the plumber's services after all.'

She opened her eyes and saw a dark splotch on his T-shirt where her waterlogged bra had been trapped between them. She lifted her gaze to his and, just for once, allowed herself the comfort of having someone to lean on. 'What happens now?'

CHAPTER SIX

AT HIS insistence, Blake made the necessary calls and organised to have the houseboat refloated and towed away. Lissa was grateful to Blake for his cool, calm and sensitive handling of the whole situation. A man to lean on in a crisis. It gave her time to regroup. Most of her artwork was gone. Photos, jewellery, books.

She sat on her bed and looked about her. She also needed time to absorb the fact that until she was making an income, this was her bedroom. She needed to pull herself together and decide that she could still be that independent woman she wanted to be but there was nothing wrong with accepting help now and then.

But did it have to be Blake's help?

She stared at herself in the full-length mirror on the bedroom wall. The boat disaster had briefly obliterated the excitement of the new business agreement she'd made…and that kiss. Oh, that kiss…and *more*. Her whole body burned and churned with the memory and she saw its instant effect in her reflection.

She shook it away and concentrated on applying make-up to mask her distress. She needed to forget that momentary indulgence. And to accept Blake's insistence that she remain in his home.

'Here?' She'd glared at Blake through narrowed eyes,

fighting it all the way. *Nuh-uh. Not going to happen. Not after that kiss and a half.*

'You have somewhere else in mind?' He'd waited for a response but she hadn't had a ready one. Not one of any sort.

Returning to Surfers and facing Jared with her failures was not an option after the regrettably immature way she'd walked out eighteen months ago. And in an hour she'd be signing papers and making Blake her business partner. She had to remain in Mooloolaba. Rental accommodation was high in Mooloolaba.

Sharing with a guy was something she'd sworn she'd never do again. Living with Todd had been the most harrowing time of her life. Not only the physical abuse but the lies and degradation. Made worse because she'd kept it a secret from those who would have helped her. She'd been so naïve, so ashamed, and, for a while, so broken.

'What are you afraid of, Lissa?'

She'd stared up at Blake and into those beautiful blue eyes. Blake wasn't Todd—was nothing like Todd—but she no longer trusted herself when it came to choosing the right kind of man.

'Nothing. Why would I be afraid? I'm certainly not afraid of you,' she'd told him when he'd scrutinised her face more closely. As if he knew her secret... *He couldn't know.* 'Thank you. I accept.'

She'd arranged to meet Blake in the living room before leaving for their rescheduled appointment with the solicitor. In her jeans and faded T-shirt. She groaned inwardly. The T-shirt with the two faintly creased circles on her chest. Now there'd have to be an additional clause with the expenses incurred to replace her belongings.

She descended the stairs at the arranged time. Blake had changed into smart casual clothes and her thoughts scattered like confetti. The white button-through shirt, open at the neck, enhanced his tanned skin and accentuated his broad shoulders and muscular frame, the trousers were slim-fitting, showcasing well-defined thighs and…

She swung her gaze to the wood-panelled wall, embarrassed at being caught checking out his masculine shape, and said the first thing that came to mind. 'Definitely the deeper turquoise. And a modern painting here that encapsulates the essence of Mooloolaba.'

'You're the expert.'

His eyes glinted and she knew that he knew what she was really thinking about. His hot, toned body against hers.

'Let's get the documentation over with first,' he said. 'Then we'll pay a visit to the bank and then you can go shopping.'

What could she say? She needed clothes. 'I'm… I'll pay you back. Every cent. You can take it off my fee when the room's done.'

'Don't worry about that now. But I've got some matters to attend to back here so I'll arrange to meet you at this address later.' He handed her a card and a key. 'It's a building I own. It was used as a prestige car showroom but it's been vacant a while. I was going to sell it, but it might be a good location for an interior design business. Maybe you could take a look, come up with some ideas and tell me what you think. Don't forget to key in the security code. Panel's on the right of the door.'

Her spirits lifted a little. 'Thanks.' She tucked the card in her bag.

'What about Jared?' He paused. 'I assume you're in contact while he's overseas. Shouldn't you let him know what's going on?'

Yes, but she had more than enough stress to deal with right now. Besides… 'I don't want to spoil his holiday.'

'He's your brother.'

She didn't look at him as she slung her bag over her shoulder but she felt a vague criticism aimed her way and shrugged off the prickly sensation. What was between her and her brother was none of Blake's business.

'I'll get around to it, okay?' Tonight. It would be morning in Milan then. She'd make herself comfortable and alone and phone him tonight. Maybe in a few hours she wouldn't be so likely to dissolve into tears in the retelling of it.

'What do you want to do about your belongings?' He sounded as if he was finding his way barefoot around broken glass.

'Of course I want to save what I can. But it's probably already ruined with salt and river grime and heaven only knows what else.' She bit her lip to stifle the sob. It made her want to throw herself into his arms and weep.

And perhaps, she thought, as she moved directly to the door without waiting, that was his intention.

Deanna Mayfield was just the sort of woman Lissa imagined Blake would find attractive. Any man would find attractive, actually. As tall as him, silver-blonde hair, trim figure. Even in her grey pin-striped business suit she exuded a sultry kind of glamour.

If you went for that kind of thing.

'Blake!' Her smile was pure toothpaste advertisement. She ushered them into her office. 'What a pleasant surprise to get your call.'

Ms Mayfield and smartly dressed Blake looked like an ideal couple as they reminisced about a past Lissa had no part in. Had they ever been lovers? She couldn't help thinking of the bad-boy reputation. Yep, she thought, Ms Mayfield would definitely go for bad boys.

Even when they eventually got down to business it was there. That…something. While Lissa sat within arm's reach feeling out of the loop, uninvolved and insignificant.

'We'll need a signature here.' Leaning over the desk,

Deanna flicked her hair and indicated with a passion-purple fingertip, then passed Blake her pen.

Lissa's lip curled, then she pressed a hand to the tender spot just beneath her breastbone while Blake signed and passed the pen back. With a smile. The knot was hunger, not jealousy. Good heavens, she couldn't begin to imagine how many women Blake would have been with over the years, no doubt all as glamorous as Miss Sunshine here.

Then Deanna smiled at Lissa as if suddenly remembering she was there and handed her the pen. 'Melissa. Your turn, sweetie.'

Sweetie. Condescending cow. Lissa stretched her lips into a smile over her clenched teeth as she took the pen and signed.

Blake dropped her at the Sunshine Plaza with her new personal debit card. The arrangement was that she should catch a cab to the address on the card he'd given her when she was done and they'd meet at five-thirty.

She headed into the mall to buy her blues away. She refused to get carried away however, knowing she needed to repay whatever she bought at a future date. Sticking to basics, she purchased underwear, toiletries, casual wear, a couple of business suits and skirts and a cream jacket...and, of course, the obligatory little short black dress.

She couldn't resist a tiny bottle of her favourite perfume and a couple of CDs—for therapeutic reasons. At an art shop she bought a new sketch pad, charcoals and pencils so that if she arrived at the premises before Blake she could keep busy. If she was busy she wouldn't think about the boat.

Fighting the dull pain that had been throbbing away at the back of his skull for the past couple of hours, Blake walked towards the shop. Standing across the road, he watched the lowering sun paint the upper half of the unique building a burnt orange. When he'd bought it, he'd been impressed right off with its central location—near other businesses but not overcrowded—and the interesting canted windows out front. Dodging a steady stream of slow-moving traffic, he let himself in with a takeaway meal, drinks and cutlery in a cardboard box.

The empty interior still blew him away. A gleaming expanse of polished floorboards flowed like a golden lake to cream walls on all sides. But the feature that really sold it for him was the main source of illumination. Two metal wheel-like structures a good couple of metres in diameter studded with down-lights and suspended at an oblique angle to each other and to the floor.

The building had a vaulted wooden ceiling and odd-shaped windows. Their topaz and sapphire glass threw out a rich palette of colours, glinting on the brass rail of the spiral staircase to one side, which led to a mezzanine level, which in turn floated above the rear third of the cavernous space.

It might have reminded him of a church except for the sound of a CD player crackling away with the unmistakeable voice of Robbie Williams from somewhere up those stairs.

With his box under one arm, he crossed the floor, appreciating the warm ambience. What better venue to launch an interior design business? With his mother's contacts and Lissa's obvious expertise, they couldn't lose.

But when he reached the top of the staircase he came to a silent halt.

Lissa was dancing, bare feet moving lightly in time with the song. A pad of some description lay open on the floor beside her. She'd been sketching…something. Didn't matter—he didn't even cast his eyes in the pad's direction. It was the woman he wanted to feast his eyes on.

The day's last vermilion beams lasered through the only upstairs window high above them, turning her magnificent crown of hair to flame, painting her limbs gold and leaving the shadowed spaces a dusky purple. He stood, transfixed in the stairwell's dimness. Held his breath, though he doubted he had any breath left in him to hold.

She'd changed into a loose white top that dipped low at the front. Beneath it she wore short white shorts leaving her legs bare.

Those feet moved fast and light, as if she were dancing on air, but her arms moved above her in a graceful arc, her gaze wholly focused at some point in the middle distance, her lips turned up slightly at the corners as if delighting in the moment.

It was like watching an angel.

Would she wear that same expression if he were lying beneath her? Would she make love with that wholly focused gaze and delight?

He shook his head to clear the lusty thoughts. Angels were supposed to be pure asexual beings, weren't they? And as far as he knew, they didn't make love. *Virginal.* But he could have watched for an eternity, absorbed in the beauty of the moment—and her—but she turned and saw him and that golden moment was gone.

For a breathless heartbeat she watched him with those wide clear eyes. Then she blinked as if coming out of a trance and slowly lowered her arms. Perspiration dewed her skin and her breathing was elevated, drawing his attention to her breasts as they rose and fell. He couldn't look away.

'Hi.' He kept his voice casual, breaking the sudden tension.

She lifted a self-conscious shoulder and colour rose up her neck. 'Hi.' Bending so that her hair curtained her face, she flipped the pad shut, creating a draught across the floor, and he caught the fragrance of some exotic perfume she'd not been wearing earlier today. It reminded him of midnight madness on a moonlit beach.

'I found an old CD player someone left behind.' She moved

to it, squatted down and lowered the volume. 'Have you been standing there long?'

'Not long.' Not long enough. Too long.

'Dancing's my stress reliever of choice. And chocolate, of course.' She helped herself to a four-square row from the half-eaten block beside the player. 'I guess I got carried away.'

'You don't share?'

'Sure, sorry.' She grabbed the bar, held it out. 'Help yourself.'

'Not the chocolate.' He gestured towards the pad. 'Your art or whatever you were sketching there.'

'Ideas for your living room. But you don't get to see them until I'm done.'

With the tip of her tongue, she licked a small fleck of chocolate from the corner of her mouth. He watched her, wishing he could've been the one to sample that sweet taste on her mouth. Then she wiped the spot with a finger for good measure and said, 'What have you got there?'

He'd forgotten all about the box. He withdrew the aromatic bag, held it up. 'I thought you might be hungry but I see you're already well supplied.'

She shook her head. 'Chocolate doesn't count. I'm starving. And that, whatever it is, smells delicious. Let me guess.' Closing her eyes, she inhaled slowly. 'Mmm…Indian.'

'Hope you like butter chicken. It's full of calories and comes with jasmine rice and assorted delights.'

'Ooh, yes. Hand it over.'

She reached for it but he lifted it higher. 'Not quite yet.'

She did the pout, her hands on her hips, but a glimmer of a smile teased the edges of her mouth. 'Hey, that's just mean.'

'First, answer a question for me. Earlier today you said you hated me. Is that still true?'

'I… No.' The tiny smile vanished and she frowned. 'Did I say that? I don't remember saying that. Of course I don't hate you.'

'Good. I don't hate you either.'

'Even though I've been such an idiot?'

'You're n—'

'But I am. I hold myself responsible for the mess I'm in and…and the trouble I've caused you.'

'And now we'll move on.' He mentally kicked himself for bringing up this morning's disaster and wiping away her smile just because he wanted some sort of petty reassurance. What the hell was wrong with him?

'That's a relief, since we just signed an agreement to work together, but can we have the rest of this conversation *after* we've eaten?'

He moved closer to better catch her scent. 'I've been thinking about you.'

'You mean that kiss.' She shrugged and turned away, refusing to play his game of grab-the-bag, but he saw her fingers tremble slightly as she popped the last piece of chocolate in her mouth.

'Ah…that kiss,' he said, slowly, and watched her cheeks pinken. 'Since you've brought it up…'

'*I* didn't, *you* did.' She dropped to her knees and busied those small hands putting her art purchases in a pile. 'I've had more important matters on my mind, actually.'

'So have I.' He set the food and the box holding the rest of the stuff on the floor, then shook out a rug he'd found in the boot of the rental and spread it out. 'Fact is, you're right in there with all the other stuff that's going on.'

She set the containers out on the rug and began removing the lids. 'I'm sorry if that bothers you.'

It did. More than she could possibly know. He watched the way her auburn hair swung down in an arc, hiding her face from view. 'I'll manage.'

'Of course you will, you're very capable. What is it you do again?'

Now her eyes flicked up to his. They were full of questions he wasn't going to answer. Not to anybody. The headache burgeoning behind his eyes intensified. 'I was a clearance diver. Like I told you, I've resigned from the navy.' *End of story.*

She blinked. 'O-kay...' When he didn't elaborate she glanced at the window. 'It's going to be dark soon. The lighting up here doesn't seem to be working.'

He welcomed the encroaching night and a change of topic. He wasn't going to spill his guts to Lissa Sanderson. Knowing her family background as she did, she'd be the kind of woman who'd want to try to nourish his soul.

If he still had a soul, that was.

'Lucky I brought these, then,' he said, pulling out a box of tea lights. He set half a dozen along the balustrade.

'You think of everything, don't you?' she murmured.

'It's my practical streak.' He shot her a quick glance as he lit them. 'I wasn't sure if the power company would make it here to switch on the electricity in time.'

He lowered himself to a corner of the rug on the other side of the feast and passed her some plastic cutlery and a plate from the box. She piled up her plate as if she hadn't eaten a square meal in a week.

'So, what do you think of the building?' He spooned some rice onto his plate.

'It's gorgeous,' she said around a mouthful of chicken. 'Absolutely gorgeous. Just what we need.'

He popped the cork on the champagne bottle, poured it. 'Have you had a chance to decide how you want to set it up?'

'Yes. I'll take you downstairs and show you after.'

He handed her a foaming glass, raised his own. 'A toast to our new partnership.'

'To success.' She clinked her glass to his.

To us, Lissa wanted to say. But despite the candles' soft glow caressing his face with bronze fingers and casting shadows in the violet spaces between them and the love song's words on the tinny player, this wasn't supposed to be a romantic dinner.

And she'd had to go and mention that kiss.

Obviously he'd not been thinking about it at all. Just because he'd said he'd been thinking about her, didn't mean he'd been thinking about her in any *romantic* sense. He probably had loads of women who'd been waiting ten years just for his call. Naturally he'd think about her, and it wouldn't be good.

She'd just managed to lose all her belongings and the boat he called his. He'd inherited a house-mate he hadn't asked for. And that wasn't all. He'd had no intention of being involved in a business, let alone an interior design one. He'd rather have his luxury sail boat. Was it any wonder he'd been thinking about her?

'Wine not to your taste?'

His voice dragged her back to the present and their surroundings. 'Yes, it's lovely. Thank you.' And so it should be, at the price she knew it sold for. French, too, always her favourite. She took a sip and said, 'So, the navy must pay you *very* well.'

He shrugged. 'I do okay.'

'Just okay?' Clearly he didn't want to talk about any aspect of his working life—his *previous* working life—or how they happened to be drinking one of the most expensive celebratory champagnes available.

'I live in military accommodation when I'm not at sea. I've never had a mortgage so I've put my money into buying property. This building for example.' He forked up a morsel of meat, but didn't put it in his mouth. 'If you're wondering whether I am, in fact, a secret international drug lord, maybe I should tell you my mother also left me a sizeable inheritance.' His expression betrayed nothing of his emotions regarding the loss of his mother.

Lissa remembered the car accident that had claimed Rochelle Everett's life and brought Blake home that last time. She'd been a popular social celebrity and famous for her charitable work from Surfers all the way up to the Sunshine Coast.

'I was sorry to hear about your mother, Blake. She did so much good for the community.'

He studied the meat on his fork. 'Can't deny that.' Then he jammed it in his mouth, chewed a moment and washed it down with a long, slow swallow of champagne.

Lissa felt the wall go up so hard, so fast, it made her head spin. Impenetrable. Insurmountable. What made a man so unwilling to talk about himself? Every aspect, every topic she broached, every time she tried to get him to open up, he stopped her cold. And it wasn't only pain she saw in his eyes, there was bitterness too.

She'd never known her mother, who'd died when Lissa was born. She'd also discovered a few years ago that she was the result of her mother's affair with an itinerant artist. The man she'd known as her father was dead and good riddance. But she couldn't begin to imagine the pain of losing Jared, who'd been both a mother and father to her in her formative years, or Crystal, her older sister.

But Blake's mother had been a *good* person, a caring person who'd worked tirelessly for charity and the community. What was it with him?

So she spent the rest of the meal covering easy neutral and safe topics, like her family. She told him how Jared had met Sophie when she'd emailed her not-so-secret diary to him on her first day as his PA and he laughed the bubbles off the top of his champagne. Then she regaled him with entertaining stories about her nieces and nephews.

He opened up enough to reminisce about his surfing days with her brother. She didn't ask him about his work or what he intended doing now or his family again.

When they'd finished the meal, Lissa switched off the CD player, stacked the plates and Blake packed everything back, standing the half-finished bubbly in one corner of the carton.

Finally out of safe conversational topics, Lissa waited for Blake to speak or fill the void with...anything. He looked at her for a long, hushed, tension-packed moment, his eyes glinting in the candle's seductive glow.

Anticipation swarmed through her body, her pulse picked up and her breathing quickened. She swore she could see the sexual sparks dancing between them on the candle-light.

But Blake didn't kiss her. He wasn't seduced or persuaded by those sparks. Instead, he rose, walked the couple of steps to the balustrade and blew out the candles, leaving only the light filtering up from downstairs. Back-lit, he was all stern lines and sharp angles and shadows. *Who are you really, Blake Everett? What's made you this way?*

Then he bent down, picked up his box and said, 'I think it's about time you filled me in on your plans for this place.'

CHAPTER SEVEN

LEAVING Lissa to follow, Blake blew out a strangled breath as he descended the stairs. A beautiful woman, a *willing* woman, champagne and candles. He could have had her. Right there on the floor, he could have given into the temptation that had kept him hard as granite all evening and most of the day.

He could have stripped away her clothes and watched her body bloom beneath his hands. He could have slid inside her, watched her eyes darken in surprise then pleasure. And he was walking away.

He shook his head. Some other man would have to introduce Lissa to the joys of sex because she was strictly out of bounds to him. And the pain in his skull was intensifying by the minute. Strobes of light impeded his vision, nausea rose in ever-increasing waves. The alcohol hadn't helped. He shoved the discomfort away. *Never allow another to witness your vulnerabilities.* He'd lived by that personal mantra all his life and he wasn't changing now.

On his arrival earlier, he'd had the unnerving feeling she was looking right into him when she'd caught him watching her at the top of the stairs. He hadn't enjoyed the sensation one bit.

Nor had he intended a seduction scene as such. One always celebrated a new venture with champagne. And the candles… He really *had* expected the power to be off.

Beneath the twin circles of light, he slowed to allow her to catch up. The empty building echoed with the sound of footsteps on wood as they crossed the polished boards.

A big hollow space, waiting to be filled. Kind of like where he was in his life right now. A place full of endless possibilities. He stared past the lights' glare to the darkened ceiling. Darkness into light.

He swiped a frustrated hand over his hair. Today had been one hell of a day and he wasn't going to end it by making an even bigger mistake with Lissa. A mistake that could cost them this partnership, and he knew she couldn't afford for that to happen.

She walked up and stood beside him, her shoulder brushing his arm, and said, 'Right, where shall we start...?'

He liked her ideas, suggested a few of his own. Her vision for the premises was well thought through considering she'd seen it for the first time this afternoon, the energy running through her commentary boundless. She pointed out a proposed office area, another space where clients could wait in comfort and browse catalogues. Areas for displays of soft furnishings and colour swatches, wallpaper, shelves to display interesting and unusual glassware or pottery. Another where clients could play with mock-up designs on touch-screen computers.

Eventually Lissa had said all there was to say. She looked to Blake for his response to her suggestion that she hang some of her own artwork on the walls. She'd saved a couple of her favourite pieces from a watery grave and she could create more.

He only nodded and she couldn't tell what he was thinking.

'If it's all right with you, I could set up at home in one of the spare rooms so it doesn't interfere with anything you might want to do,' she said.

'No problem. I don't have any plans for entertaining. Besides, I've never watched an artist at work.'

The thought of him watching unsettled her and she rubbed her arms in the cool swirl of air. 'Oh, I don't know about that.' A half-laugh trickled out. 'I've never worked with an audience.'

But when she looked at him her smile faded. His eyes. Haunting, hurting. Hungry. A well of conflicting emotions churned like a choppy sea behind that carefully neutral stare. A stare that defied anyone to try and find a way through.

She wanted to see the pain gone. She wanted to be the one to make it go. Right now she didn't care that she'd warned herself to keep away, that the business came first, that she didn't want her heart broken. She rested her hands on his crossed forearms and looked up at him.

She wasn't going to let their difference in height intimidate her. Rising on tiptoe, she reached behind his head and pulled it down towards her, keeping her hands slow and light, craving his taste again.

She felt his tightly crossed arms loosen, his body give as he leaned closer. So close. The scent of his skin surrounded her, his quickened breathing feathered over her mouth.

And then his lips brushed hers and her pulse went wild. How long had it been since she'd been brave enough to invite any kind of sexual contact, let alone initiate it? She crept her fingers between his forearms so that she could open them wide and fit herself against that broad hard chest—

He muttered something against her mouth that sounded like something a sailor would say. She felt the stiffness in his neck, resisting her, pulling back. Pulling away.

He uncrossed his arms all the way. Not to wrap them around her but to let them hang at his sides, leaving her own hands to drift down, useless.

'Lissa.' He looked down at her, the heat she'd felt emanating from him banished somewhere behind that shuttered gaze. 'I phoned Jared this afternoon.'

Pardon? 'You phoned Jared?' It took her a moment to gather her wits, pull her scattered self together and absorb what he'd said. Another before the feeling of betrayal slid cold and slick between her ribs. What had happened to keeping it between them? *Our little secret.*

'You made an agreement with me and you broke it.' The intoxicating moment fled and she clenched her fists against her stomach to stop the feeling of nausea welling up there. 'What did you do—scroll through my address book behind my back?'

'I looked up Crystal and Ian's phone number. Ian remembered who I was and gave it to me. I—'

'No.' She couldn't look at him. 'You had no right.'

'Wrong. It was the responsible thing to do. The only thing to do.'

'No.' She jabbed a finger at her chest. 'What I tell Jared is *my* business.'

'What, you'd have him drop by on his way home from vacation and find no boat? No Lissa? No way of knowing where you were?'

She shook her head. 'He'd never drop in without phoning ahead. It's called *communication.*'

'You weren't doing a very good job of communicating with him, then, were you?'

'What about you? Did you *communicate* with me about this first?'

'You were shopping.'

She lifted her head and glared at him. 'So?'

'I didn't want to have this conversation with you over the phone.'

'I told you I was going to let him know.'

'When? He loves you and you left him out of the loop.'

She knew, and it stopped her in her tracks. Worse, it had

taken Blake to point it out. 'That still doesn't give you the right to go over my head or mess with my affairs.'

What exactly had he told Jared? Had the two of them discussed her as if she didn't have a voice—or a brain? It made her want to slap something. Or someone.

'So you had a chat about Lissa's lapsed insurance too, then? The boat's state of disrepair? *Did you tell him you own it?*'

She stopped because she'd run out of breath. He wasn't attempting to deny her accusations. He was waiting for her to finish her little tirade. Calmly. Rationally. Only a tic in his jaw betrayed him.

'The boat's gone,' he said coolly. 'I've decided there's no point telling him my father sold it twice over. I assume Jared has insurance to cover it. He can make his own decisions about whether or not to replace it.'

Oh. 'That's very—'

'I told him what happened,' he continued, in the same unhurried voice. 'And that you were safe and unharmed and with me.'

With me. Why did those words claw so at her belly? She tightened her stomach muscles against the odd sensation and said, 'Nothing about our business arrangement?'

One eyebrow rose. 'You and I have an agreement.'

She nodded. She felt small. *Really* small. She'd jumped in feet first without thinking, without seeking clarification.

He went on, 'But it doesn't mean you keep him in the dark about it for much longer.'

What about that kiss? Did he intend not keeping him in the dark about that too? Oh, she did *so* not want to think about him talking guy talk with Jared about that. She comforted herself with the knowledge that they were mates, she was Jared's sister and Blake wasn't likely to spill that piece of information to her brother. Still, guys were guys…

And to think she'd been tempted to kiss him again. *Only to make him feel better.*

And he'd wanted to kiss her, it had been as obvious as the horn on a rhinoceros. And then at the last second he'd suddenly remembered he'd phoned Jared? He'd have known she'd react to that. It was almost as if he'd been looking for a reason, any reason at all, not to give in to that sexual hum between them.

She rubbed her arms to ward off a sudden chill. She should be relieved he'd put a stop to it. After all, she'd told him only hours ago that they were moving too fast.

'Okay.' She worked hard to keep her voice reasonable when what she wanted to do was yell why did he have to be so remote? As if he'd flicked a damn switch. 'But I wish you'd told me before you rushed into it. I'd intended phoning him this evening.'

'You still can.' His disbelieving look negated the barely there nod, making her feel like a kid again, and then he was walking away, cutting their conversation short with, 'It's late. Where's your gear?'

They didn't speak as they piled everything into his rented SUV. On the short drive home she pressed her lips together tight to stop the words she wanted to say spilling out: Frustratingly Infuriatingly Complicated Gorgeous Man.

When he pulled into the kerb outside the house, she glared straight ahead. 'I've changed my mind,' she murmured. 'I think I hate you after all.'

'I'll try to take it in my stride.'

They unloaded the car, both avoiding the other. When it was done, he muttered something about checking his emails and she saw him heading to a room off the living area that looked like a study. Or a cave. And he was damn well going to shut himself in there.

'Hang on.'

When he didn't stop, she caught up, planted herself in front of him, then waited until he looked down and at least acknowledged her. 'If you don't want to kiss me, you don't need to fake some spur-of-the-moment excuse to push me away. I'm a big girl these days, I can cope.'

He stood unmoving for a few unsteady heartbeats. 'Be very careful what you say to me right now, Lissa.' His husky warning sounded more like a promise than a threat.

But his non-committal expression just plain got to her. Did he have to be so...lone wolf? It made her want to push and prod until she got a reaction. Any reaction. She wanted to understand the demons she saw in his eyes in an unguarded moment. She wanted to understand *why*.

She pushed harder. 'I can handle rejection, I can handle disappointments. I can handle y...' She trailed off at his unforgiving stare, realising she'd let her mouth run roughshod over her thoughts, and took a step back, away from the intensity battering her.

His nostrils flared, his jaw clenched and something deeper than indigo flickered hotly in the depths of his eyes. He stepped forward, crowding in on her. Now she saw gold flecks among the blue in his gaze. Alive, like a flame. Raw and hot and primitive. For a brief moment he looked like a stranger—or that dangerous lone wolf—and instinctively she took another step back.

'You think you can handle me?' His hands shot out and his fingers curled around her upper arms, his thighs bumping hers as he walked her backwards with him until her spine came up against the wall. His unrelenting gaze didn't waver from hers.

He dragged her against him and kissed her. Hard. No time to react as his body flexed against hers, unyielding and unforgiving while his hands fisted tightly in her hair.

Then, before she knew it, he lifted his head to mutter against her shocked lips, 'You're not ready for what I'd like to do to you.'

The images his harsh words invoked sent a thrill pulsing through her. It throbbed low and heavy between her legs.

He untangled his hands from her hair and backed off. Without the support of his body, she slumped against the wall, dazed and dizzy and not a little delirious.

She knew her eyes were too wide, her breath too choppy, her limbs too trembly. She'd blown it, she could tell, and she saw a muscle twitch in his left jaw, felt him grow distant as he watched her through half-lidded eyes.

'And what would that be, that you'd like to do that I'm not ready for?'

His Adam's apple bobbed, his hands fisted at his sides and she swore the air vibrated with shared images... Blake pushing her back against the wall, tearing away her clothes with impatient fingers until she stood naked and trembling with need. Using his hands and mouth and tongue to bring pleasure to every square centimetre of quivering flesh, then ploughing into her where she stood...

Dull colour sprinted high along his cheekbones as if he'd been having the same thought. 'That'd be a mistake.'

She licked lips gone dry. 'How do you know it would?'

He shook his head but she could see she'd put a dent in that composure. 'I suggest you go upstairs and get some sleep.' Turning on his heel, he walked away.

'The night is young,' she called to his retreating back with a brightness she didn't feel. She watched him walk to his cave, his shoulders tense, his strides long and swift. 'I think I'll go to that party after all.' She said it loud enough for him to hear as he reached the door. He hesitated before closing it behind him with a firm click.

She sighed, a weird cocktail of frustration and satisfaction simmering through her. She'd had no intention of going anywhere but he didn't need to know that.

Forget the way he'd stalked off, she'd got to him. Rattled his cage. Woken the primitive man beneath the civilised exterior. A quiver of excitement jagged down her spine. Was she really ready for that?

But she wasn't the only one with something to fear, something to hide. And what would stop a man like Blake from acting on their obvious attraction?

His own code of honour. His integrity. She'd seen it in action. More than once. Her fingers tightened into fists. Damn the gossip-mongers. He didn't deserve to be talked about that way.

But the man clearly didn't do emotion. Never had. And she'd never understood how he and Jared had got along so well. Back then she'd been too young to question it, but not too young to imagine herself offering him solace any way she knew how.

There was pain too, recent and raw in his shadowed eyes. And he was alone here with no support base. She couldn't begin to understand how someone dealt with that. He could try and block her out but she was going to reach him eventually. No one should be an island.

Someone was playing the harmonica. Blake pressed the heels of his palms to his eyeballs as the familiar childhood sound drifted over the pool's still blue water and through the open window.

Tipped back as far as the recliner would go, he lay in the study's darkness while a bevy of hammers battered away at the back of his skull. Darth Vader and Luke were fighting their all-time classic laser battle inside his eyeballs. The nausea was still at the high-tide mark.

Had Lissa gone partying? Probably, after that scene against the wall. He'd had to get rid of her—it was that or lose his pride. Throwing up at a woman's feet was never going to be a good look.

The tune switched to a country and western ballad he remembered playing as a kid. It had been an old distraction. He'd taught himself to play harmonica while he waited alone for his mother to come back from one of her endless meetings.

A foster home would have offered more. Lissa's mention of her tonight had brought the memories back and reminded him why he didn't allow emotion to clutter his life.

His father had been no better at the parenting game. Predictably he'd tired of the marriage and lived a separate life under this very roof. But by some miracle they'd conceived Blake. What a joke.

He'd learned early on not to depend on others for emotional or any other kind of support. Janine had reinforced that learning in his late teens. *Love equals vulnerability.*

Women looking for more than the casual date soon discovered he wasn't that kind of guy. As long as they were on the same wavelength he was happy to indulge whatever games they wanted to play, but the moment he got a glimpse of those stars in their eyes he was off.

And now there was Lissa.

Too young, too inexperienced, too-delicate Lissa. He hadn't missed the flicker of real fear in her eyes when he'd backed her up against the wall just now and guilt sat uncomfortably alongside the roiling in his gut.

Definitely off-limits to guys like him.

The strip of golden sand was strewn with shells, driftwood and dead palm leaves where the rainforest met the sea. The heavy pounding at the back of his skull was gunfire and the sound of his boots on the hard-packed sand.

Blake looked over his shoulder.

Torque crouched on the sand, frozen.

Blake dodging bullets. Dragging him across the beach. Torque's cry as he fell, knocking him off balance. Rocks coming up to meet him as he fell...

'Blake. Blake, wake up.'

He jerked awake like a panic-stricken diver out of oxygen. Lissa's voice, her tone calm but firm and instantly grounding.

A wave of relief flooded over him as his eyes blinked open. Ghostly light from the muted TV screen lit the living room.

He was on the couch and she was perched on the arm rest, watching him with concern in those pretty eyes. He remembered coming out here, unable to find sleep in the study.

Relief quickly turned to a storm of humiliation and he started to lift his head, which felt like a ripe watermelon. *How long had she been watching him?*

'You okay?'

Her cool light fingers on his brow both soothed and embarrassed. A bloody rerun of last night.

He pushed her arm away. 'Yeah.' His mouth was dust dry. He didn't know if it was the result of being caught napping or the sight of her in nothing but that wispy white nightdress. In the TV's soft glow he could see the outline of her nipples against the sheer fabric.

He closed his eyes and imagined diving back into the cool, dark ocean.

'Are you still in pain?'

His eyes blinked open again. She was looking at his pack of prescription painkillers on the coffee table.

'No.' *Not the kind of pain you're referring to.* 'I'm fine.'

'You didn't sound fine.'

He swore silently to himself. Had he called out? Made an idiot of himself? Ignoring the vague residual dizziness, he pushed up, set his feet on the floor and said, 'How was the party? I didn't hear you come in.' He hadn't realised how he felt about her enjoying herself until he heard the sarcastic edge to his voice.

'If you didn't go, you'll never know.' She passed him a tumbler of water. 'Seems like you need this more than I do.'

He gulped half of it down, returned the glass to her. 'Thanks.'

Obviously in no hurry to go upstairs, she curled her feet beneath her and sipped at the water. 'Something horrible happened to bring you back to Oz after all this time. I've been wondering what.'

Right now he wondered the same thing about his choice of location to recuperate. He could have gone to Acapulco or Hawaii. Found some warm and willing local girl to recuperate with. But for some reason he'd yet to fathom, because it certainly wasn't for the love of family, he'd decided to return to Australia.

Bad things happened but he didn't want to talk about it. Not with the party girl who saw the world through a rainbow prism. What the hell would she know about real life? How could she ever understand what he did or why he did it? Nor did he want her to know. God knew, he wanted to protect her from all that.

And yet…he'd never had someone like Lissa interested enough in his life to ask. Maybe because he'd never been around a woman long enough. A strange warm sensation settled somewhere in the region of his heart.

'I'm not going to pretend I didn't hear you in your sleep. Post-traumatic stress isn't something to be ashamed of. Perhaps I could help,' she finished softly.

'*Post-traumatic stress?*' A rough laugh rasped up his throat. 'You don't know what the *hell* you're talking about. I get the occasional migraine, so what?' He pushed off the couch and headed for the stairs.

'Maybe you should let others do some looking out for you for a change,' she said behind him.

He reached the first step, didn't stop. 'With you around why would I need to?'

CHAPTER EIGHT

LISSA barely paused to breathe in the front garden's tropical scents as she stepped outside. The warm Mooloolaba morning wrapped around her but she barely noticed. A gazillion thoughts were running through her mind—*not* Blake and that kiss that had turned her inside out last night.

Although she did spare more than a passing thought for his nightmares. His haunted groans in the dark of night had chilled her to the bone. But unless and until he was willing to talk, what could she do? She shook her head. And he'd called her stubborn?

So for now Blake's living room was top priority. The living room was her *focus*. She had furniture and soft furnishings to select and order, paint to choose…

But she glanced down at the unfamiliar sharp staccato on the paved garden path and slowed to admire her sassy red sling-backs. Nice. They brought a smile to her lips. She'd not bought a thing for over three months. Even if they were only bargain basement, they were shiny and brand spanking new.

'Lissa.'

She heard her name spoken in that deep sexy drawl and saw Blake coming through the front gate. No sign of last night's terrors in those azure eyes. As he jogged across the lawn towards her every other thought flew out of her mind.

She came to a halt, her pulse doing a blip at the blinding sight of all that exposed bronzed skin. His upper arms gleamed with sweat, his navy blue vest-top was dark and damp. Short shorts revealed tanned, toned muscular thighs peppered with dark masculine hair.

Last night he'd pressed those thighs against hers.

She forgot she was on a mission. Forgot she had no time to waste, no time to linger over mere distractions. Even if the distraction was Blake Everett, with his musky scent wafting towards her. He looked like some sort of divine being sent from above. She blew out a heartfelt breath. Her shoes weren't the only things worth a second look around here.

'Wait up, I'm coming with you.' He was watching her as he approached and she knew by the way his eyes suddenly darkened that he was thinking about last night too. *You're not ready for what I'd like to do to you.*

Until he'd walked off.

Dragging her gaze away, she lifted her chin. His loss. 'No time,' she told him. She didn't want him with her, reminding her of whatever shared delights he'd decided she wasn't ready for and taking her mind off what she needed to buy. She keyed the remote to raise the roller door, then unlocked her car and tossed her bag on the front passenger seat.

'Are you sure that's all?' He studied her far too astutely while he lifted a bottle of water to his lips.

'What else would it—?'

'Blake?'

Lissa turned at the interruption to see Gilda from next door slipping through the front gate.

'Blake?' she called again. 'It *is* you!'

'Gilda Matilda!' His face broke into a broad relaxed smile, something he hadn't bestowed on Lissa, she noted with a curious feeling in the pit of her stomach as he changed direction and jogged towards the woman.

Flawlessly made-up, their neighbour wore a stunning white

sundress that no doubt came from some exclusive European collection. Lissa, in her new off-the-rack red skirt and cream jacket, instantly felt outclassed.

Blake leaned down, dropped a kiss on her cheek. 'You're still living here, I see.'

'Yes. And about time you came home, you long-lost sailor, you.' The dark-haired woman returned the kiss and gave him a heartfelt hug, the clutch of rings on the third finger of her left hand sparkling in the light. She turned and smiled Lissa's way. 'Hello, Lissa. How are you? I didn't realise you two knew each other.'

'Hi, Gilda. Yes, we knew each other in Surfers. It was a long time ago.' She glanced at Blake and saw something flicker in his gaze before he turned his attention back to their neighbour.

Lissa wandered towards them. She wanted to watch their interaction and see if it was just herself he didn't let in on his life's details.

Gilda beamed up at him. 'Well, what extraordinary activities have you been up to all this time?'

'I can see what *you've* been up to.'

Neatly diverting attention away from himself. Again.

His gaze dropped to the woman's gently rounded belly. 'Congratulations. Or have you popped out a couple of others since I last saw you?'

She laughed, breathless and happy. 'No. This is our first.' Her gaze softened and turned inwards and her voice grew almost reverent. 'It's a miracle. Fifteen years of trying and now I'm six months along. I still can't believe it.'

'You've waited a long time, Gil. Enjoy it.'

'Oh, I am. Every minute.' Her smile flashed wider. 'I'm in the throes of preparing the nursery. It's a girl and I can't decide whether to go with traditional pink or something completely unexpected. Whatever we decide, it's got to be something spectacular. But I guess you men are all the same.' She flapped a hand and smiled knowingly at Lissa. 'Put off by women's talk of nurseries.'

'Maybe your neighbour can help you out.'

'Oh?'

'Lissa's an interior designer and, believe me, you'll want to see her ideas.' He cast a conspiratorial smile Lissa's way. 'She's working on my living room at present, but I'm sure she'll find time to fit you into her schedule.'

'Really?' Gilda's eyes lit up. 'I had no idea, Lissa. What a timely surprise. And I'd love your input.'

Lissa's spirits soared and she cast Blake a grateful glance. What better opportunity would come her way than the chance to impress this wealthy suburban socialite with her expertise?

'I'd be happy to give you some options to consider, Gilda. Would this afternoon be a convenient time for me to look at the room?'

'Oh, that'd be wonderful. Shall we say 2:00 p.m.?'

'That'll be fine. I'll see you then.'

Gilda paused, her eyes darting between both of them as if deciding whether they were an item or not. 'Are you two doing anything tomorrow evening? I'm having a little party and I'd love it if you could both come.'

'We'd be delighted,' Blake answered for both of them.

'Can we bring something?' Lissa offered and immediately wished she'd kept her naïve mouth shut. Gilda didn't do anything so simple as pot-luck dinners.

'Just your wallets,' she said with a grin. 'It's a fundraiser for childhood cancer awareness, so it's gold tie or gold ribbon for you, Blake, and a gold dress, Lissa.'

Oh. Not even a semi-formal occasion then, but one of her famous extravaganzas. Obviously Gilda assumed everyone had a gold gown hanging in the closet. Her society friends probably did. Lissa wanted to go. It was an exciting, timely opportunity, but who'd give her a second glance in her chain store's little black dress?

But Blake…he wasn't a party kind of guy. She could see it in his stance, in the set of his jaw. He'd accepted because he knew it was a chance for her to make some contacts.

'About tomorrow night…' she began as they waved Gilda goodbye and walked towards the car. 'I—'

'I suspect this type of party's not exactly your thing but—'

'That's *not* what I was going to say.' At the car door, she swung round to look at him. 'If you'd rather not attend, I can go alone.'

He stared her down. 'Not a chance.' His fingers curved over the door frame as he held it open for her. 'Now hop in. You've got shopping to do.'

She wanted to thank him but she knew now that it would make him uncomfortable.

'Why couldn't it be a simple black tie dinner?' she moaned, climbing in. 'I don't have a suitable dress and I'm so busy today.' She slid the key into the ignition. 'I have an appointment to look at office furniture…' she glanced at her watch '…in half an hour.'

'Not much point looking at outfitting the shop if you don't have clients. You've got two days. Plenty of time to look at dresses.'

'What about your room? That's a priority.'

'You can do both. I've every confidence in you.'

'Gold, for heaven's sake.' She turned the key and the old engine, badly in need of a service, coughed into life. 'Where will I find a gold dress?' More to the point, where would she find one that didn't cost an arm and a leg?

'You're a woman, you'll find one. Use the new account. We'll claim it as a business expense.'

'We can do that?'

He shook his head. 'Let me handle the finances for now,

Lissa. And see if you can find me a gold tie while you're at it,' he said. And swung the door shut.

Lissa pulled into the drive at two minutes to two. Leaving her supplies in the car, she rushed inside. Blake was nowhere to be seen so she grabbed her portfolio, then hurried next door to Gilda's impressive home.

'Hello again, Lissa, it's good of you to come.' Gilda held the door wide. 'I'm so looking forward to hearing your ideas.'

Lissa smiled all the way down to her toes. 'I'm happy to help out.'

Gilda ushered Lissa through to the spacious living area overlooking the pool. Every surface from the polished furniture to the marble floors and gold fittings gleamed. Urns of flowers filled the air with fresh fragrance. A cleaning service was in full swing on the patio.

'Preparations for tomorrow night,' Gilda explained, indicating a seat on a silk upholstered couch.

'I'm surprised you have the time, being pregnant and all.' Then again, having a cleaning service no doubt helped.

She set her portfolio carefully on the marble topped coffee table and said, 'Before we get started, I'd like to do my bit and donate a portion of my services for the nursery makeover towards your cause tomorrow night.'

A pot of steaming aromatic coffee and a jug of orange juice sat on a tray on the sideboard along with a plate of Kourabiedes, Greek shortbread biscuits that Lissa loved. Gilda picked it up and set it down in front of them. 'That's a thoughtful gesture, Lissa, are you sure?'

'Of course.' She knew without asking that Blake would be the kind of man who'd wholeheartedly approve.

'Thank you so much, you're very generous.' Gilda lifted the pot. 'Coffee?'

'Yes, please.'

'It's lovely to see Blake back home again after all this time.' Her voice softened at the mention of his name.

'You two seem close.' Lissa took the proffered cup, hoping to hide the colour she could feel in her cheeks. She shouldn't have asked. It was none of her business. She was here in a professional capacity.

'Yes. We are.' Gilda watched Lissa with a woman's understanding in her eyes while she poured herself a glass of juice. 'You probably don't know, because he's not the kind of man to tell, but he saved my life.'

'Really?' Lissa's cup stopped halfway to her lips. 'What happened?'

'Blake was living on the houseboat at the time. I slipped on the pool surround, broke my leg and fell in. It was the housekeeper's day off. If he hadn't heard my calls and come to my rescue I'd have drowned.'

'Oh, my goodness. You were lucky.'

'Indeed I was. It could have stopped there, but no. He helped me through the two months when I was housebound on crutches. The housekeeper came in daily, of course, and I had a nurse for a while, but Blake provided the company.

'We were both keen chess players and loved adventure movies so that passed time, but, more than that, we were both lonely. Stefan was away on business for weeks at a time and Blake's father...' She waved him off. 'And his mother was too busy to notice.'

Gilda's mouth pursed as if she'd bitten into a sour pomegranate. 'As much as I respected Rochelle's charitable work, I couldn't come to grips with how she neglected her only child.' She shook her head, setting her earrings jangling. 'There was Rochelle with a son she'd never taken the time to get to know, and I'd have given anything for a baby yet I couldn't get pregnant.'

Blake had been a neglected child? No wonder he'd closed

up when she'd praised his mother's tireless charity work. Yet he'd never said a bad word about her.

And here was Lissa with a brother who'd given up his teenage years for her to make a loving home, to keep her safe. Blake hadn't had that security, nor obviously had he known the feeling of being loved as he grew up.

'So there we were,' Gilda continued. 'A bit of an odd pair to the rest of the world. But there was honesty and I like to think there was a trust between us despite the difference in our ages. Stefan thinks the world of him.'

Lissa felt an odd twinge around her heart. It seemed he wasn't an island. He confided in someone after all. Just not Lissa. And why would he? she asked herself. The last time she'd seen him she'd been thirteen.

And when it came right down to it, what would be the point? He was leaving.

'Then he joined the navy.'

Gilda's words had Lissa's thoughts spinning in another direction. 'Was that a sudden decision?'

'He spoke of it often enough, but in the end, yes, it was.'

Janine.

Gilda eyed Lissa over her glass and both knew what wasn't being said. 'You can be sure if he'd made a mistake he'd have stayed to fix it.'

Lissa looked down at her cup. Maybe he had stayed. A couple of days, a quick private trip to a clinic, problem solved. But even as the thought came to her, she knew it couldn't be true. She'd learned more about Blake in the past couple of days than she'd ever known. It wasn't in his nature to run away from his problems.

She could feel the other woman's gaze and set her eggshell-fragile gold-rimmed cup on its saucer with the faintest tremor. 'Of course he would have.'

She wasn't here for a history lesson and she wasn't going

to talk to Gilda about her own relationship with Blake. That would be unprofessional.

She reached for her portfolio. 'Why don't you have a look through this? Then you can show me the nursery and we can start things happening.'

When Blake arrived home early evening, he found Lissa cross-legged on the floor in the living room surrounded by a maze of sketches, designs and scribbled notes.

She looked up as he approached, taking in his sand-covered legs. 'Hi. You've been to the beach, I see.'

'Thought I'd test the surf—wind's up today and there was a good swell.' He sat down opposite her, against the wall, plonked his damp towel and two boxes on the floor. Now he'd made up his mind Lissa was off-limits, he concentrated on thinking of her as a friend. A business partner. Easier said than done when her perfume filled his nostrils and his eyes couldn't seem to focus on anything but her tanned knees. 'How did it go with Gilda?'

'Very well.' Her eyes glowed with enthusiasm. 'She's going with a fairy-tale theme. Pastel colours. I saw this gorgeous little pumpkin-shaped cot today…I can't wait to get started.'

'If you want to postpone this room—'

'I can do both. You told me so and it's good practice. I've already organised the painters here for next week and the furniture's been ordered.'

For the first time since he'd come back he took a good look at the room, visions of the way it used to look swimming before his eyes. 'I can't wait to see this transformed. It always reminds me of…'

She looked up. 'What?' she asked softly.

'Dad used to have his poker nights in here. Four nights a week. I remember the first night I came to live with him. I was fourteen. Mum had gone overseas so I was sent to Dad's.' He leaned his head back against the wall, the bad old memories coming thick and fast. 'Dad had forgotten to pick me up at the bus so I walked. With my luggage.' He closed his eyes, felt the old tension grab at the base of his skull.

'Go on,' she urged. Her voice was gentle. Oddly calming, like the trickle of water over a moss-covered rock. So easy to let it flow over him.

'The place was a garbage tip. Beer bottles, pizza boxes, spilled cigarette ash, you name it. I thought after his buddies left he'd clean it up, but no. It was still there a week later.

'The rest of the house was just as bad. In the end I couldn't stand it so I asked if I could live on the houseboat. He was more than happy with the arrangement. I taught myself to cook. At least I could study in peace...'

A long silence followed. 'I never knew my father,' Lissa said into the hiatus.

He opened his eyes. 'What?'

'That man you knew wasn't my father. My biological father was just passing through town one summer. I must have looked liked him because Dad hated me. I was a reminder of my mother's infidelity.'

She smiled suddenly. 'This sounds like True Confession time.'

He smiled back, feeling as if a load had been lifted off his shoulders. Feeling something like companionship. He'd never told anyone his troubles. Somehow Lissa had got him to talk. To open up. And it felt good. Freeing. Connected. 'How about we go eat some pizza? I saw a live band setting up in an outdoor café on the esplanade. Oh, wait up.' He picked up the boxes, reached over and set them in front of her. 'This first.'

Lissa reached for the larger one. 'What is it?' When he didn't answer, she opened the flaps. Her jewellery box sat on the top. 'Oh...' Eyes filling, she pulled it out and opened it. It was still damp but she lifted out the bluebird brooch. 'This was Mum's. You rescued my things.' She could barely see him through the tears.

'I had the boat moved yesterday while you were at the shop. I didn't get everything, most of it was too far gone, but the stuff in the box was salvageable. And what I thought you might like.'

She ran her hands over a white porcelain bowl with blue dolphins around the edge. It had been a gift from Crystal when she'd moved here. He'd thought enough to sort through her things. 'Thank you. So much.'

She opened the other box. It was full of new lingerie. All different colours. Sexy as sin. She sifted through the silky bras and panties, her cheeks blooming with heat. She found two nightgowns. A teal blue and a deep gold.

'I noticed you didn't buy enough stuff yesterday,' he said, his voice oddly gruff.

The heat intensified. 'How did you know my size?'

'I checked the ones you bought. If you'll forgive me for looking.'

'Oh, yes…and they're beautiful.' She bit her lip. 'I don't know what to say.'

'Your smile's enough.' He reached out a hand, lifted her chin up. 'You should smile more often—with those eyes, like you're doing now.' For a fleeting moment his gaze turned almost reverent.

And she felt her heart melt.

Then he pushed up, as if uncomfortable with the moment. 'Let's go eat.'

CHAPTER NINE

FOR this evening, at least, it was enough to simply share pizza and enjoy each other's company while the waves thumped on the beach. To see the ocean change from aqua to indigo to black and to watch Blake finally relax as they listened to the jazz quartet.

It gave Lissa time to think about what Blake had told her about his father. No wonder he was obsessed with order and tidiness. She resolved to make more of an effort while she was staying in his house.

When the band packed up, they drove home and went their separate ways to bed. The ever-present hum between them was still there, but also a feeling that barriers had been lowered a little. As if a bridge had been crossed.

Lissa spent the following day working on the living room and plans for Gilda's nursery. Blake offered to be at the shop in the morning to receive the office supplies she'd ordered. He refused her suggestion to accompany her shopping in the afternoon and went surfing instead.

The last item on her list was what to wear to Gilda's party.

He should have insisted on going shopping with her, Blake decided that evening as he stood at the bottom of the staircase looking up.

He resisted the urge to loosen the gold bow tie that threatened to strangle him as he stared at the woman descending the stairs.

No way he'd have agreed to the skinny tube of shimmering gold lamé and its row upon row of bright coins that jingled and winked in the light as she moved. What there was of it. Her 'find' was strapless and covered precious little of those sun-kissed thighs that he'd thought about constantly since that first night on the houseboat.

His brow wrinkled. Except now she was coming closer he could see that those thighs seemed to be dusted with something like…gold dust… She'd threaded gold ribbons through her hair and piled it on top of her head and he noticed her shoulders gleamed with the same fine gold glitter as her thighs. Strappy gold stilettos completed the look.

An uncomfortable heat burst into flame below the surface of his skin and spread all over his body like a rash. How was he going to get through the evening without thinking about what other priceless treasures she had hidden beneath that slinky scrap of fabric that looked as if she'd simply wound it around her? He was going to spend the whole night wondering if it came off as easily.

'What do you think?' she said, reaching the bottom of the stairs.

'It's…certainly eye-catching.' Not to mention snagging on a few other sensitive body parts.

'That's the idea.' She shimmied like a belly-dancer and the whole thing glittered and jingled. 'Not bad for a few moments' work and a couple of quick threads, huh?'

Quick threads? He swallowed. It was held together with a few threads? 'You…constructed it yourself?'

'I'm not wasting money when I don't have to. I found it in an off-cut bin at a belly-dance studio.' She held up a hand and thin gold bangles danced along her arm. 'No, don't ask how it holds together. And no, it's not going to unravel. At least I hope not.'

By God, so did he.

'But just in case…' She flicked at a string of tiny gold safety pins tucked discreetly into the top.

Music, voices and a tinkle of feminine laughter drifted from next door as she reached down to adjust a strap on her sandal then straightened. 'Still, I hardly think I'll be noticed among the Beautiful People.'

Blake gave his head a mental shake. It was she who was beautiful, and, going on his memory of these charity dos, the majority of party-goers were generally over fifty. She was going to give some old geezer a heart attack.

If he wasn't careful she was going to give *him* a heart attack.

'Nice look.' Her gaze slid over his dark suit rather too slowly for his comfort. 'Do you get a lot of wear out of that attire in the navy? Lots of military functions to attend, admirals to salute? Wives and daughters to charm?'

He didn't miss the glimmer of dark in those clear eyes at her pointed mention of the last.

'But of course,' she ran on before he could get a word in. She shook her head and a single auburn curl beside her ear bobbled. 'You'd wear one of those gorgeous naval dress uniforms, wouldn't you? All blinding white with gold buttons.' Her gaze clouded momentarily as if she saw him dressed so.

And if they didn't get going, he was going to have to reach out and smooth that curl behind her ear…and then…his stomach tightened…they'd be in a world of trouble. He turned away, towards the door. 'Shall we go?'

Lissa tried not to look impressed but Gilda and Stefan's magnificent mansion had been transformed into a Grecian paradise. In the balmy air, multicoloured lanterns hung overhead and reflected like fireworks in the sapphire pool while guests wearing the latest in gold designer fashion feasted on a multitude of delicacies and drank champagne from sparkling crystal glasses.

The patio doors had been flung open and, inside, tall orchid spikes speared from gilt-edged vases set on ornate polished mahogany or marble pedestals, their exotic scents mingling with expensive French perfume. Somewhere a blues singer accompanied a clarinet, crooning come-hither World War Two songs.

She didn't have time to absorb it all because as soon as they arrived they were handed drinks and Lissa was whisked away by her hostess to meet a trio of women who'd known Blake's mother, wealthy middle-aged matrons dripping with diamonds. And gold. It was like being in the house of Midas.

Blake was still watching her as she cast him a backward glance. He raised his glass. *Enjoy the evening*, he seemed to say. *I intend to.* From the corner of her eye she saw why: tall, blonde and busty heading his way.

So there was Lissa, hearing all about Muriel someone's latest fashion disaster while waiting for a lull in the conversation so she could get a word in about her business—*their* business—while he indulged in…whatever it was he was doing behind her back.

'Oh, and did you hear that the Bakers from Surfers heard Rochelle's son was coming and cancelled at the last minute?'

Lissa's ears pricked up.

But at sharp glances from her friends, the woman who'd delivered the news found a sudden interest in the bottom of her crystal flute. 'Oops. Sorry.'

The words, obviously aimed Lissa's way and tossed out with malicious amusement, stunned her. Then filled her with anger. A red-hot ball in her chest. She felt it build and build until she felt as if she might explode.

This was Blake they were maligning. Who'd risked his life for fourteen years and suffered God only knew what horrors to keep their country safe. A man she'd learned was much more than she'd ever given him credit for. Once upon a time she'd listened to the rumours too. She didn't know the circumstances with Janine. She didn't need to—she knew Blake.

And she'd trust him with her life.

The sudden realisation stunned her anew. She'd never thought it possible to feel that way about a man again. Armed with that knowledge, she took a sip from her glass before seizing the opportunity in the lull to ask, 'Are you talking about Janine?'

There was a startled 'Was she a friend of yours?'

'No.' She looked straight into the other woman's eyes. 'But Blake is.'

More glance-swapping. Frowns exchanged. A conspiracy of silence. Awkward moment.

'I hate innuendoes and gossip, don't you?' She tilted her champagne flute towards the women, looking at each one in turn. 'Especially when we all know it's based on lies and hearsay and spread by ignorance.'

For a few tense seconds there wasn't a murmur. Not so much as a flicker of movement from any of them. It was as if they'd been turned to stone. Or solid gold.

Then the oldest of the three smiled slowly. 'Well said, my dear. I like a girl who's not afraid to stand up for herself.' Looking Lissa up and down, she nodded approvingly. 'My name's Jocelyn. Rochelle Everett was one of my closest friends. So tell us how you met Blake and then we'd love to hear all about your new business.' She turned to the others. 'Wouldn't we, ladies?'

Lissa mingled with the crowd, feeling extraordinarily satisfied. Jocelyn had given her a business card and told her to make an appointment to look at renovating her kitchen. She made two other appointments with potential clients over the next hour.

Finally, excusing herself from the airless room, she made her way outside to the patio and the younger set. A couple of women in gold bikinis were splashing about in the pool and laughing.

And like any other unattached male, where else would Blake be but watching on from the decking? Tossing their big plastic ball back to them with a grin?

The pain that twisted beneath her ribcage was nothing to do with the way they were deliberately throwing it in his direction, nor the fact that he was obviously enjoying the attention. It was just the way she'd tied the length of fabric too tight beneath her breasts.

He must have felt her glare because he looked up and their eyes met over the cavorting mermaids. He'd removed his jacket and his white shirt clung to his body like a second skin, making his skin appear even more bronzed. She refused to notice. *Fun for some.* She was sweating contacts and appointments while he was sweating…bimbos.

Turning away, she headed for the nearest waiter.

What? Blake mouthed, watching her. Too late. She was already stalking off, disappearing among the crowd, her undulating gold-wrapped hips a magnificent memory.

He rolled shoulders suddenly gone tense. He'd kept out of the way to give Lissa a chance to do her thing. He knew it was important to her that she make a success of this on her own. She wanted independence. He was giving it to her. Though he had to admit he had no inclination to schmooze with his mother's cronies unless they found him. To his vexation, a few of them had. But he'd played nice. For Lissa's sake.

And all he'd got was a glare for his trouble.

Frowning, he skirted the pool in pursuit. What had he done to tick her off?

He caught sight of her near one of the glittering supper

tables, her expression animated as she spoke to an elderly woman with lavender hair, and found himself stalling. To watch her, simply watch her.

The grown-up Lissa wasn't what he'd expected. And different from the other women he'd associated with over the years. She didn't fawn all over him; she had too much dignity. Nor did she give herself unrealistic airs. She was down-to-earth. She had guts. Moxy. Pride. When she'd lost her boat and almost everything she'd owned, she'd picked herself up and moved on.

And...*for pity's sake*...when it came down to sheer sexuality, she attracted him like no other.

At that moment some of the guests nearby moved away, giving him a clear view of those attributes. Feminine curves. Shapely legs.

How would those thighs feel wrapped around his waist?

Lust clutched him low and hard and his vision blurred. He grabbed a beer from a waiter's tray as he headed towards her. When he looked her way again a dude in a shiny gold suit had struck up a conversation with her.

Blake scowled. Typical indoors type—pale skin and smooth manicured hands. Wrong haircut. Apparently it didn't bother Lissa because her eyes sparkled and that luscious mouth curved as she laughed at something he said.

Then, as if she felt the heat of Blake's gaze, she turned her head slightly and their eyes met. A ribbon of heat arced across the space between them.

But then Midas Man shifted, leaned closer, blocking Blake's view. Simmering with impatience, he threw back his beer, plunked the near-empty glass on a marble pedestal bedecked with gold-painted leaves and closed in.

He circled behind her so that he could lay his hand on the middle of her back and lean in close to catch the heat of her skin and inhale her scent. *To claim possession.* He felt her tense beneath his touch. Then she jerked round, and those stunning eyes blinked. Just once.

'Blake.'

She sounded surprised. As if she wasn't expecting to see him there. Damn it. Clearly that look they'd exchanged less than thirty seconds ago hadn't meant what he'd thought it meant. His impatience reached flash point.

Ignoring her conversation partner, Blake leaned even closer, so that his lips grazed the tip of her ear, and murmured, 'We need to leave.'

'Now? But—'

'Something's come up.'

'Oh? What?'

A heart-pounding beat. The tiny space between them crack-led with something like static electricity. He knew she knew by the spark of realisation in her eyes, which were focused carefully on his. 'Oh.'

'And it needs immediate attention.'

She turned to the Midas Man. 'Excuse me…'

Her voice trailed off as Blake grabbed her hand and towed her away.

'What are you doing?' she muttered breathlessly.

'Saving you from terminal boredom.'

She shot a quick look behind her. 'That's mean, he was very sweet…not to mention mega-rich with a mansion to renovate. And we're here in a professional capacity…'

'Don't change the subject,' he snapped. His pulse was drumming in his ears. 'We're here as Gilda's friends.'

'What subject?'

Ignoring her question, he continued tugging her away from the crowd towards a wide chandeliered hallway, past alcoves where Grecian alabaster goddesses posed until he came to a narrower passage. He found the nearest closed door, pulled her inside and slammed it shut behind them. The party noise evaporated. A lone gold candle flickered on the bathroom vanity and he got a glimpse of his own reflection and Lissa's wide eyes before he turned away.

The sound of the lock turning sounded preternaturally loud in the sudden silence and he heard her sharp indrawn breath as she pressed a hand to her chest.

'What's wrong?'

'I… You startled me for a moment.'

'You startle easily, party girl,' he murmured. He could feel the warmth of her body beneath her dress, the silken slide of her arm as he twisted her so that she was wedged between him and the door.

'What was all that stuff you said earlier about drumming up clients?' In the dim light he saw her eyes spark as she looked up at him and her voice took on a clipped edge. 'I noticed *you* weren't d—'

'Shut up and kiss me,' he said, and laid his lips on that luscious mouth as he'd wanted to do all evening.

CHAPTER TEN

As HIS lips claimed hers, everything else flew out of Lissa's mind except that this was Blake kissing her and she was kissing him back. His hands on her shoulders, her waist, her hips. His body heat searing her from neck to knee and every place between. His forest-fresh cologne and the musky scent of clean male sweat.

But mostly it was the way he kissed her. Hot with impatience, rich with desire. And with a fast-burning energy that threatened to spontaneously combust her right where she stood. His tongue plunged between her lips then withdrew, and again, making love to her mouth over and over until she felt her legs turning to jelly.

Somehow her desperate arms found their way around his neck, and she clung to him as if he were the one dependable reality in a world gone momentarily crazy.

He lifted his head and watched her through heavy-lidded eyes as he slid one hard palm between her thighs. Anticipation danced along her nerve endings, heat shimmered on her skin and she shivered all over. 'Yes...'

He continued to watch her as his hand moved higher. As his long fingers found the edge of her panties and crept beneath. As his thumb stroked her swollen sex, just once. Liquid heat rushed to her core and she sucked in a sharp breath as her intimate flesh quivered. 'Oh, *yes*.' Her head fell back against the door and her eyes slid shut.

'Do you like that?' His breath tickled as he nibbled her ear lobe.

'You know…a woman…who doesn't?' She wondered vaguely whether she was going to hyperventilate.

He stroked her again, then dipped a finger inside her. Drew it out slowly—a long smooth glide that sent her soaring halfway to the moon. He slid in once more. Two fingers. Deeper, more insistent.

Ribbons of colour played behind her eyelids, she felt the familiar rippling sensation building, building… So soon…a mere touch and she was already on the edge…

'Look at me,' he demanded, his voice harsh.

As the wave crashed over her and her internal muscles contracted around his fingers she opened her eyes and tumbled into his gaze. Candle-light flickered over his features and the room smelled of lilacs. 'Yes, yes, yes-s-s.' She felt herself start to slide down the wall and clung tighter to his neck.

'Gotcha.' With his hands beneath her bottom, he lifted her so that she was pinned against the door. She started wrapping her legs around his waist until the harsh sound of fabric ripping filled the room.

'Oops.' Her slightly hysterical, trembly laugh seemed to ricochet off the tiled walls.

They both heard the tap on the door and turned to stone, Blake's hands clamped on her bottom.

'Excuse me…' An elderly woman's voice.

'Uh-oh,' Lissa whispered. 'Now we're in trouble.'

Another knock, louder. 'Is everything all right in there?'

'Everything's fine,' Blake answered smoothly.

Before Lissa could disengage her arms from around his neck, he was fumbling for the pins at her bodice. His hands brushed her breast as he worked. Her nipples took no account of the fact that she and Blake were locked in a bathroom and some old lady was right outside the door probably waiting to use the loo, and puckered up even more tightly against his palm.

He pressed the pins into her hand, then stepped back to give her room to fasten the frayed edges, but her fingers shook so badly she barely managed the task. 'I'm not sure it'll hold for long.'

'It doesn't need to.' His voice was tight and gruff as he took her firmly by the arm, unlocked the door. 'You first.'

'Why me?' she whispered back. Oh. She unlocked the door, pulled it open.

Gilda was waiting with a concerned elderly lady hovering behind her. 'Oh, Lissa. Blake…?' Her voice rose slightly on the last. 'Margaret heard noises…'

Lissa stifled a nervous giggle that bubbled up.

Blake stepped behind her, his hands on her shoulders, and she felt an immediate surge of guilty embarrassment. She knew her face proclaimed to the world what she'd just been enjoying. Heat climbed into her cheeks. She didn't dare look down at the hem of her dress.

But Blake, cool and in control, at least to outward appearances, said, 'Wardrobe malfunction,' his voice betraying none of the huskiness and dark passion she'd heard moments ago. 'I'm taking Lissa home.'

'Oh…that's probably best.' A tiny line creased Gilda's brow. Obviously the shredded reason for their sudden departure wasn't apparent to her, even if their exit from the bathroom together left little doubt as to what they'd been doing.

'Thank you for coming, and thank you, Blake, for your very generous cheque.'

'You're welcome. I hope it'll do some good.' He dropped his hands and edged Lissa along with a firm palm at her back, obviously mindful of the fragility of those pins and her super-stiletto shoes. 'Thanks for inviting us.'

'Um,' Lissa agreed, vaguely. Her power of speech seemed to have deserted her. ''Night.'

The moment they were away from prying eyes he swung her into his arms and carried her down the paved path. Under the street light his jaw was rigid, his eyes focused dead ahead. She could hear his heart thumping against her ear as he strode to the front door, keyed the security code and shouldered the door open.

He flicked on a light and they made it as far as the second stair—not far at all—before he bent his head and touched his brow to hers and said, 'Lissa,' in a strangled voice that spoke of barely restrained control.

He released her in such a way that her body slid slowly down the front of his, her feet landing on the step above where he stood. His lips were pressed together tight, eyes blazing with a passion that seared all the way through to her crazily beating heart and she wondered that it didn't stop altogether.

But then he said, 'Go on up to bed.'

Her heart did stop then, with a terrifying jolt before resuming its crazy rhythm. He didn't mean that. He *couldn't* mean that. Not after that mind-blowing trip to the moon he'd given her. Not with those eyes, not with that steel rod she'd felt as she'd slid down his rigid torso.

You're not ready for what I'd like to do to you.

Maybe she *should* go while she had the chance. Flee straight up those stairs to her room and lock the door tight.

Her legs barely held her upright but she remained where she was. This was Blake, and a night of pleasure in his arms beckoned. She stared him down. 'I'm not tired.'

A muscle in his jaw tightened and he growled through clenched teeth. 'Go, Lissa. Before I do something we'll both regret in the morning.'

'I'm not going anywhere.' Regrets were not on her agenda.

'You want me,' she said, and watched his eyes turn to smoke. 'And I want you.'

If they made love, she was going to fall hard. She was risking her heart. But hadn't her heart been his all along? 'I've always wanted you.'

She felt him go still beneath her palm. His entire body seemed to turn to stone. *That's right, Blake, think about that not-so-little confession.*

The impact of her words took a moment to sink in. 'Sweet heaven,' he groaned softly, and closed his eyes. 'You were only thirteen last time I saw you. For God's sake, go. Go now.'

'Blake, what I'm trying to say here is, it's not a whim,' she continued. 'It's n—'

'Do you realise what would have happened back in that room if Nanna Margaret hadn't knocked on the door and given me a moment to regain some sense? I'd have taken you where you stood without a moment's hesitation and to hell with the rest of the world.'

Lava geysered through her veins and she thought for one moment she might faint with the thrill.

'And with not one damn thought of protection,' he finished, his voice scraping like rough stone over her senses.

Her mind spun back to those rumours. The rumours she refused to believe. The rumours she'd condemned only hours ago. But even so, the heat cooled and congealed in her blood because there was one indisputable fact—he *had* been dating Janine.

Had he lost control with her? Had he been so driven, so lost, so crazy hot for her that he'd forgotten birth control? Sharp images of his hands, his mouth on the girl's flesh, that hard masculine *unprotected* part of him plunging into her where she stood tore at Lissa.

'And now?' Her throat was clogged, her voice tight. 'What, you've suddenly developed a conscience in the last few minutes?'

'No.' His eyes blazed. 'That's the problem, Lissa. You make me crazy. When I'm with you, when I'm anywhere near you, I don't *have* a conscience. And I don't seem to be able to function rationally.'

'And you need to be in control at all times.'

His non-answer and the blue flame in his eyes told her all she needed to know, but she could lure him over to the dark side. She could. 'You've been trying *not* to wonder how this dress comes off all night, haven't you?'

Blake didn't move a muscle. His eyes…it was as if they were glued in place. He could *not* tear them away from those sun-spangled thighs. The twist of gold and the curves beneath.

'It's one long strip of fabric,' she said. 'Like a scarf. You start at the bottom—or the top—and unwrap it. Like a birthday gift.'

Birthday gifts? His mother hadn't believed in such indulgences. Instead he'd been allowed to choose which charity he wanted to donate to. 'I'm warning you now, I don't do emotion, Lissa.'

'Fine. We won't do emotion. We'll just have sex.' She stepped out of her shoes.

Still facing him, she took a backward step, up one stair. Slowly, hypnotically, making the little coins on her dress jingle and drawing his gaze up and over her flat belly and full breasts. It also caused the air around her to eddy, bringing her sweet and sinfully tempting perfume to his nose.

The reincarnation of Circe, he thought, seducing him with a feast of the senses. Weaving a spell around him with those captivating eyes. Drawing him closer. Making his hand reach out in front of him as if it belonged to someone else.

But it wasn't someone else's fingers that tingled as they touched that warm flesh once more. And it was his hand that burned as it traced an invisible line inside the fabric and up the smooth line of her leg. Ankle, calf, the back of her knee. The long firm length of her outer thigh.

His fingers retraced their journey down to the tattered hem of her dress and closed over the fabric, knuckles brushing her skin and feeling the quiver run through her like a tiny electric current.

Need. This ferocious and urgent and *soul-deep* need... He'd never experienced anything remotely like it. One yank and he could have her naked. Sprawled on the stairs while he plunged into her, her precious innocence gone in a few seconds flat.

She deserved better. So much better. He closed his eyes briefly, then looked at her. 'I don't want to hurt you.'

A flash of something lit her eyes and a small frown puckered her brow. 'What do you mean...hurt me?'

'You're a virgin...and this...this... It isn't—'

Her eyes widened. *'Virgin?'*

'You mean you're not?' He stared at her while his mind reeled and his whole body tightened.

'Whatever gave you that idea?'

'You said... Never mind.'

'Blake.' A smile stole across her lips. 'I'm not a virgin. I haven't been one in quite a while. I've had a few lovers in my time—just don't tell Jared that. You really need to stop thinking of me as that kid you knew.'

'I don't,' he muttered, his blood surging south, pulse hammering in his ears. 'Believe me, I don't.'

He wound the lower end of the fabric around his hand, tightened his fingers into a fist and tugged. 'Come here.'

But she shook her head. 'I feel like a swim.' Her smile was wicked as she stepped past him on the step, twirling a circle as she went, the gold strip unravelling like a streamer behind her.

She continued whirling across the room towards the patio, shedding any inhibitions he'd thought she had along with her scarf. He saw that she was wearing a tiny triangle of tarnished gold lace, her luscious breasts spilling out of a matching strapless bra.

She ran out of scarf and jerked to a stop. Blake growled low in his throat and walked towards her, gathering up the fabric. Reeling her in. But before he got within reach she tossed her end to the floor and was off, flinging the patio doors wide.

Her bare bottom flashed in the light spilling from the house as she danced across the slate tiles. At the edge of the pool she turned and met his gaze. Peeled the bra off and threw it over her shoulder. Slid her hands down her hips, taking her gold thong with them.

He felt a momentary disappointment that she'd robbed him of the opportunity to perform the task himself, then again, he shrugged. What a view. He breathed out a sigh. *Per*fection. Every tempting hollow, every inviting curve.

'Stay right where you…' she smiled at him, then stepped backwards into the water '…are,' he finished.

She bobbed up again almost immediately, her eyes laughing. 'Feels good.' Her voice was as sultry as the night. 'Don't you want to feel good, Blake?'

Oh, yeah. 'Get out so I can see you.'

'Sure you don't want to join me in the water?'

'Maybe later.' He beckoned her. 'Out. Now.'

She shrugged and moved to the ladder, climbed out. Water sluiced off her body, leaving droplets clinging to her skin like diamonds, her dripping hair a dark crimson threaded with gold ribbons.

He didn't take his eyes off the glorious sight as he quickly stripped down to skin. He saw her eyes widen at the sight of his throbbing erection, felt the hot stroke of her gaze clear across the patio.

His mouth watered at the sight of her glistening nipples puckered up with the pool's chill. As he watched water gathered at the rosy tips and dripped onto the slate. Urgency whipped through his body like a loosened high-tension wire in a blustery wind, but he refused to hurry.

She was the birthday cake he'd never had and he was going to take his own sweet time over her and indulge. Before they were done he was going to sample every delectable square centimetre.

He stepped onto the soft emerald grass. 'Come here.'

She moved towards him with that same stunning grace he'd seen when she'd danced. And then she was there, looking up at him with wide turquoise eyes.

'You're a temptress, you know that, don't you?'

'Uh-huh.' She was breathing fast, her breasts rising and falling. 'Did I tempt you?'

'Oh, yeah.' He smoothed his hands over her damp shoulders.

She gasped softly at the first contact and her hands slid into his hair. Her musky feminine scent with a hint of chlorine surrounded him, drawing him closer. He lowered his lips to her neck. The taste of her skin was sweet and fresh.

His hands took a journey over smooth firm breasts. Beneath his palms he felt her hardened nipples. He rolled them between thumbs and forefingers, heard her whisper something as he closed his lips over one perfect bud.

'Touch me again, Blake.' Her voice had turned from teasing to seriously turned on. She shifted beneath his lips, lifting her hands to tug at pins and ribbons so that her hair fell loose and wet over her shoulders, a wildfire of curls. 'Come inside me.'

Her impatience urged him to take her now where they stood and his own need chafed at him but he would *not* be rushed.

Lifting his head, he slid his palms over her hips and let his gaze wander. Naked had never looked so perfect and he drank in the sight before him like a man too long between beers. He could feel the need radiating from her like a blush and lifted his gaze to hers.

Clear eyes stared back at him, drenched with desire, and

the air around her shimmered like the gold she'd dusted on her shoulders. His body burned with something more than lust. She was feminine perfection but she was still tiny. And she looked even smaller naked, and so fine-boned and fragile, as if she'd break with one touch.

'Don't think about whatever it is you're thinking about,' Lissa whispered, her heart racing as she leaned forward to place her lips on his chest. Circling his hard male nipples and learning their texture. Bending her head and discovering their taste—salt and sweet and...Blake.

He groaned with a sound that was part pleasure, part pain. 'You're exquisite,' he muttered with an almost savage growl. 'And, God...what I want to do with you...'

Twining her arms about his neck, she looked deep into his eyes. 'Glad to hear you still feel that way.'

And then he was sweeping her legs from beneath her and laying her on the softly damp grass. It was like falling end-lessly into her dreams.

Silvery moonshine slanted across one sharp cheekbone as he stared down at her. Then darkness as his head blocked the light and his mouth closed over hers with a deep desperate kiss that told her he was as lost in the moment as she.

Her water-chilled, droplet-covered body all but steamed against the heat of his skin. She revelled in his rich, dark taste, her tongue sliding against his as she traced the hard planes of his shoulders with her fingertips, the bunched muscles of his upper arms. Loving the rasp of masculine hair against her breasts, her belly.

The hard hot length of his masculinity surged against her hip, but he made no move to use it. He lifted his head and watched his hand as he stroked a slow path from her neck and over one tingling nipple, then lower, to circle her navel with one feather-light fingertip. Her body arched instinctively against his touch like a flower searching for sunlight.

She held her breath… 'Oh, yes…' Finally, finally, oh… Her thighs fell open and she heard herself moan, closed her eyes and prepared to give herself up to the ultimate sensation for the second time in less than an hour.

'So hot,' he murmured as he opened her and pushed a finger inside her. 'So wet for me.'

His last possessive words and their simple truth squeezed at her heart. 'Yes,' she murmured back. *Only for you*.

Gentle. She'd never experienced such gentleness. She could feel the strength and the tension hum through his body and knew he was holding back. Unlike Todd who'd always raced to the finish without a thought for her needs. And unlike the man who'd betrayed her, she trusted Blake, wanted him to lose that control, wanted that heat and strength inside her. 'Blake…now.'

Eyes still closed, she trembled, poised on the thin edge between anticipation and something like fear. Fear that he'd stop.

He did. Then he swore, a strangled sound that had her opening her eyes. His expression was frozen. 'Protection.'

'I'm on the pill,' she gasped. 'I take care of my own.'

'My kind of girl,' he muttered and lowered himself slowly on top of her.

He slid inside her in one long smooth motion and her entire being quivered with the new intimacy. The pressure invaded her, expanding and radiating to every part of her body in a thousand glorious explosions and sending her hurtling towards climax.

The shock of the speed staggered her and she opened her eyes so she could see him, to know it was him inside her as she crested that stunning peak. His jaw was tight, his face almost grim with intensity as he watched her fly away.

'Blake,' she whispered. The tension spiralled then snapped

and she felt her limbs grow limp, sated. She'd been waiting her whole life for this moment. *Welcome home.*

But, oh...no... She couldn't let herself think that way. She'd told him herself that it was just sex. His home, and his *emotionless* life, were on the ocean.

Still...his eyes glittered like fire in the dimness as he moved inside her. And, at last, at long last, *she* was the woman who'd made them turn to indigo.

She was the woman whose hands skimmed that hot, taut skin, whose legs were wrapped around those powerful thighs as he plunged deeper, faster. She was the woman who arched against him as he found his own climax. He dropped down beside her and she cradled his head against her breast in the aftermath.

'Lissa...' Her name, murmured in that deep voice, curled around her like a sigh and told her more than he'd ever say.

So she could enjoy the masculine texture of his jaw against her breast a little while longer, she touched the side of his face and smiled to herself while the night's tiny wildlife rustled nearby. She could smell the fragrance of the new-mown grass, feel its soft scratchiness against her skin.

The sky was alive with stars, and, in the east, the waning moon on its ascent. Her life with all its twists and turns was suddenly, and for the moment at least, perfect.

He looked up at her, eyes searching hers. 'No regrets?'

'Not one.' She traced his eyebrows. 'You?'

He stroked a finger over her nipple, watched it pucker. 'You were amazing.'

Which didn't answer her question, but he was the master of evasion and she wasn't about to spoil it, especially when she felt him harden again against her hip. Already. 'It was pretty amazing, wasn't it?'

'So...' He leaned up on one elbow. His eyes were the colour of smoke and he smiled a wicked sailor's smile as he curled one hand around the back of her neck. 'What do you say we do it again? In a bed this time?'

'Or the pool.'

'I like the way you think.' He rose, sweeping her up with him and heading to the water. 'We've got all night. We can enjoy both.'

CHAPTER ELEVEN

YOU had to worship a man who brought you breakfast in bed on a silver tray after a night of carnal pleasure, especially if he was naked and built like a bronzed god. A bowl of fruit, poached eggs—hard—with toast and jam to follow. In addition to his pot of tea, he'd made her an instant coffee. She'd have preferred her early morning latté but he'd not familiarised himself with that piece of kitchen technology. And it wasn't early. It was well after midday.

'So what made you think I was a virgin?' she asked, around a mouthful of mango.

He grinned at her. 'Could be because you mentioned "after all this time" the first time I kissed you.'

She smiled, took another bite. 'That's because I'd only been waiting years and couldn't believe you were attracted to me.'

Blake leaned forward, licked the juice from her mouth. 'Believe it.' He smoothed her back and studied her. She wore the smile of a well-satisfied woman. 'You know, you have the most beautiful eyes I ever saw.' He hesitated. 'But some-times…there's something there…like last night, when I hauled you into the bathroom at Gilda's.'

Her smile dropped away. 'I was surprised, that's all.'

He shook his head. 'Not all.'

Something didn't fit with her normally casual, easy-going

style. And he was absolutely, one-hundred-per-cent through seeing that startled, hunted look that stole into her eyes at odd times. All the more concerning when she was usually warm, willing and with him on so many levels.

A man, he was sure of it. 'What happened, Lissa? Who hurt you?'

'No one important.' Her eyes turned dull, flat. Distant.

A knot tightened in his chest. He touched her chin lightly and turned her head so she had no choice but to face him. 'What did he do? Tell me,' he demanded, when she didn't reply.

'I don't want to talk about it.'

'Would you rather I asked your brother?'

She stiffened, her eyes widening. 'You wouldn't.'

'If it helped, yes, I damn well would.'

'Jared doesn't know anything about him and I want to keep it that way.' She pushed his hand away. 'I'm not a kid and I don't need him or anyone else to fight my battles. He was a guy I met a year ago. Todd. We had a relationship.' Hesitation. 'An abusive relationship. He got a real kick out of seeing me scared.'

Anger didn't begin to describe what boiled up inside him as he looked at Lissa. So small and delicate. So vulnerable to the wrong sort. What cowardly scum got off on scaring a woman who'd put her trust in him? Worse, Lissa had called him abusive. What else had the low-life done?

Blake didn't need her to tell him. His imagination filled in the rest. 'The bastard.'

'That's what I told the cops. There was a restraining order. Haven't seen him for months. Last I heard he'd moved interstate.'

'You should've told Jared.'

She shook her head. 'No.'

'Yes.' He cupped her cheeks in both palms. 'Why the hell not?'

'Because I told you. We had a disagreement.' Her voice was clipped. Angry. Hurting. 'He's made a point of not coming here unless specifically invited ever since.' Her eyes filled with moisture. 'And there's a distance between us that was never there before.'

He tightened his fingers on her face. 'Ah, Lissa. He's your brother and he loves you. That'll never change.'

'I know,' she whispered, those tears spilling over.

Lissa covered his hands with hers on her cheeks, wanting to put this conversation away before she lost what was left of her composure. 'But the bad's in the past and I just want to move on. In lots of ways you've helped me do that. And the best thing you can do for me now is not to mention it again.

'You made me happy, Blake, last night and I hope I did the same for you. I haven't felt this good in a long long time. And it's not just the sex. It's you.'

'Lissa...'

She could almost hear his alarm bells ringing. 'It's okay,' she said quietly, drawing his hands away. 'You've been a true friend in my hour of need and you're already a great business partner, but sex does have a way of complicating things and we'll deal with it. The thing to remember is that you're not looking for an ongoing relationship and neither am I.'

Except this was Blake. The man she'd never got completely out of her thoughts. She picked up her coffee, stared into its depths. She wanted what they had for as long as it lasted and her heart was so going to pay for this later, but right now she couldn't see the thorns for the roses.

He was silent a moment, then nodded slowly. 'Let's take it one step at a time, then.' Darkly clouded eyes clashed with hers. Not the kind that wept soft rain but clouds that promised a cracking good lightning display, all light and heat and unleashed power.

'The business first,' he said. 'We should have a launch party. Get your name out there.'

'A party.' Taking his cue, she made a concerted effort to shake off the intensity of the last few moments. 'That's a brilliant idea. I've thought of a name. Lissa's Interior Design. Gilda— Oh-my-gosh…'

She grabbed her mobile, checked the time and sprang off the bed, spilling crumbs over the sheet. 'I arranged to be there in twenty minutes to check with her about the curtains. I'd better shower and get my act together.' She took a last look at the naked man ogling her bare butt as she slid through the doorway. 'Thank you, Blake. For every thing.'

Blake watched the pool's sunny reflections ripple across the ceiling. He'd been so relaxed last night he'd woken pain free from a dreamless sleep. In a bed that smelled of a warm, sated woman.

A woman who'd been used by a man in the worst possible way.

His fists tightened against the mattress. *Pond scum. Lowlife.* He threw back the sheet and stalked to the window where he glared at the sun sparking off the river. Lissa wanted to forget and move on. So he'd not mention it again.

But he wouldn't forget.

He turned from the view and, in an automatic move, picked up his clothes from the floor, folded them and set them on a chair. And what of Blake Everett? Was he any more worthy of someone like her? He was a wanderer. A loner. A lasting relationship for him and someone like Lissa, or anyone else for that matter, was never going to happen. Home and family weren't in his destiny.

Lissa, on the other hand, needed that security, that bond of family. If there was one thing he could do for Lissa before he left, it would be to get some open and honest conversation between her and Jared happening again.

She'd told him she wasn't looking for an ongoing relationship and he could understand why she might feel that way at present. But given time to heal, that might change.

Whereas for them…they'd had great sex. Mutually satisfying sex.

And mutually satisfying sex was all it was. All it could be. He refused to acknowledge anything more. He'd been cruising through life just fine on his own. Okay, his ship-mates were as close as family and navy life offered little privacy, but on shore leave or one of his rare recreational night dives—in the quiet, solitary times he'd found peace. Or close to it.

Until last month.

His bare toes connected with the brass bed base and pain ricocheted up his shin and he swore like the sailor he was. Yeah, he thought almost savagely, Lissa, with her sheltered upbringing, knew nothing of the murky depths beneath the surface of his civilian persona. She'd never understand the trauma of watching someone dying before her eyes and to wake up and know there'd been nothing she could have done to stop it.

And yet she'd offered him comfort when he'd woken downstairs the other night. She'd listened. Really listened. She'd talked—sensibly, with maturity and sensitivity—about post-traumatic stress. He'd been the one to cut off the communication because he still refused to believe that was what he suffered from. *Never reveal your weaknesses.*

He stared down at the place where they'd made love. Last night, lying beside her, he'd felt something he'd never experienced. Something warm, something worthwhile, like… trust?

Jaw tightening, he turned away. *No.* His father had wanted nothing to do with him. His mother had been trusted to put on a good benefit show, but when it had come to her only son, she'd fallen far short. That innate trust in the love and comfort of family had been wiped clean at an early age.

He thought of Janine. He'd fallen for her hook, line and

sinker. He'd ripped out his scarred heart and laid it at her feet and she'd crushed it beneath her heel with her lies and betrayal.

So much for trust. He would never lay himself on the line that way for anyone, ever again.

He stalked to the bathroom and had just switched on the spray when his mobile buzzed on the bedside table. He switched the water off again, swiped a towel from the rail and went to answer it. Jared's familiar voice caught him off guard.

'Hey. What are you doing up so early?' Blake turned from the sight of sex-rumpled sheets and one of Lissa's gold hair ribbons and moved away from the bed. The last person he wanted to talk to with the scent of Lissa on his body was her big brother. 'What time is it there?'

'A tick before the crack of dawn. Isaac's an early riser.' Blake heard a muffled sound then a distant, 'Hey buddy, put that down, Mummy'll have my b— Isaac…' A crash. 'Never mind, I'll buy her another one.' He sounded resigned, then spoke into the phone again. 'You still there?'

'Still here. Kids, eh?'

'Yeah. Who'd have 'em?'

But Blake heard an exuberance of love in his mate's voice. 'I bet he's a firecracker.'

'You got that right.' There was a hesitation through the phone, then Jared's voice turned serious. 'Before I speak to Lissa, I've been talking to Soph and we're wondering if we should cut short our trip and come home.'

And wouldn't that throw everything into a spin?

No mention of the business, Blake noted, and cleared his throat. Damn it. Lissa obviously hadn't contacted him herself yet. 'She hasn't called?'

'No. And her phone's been switched off for hours.'

'We were at a party till late—'

'You and Liss…?'

He heard the surprise in his old mate's voice. 'Yeah.' *Moving right along.* 'She's next door at the moment, doing up a quote for a nursery. I'll get her to call you when she comes back.'

'So she's getting some work. That's one good thing I suppose. How's she taking the boat disaster, do you think?'

'She's doing okay. Still a little shocked but—'

'Not enough to prevent her from partying obviously.'

'It was a charity thing,' Blake felt obliged to point out in her defence.

'She wants to start her own business. It concerns me a lot. I don't think she's ready for it. Has she mentioned anything about that to you? I guess she's got enough to think about right now.'

Blake paced the carpet, feeling as if he were sinking further into quicksand with every step he took. Yet here was an opportunity to get them talking. 'I'll let her tell you about it.'

'I was hoping to hear your opinion.'

Blake really didn't want to get into anything serious here after doing the wild thing with her all night. 'Better coming from her, mate,' he said, scrubbing a hand down his face. 'She'll call as soon as she gets in.'

'Blake…we were buddies a long while. Is there something I should know here?'

Hell. His grip tightened on the phone. He couldn't talk about their business arrangement because he'd given his word to Lissa, even though he knew that wasn't what his mate was asking. 'She's an adult, Jared. She makes her own decisions.'

Silence. 'What the hell's that supposed to mean?'

'Like I said, she'll tell you herself.'

'So there *is* something going on.'

'At ease, mate, nothing to be alarmed about.'

'She's my sister. I don't want to see her hurt.' There was an edge to his voice that could slice through steel.

'Nor do I.'

'Tell her to call me via webcam. I want to see how she's taking this—and whatever else—for myself.'

'No worries. The moment she's back.'

Jared disconnected without another word.

Blake stared at the dead phone. 'That went well,' he muttered, and headed back to the bathroom to take his shower.

He thought about Jared's concern as he put his room back into some kind of order. Despite her pride in her independence, Lissa was a family girl at heart. She'd probably tire of her party ways eventually and settle down. Marry an easygoing Mr Joe-Average Nice-Guy with no emotional baggage and have two stunning kids, a boisterous dog and a comfortable four-bedroom home overlooking the beach.

Not for him. It was time to look at purchasing his own boat. Time to get moving, explore all the dives along the coast. Use the stars as his compass and live the dream before it was too late. Wasn't that what it was all about?

He collected Lissa's ribbons and hairpins and took them down the hall, but stopped in her bedroom doorway. Was there a bed somewhere beneath those shopping bags? How did someone who'd just lost everything manage to accumulate such a chaos in a single day?

The en-suite fared no better. Lotions of every description and bottles with tops off littered the vanity. A wet towel trailed from the basin. He left her ribbons beside her hairbrush and screwed the lid back on the toothpaste. Another reason they'd never work out. He liked his life ordered. He liked his space clear. She'd drive him crazy.

What they had was just temporary, he assured himself again as he walked away. A fling. She'd drive someone else crazy some day.

CHAPTER TWELVE

She'd drive someone else crazy some day.

Blake needed something else to take his mind off the persistent and distracting thought rattling around in his head. Problem was, his day's routine was shot. He'd not had his morning run—he'd been 'otherwise occupied'. And now the afternoon was slipping away and Lissa was still busy with Gilda. Probably catching up on last night's success. He needed a diversion.

Food. He'd cook something for dinner. How long since he'd enjoyed a good home-cooked meal? He checked the pantry supplies, began compiling a list, then stopped. He had no idea what Lissa liked. Still, who'd not enjoy a good old-fashioned Aussie lamb roast? It could cook while he…what?

Waited for Lissa to come home?

The scene played before his eyes:

He's just put the finishing touches on a complicated dish that took all afternoon to prepare. The leafy salad with a new mustard/pepper dressing is chilling in the fridge along with a bottle of chardonnay. He's thinking cheese for afters, with a little quince pâté, some grapes…then a leisurely bubble bath and an early night…

Lissa rushes through the door, her blouse askew, her hair dishevelled from driving the convertible with the top down. Dinner meeting—sorry, did she forget to tell him? She fishes a couple of cherry tomatoes from the salad bowl in the fridge then a peck on his cheek on her way past. Don't wait up, it's going to be a long one—some after-dinner function to attend and, oh, would he mind collecting her dry cleaning before the shop closes?

Blake stumbled back a step, scowling. What the hell had happened to that bubble bath? What—

'I'm back,' Lissa sang out as she danced into the kitchen, her face glowing, her hair flying behind her. 'Oh, you should see how the nursery's coming along.' She did a quick twirl. 'It's going to be stunning. And she loves the colours. And Gilda's offered to make it a glittering affair with all her rich friends and Stefan's going to take pictures for the PowerPoint presentation at the launch and everyone will see it…and… Hi.' She exhaled hugely on the final word and smiled like sunshine.

Blake blinked, feeling as if he'd just been flattened by a runaway lawnmower. 'Hi.' He screwed up his shopping list, tossed it on the sink. She was wearing a lettuce-green sundress with cherries on and tomato sauce spaghetti straps. Damn the roast, he wanted to take her on the nearest available surface and feed on her instead.

But the domestic role-reversal scene continued to shimmer dangerously before his eyes. Damned if she was going to leave him home alone all night while she got up to…whatever.

Her smile faded a little. 'You could sound more enthusiastic, it's your business too.'

'You're enthusiastic enough for both of us.' With an effort, he snapped himself back to the present and the vision of delightedness before him. She was here now, and for now she was all his. He pushed the uneasiness aside. 'Come here.'

She stepped unhesitatingly into his embrace with the ease and comfort of a familiar lover, linked her arms around his neck and tilted her head up, her lips a breath away from his. 'Have you any idea how I feel right now?'

'Yeah.' He smoothed his hands over her shoulders beneath the straps of her sundress and pressed his mouth against her neck. Impossible not to linger a moment, to feast on that almost translucent skin. 'Oh, yeah.' He lifted his head to watch her face as he ran his hands down her sides—the dip of her waist, the flare of her hips beneath skin-scented cotton. 'You feel incredible. Good enough to eat, in fact.' Lowering his lips, he rubbed them lightly over hers and tasted the faint bitterness of coffee, the stronger, sweeter hint of vanilla and almonds. He flicked his tongue out, sampled the corner of her mouth where the flavour was more delicate. 'Gilda's been feeding you.'

'Mmm.' She wriggled closer, tightened her hold and her breasts rubbed against his chest. 'But I'm still hungry.' She opened her mouth, took his lower lip between her teeth and bit down. 'So hungry...' she soothed the tingle with her tongue, then sucked gently '...I could eat you too.'

He lifted her off the floor and she clamped her thighs around his waist, her eyes hot, her rose-bud lips parted. His blood thundered in his ears and hammered in his groin.

'Yeah. Who needs a lamb roast?' he murmured against her mouth as his fingers clenched around her bottom, bringing her intimate heat into contact with his belly.

His gaze remained fused with hers as he carried her to the kitchen island, set her on the edge of the smooth marble and pushed her thighs apart. Then he braced his hands on the counter top and leaned in while she twisted her fingers in his T-shirt, knuckles white, pressed against his chest.

Falling into the kiss was like leaping out of a plane and into the clouds. Fast and exhilarating, destination uncertain. And for the moment he didn't care. The journey was enough.

The skinny strip of white lace was no barrier—a flick of his wrist, a quick tug and it was gone. Freeing himself, he plunged inside her. He heard her gasp; her eyes were wide and dark as he withdrew slowly. Plunged again. Harder, deeper. Faster.

He feasted on her sweet taste, swallowed her sighs as she met him beat for beat with an enthusiasm that rivalled his. They gorged on each other with mouths and tongues and teeth, the past forgotten, the future unclear.

She surrounded him, slick heat and damp, dark desire, the tight liquid tug pulling him towards completion too fast. Way too fast. The notion that he was *here at last* registered vaguely on some distant horizon.

Then no words, no time, no thought, just a fierce, fast, furious coupling. The need to possess her, a demand to drive reason from her mind so that he was all she knew— all he knew—hammered through his mind in time with his thrusts.

Lissa had never known such a frenzy of wants and desires, needs and demands. Her hands rushed beneath his T-shirt to find all those hard muscles beneath damp skin. He didn't try to hold her or pin her down in any way and rational thought fled as she gave herself up to the whirlwind of sensations battering her. And, oh, how liberating to allow herself to be swept along in its wake, knowing she was safe, that she'd found a haven in Blake.

And somewhere amidst the maelstrom she found the eye of the storm, the calm, her centre.

She held tight to it as they raced together to the finish.

Moments later she slid her hands from beneath the soft cotton tee to wrap them around his forearms braced either side of her. Her thighs trembled, her whole body was limp and tiny exquisite aftershocks still shuddered through her body.

'Lissa.' Breathing heavily, he looked into her eyes and she saw a glimmer of concern. 'I'll replace the underwear.'

If that was all that was bothering him... She opened her mouth to answer and discovered her throat was dry. This new physical facet of their relationship was moving at warp speed and she was still trying to catch up.

But emotionally, Lissa knew she was light-years ahead. He would *not* want to know she was falling in love with him.

'Lissa?' He lifted her chin with a finger, searching her eyes. And she knew he was remembering their earlier conversation about no complications. No ongoing relationship.

She leaned forward, pressed a quick kiss on his lips. 'No need. Thanks to you I have a whole new drawer full of undies,' she assured him, swallowing the ball of emotion that had rolled up her throat. 'And it was so worth it.' *Sunny but casual.* 'That was...*fa-a-a*-n-tastic.' She stretched her arms, let them relax onto his shoulders and smiled. How could she not? She'd just been ravished on a kitchen counter. 'Did I hear a lamb roast mentioned somewhere?'

His smile was...smug? 'Too late to start now but I can do tuna cakes with a side salad.'

'And he cooks too,' she murmured, and kissed him lightly on the lips. 'I'll make the salad.'

'No.' He slid her off the counter and deposited her on the floor. His smile disappeared. 'You'll call Jared. He phoned while you were gone.'

Oh. 'Right.' She heard the message in Blake's tone. She should have made that call earlier. 'I take it you didn't tell him about the business?'

'That's your task.' He walked to the fridge and began pulling out ingredients. 'He asked you to call him via webcam. He wants to see how you are for himself.'

With the satisfied glow of love-making in her eyes? Not flipping likely. 'Oh, *bother*—the computer's down, right?' And her phone was too old for image-to-image capabilities.

'I guess it is.' He glanced at her as he set a bowl and chopping board on the counter where she'd been sitting moments ago. She felt herself colour. She'd never look at that counter in the same way again.

Taking her phone outside, she settled herself on a lounger by the pool in the fading afternoon's warmth and called Jared. She started with an apology, briefly summarised what had been happening with the boat, then talked to little Isaac a moment, which gave her time to psych herself up for the next round of information.

'Blake and I have gone into business together.' As quick and easy as that, she thought.

'I see.'

Clearly he didn't.

She lay back and watched the palm fronds move in the breeze and told herself not to overreact. 'He didn't tell you because I asked him not to. I wanted to do it myself. Just listen first, will you?'

She hurried on with a quick overview, then outlined the details of her new partnership with Blake, his living-room makeover clause, the new clients she'd got and how fortunate she was to be getting her own business ra, ra, ra.

'So, it makes sense to stay at Blake's for now,' she finished.

Silence.

She tracked the calming sight of flight of a flock of water birds as they skimmed the water. *Calm, calm, calm.*

'Is that wise, Liss?'

Calm vanished and irritation prickled between her shoulder blades but she kept her voice steady. 'What are you implying?' She flicked at an insect on her dress with a fingernail, then tapped on the lounger's metal arm. 'You know Blake—it's not as if he's a stranger.'

'I know you had a little crush on him as a teenager but he's been in the navy for fourteen years apart from that brief trip home when his mother died. He's a sailor, for God's sake.'

'A clearance diver, to be precise.' *Jared knew about her crush?* Her calm slipped another notch. 'The naval equivalent to the Special Air Services.'

'So he informed me,' he replied coolly. 'I *am* aware of what they do, Lissa.'

'At least you know he's not just any guy I picked up at a party.' Like Todd.

'Are you sleeping with him?'

She jerked upright. Forget calm, forget irritated, *now* she was angry. 'Is that *any* of your business?'

'My God, you are. It's been what...days?'

'Careful, Jared. Glass houses.' She fought for composure; she didn't want to argue long-distance.

There was a long pause. 'He's not going to hang around for long, honey. He's buying himself a boat. Are you prepared for that?'

She knew. And she'd never be prepared. The heartache would come and the knowledge stabbed at her. She wished she'd thought to bring a drink with her to wash away the dry taste in her mouth. 'I know all that. I'm not a kid.'

'A man like Blake is not the settling-in-one-place kind of guy. He—'

'Oh, for heaven's sakes, didn't you ever have a fling in your life? One wild, crazy no-strings affair with no unrealistic expectations?' Then she frowned, remembering he'd been too busy being a parent to her, and said quietly, 'No, I guess you didn't.'

'Is that what this is?'

She blinked back a sudden moisture, already storing memories of Blake in her heart. 'What else would it be?' What else *could* it be? She gave a light laugh for Jared's benefit, but it came out loud, brittle and over-bright. 'You know me. Always busy. Too busy for anything more and that's not going to change any time soon.' *The world's worst fibber.* 'Don't worry, he'll be gone and it'll be over before you know it.'

'What about the business?' he said. 'I hope you—'

'Of course. Priority number one, but, as I used to tell you often enough, all work and no play...'

'Just…look after yourself.'

'Always.'

'We love you.' Gruff and stern. Not happy. Not happy at all.

'Love you too.' She did. She really did. But she forced a sunny-as-you-go smile into her voice. 'Bye for now.'

She disconnected, leaned back and closed her eyes, moisture clinging to her lashes. Let him get used to the idea. No surprises when he came home from overseas.

Blake might already be gone by then.

Relax. Breathe. Don't let Blake see you like this.

So while she got her emotions under control she reminded herself of the conversation and why she needed to listen to her head and not her heart. She didn't need Jared to tell her Blake wasn't the right man for her. Not long term.

She'd want too much from him—already wanted too much—and an ongoing relationship with a man who lived a million miles away on a boat just wouldn't work. It was vital for her own well-being that she accepted their liaison for what it was and lived the next few weeks accordingly.

A short-term affair.

Blake leaned a shoulder against the open doorway and watched Lissa through narrowed eyes. He couldn't see her face from this angle but she'd disconnected and stretched out as if she didn't have a care in the world.

He'd been about to step outside when he'd heard her spill the status of their relationship to her brother.

He'll be gone and it'll be over before you know it. He'd seen the flip of her hand as she said it. Chuckled it even.

Amused and casual about it all, was she? She'd been anything but amused and casual last night, he remembered darkly.

She'd told it how it was—fun and games for as long as it lasted. *A wild, crazy no-strings affair*, he'd heard her tell Jared.

That was what Blake wanted too, he told himself. And what better way to de-stress than a fling with a gorgeous, fun-loving woman who knew where they stood? It had always worked before.

So why did he feel as if he'd been trussed with barbed wire and tossed overboard into a storm-ravaged sea?

He was a navy man, he reminded himself. He knew how to swim. Tension coiling through every muscle in his body, he pushed off the door frame. 'Food's cooked,' he said. 'You about ready to eat?'

She jumped at his voice and scrambled upright. 'Sure am.' Facing away from him, deliberately, he guessed, she rose, all loose-limbed grace, and stared at the tangerine-smeared sky. 'I never tire of this view.'

'Me neither,' he agreed, willing to stand there for however long it took and watch her with the balmy breeze carrying her scent to his nose and the languid sound of a clarinet drifting from a house across the river.

Then she turned and she was smiling and the force of it hit him smack in the chest. He rubbed a hand over the tender spot, then said, 'I'll miss it when I go.'

Her smile remained but something in her eyes changed. His words had hit their intended target and he wished he'd kept his mouth shut. He wished he knew what she was feeling.

He wished to hell he knew if he was the only one suffering the same gut-rending, devastating force that held him motionless.

Rubbing her upper arms, she glanced away over her shoulder, as if a chill were stalking her. 'It's gorgeous outside. Why don't we eat by the pool?'

They shared a bottle of white wine with their meal as the violet dusk settled into night and the insects chittered. He lit the tea candles he'd brought out with them so he could enjoy the way the light glinted on the gold highlights in her auburn hair.

He didn't pay much attention to their conversation. He was too distracted by the sound of her voice and the way her hands moved as she talked and his own thoughts racing inside his head.

Until she said, 'Gilda was telling me how you saved her life. She had other good things to say about you too.'

Thanks a lot, Gil. What he didn't need right now was to have his life dissected, however well intentioned. The less Lissa knew, the less involved she'd be when he left. 'I just did what anyone would have done.'

She spread her hands on the table. 'I guess you've saved a lot of lives over your time in the navy.'

He shifted, uncomfortable with the conversation, and poured himself another glass of wine, drank half of it straight down. 'It goes with the job.'

'And do you—did you—like your job?'

'It has its moments.' He'd been thinking a lot about that over the past couple of weeks. He'd reached his personal horizon as far as the navy was concerned. It had been time to leave and plot a new course for his life.

'So why did you join the navy?'

'I always loved the sea. Its vastness. The solitude.'

'Solitude? In a navy vessel?' She grinned.

'Yeah, okay, you got me there.'

'I still remember when you left. Here one day, gone the next.'

He shook his head. 'Not quite but it might have seemed that way.'

'Heartbreaker,' she murmured. 'I cried for a week.'

He stared at her, remembering the young teenager and felt…odd. He was still uncomfortable by the whole idea that she'd more than likely projected her sexual fantasies onto him, a guy nine years her senior. 'You did not.'

She lifted a shoulder. 'Okay, maybe it was only a couple

of days, but I might have if I… Not after… Never mind,' she finished quietly. 'It's not important.'

And as if Lissa had conjured her up, an image of Janine shimmered in front of his eyes. The Ghost of Mistakes Past. His mood darkened. 'Don't stop now, it's just getting interesting.' He drained his glass, leaned back and gestured for her to continue.

She was silent a moment, then said, 'Okay. I'm not going to pretend I didn't hear the rumours.' Her voice was as soft as the evening air.

'Why would you?'

'To spare you pain…or embarrassment maybe?'

He shook his head. Not pain, not any more. He'd taught himself not to react every time he thought of Janine. Not embarrassment because he didn't give a rat's ass what others thought they knew. 'Don't spare my feelings, Lissa. Either you believe the gossip-mongers or you don't.' Watching her, he reached for the wine bottle, raised it to his lips but didn't drink.

'I didn't really know you back then. You weren't real. You were more a…fantasy.' She looked down at her hands, then back at him. 'But I'm beginning to know the man you are now. You're kind and generous, you're a good listener, you care about others—'

'But you don't know whether to believe the rumours or not.'

She lifted her glass, sipped from it, set it down again. 'Of course I don't believe them.'

Was she telling the truth about how she felt? Or was it a carefully disguised attempt? He realised that what she thought mattered to him a great deal more than he'd have liked.

'You can't decide,' he said, watching her. 'You want to believe they're lies but deep down inside you, there's always been that doubt. Who is Blake Everett? Not the man you wanted to see, but the real man? Could he make a girl pregnant then walk away? Could he walk away from his own child?'

'Stop it, Blake.'

'And now we've had sex, you think a bit further…and you wonder, what if, just once, your pills don't work? You ask yourself, 'Would he walk away from me? Would he leave me to raise our child alone?''

She shook her head, closed her eyes. 'Stop.'

'Maybe I could walk away. Maybe my upbringing convinced me that alone was best, that responsibility didn't matter.' He turned the bottle in his hands, studying the distorted image of the burning candle through the glass. Everyone had their own way of looking at things.

'Or perhaps back then, I simply made the problem go away. Don't tell me that never crossed your mind.' He looked into her eyes, read the answer.

'Blake, please, I know you better now.'

He picked up her glass, downed the rest of her wine in one long swallow and said, 'Let me tell you about Janine.'

CHAPTER THIRTEEN

'You don't have to. I know you'd never do what they say you did.'

He challenged her clear-eyed gaze. 'Maybe I want to set the record straight.' *For you at least.* He cared more than he wanted to what Lissa believed and what she thought about him.

He looked up, away from the warm distraction before him, to the cold blue emotionless stars. 'I met Janine at the beach. She asked me about life-saving. Said she was interested in joining. She lived in a small apartment on the edge of town and was studying law and pulling late-night shifts at a nearby club to pay her fees.

'Her body was every teenage guy's fantasy but she didn't even seem to be aware of it. She had a freshness about her and a keen mind and I found the combination irresistible.

'We started dating. I saw her every day for lunch and in the evening before she had to go to work. We were together for two months. The houseboat didn't feel right so I told her I intended getting us a bigger place and supporting her so she didn't have to work nights. I'd already bought and sold my first property and was making a reasonable income at the dive shop.

'But before we'd met I'd arranged to sail from Perth to Port Lincoln. I wanted to test my sea legs and the Great Australian

Bight has some of the world's roughest seas. Throw in some scuba diving and I was supposed to be gone five weeks. She cried all over me the day before I left and told me how much she loved me and how she couldn't bear to be without me. I cut my journey short by ten days for her.

'Then a week later she told me she was pregnant and that we needed to get married fast. I hadn't known who her parents were until then. She'd kept very quiet about her privileged upbringing.'

Lissa frowned, doing the calculations. 'How pregnant?'

Exactly. 'She didn't say and it didn't occur to me to ask. She said it didn't matter since we loved each other and I'd forget the navy now we had a baby on the way.' He blew out a breath. The old pain still had the ability to crush. 'You know, she nearly had me. Then I saw her due date on a report she'd carelessly left inside a pregnancy advice book on her bedside table. There was no way I could have been the father.'

He'd been devastated. He'd let himself be drawn into love only to be betrayed again. *It had been the last time.*

He jerked himself out of the memory. 'So I did some quick investigating. Turned out her night shifts hadn't been of the waitressing kind. I went to Sydney and joined the navy a week later.'

'How could someone do that?' Lissa's voice seemed to come from a long way away.

'Quite easily, it would seem.'

'Blake, I'm…' Lissa swallowed. He wouldn't want her pity. 'That must have been tough.' She reached out and covered his hand with hers on the table and felt him flinch.

Before she could think of how to tell him she understood his anguish, she stopped. Because she *didn't* understand. She had no idea how he felt. Whether he'd have given up his navy dreams to be a father. To make a home with her and the baby.

He pulled his hand away, flexed it at his side and rose abruptly. 'I'm going for a run.'

Lissa's heart ached on his behalf. She'd tried reaching out and he'd rejected that, so she just said, 'Take care,' as he stalked away.

There was a coolness in the air and it wasn't just the evening's breeze from the river. Janine's deception had broken something inside Blake and talking about it tonight had scraped at the old wounds. She knew he needed that alone time.

She cleared the dishes, hoping Blake would come back soon and she could see how he was. When he didn't, she went to the room where she'd set up her artwork. She pushed the window wide to let in the evening.

Ears strained, she listened for the sound of Blake's footsteps on the pavement. She could hear nature's soft night music, the distant sounds of a party in progress. The frangipani's scent from outside mingled with the tang of turpentine and charcoal.

With a sigh, she tucked her legs beneath her on the tarpaulin she'd set on top of the carpet, letting her gaze meander through the window to the river with the spill of moonlight shimmering like pearl beads on black velvet.

The moonlit scene reminded her that she loved working with black and white. She opened her sketch pad. If only problems were as clear-cut. She selected a black pencil with a blunt smudged tip and drifted it at random over the blank page.

She wasn't aware of time or her cramped fingers or the moon's slow arc across the sky. Nothing took her attention from her work. Until she felt the hairs on her neck rise.

For a few seconds she froze, remembering how Todd used to creep up on her, finding it funny to see her jump.

She looked over her shoulder. And her heart started beating again...*Blake*.

'I startled you.'

'Only a bit. I'm all right.'

He watched her a moment without speaking.

'You okay?' she asked.

He barely nodded.

No words could describe the moment. The way he looked at her. The way she felt. No words necessary as he crossed the room and stretched out behind her on the tarp. No words spoken as she turned and slid down beside him.

They undressed each other with only the sounds of their breathing and the whisper of clothing being shed in the silence. Slow in the intimacy of night's darkness, skin slid against skin. Heart beat against heart. Fingers entwined. Mouths coming together, clinging a moment then moving on to sip and soothe.

And Lissa knew, with every touch, every murmur, every lingering look, that this understanding could only be forged from love.

If only he knew it too.

Over the next couple of weeks, Lissa barely had time to turn around. Gilda's nursery was finished, photographed and filed for future reference. It was a magical 'Cinderella meets Snow White' theme with a pumpkin-shaped crib and a fortune in fabrics and fittings. Blake praised the new-look living room with its deep turquoise walls and mustard and dark gold furnishings. Another nursery was completed for a client she'd met at Gilda's party. Primrose walls, clean white furniture and a black lacquered crib for the central focus.

The rest of the furniture for the shop arrived. Spacious sofas, unique lamps, wallpaper hangings for customers to browse and office supplies. All were pulled together with the use of vivid colours and hours of hard slog.

They worked as a team. Blake handled the finances, any purchases needed and worked with an IT tech to build a website. When she wasn't trawling catalogues and home-living stores, Lissa was visiting clients, sketching ideas, giving quotes and working on the publicity for the upcoming launch.

But at night they fell asleep together. There were some days when those few precious hours were the only time they saw each other and Lissa grew accustomed to waking with someone beside her again.

She'd learned to read Blake's pain. She was happy to note that he'd only had one headache since that first time she'd found him on the couch. He'd needed the break to recover. If only he would come clean about his military past. He'd done his duty for his country and it was time he tried something else, even if it took him away from her.

Lissa knew he wasn't going to be around for ever. The business was her dream, not his. As if to reinforce that point he'd gone to Surfers one day to look at boats. He'd come home with a renewed enthusiasm...and it scared her.

Requests for work came in, thanks to Gilda's abundantly wealthy friends. Blake had suggested it might be time to start looking for a suitable part-time employee. 'You don't want to lose business because you can't keep up the pace.'

Because he wasn't going to be here to help, she thought, and another piece of her heart broke. The reality was, he'd never said he would be and he'd been up front about it from day one. Silent partner.

The night before the big event, they celebrated their hard-won achievements with oysters, Thai fish cakes and French champagne beneath the white shade sails of an open-air restaurant on the esplanade and watched the night-darkened waves lap the shoreline. Then they took off their shoes and strolled along the beach, which was still populated with tourists and locals alike enjoying the warm evening before heading home.

When they arrived back at the house, Blake kissed Lissa the moment he switched off the car's ignition. A long, deep kiss that reached right down to her toes and left her breathless and had every cell in her body clamouring for more.

'I've wanted to do that all evening,' Blake murmured when he at last lifted his head.

'And I've been waiting for it all evening too.'

His gaze darkened within the car's confines and dropped to her tingling lips. 'Have you now?'

'Seems like for ever. I have to tell you I can't wait much longer...' Feeling bolder than she had in a long, long time, she reached across and rubbed her hand over his crotch. She watched him harden against her fingers and felt its heat reflected in her cheeks as she looked up at him. 'Obviously you can't either.'

Humour danced around his mouth as he yanked the car key from the ignition and their gazes locked. 'And who's responsible for that?'

Still watching him, she pulled her house key from her purse. 'Race you to the bedroom.' She swung open the door and was out of the car like a rabbit. She laughed when she heard Blake swear, kicked off her shoes and kept running, urgency skipping through her veins.

He'd gained ground by the time she'd unlocked the door and pushed inside. Just behind her on the stairs. She screamed when she felt his fingers touch her hair and threw herself onto the bed. 'I won.' She let out a slightly inebriated whoop and flopped back onto the quilt.

'I was at a disadvantage.' He flicked on the bedside lamp, filling the room with a warm glow.

'No.' Out of breath, she stared up at him and bit her lip to stop the smile. 'You have longer legs.'

She watched him whip off his belt, slide it through his fingers. His eyes turned to smoke, the humour faded, replaced by an intensity she'd never seen before, and a sliver of uncertainty shimmied down her spine.

Her pulse stuttered, but not in a good way. 'Okay, call it a draw. It's over.'

'It's only just beginning,' Blake told her, and followed her down.

In a lightning move she wasn't prepared for, he grasped both her wrists, propelled them above her head as his mouth swooped on hers. The weight of his body pushed her into the mattress, one rock hard thigh pushed her legs apart.

Her heart pounded in her ears. She couldn't get enough air. She couldn't *breathe*.

But the instant she tried to pull her hands free, his hold loosened. 'Lissa?'

She dragged in a much needed breath. 'It's okay. I'm okay.'

Guilt steamed through Blake. What the hell had he been thinking, going at her that way after what she'd told him? He knew she didn't want to talk about it so, without a word, he leaned down and kissed her. Then he rolled over, bringing her on top of him.

Her hair fell in a curtain, cocooning both of them in its fresh fruity fragrance. He soothed her back with light strokes for a few moments, then kissed her shoulder and said, 'How about you doing all the work this time?'

'Me?' she murmured against his chest.

'I don't see anyone else here.'

She lay so still he wondered if he'd got it wrong but then she stirred. A slow sinuous movement that made his toes curl and his stomach muscles spasm as she pressed her lips to his chest and stretched. 'Hmm. If you insist. But it has to be my way all the way.'

He jerked when she scratched his nipples with the tips of her fingernails. 'Your way, sweet cheeks. I'm waiting...'

She sat up, her thighs gripping his hips, the hem of her loose-fitting dress sliding up to her waist. Wordlessly, she began undoing his shirt buttons. When she'd finished that task she pushed the fabric aside and smoothed her hands over his chest, her eyes clear now, and focused, and he breathed a sigh—part relief, part pain, but mostly he was just plain hot.

Lissa looked into his eyes and wished she could tell him what he'd done for her with his one simple suggestion that showed he understood. He'd given her her soul back, this man.

This man she loved.

Her heart both swelled and wept. She'd been so stupid. She'd fallen into the trap she'd told herself to steer well clear of. And he'd warned her, hadn't he? He'd been up front with her from day one. He was a sailor, he had a life and he didn't want to share it. With her unrealistic romantic fantasies, she only had herself to blame.

So no tears. And above all, no regrets.

'Jeez, woman, you're killing me here.'

His edgy demand brought her back to the present, and that was about all she had left. 'Patience,' she told him.

He reached for her hem but she batted his hand away. 'No.' She did it herself, lifting it up, throwing it to the floor. And, oh, the rush of feminine empowerment as she reached behind her back to unsnap her bra and toss it behind her.

He eyed her bare breasts with barely restrained hunger but she shook her head. 'No touching. Not yet.' Then she leaned back and took her weight on her hands and ordered him to, 'Take off your shirt.'

A difficult task, she conceded, since she was sitting on the tops of his thighs, but he managed to free his arms. He stuck them behind his head and lay back to await further instructions.

What freedom. What joy. What delight to have this man at

her mercy beneath her. 'You know, I used to fantasise about doing this,' she told him, and watched his eyelashes flicker.

'I don't think I needed to know that,' he murmured, his voice thick.

'Then I won't tell you what else I imagined…' She slanted off him to one side and gestured at his crotch. 'Now the pants. Then hands back behind your head.'

When the clothing was gone and he'd resumed his semi-relaxed pose, she moved back on top of him. She took him in her hands and slowly slid herself down his length. 'Ooh, that feels so good…'

She raised herself up, sank again and he thrust his hips to meet her, pushing further inside. Slow and slick and slippery. Watching his face now, she ran her hands through her hair, relishing the moment as they moved together. Glorying in the final rush to fulfilment.

Moments later she slid off to one side and stretched, before flopping an arm over Blake's chest and cuddling into his side.

'So…tomorrow's the big day,' he said, lifting her hand and rubbing her palm with his thumb.

'I wish Jared could've made it but he's been held up in Singapore with work. He was *supposed* to be on vacation.'

Blake brought her fingers to his lips and kissed each of them in turn. 'Crystal and Ian are coming.'

'Yes.'

But he knew it was Jared she wanted to see. At least they were talking more and, from what she'd told him, Jared sounded happy with the way the business was shaping up. 'He'll be there in spirit.'

'I know.'

'You still haven't told me what charity you're raising money for.'

'It's a surprise. Only Gilda knows.'

'I'm not a big fan of surprises.'

'Then toughen up, big boy, because I'm not telling you. You'll find out tomorrow like everyone else. Now go to sleep.'

He was back on the beach that haunted his dreams. But this time he found himself suspended in mid-air, looking down. Torque was gone, Lissa stood on the sand instead. The breeze caught her hair, twirling it about her beautiful face, which was turned towards the sun. She looked up, smiled at him, waved, then set off down the blinding strip. His heart stuttered. He wanted to wave back, tell her he was coming and ask her to wait but he couldn't move his arm.

And then she was sinking into the sand, her face contorted in horror as she screamed his name, over and over. He tumbled down to earth and onto the beach and started running but his legs were columns of concrete. Then the world turned dark as he pin-wheeled towards a rocky outcrop on the water's edge...

'Blake. Blake, you're having a bad dream.'

Lissa. Not screaming. Her soothing voice washed over him. He felt her hand on his chest and opened his eyes to see her leaning over him, her silhouette outlined against the grey light from the window. He could just make out her features in the darkness. Eyes wide and filled with something akin to the fear that still ripped through his body.

He'd not had his nightmare for weeks. He'd thought they were gone. But this dream was different. His subconscious was warning him to stay away from her, to keep her safe from him and harm.

'You're not going to shut me out any longer,' she said firmly. 'And you're not the only one who reads eyes.'

He turned his head away on the pillow. In the shadows, he could still see her on the beach and it was as if sharp talons had shredded what was left of his heart. 'Turn on the lamp,' he snapped out.

He felt the mattress dip and the room filled with a soft rosy light, chasing away the shadows and images. He blinked awake, desperate not to see her falling back into that hell hole.

And then the words, the pain, the memories were tumbling out. 'We were attacked by an unseen enemy on a beach. My youngest recruit was killed. I was in charge, I was the one responsible. It should've been me who died that day.'

'Oh, Blake.' She brushed her fingers over his brow. 'Why would you say that about yourself? It shouldn't have been anyone. Let me in…please.'

He turned and looked at her. 'You're a good listener, Lissa. The only one who ever listened.' The only woman who ever cared what was inside him.

She stared down at him, her eyes wide and full of compassion. 'Start at the beginning and don't stop till you're through.'

He put a hand behind his head and stared at the ceiling. Then he took a deep breath. 'We were on a routine training exercise…'

Lissa's heart wept for him as he told her, his gaze fixed on horrors she couldn't see.

'I woke up in a military hospital,' he said at last.

'Thank God,' she whispered.

'They called me a hero.' He drove a hand over his head. 'If I'd been doing my job right I'd've seen the signs earlier and Torque might still be alive today.'

'No. You did what you could. No one could have done more. You're a good, good man, Blake. The best. You couldn't save Torque, but you've done so much for others. You've spent years protecting our country. Protecting us. Think about Gilda. And me—think about all you've done for me. The boat. *Your* boat. You never told Jared the story behind that, did you? The business you've helped me build. Todd.

'Forgive yourself, Blake. Let me help you.' She closed his eyelids gently with her fingertips. 'Sleep now. I'll be here.'

CHAPTER FOURTEEN

'I SHOULD'VE bought a new dress.' Lissa surveyed her reflection, less than satisfied. It was her big night and her little black dress was strapless and short and simple. Everyone else would be blinged to the eyeballs and the party princess was a plain Jane. But she hadn't had time to wander the boutiques.

'That is a new dress,' Blake said, behind her.

'And that is such a typical male response.' She glanced at Blake in the mirror to check he was okay after finally opening up to her last night.

He was buttoning his shirt. Covering all that gorgeous bronze skin. He looked amazing. Semi relaxed. She knew he wasn't looking forward to facing a crowd of people. She stared back at herself. 'It's not what I imagined myself wearing tonight. I look so…stark. And boring. Maybe a brighter lip-gl—'

'Perhaps these will help.' Blake's reflection appeared behind her. He lifted his hands above her head and she saw a single strand of cream pearls.

'Oh…' She met his eyes in the mirror—warm and incredibly blue, like a tropical day, and for a heart-stopping moment she forgot to breathe.

Then he broke eye contact, as if he'd seen something he wasn't comfortable with. 'Lift your hair.'

Unable to speak for the lump in her throat, she did as he

asked. He fastened it around her neck, then adjusted its princess length so that the diamond-crusted clasp sat below the line of her collarbones. It sparked like fire in the bedroom light.

'Oh, my...I don't know what to say.' She touched the smooth orbs, cool against her suddenly flushed skin. They must have cost a fortune. 'They're beautiful. And absolutely perfect.'

'They match your complexion.' His hands drifted over her bare shoulders as he turned her to face him, dropped a kiss on her brow. 'Good luck for tonight. You deserve it.'

'Thank you, Blake.' In turn, she leaned in to press her lips lightly against his neck just above his collar. 'For everything.'

But as she walked out into the night with him, something shivered down her spine. Hadn't she read somewhere that when a man gave a woman pearls, tears weren't far behind?

By eight-thirty the vaulted room where Lissa's Interior Design was to open for business on Monday morning was a sensory hive. Animated conversation. A fortune in fashion and fragrance and diamonds. Exotically perfumed pine-cone ginger stalks and Singapore orchids among tropical foliage. Colourful canapés, pink champagne. And over it all, the sounds of Vivaldi drifting from a quartet on the mezzanine floor.

Lissa mingled with the guests. Some she knew, others she met for the first time. Gilda, with her rapidly growing baby bump swathed in midnight blue, introduced her around. Blake was working the room from the opposite end.

Suddenly, she was enveloped in a tight warm hug and a familiar voice over her shoulder said, 'Hello, gorgeous.'

'Jared!' She turned in the circle of his arms and hugged him tight. 'I didn't know you were back.'

'We wanted to surprise you.'

'You did.' And for a moment she wanted to cling, to breathe

in his familiar aftershave and tell him she loved him, how much she appreciated him.

How much family meant to her even though she didn't always show it.

'Missed you,' she said, against his cheek.

'Same goes. Don't worry, sis,' he whispered for her ears only. 'I'm not going to rain on your parade.'

'I know. Thanks.'

He let her go and she stepped back, feeling unaccountably emotional. 'Sophie. You've cut your hair. It looks stunning.'

Sophie, gorgeous in a teal-coloured dress, flicked at her new bob with a smile. 'Easier to manage when travelling.'

'Crystal.' Lissa hugged them both. 'Thanks for coming. And Ian too. You all made it.' She soaked in the sight with all her senses. Her family loved her and they'd always be there for her, no matter what. They'd always be around to celebrate her successes.

She tried *not* to think about her business partner but her hand rose to the pearls at her neck. Blake would never be part of her inner circle. He wouldn't be here with champers when the business turned a profit for the first time. He wouldn't be here when it came time to decorate the office with Christmas cheer. He wouldn't be here to share their milestones *because he sailed alone*.

'Are you all right, Lissa?' Sophie asked, with a small frown.

'Are you kidding? With all this happening?' Waving an encompassing hand, she shook off the melancholy and smiled. 'Where are the kids?'

'Ian's parents are baby-sitting the lot,' Crystal said, then grinned. 'Overnight. So we're all staying at the Oceans Blue.' She glanced at Jared as she said, 'We're hoping you and Blake will join us for brunch tomorrow morning before we head back.'

'Love to. I'll ask Blake when I can catch him.' She glanced

about her. She'd hardly seen her partner in crime since they'd arrived. She saw him among the crowd, conversing with an elderly couple beneath the 'rings of fire', which they'd taken to calling the magnificent circles of light above them.

Her heart leapt against her breast at that first glimpse. It always did. It always would. The tanned skin and glossy dark hair, those brilliant blue eyes that she just wanted to drown in. His smile. He was smiling now as he talked, that delicious mouth kicked up at one corner, one hand holding a champagne flute, the other gesticulating as he made a point. Even though she knew he'd prefer to be alone or perhaps with her on some secluded moonlit beach.

But it wasn't only his physical beauty she saw. She saw the man behind the masculine perfection. A wounded man who'd only just begun to open up to her. His troubled family history.

She also knew him as a man of patience, understanding and integrity. He put up with the chaos she'd turned his house into with her work gear and her seeming inability to leave a room tidy.

He'd drawn out her deepest fears and soothed them with a gentleness she'd never have expected a man of his solitary background to be capable of.

But she kept the knowledge and her feelings deep. They'd agreed that if a more suitable partner came along, he'd be happy to bow out of the whole deal. More than happy, Lissa knew. He'd talked about sailing. He'd found a boat he was interested in. She knew he was leaving, it was only a matter of time.

Would he change his mind and stay if he knew she loved him?

Would it be fair to lay that on him?

No. Because with the emotional baggage he carried, to him they'd be empty words. And what would be the point? He didn't want to be tied to one place and she wanted this business so badly her eyeballs ached. They could never be together long term.

Jared's voice sounded over the microphone set up in the middle of the room, jerking her out of her thoughts. The guests quietened and gathered around.

'Ladies and gentlemen, welcome to Lissa's Interior Design.' Her brother smiled her way as the onlookers clapped. Emotion choked her. She lifted a hand in acknowledgement. She glanced at Blake but his attention was focused on Jared. She tried to interpret his expression without success.

When the applause settled down, Jared continued. 'Gilda's asked me to say a few words and I'm going to start by telling you about my kid sister…'

A few moments later, he finished by saying, 'And now with great pleasure and no small amount of pride, I want to introduce the talented woman who's going to transform your homes into magazine-worthy masterpieces. Lissa Sanderson, ladies and gentlemen.'

He handed her the mike, with a murmured 'Congratulations, sis,' and a brotherly pat on the back.

She clenched one hand around the microphone. 'Thank you, Jared.' Her voice resounded through the room. She blew him a kiss on a wide smile. 'That was quite a speech.' She glanced down at the scrap of paper in her hand.

'First off, I'd like to thank you all for coming and making the evening such a success…'

Crossing his arms, Blake stood well back from the crowd, out of the spotlight, and watched the exchange of fond smiles between the siblings. And an odd sensation tugged at him. He felt as if he were standing on a ship's splintering deck watching the rest of the crew cram into the only lifeboat and sail away. He tried to shake it away, but the feeling persisted.

She continued her speech but he wasn't listening to the words, he was listening to her voice—clear and crisp and calm, like the sound of a church bell over still water at sunset.

He couldn't take his eyes off her. The scrawny little red-head now the voluptuous Titian-haired beauty in a short black dress and taking on the world of interior decorating. If she'd left him at sea all those years ago, it was nothing to what she was doing to him now. He could imagine her in ten years. Twenty.

And she'd still be the only woman he wanted to look at.

'As most of you would already know, the evening's not just about Lissa's Interior Design. It's also about charity. Tonight I want to pay tribute to the men and women in the Armed Forces. Our own Aussie Diggers...'

Then those crystal clear eyes looked right at him. As if she'd known exactly where he was. In some still-functioning corner of his brain he registered her recognition to his line of work, even though he'd barely scratched the surface of that aspect of his life with her. With any woman.

'For those of you who haven't heard of it, the 'Support our Diggers' campaign provides health care, counselling and legal support for our troops overseas and for returned soldiers.

'Each and every one of them makes a huge personal sacrifice to protect us here in Australia. They leave their families and loved ones and endure life-threatening situations on a daily basis. Some pay the ultimate price. Others return, changed for ever.'

Changed for ever. The words reverberated in his skull. Lissa had changed him. For the better. She'd shown him a different view of the world. One he liked. One he wanted. He rubbed a fist over his chest. Something was shifting inside him.

'So we want to champion the very worthy and valuable charity, 'Support our Diggers'. Make sure you see our charity diva, Gilda, and donate as much as you can before you leave.

'There's someone else, someone special, I want to acknowledge. Blake Everett. Most of you will remember Blake's mother, Rochelle, who worked tirelessly for charity from Surfers to the Sunshine Coast. Blake's the man responsible for making this dream of mine happen.'

Blake barely heard the resounding applause over the roaring in his ears.

I've been waiting my whole life for you.

He didn't know what to do with the feelings crashing around him. He'd heard her tell Jared what they had was a fling. *A wild, crazy no-strings affair with no unrealistic expectations.*

He needed to get outside, breathe some fresh air and think, because maybe this was the most important question he was ever going to ask himself, but before he could make his getaway a hand clapped his shoulder. 'Long time, no see, my friend.'

Blake turned at the voice and curbed his impatience. Jared's eyes pierced his as Blake extended a hand. 'Jared. It's good to see you.'

Jared nodded. 'Thanks for your phone call. It was reassuring to know Liss really wanted me here that badly.'

'You mean the world to her. Even if she doesn't always show it.'

'Same goes.' Jared cleared his throat. 'I want to thank you for helping her out with the boat.'

'Not a problem.'

'And with the business. I'd have helped but she's got that stubborn streak a mile wide.'

Blake felt a smile tug at his mouth. 'Believe me, I've seen it.'

She was also loyal and caring and all-the-way committed to making this venture a success, something he'd not been sure about at the start.

He looked about him, at the amazing job she'd done in transforming the building in such a short time. 'She's got talent and a good opportunity here. She'll do well.'

When he looked back, Big Brother was still watching him. 'So, what are your plans now?'

Blake heard the question behind the casual tone. And Lissa's words to Jared: *He'll be gone before you know it.* 'I've negotiated the price on a sailing yacht. Thought I'd sail north first and check out the Barrier Reef and the islands up there. Take in some diving. Recreational for a change.' He heard himself reciting the words as if from a dry school text. Why didn't he sound more enthusiastic? He'd been thinking about this for over a year, planning it for weeks.

'And the business?'

Lissa had always known how it would play. They'd both known. 'If she needs some advice and I'm out of contact—'

'She'll be just fine.' Jared watched him. 'She's got her family's support.'

Family. Yes, Lissa needed family. A house and a husband all the way committed. To settling down, raising her own kids.

'Blake…' A female of indeterminate age excused herself for interrupting but she'd known his mother…

Jared left them at some point and Blake was caught up with guests, then Gilda took the mike and proposed a toast. And everyone looked towards the spiral staircase where Lissa stood halfway up with a huge pair of gold scissors with purple foil streamers dangling from them. She cut a ribbon and a rainbow of balloons and foil confetti drifted down from the ceiling.

Cameras flashed, glasses clinked. Everyone cheered and clapped. Except Blake. Forget Helen of Troy, he thought as he watched her. Lissa's smile could launch a thousand ships ten times over.

As the metallic confetti swirled down around her, she locked eyes with him and it was like being sucked into a whirlpool of wants and needs and hopes, his or hers, he didn't know whose—just that they pulled him in a direction he'd never had any intention of going.

And all he knew was that he wanted to follow wherever it led. As she descended the steps he made his way towards her, his heart thumping like a piston in his chest. He didn't want to be a silent partner. He wanted a full partnership. So he didn't know much about interior decorating but he could learn, couldn't he? They could learn together. She could be the creative genius and he'd... They'd figure something out. But first he had to know how she felt. How she *really* felt about the two of them. Together.

She waved and headed straight for him, her smile glowing. 'I've got such exciting news.' She grabbed his arm. 'I'll tell you on the way...there's a party at Brandy's house and...' She trailed off, her brow creasing. 'You haven't got a headache, have you? You look pale...'

'I'm fine, in fact I—'

'So you'll come? Please, please, Blake, I want you there with me.'

'I need to talk to you first.'

'What about?'

'Not here.' He gestured with his chin. 'Outside.' Without waiting for a response, he took her elbow, and guided her past the crowd and out to the footpath. The sea air laden with the aromas of Asian stir fry and warm bitumen met them. He turned her towards him. 'Lissa, I—'

'Can it wait?' She all but jiggled on the spot, her beautiful face brimming with delight, clear eyes sparkling. 'The party's for—'

'This is important.' He grasped her upper arms, suddenly desperate.

'So is my career. Didn't you say to focus on my career first? Okay, I can't wait, I'll just have to spill it now...' She clasped her hands together beneath her chin, her eyes sparking with life and energy, bits of foil glinting in her hair. 'Maddie Jenkins wants in on the business as a full partner! You wouldn't be aware but she's got interior design shops all the way down the coast from Cairns to Brisbane and she wants Lissa's to be a part of it.'

Inside, Blake turned to stone. He loosened his hold. Who the hell was Maddie Jenkins? 'You haven't discussed it with me.' His lips felt numb; he felt as if someone else were pushing out the cool, clipped words. 'It's good manners to discuss any changes with your current partner first, don't you think?'

She stilled. 'Oh, Blake. I should have, I'm sorry. But it just happened moments ago.'

Her smile faded and the sparks in her eyes changed and he hated himself for being the cause but he couldn't find it in him to accept her apology.

When he didn't respond, she continued, 'You and I...we agreed it was a temporary arrangement until I found another interested party. Maddie's got years of experience and contacts all over the country. It'll still be Lissa's Interior Designs but this arrangement is just...so perfect. For me...*and* for you.'

Her eyes changed again, shadows stealing the light, but they remained level on his. 'You never really wanted to be involved in an interior design business. You only did it to help me out, we both know that. Because you knew I wouldn't accept charity. But you believed in me and I'll never forget it.'

He tightened his jaw. She was right, all the way right. 'You've got it all figured out.'

'It makes sense—for both of us. You're free now. Totally free. You can go off and do what you want, wherever you want. If that's what you want...'

'If I asked you to, would you come with me?' The words spilled out before he could stop them.

'What?' For a heartbeat he saw a flash of something like yearning in her eyes and his heart skipped a beat. 'Where? When?'

'Anywhere. Everywhere.' *For as long as for ever.*

'Why?' she asked quietly.

And he knew it wouldn't work, even if her eyes were telling him something else. Her new business was where she needed to be. She'd regret it for the rest of her life. Because he couldn't be the man she needed. He couldn't give her the kind of life she wanted.

So he shrugged as if his gut weren't tearing him up. *A moment of madness.* 'I just wanted to satisfy myself that you really are committed to this venture.'

She nodded, crossed her arms over her chest. 'And now you know. I can't believe you'd think I'd give up my career on a whim. You made this chance possible and I've worked towards it for so long. I'm going to take Maddie's offer while it's still on the table.' She searched his eyes for the longest time, as if committing them to memory.

He was vaguely aware that a group of younger party-goers stepped onto the footpath, that someone called her name. Still watching him, Lissa backed away towards them. Someone put a glass of champagne in her hand. She didn't seem to notice. 'You sure you won't come with us?'

He shook his head, barely managed a quick smile. 'Go do your thing, party girl. I've got some business of my own to take care of.'

'Someone'll drop me off, so I'll see you back at home, then.' She lifted her glass in a kind of salute.

Home? She'd never referred to his house as home before and warmth flickered deep inside only to cool instantly as he watched her walk away, his jaw so tight he wondered that he didn't crack a tooth.

Then she seemed to change her mind. She turned around and ran back, clutched at his shirt and blinked up at him. And for a pulse-pounding second a new dawn beckoned.

'Thank you, Blake, you're the best partner I ever had.' She reached up, pulled his head down and pressed her warm lips to his. The cold bubbly spilled out of her glass and down his shirt.

He pulled her closer, skimming the edge of something that felt eerily like panic. He'd faced enemy fire, unexploded mines and been life-threateningly close to running out of oxygen in the ocean's depths and always kept his cool. Used reasoning and logic to see him through.

There was nothing cool or reasonable or logical here.

When she broke the kiss and eased her heels back down to the footpath, the feeling didn't go away. It deepened.

She smiled and stepped back. 'The cleaning crew'll lock up when they're done.'

He jutted his chin towards the group up ahead. 'Your friends are waiting.'

She nodded. ''Night.' *Don't wait up.* He swore he heard those words on the balmy salt air.

CHAPTER FIFTEEN

HE SHOULD have enjoyed coming home alone. That was what
he wanted, right? His temples throbbed with tension. Not
wanting the light's harsh glare, Blake walked through the
darkened house. The silence was shattering. He stopped outside Lissa's bedroom. The subtle fragrance she wore lingered
on the air. He stepped through the doorway and looked about.
It was the usual disaster area. A jumble of clothes, boxes,
shopping bags.

Her presence extended to other rooms. Where she stored—
and he used the word loosely—her tools of trade, where she
sketched. Even his room didn't escape unscathed. Make-up
and hair products. Her two pillows propped at a crazy angle
against his headboard.

Damn. He'd become accustomed to it. It was…comfortable.
Too comfortable.

His gaze moved to a photo he'd snapped of the two of them
at the Loo with a View, a popular local spot overlooking the
esplanade. She'd framed it for him to take with him when he
left.

Their relationship had never been anything other than temporary. No misunderstanding on that score. It had been fun
while it lasted.

Stretching out on the bed, he tucked her pillows behind his
head. *Waiting for Lissa to come home.* What if…?

In his mind's eye he saw Lissa setting a birthday cake glowing with candles in front of him. Gifts on the sideboard. Smiling faces around the table. Jokes and laughter. Sharing his special day. Being part of a family. Shaking his head, he dismissed it before it could seize his heartstrings and never let go.

He'd made her, and himself, a commitment to stay, or at least remain in contact until Lissa was on her feet and able to manage without him. They'd come to that point. Closing his eyes, he made a mental list of all he needed to do.

Lissa quietly let herself in as the first line of scarlet smeared the sea's horizon. She grimaced as the door squeaked on its hinges. She hadn't meant to be out so late but she and Maddie had had a lot to discuss and the time had flown by. She'd texted Blake over two hours ago and left a message to tell him she was okay but she'd had no response.

Now the festivities and celebrations were over, everything else came flooding back. Fatigue hit her like a bomb. Not wanting to wake Blake, she slipped off her shoes, crept to the staircase and sat on the bottom step.

If I asked you to, would you come with me?

And for a moment there, at the party, looking into his eyes, she'd wavered. To sail with him off into the sunset. To live and love and grow old together. Her heart had yearned with the beauty of it, cried with the pain of it.

But he'd thrown it out there to test her *commitment*. Her sense of *responsibility*. To see if she was as good as her word.

So she'd given all the right reasons, all the logical reasons why she should say no. She'd struggled for independence most of her life and Lissa's Interior Designs was her passport.

But deep inside, where reason didn't exist, she'd wept.

Gathering up her shoes, she climbed the stairs. Blake's bedroom door was part-way open.

Suddenly unsure, she tapped before entering and was met by a brooding man with a surly tone. 'Morning, party girl.' He wore the same black jeans and ratty T-shirt he'd had on the night he'd landed on her deck. His hair had grown in the weeks since, and was furrowed now, as if he'd been running his hands through it. There were dark smudges beneath his eyes.

'I texted you,' she said.

One glance at the bed and she saw he was packing. Packing? Now? Swift and devastating pain stabbed at her. She'd known it was coming, but today?

'Yeah. Thanks for letting me know.' He folded T-shirts, laid them in his bag. 'So, you and Maddie got it all sorted?'

She barely heard him. 'You're leaving.'

'It's time. You've got what you wanted and my boat's been ready for a week. I'm picking it up tomorrow. I wanted to wait until the launch was over. Didn't want to spoil the fun.'

Her brain whirled with the shock and the details that needed sorting. 'Your loan. We have to arrange—'

'I don't need the money, Lissa. Keep it as a gift. I'll arrange for the paperwork.' He moved to the wardrobe and pulled shirts off hangers.

'I can't do that, it's not right. And it doesn't sit well with me. You know it doesn't.'

'Then donate it to the charity of your choice.'

'What about the house?' She'd need to find somewhere else to live.

He didn't look at her as he folded each shirt with the same precise care, laid it on the pile. 'There are no bookings for the next couple of months. I've just emailed the agent and informed him you're here for as long as you need to be. Till you find somewhere decent that you can afford.'

'I can't stay here.' *You're all around me.*

'Then do me a favour and house-sit for a while. It's always safer when someone's living in a place. And for God's sake stop telling me you can't. I know you can, and it's really not a word I want to hear right now.' Jaw tight, he slammed the bag's lid down, wrenched the zip closed.

He looked at her and his eyes did that magic thing she'd seen on rare occasions. They turned from hard flint to the softest tropical blue, just for an instant before reverting to hard once more. 'I need to leave. And it has to be now.' His voice was scratchy and raw, as if he'd swallowed sandpaper. 'Do you understand?'

No. 'No. I *don't* understand.' The full impact had taken a few moments to sink in and now shock turned to desperation. But she kept her voice steady. 'I do understand you need time to heal. But I can help you with that. Now you've talked about it, we can work on strategies together. If you want, we can see a counsellor…'

He shook his head. 'It was always temporary, Lissa. We knew that.'

'So that's it, then.' No tears. Her eyes were as dry as dust and she was grateful for it. A swift clean break now would allow her to focus on her new career. She'd be so busy she wouldn't have time to miss him.

'Why don't you go make us some breakfast?'

She couldn't seem to drag her eyes away from his face. This was what he wanted and she so wanted him to be happy. He deserved to be happy, to live his life in peace and solitude if that was what he wanted. But why did it have to hurt so much? Why did it feel as if her very soul were being torn apart?

'So you're walking away.' She'd sworn she'd not say it but it was as if someone else were speaking through her. 'After everything I've just said. After all we've been through. What we've come to mean to each other. You can pack up and move on *just like that*?' She clicked her fingers in front of her face.

And for one thudding heartbeat she thought she saw the same emotions rip through his gaze, but maybe she was hallucinating because when she blinked her vision clear there was nothing but that flinty-eyed, self-contained remoteness.

'On second thought, forget breakfast, it's best if I just go,' he said, with that same wretched aloofness. 'You're dead on your feet and you always did have that flair for the overly dramatic.'

He crossed to her, took her hands in his and she wanted to pull away from his touch, to prove she could, but her hands were numb. 'It's not the end of the world, Lissa, it's just the beginning. You'll thank me later. A good eight hours' sleep and everything will fall into perspective. You'll wake rejuvenated and ready to take on the next challenge in your life.

'We want different things. You need stability. A home, family. I want to feel the salt air on my face and drop anchor wherever I please. And that's not the kind of man you need. We had some good times but we always knew it was just a fling.'

She flinched at his tone and the word. *Fling.* It sounded almost sordid, an abomination for what she thought they'd had. Had she been the only one to feel that intensity? Or the only one dumb enough, naïve enough to let it matter?

'You know something? I don't *need a man* in my life. Why do you men always think you're so indispensable?'

'I guess we've said it all, then.' He picked up one of his bags, slung it over his shoulder.

'I guess we have.' Damn him, she wasn't going to watch him walk away. Their talk had drained every last drop of energy from her and she didn't know how much longer she could remain standing. 'I hope you enjoy your freedom. And I'll always be grateful for your helping hand when I was down, so thank you for that.' She stepped away. 'I think I'll go take that nap. You'll probably be gone when I wake up, so…I'll say goodbye now.'

He nodded once, then tore what was left of her heart out when he kissed her cheek lightly and said, 'I'll see you around some time.'

Not in this lifetime, she vowed later sitting on the couch with her arms around his pillow watching the afternoon shadows creep over the pool.

And she'd been left to explain why *he* wasn't going to be coming to brunch with her family. She'd opted out too, pleading fatigue. She squeezed her eyes shut to stop the tears.

In one evening she'd been handed her dream career, her independence, her new life. And lost the man she loved.

The shop opened on Monday. Jill, one of Maddie's staff from the Noosa branch, had come down to help for a couple of weeks with a view to looking at relocating there to be closer to her family. Older than Lissa and with a few years' experience under her belt, Jill was bright and enthusiastic and Lissa hoped she'd stay on.

People dropped in to wish Lissa well and share the bubbly Maddie had sent. She didn't think about Blake *at all*. No way. Not for a minute.

She did *not* imagine him sharing the excitement of her first day or seeing him walk in at closing, eyes hot for her, hair glinting under the rings of fire when he came to whisk her away for a celebration dinner.

Then mid-morning a massive floral arrangement arrived. Three dozen fragrant yellow roses spilling from a ginormous glass bowl. 'Someone loves you.' Jill grinned as the black-capped delivery guy in his crisp black shirt with its gold logo set it on the coffee table in the display area.

A little tag gave instructions for care of cut flowers and a hand-written explanation that yellow roses celebrated success and new beginnings.

'My brother.' Lissa smiled back, tugging at the attached

envelope. 'He's always…' Her voice trailed off, her smile dropping away as she read the card inside.

Congratulations! Thinking of you today. Blake.

The surprise caught her off-guard. Her nose stung, her eyes brimmed and something huge and heavy lodged in her throat. He'd thought enough to choose the exact right flowers and, what was more, he'd wanted her to know. 'They're from my… They're from Blake.'

'You mean that dishy navy guy from Saturday night?'

Lissa heard Jill's appreciative murmur and shuffled the card quickly back in its envelope. 'He's left the navy. Bought himself a yacht. He won't be coming back any time soon.' She turned her back on the flowers and headed for her desk, aware of Jill's gaze boring into her neck.

But she slept in his bed that night. The following night she moved her stuff there. Just for the short time until she found her own place. She told herself she liked the view of the river from there.

In the evenings after putting in hours of overtime at Lissa's, she sketched. She finished the piece she'd been working on. After all, she knew every plane and angle of his face. A portrait of Blake. She'd give it to him some time when he was passing through.

She put on some music and danced in the living room until she was physically exhausted, then tossed for hours, unable to sleep. Citing work as the reason, she put off visiting her family.

Work, work, work. It gave her a reason to get up in the morning. She enjoyed the long hours. She loved seeing the process move from plan to finished perfection. The income allowed her to start repaying the debt into the bank account Blake had set up.

To her surprise, over the next few weeks she discovered she could live without Blake and not fall to pieces every time she thought of him. She knew she could lead the fulfilling, independent life she'd wanted.

But now she knew Blake as well as anyone could, she'd always feel as if a part of her were missing. One day she might even be able to think about dating again. It was ironic that it had been Blake who'd given her back that confidence.

She'd not heard a single solitary word from him, nor had she contacted him. She told herself it was better that way. One email or text, one phone call and she'd want more.

Blake didn't.

Blake cradled his mug of tea while he watched the sun lift out of the water. It swam on the horizon, a ball of fire shimmering in the early morning haze. Fingers of crimson spread along the yacht's decking and stroked his skin with sultry warmth. The air was thick with humidity and the smell of the ocean, the way he liked it.

To his right, tropical rainforest capped a steep peak, then dipped all the way down to a golden ribbon of sand. If he looked to his left he could see the conical shape of one of the Barrier Reef's unspoiled islands rising out of an indigo and turquoise sea.

This was paradise.

Who wouldn't give their all to be in his place right now? He breathed deep as he watched a flock of seabirds dip and dive, and took a bite out of his toasted bacon sandwich. The water lapped at the hull, the sails flapped lazily.

This was freedom.

He could take the time to enjoy the wind in his hair and the sun on his back. No one to tell him what to do and how to do it. No one to tell him when to get up, where to go.

No one.

He shook off the edgy feeling. He wasn't lonely. He could drop anchor at the nearest marina any time and chat with the locals at the yacht club. He didn't need company.

Why waste time building relationships that always ended? Why build a home, settle in one place when he could take his seafaring home anywhere he wanted?

This was living the dream.

All he needed was a seaworthy boat, food on his plate and a comfortable bed. He curled both palms around the railing. All he wanted was peace and solitude and a blue horizon.

The hell it was.

One night after she'd closed up, Lissa looked at a tiny apartment that was becoming available at the end of the following month. No sea views but she couldn't afford to be choosy. She drove home feeling happier than she had in a while.

As she pulled into the driveway she saw a stretched limo out the front of Gilda's house. Off to one of her charity events, no doubt.

It wasn't until she was walking along the path to the front door that she heard the footsteps behind her.

'Ms Sanderson?'

'Yes?' She turned as the uniformed driver approached and it occurred to her that she'd felt none of that tingling alarm that had dogged her for so long.

'Good evening.' He took off his chauffeur's cap. He was medium height with an easy smile and greying hair and he handed her his ID. 'My name's Max Fitzgerald and I've been asked to give you this package then wait until you're ready. I'm to transport you to your dinner meeting.' He handed her a large flat box.

She frowned at the ID. He appeared to be who it said he was. Should she be suspicious? 'I don't have a dinner appointment,' she said. 'I bought a frozen meal on the way home.'

'You didn't receive a text message explaining?'

Oh? 'I haven't checked, I've been…busy…' She fished in her handbag for her phone. The screen lit up at her touch and she opened the text.

Lissa, you can trust Max. It's time we discussed moving on with the rest of our lives.

She recognised Blake's number.

For a few stunned seconds she couldn't move. Then her heart flipped over and dropped like a stone. *Now* he wanted to talk? Just when she was getting used to not having him around?

He probably had tenants waiting to lease the house and wanted her to vacate. *He wanted to get on with the rest of his life.*

Or did he think that he could just turn up out of the blue and whistle—or text—and she'd come running? Other women might but not Lissa Sanderson. He couldn't even be bothered inviting her personally to have this discussion or collecting her himself?

'I'm not free tonight,' she told Max, slipping her phone back into her bag. 'I'll text him. Thanks, you can leave.'

'He told me you might say that. He asked me to beg you to reconsider.'

'I don't—'

'Please, Ms Sanderson.' Max ran his fingers over the cap in his hand. 'He asked me to get down on one knee if I had to and I'm getting too old for all that.' His eyes lit with humour. 'My joints aren't what they used to be.'

Lissa stared at him. Blake had begged? Pleaded? He wanted to see her that badly? A glimmer of something like hope flickered inside her but she pushed it down. 'There's no need for that.' She looked at the smooth, white, expensive-looking box in her hands. 'Why don't you come inside and I'll just see what's in this package…?'

'I'll wait in the vehicle, if that's all right with you, ma'am. Take your time, I'll be here till dawn.'

'Dawn?' Was he serious?

'Mr Everett explained you like to party on occasion.'

'Did he?' she murmured. Obviously he thought she'd got on with her life. She didn't know whether to be amused or offended. 'Okay, Max. I'll be sure to let you know my decision soon.'

The moment she was inside, Lissa pulled the string off the box. Her heart raced as her fingers scrabbled through the mountain of tissue paper.

A slimline gown of the palest aquamarine. It shimmered in the light as she drew it out. Or maybe it was the tears that sprang to her eyes making it seem so.

'Oh, my…goodness.' She'd never seen anything more exquisite.

Her arms shook as she held it against her. It flowed to the floor like a slender stream of clear spring water. Shoestring straps and a low back that dipped to her waist.

As she raced upstairs to try it on she didn't let herself think, dared not allow herself to hope.

CHAPTER SIXTEEN

MAX was out of the limo the moment she stepped through the front door twenty tension-fraught minutes later. 'Very becoming,' he said, nodding as she approached. 'You look lovely.'

'Thank you.' She smoothed a hand down the slippery fabric. It fitted like a dream. She wondered if that was what this was. Just a dream. Like the ones she'd had so many years ago.

He reached into the vehicle and withdrew a small bouquet of creamy gardenias and presented them to her as he opened her door.

'Oh…' She inhaled their delicate green fragrance. 'Thank you, again.'

She slid inside and set the flowers beside her on the soft leather seat. Through the speakers, Robbie was singing about angels. A bottle of champagne chilled in an ice-bucket beside a crystal flute.

'Can I pour you a glass of champagne before we leave?' Max asked.

'Oh, no.' She pressed a hand to her jittering stomach. 'I really couldn't.'

As they drew smoothly away from the kerb she tried to remember the last time she'd refused champagne. But right now her insides simply wouldn't tolerate it. And she needed a clear head to face Blake.

This might seem like a dream but she couldn't be sure it was the dream she wanted. Wouldn't allow herself to think beyond the next step. According to his text, he was expecting them to have a discussion. Over dinner. Maybe he liked women to look sophisticated when he dined. Or maybe... She shook her head and looked out at the darkening tropical sky with its anvil thunderheads building over the hinterland. She refused to contemplate any more maybes.

The journey took only a few minutes. At the Mooloolaba Marina she stepped into the deepening twilight, clutching her flowers and her bag.

Then Max was accompanying her through the security gate and towards a luxury yacht that dwarfed every other watercraft in the vicinity. Light spilled from the main deck and shimmered on the inky water. This wasn't the simple sailing boat she'd seen in Blake's brochure, even though that, too, had been a luxury in her eyes.

This was a floating palace. With its sleek white lines, it reminded her of a powerful beast waiting to be unleashed. She could visualise it slicing through the water with Blake at the helm. And that was probably where he'd be tomorrow, or the next day when his business with her was concluded.

And then she saw him. On the deck. In slim-fitting dark trousers and a white shirt open at the neck with the cuffs rolled back. Her heart stopped, then beat at double time. Their gazes met. Held for what seemed like eternity while the water lapped and the foody aroma from the nearby waterside restaurants wafted on the air. She could do this. She could.

Still watching her, he walked down the gangplank towards her. She could have a civilised meal then walk away...

'Good evening, Lissa.'

His tone was welcoming, if a little formal and, oh, how she'd missed that deep rich voice. But she could live without it. 'Hello.'

He barely glanced at the chauffeur. 'Thank you, Max. That'll be all for now.'

He reached out and sifted his fingers through the hair curling over her shoulders. She had time to breathe in his musky scent before he stepped back.

'Thank you for the dress. It's beautiful.'

'You make it so. And you're welcome.'

He leaned forward, touched cool dry lips to her cheek. Smooth skin. He'd shaved recently and smelled sinfully good for such a chaste kiss. She could feel the last of her strength draining out of her.

'I hope you haven't eaten already,' he said, placing a warm palm at the small of her bare back to guide her onto the boat.

She almost sighed at the contact before arching away and quickening her steps. She looked at the luxury surrounding her. 'This is a magnificent yacht.'

'I sold off most of my investments to buy it.'

She stared up at the stern's fibreglass U-shaped structure, which arched over a comfortable table setting with satin wicker chairs. Down-lights reflected on the table set for two with silver cutlery and white china. A candle glowed inside a tall glass.

Through a wide open doorway she could see a spacious living room. Thick blue carpet, polished wood and brass fittings, over-stuffed leather chairs and a bar with hidden lighting that sparkled with rows of bottles. 'This is all too overwhelming. You've been gone a month and now...'

'Twenty-six days, actually.'

She knew. Twenty-six days and thirteen hours.

A uniformed waiter appeared with a silver tray. Lissa recognised him from the catering company they'd used for the launch party.

'Would you care for a prawn tail with wasabi and lemon sauce?' Blake asked.

Her stomach writhed with nerves and nausea. She set her flowers on the table. 'I won't be dining with you. I came tonight because you went to such a lot of trouble to get me here, and I felt a little sorry for Max, but I need to know what you want. And I need to know now. Then I'll be leaving. We won't see each other again.'

Blake's demeanour changed. His jaw tightened and she saw his fingers flex at his sides. So his night wasn't going according to plan? Neither was hers.

He glanced at the waiter, waved him off. 'Take a break, Nathan.'

Lissa took the opportunity to move to the railing and looked out over the myriad boats bobbing on the water. From that distance she made herself turn to face him. And, oh, she wished she didn't have to because looking at him made her want to tell him things she knew he wouldn't want to hear.

'In your text you suggested moving on with our lives. I thought that's what we were doing.'

'I thought so too. Until a week ago.'

He took a step towards her but she held up a hand. 'Don't come any closer. Please, Blake.' She latched onto the only reason she could think of. 'You found someone to lease the house and you want me to vacate, right?'

He seemed to consider a moment. 'It's true, I want you to vacate the house.' His eyes were dark and steady on hers. 'Because I want you to live here on this boat. With me.'

The simplicity of his words—and the shock—pinned her feet to the deck. She gripped the railing for support. He wanted her to live with him. But he wanted it all his way. He was suggesting what was essentially a convenient live-in arrangement. She'd been there, done that, had the restraining order to prove it. No one was going to use her as a convenience again.

'We've played this scene before. I thought I already made it clear to you that I'm committed to my career—'

'I love you, Lissa.'

'That I—'

'I don't want to spend another day or another night without you.'

He took another step closer and this time she didn't try to stop him. Because she was too busy trying to breathe. To stay upright. To process the implications of what he was saying.

'And you think because you tell me you love me…' she hitched in a breath as she said the words and tightened her grip on the railing '…I'll give up all I've worked towards for you?'

'No.' His gaze reached out to her, holding her captive as he walked towards her. 'I'm going to stay here, in Mooloolaba, because here is where you are.'

What little breath she had left rushed out. She sucked in more salt-laden air. 'What happened to feeling the sea breeze in your face and dropping anchor wherever you please?'

'I thought that's what I wanted. But now I know I want you more.' He pushed a hand through his hair. 'For God's sake, Lissa, put me out of this hell I'm in and say yes. Tell me you love me back. Tell me what we had wasn't just a fling.'

She looked up at him, his face taut in the spill of light. She'd never seen such raw vulnerability in his face before. She'd never seen his expression so…open. 'I do love you,' she said softly. 'I always have and I always will. You were the one who always talked about leaving. And you were the one who called it a fling.'

'I heard you talking to Jared.'

Oh… And she felt a small smile touch her lips momentarily. 'Don't you know not to eavesdrop on private conversations?'

'Lissa…'

'It was never a fling, not to me. No, don't touch me.' She stepped away from his outstretched hand. 'Not yet. I want to know what made you come back.'

The haunted look she'd seen so often flickered behind his eyes. 'I realised I wanted to live before they bury me.'

'Torque…'

He nodded.

Then he didn't give her time to move. He gathered her up into his arms and held her close so she could hear his heart beating solidly beneath her ear. And she wanted to stay there in his safe and solid embrace for ever. He tucked her head beneath his chin and she knew he was looking out over the horizon.

'I felt his soul leave his body, Lissa, as I dragged him across the sand. I still hear the gunfire sometimes.'

'The nightmares…' Lissa whispered. 'You still have them.'

'Not as often.' He took a deep breath, stroked her hair. 'He was only eighteen. Thousands of miles from home. He'd barely begun to live and he was dead already.'

'I know.' She curled her hand against his heart. 'You need to learn to forgive yourself.'

'I'm working on it. I went to visit Torque's parents. They were so grateful there was someone with him when he passed. That he didn't suffer. It's helped. Both them and me.'

She nodded. 'I'm glad.'

He was silent a moment while the breeze blew over the deck. 'I came home to recuperate because I was looking for that familiarity I hadn't experienced in so long.

'I never expected to find you. A woman I could love. A love I can trust, a love I can give myself wholly to.'

Tears welled in her eyes and spilled over onto his shirt. He shifted so that he could cup her head in his hands, tilt it up and look into her eyes. 'A love that will last a lifetime.'

Her heart swelled to bursting. 'Blake…'

'I know you have your business and that I'm no longer a part of it, but that doesn't mean I can't be involved in some small way, does it?'

'Of course you c—'

'The marina's a few minutes' drive away from the shop. This yacht has more comfort and luxury than you've ever seen. You have Maddie and her team to help out now and then so when we want a weekend away we can just take off, up the coast, or down to Surfers to visit your family. The best of both worlds. The sea and, most importantly, you.'

Her thoughts were jumbled, spinning with the images he was conjuring with his words.

But he wasn't finished. He stepped back and drew something out of his pocket. He flipped the little velvet box open. 'Are you prepared to take on this scarred sailor who'll probably wake you up with bad dreams some nights?'

'Oh...I—'

'Marry me, Lissa. Live with me for the rest of our lives. Be my life's comfort and I'll be yours.'

Through her tears she saw a ring with a solitary aquamarine flanked by a diamond on either side. 'Oh...do you know how long I've waited to hear you ask that question?' she whispered. 'Fantasised where we'd be, how you'd ask? And it was never as perfect as this. And the answer is yes. A thousand times yes.'

'You're the only girl for me, Lissa. And I'll spend my life showing you.' He slid it onto the third finger of her left hand. 'A stone that captures the sea and the colour of your eyes. There's something of both of us in it.'

'It's beautiful,' she said softly. 'I couldn't have chosen anything better.' She watched it glitter in the light, then turned to him with a smile that came from the deepest corner of her heart. 'And now...are you going to seal this deal with a kiss?'

He smiled back and this time his amazing blue eyes were filled with sunshine and light. 'Try stopping me.'

And, oh, she'd missed his luscious mouth on hers. The taste of him, the scent of him as he drew her closer. Finally, he drew back and she knew it was only because they'd both run out of air.

'Now I want to show you your new home.'

He pulled his phone from his pocket. 'Max? We won't need your services for the rest of the night, thank you. Go home to bed.' He disconnected with a serious gleam in his eye. 'I intend to.'

Then he swept her up in his arms and carried her through the living room at a rate of knots. 'We'll do the more detailed tour later,' he told her, barely raising a puff. He paused at the galley's entrance to tell Nathan he could leave, that they'd help themselves to the meal later.

Then on through another entertainment area with wide-screen TV and concealed lighting that gave the room a pink-purple glow. Up the low polished wooden spiral staircase in the centre. Past a bathroom and its moulded spa bath with clear Perspex sides and marble vanity.

Blake set her on her feet in front of a massive double bed with a deep indigo quilt. Finally. He had her right where he wanted her. She glanced about her. 'I've got a really nice sketch that would suit this room...'

He could see her studying the décor with a trained eye. 'I think it's really you...'

'Not now, sweet cheeks.' He touched her chin and turned it so that she was looking at him. Only him. 'Take the night off.' His lips roamed her face while his hands moved over the delicate silk, reacquainting himself with her shape. Her fragrance. Her heat. 'I've missed you,' he murmured. It was a first for him. Hell, the whole evening had been about firsts.

He felt her smile against his mouth. 'So what have you missed about me?'

He kissed her again, then cupped her cheeks and looked into those clear sea-green eyes. 'I've missed your colour, your resilience. Your independence.' He punctuated each with a kiss. 'The way you listen when I talk, as if I matter. The way you push me to open up because you give a damn.'

He saw her eyes spring with moisture and smoothed the dampness away with his thumbs. 'I've even missed your chaos, believe it or not.'

'I've been trying to do something about that,' she whispered.

'Don't ever change. I love you just the way you are, feminine hygiene products on my bathroom shelf and all.'

He smoothed a hand over her breast so that he could feel her heart beating beneath his palm. 'You made me realise I've been existing but I've not been living. I've been hiding behind my navy career, too afraid to take another chance on love.'

'I was afraid too.' She closed her hand over his. Over her heart. 'You taught me to trust again.'

'I reckon we're pretty darn good for each other.'

'I reckon so. Except you forgot one thing.'

'Yeah?'

'You forgot how much you missed making love with me.'

'I didn't forget.' And he tumbled with her back onto the bed.

He was home.

* * * * *

THE SOCIALITE AND
THE CATTLE KING

BY
LINDSAY ARMSTRONG

Lindsay Armstrong was born in South Africa, but now lives in Australia with her New Zealand-born husband and their five children. They have lived in nearly every state of Australia, and have tried their hand at some unusual—for them—occupations, such as farming and horse-training—all grist to the mill for a writer! Lindsay started writing romances when their youngest child began school and she was left feeling at a loose end. She is still doing it and loving it.

CHAPTER ONE

HOLLY HARDING had the world at her feet—or she should have had.

The only child of wealthy parents—although her father had died—she could have rested on her laurels and fulfilled her mother's dearest ambition for her, that she settle down and make an appropriate, although of course happy, marriage.

Holly, however, had other ideas. Not that she was against wedlock in general, but she knew she wasn't ready for it. Sometimes she doubted she ever would be, but she went out of her way not to dwell on the reason for that…

Instead, she concentrated on her career. She was a journalist, although occasionally she partook of the social scene so dear to her mother's heart; Sylvia Harding was a well-known socialite. It was on two such occasions that Holly had encountered Brett Wyndham, with disastrous consequences.

'A masked fancy-dress ball and a charity lunch? You must be out of your mind,' Brett Wyndham said to his sister Sue.

He'd just flown in from India, on a delayed flight that

had also been diverted, so he was tired and irritable. His sister's plans for his social life did not appear to improve his mood.

'Oh, they're not so bad,' Sue said. She was in her late twenties, dark-haired like her brother, but petite and pretty—quite unlike her brother. She was also looking a bit pale and strained, whilst trying to strike an enthusiastic note. 'And it is a good cause—the lunch, anyway. What's wrong with raising money for animal shelters? I thought that might appeal to you. I mean, I know they may only be cats and dogs…'

Brett said wearily, 'I can't stand them. I can't stand the food, I can't stand the women—'

'The women?' Sue interrupted with a frown. 'You don't usually have a problem there. What's wrong with them?'

Brett opened his mouth to say, *They are usually the most ferociously groomed set of women you've ever seen in your life, from their dyed hair, their fake eyelashes, their plucked eyebrows, their fake nails and tans; they're ghastly.* But he didn't say it. Although she didn't have a fake tan or fake eyelashes, his sister was exquisitely groomed and most expensively dressed.

He shrugged. 'Their perfume alone is enough to give me hay fever,' he said moodily instead. 'And, honestly, I have a problem with the concept of turning fund-raising into society events that bring out all the social climbers and publicity seekers.' He stopped and shook his head.

'Brett, please!'

But Brett Wyndham was not to be placated. 'As for masked fancy-dress balls,' he went on, 'I can't stand the fools men make of themselves. And the women; something about being disguised, or thinking they are, seems to bring out the worst in them.'

'What do you mean?'

'I mean, beloved,' he said dryly, 'They develop almost predator-like tendencies.' For the first time a glint of humour lit his dark eyes. 'You need to be particularly careful or you can find yourself shackled, roped and on the way to the altar.'

Sue smiled. 'I don't think you would ever have that problem.'

He shrugged. 'Then there's Mark and Aria's wedding coming up shortly—the reason I'm home, anyway.' Mark was their brother. 'I've no idea what's planned but I'm sure there'll be plenty of partying involved.'

Sue's smile faded as she nodded, and tears came to her eyes.

Brett frowned down at her. 'Susie? What's wrong?'

'I've left Brendan.' Brendan was her husband of three years. 'I found out he was being unfaithful to me.'

Brett closed his eyes briefly. He could have said, *I told you so*, but he didn't. He put his arms around his sister instead.

'You were right about him.' Sue wept. 'I think all he was after was my money.'

'I guess we have to make our own mistakes.'

'Yes, but I feel so stupid. And—' she gulped back some tears '—I feel everyone must be laughing at me. Apparently it was no big secret. I was the last person to know,' she said tragically.

'It's often the way.'

'It may be, but it doesn't make it any easier.'

'Are you still in love with him?' Brett queried.

'No! Well, how could I be?'

Brett smiled absently.

'But one thing I do know,' Sue said with utter conviction. 'I refuse to go into a decline, I refuse to run away and hide and I refuse to be a laughing stock!'

'Susie—'

But his sister overrode him, with tears in her eyes still, but determination too. 'I'm patron of the Animal Shelter Society so I will be at the lunch. The ball is one of the festivities planned for the Winter Racing Carnival; I'm on the committee, so I'll be there too, and I'll make sure everyone knows who I am! But—' she sagged a little against him 'I—would dearly love some moral support.'

'I beg your pardon?' Mike Rafferty said to his boss, Brett Wyndham.

They were in Brett's apartment high above the Brisbane River and the elegant curves of the William Jolly Bridge. Sue, who'd insisted on picking him up from the airport, had just left.

'You heard,' Brett replied shortly.

'Well, I thought I did. You asked me to make a note of the fact that you were going to a charity lunch tomorrow and a masked fancy-dress ball on Friday night. I just couldn't believe my ears.'

'Don't make too big a thing of this, Mike,' Brett warned. 'I'm not in the mood.'

'Of course not. They could even be—quite enjoyable.'

Brett cast him a dark glance and got up to walk over

to the window with his familiar long-legged prowl. With his short, ruffled dark hair, blue shadows on his jaw, a kind of eagle intensity about his dark eyes, his cargo pants and black sweatshirt, his height and broad shoulders, he could have been anything.

What did come to mind was a trained-to-perfection daredevil member of a SWAT team.

In fact, Brett Wyndham was a vet and he specialized in saving endangered species, the more dangerous the better, such as the black rhino, elephants and tigers.

He dropped out of helicopters with tranquilizer guns, he parachuted into jungles—all in a day's work. He also managed the family fortunes that included some huge cattle-stations, and since he'd taken over the reins of the Wyndham empire he'd tripled that fortune so he was now a billionaire, although a very reclusive one. He did not give interviews but word of his work had filtered out and he'd captured the public's imagination.

As Brett's PA, it fell to Mike Rafferty to ensure his privacy here in Brisbane, amongst other duties at Haywire—one of the cattle stations in Far North Queensland the Wyndham dynasty called home—and at Palm Cove where they owned a resort.

'So will you be saying anything to the press?' he queried. 'There's bound to be some coverage of the lunch tomorrow, even if you'll be incognito at the ball.'

'No. I'm not saying anything to anyone although, according to my sister, my presence alone will invest the proceedings with quite some clout.' He grimaced.

'It probably will,' Mike agreed. 'And what will you be going to the masked ball as?'

'I have no idea. I'll leave that up to you—but

something discreet, Mike,' Brett growled. 'No monkey suit, no toga and laurel wreath, no Tarzan or *anything* like that.' He stopped and yawned. 'And now I'm going to bed.'

'Mum,' Holly said to her mother the next morning, 'I'm not sure about this outfit. Isn't the lunch supposed to be a fundraiser?' She glanced down at herself. She wore a fitted little black jacket with a low vee-neck over a very short black-and-white skirt. Black high-heeled sandals exposed newly painted pink toenails, matching her fingernails. She wore her mother's pearl choker and matching pendant earrings.

'It certainly is,' Sylvia replied. 'And a very exclusive one. The tickets cost a fortune, although of course they are tax deductible,' she assured her daughter. 'But you look stunning, darling!'

Holly grimaced and twirled in front of the mirror. They were in her bedroom in the family home, a lovely old house high on a hill in Balmoral. She still lived at home, or rather had moved back in after her father had died to keep her mother company. There were plenty of advantages to this arrangement that Holly was most appreciative of, which was why she humoured her mother now and then and attended these kinds of function.

Quite how she'd got roped into going to a charity lunch and a masked fancy-dress ball within a few days of each other she wasn't sure, but she knew it did give her mother a lot of pleasure to have her company. It also gave her a lot of pleasure to dress her daughter up to the nines.

Holly was quite tall and very slim, two things that

lent themselves to wearing clothes well, although when left to her own devices she favoured 'very casual'. She herself thought her looks were unexceptional, although she did have deep-blue eyes and a thick cloud of fair but hard-to-manage hair.

Today her hair was up in an elaborate chignon, and sprayed and pinned within in inch of its life to stay that way. Sylvia's hairdresser, who made house calls, had also done their nails.

Sylvia herself was resplendent in diamonds and a fuchsia linen suit.

Despite her mother's preoccupation with the social scene, Holly loved Sylvia and felt for her in her loneliness now she was a widow. But the most formative person in Holly's life had been her father, imbuing her not only with his love of the different but his love of writing.

Richard Harding, had he been born in another era, would have been a Dr Livingstone or Mr Stanley. He'd inherited considerable means and had loved nothing better than to travel, to explore out-of-the-way places and different cultures, and to write about them. The fact that he'd married someone almost the exact opposite had been something of a mystery to Holly, yet when they'd been together her parents had been happy.

But it was Holly who Richard had taken more and more on his expeditions. Amongst the results for Holly had been a well-rounded informal education alongside her formal one and fluency in French, plus some Spanish and a smattering of Swahili.

All of it had contributed towards Holly's present job. She was a travel reporter for an upmarket magazine but with a slight difference: hard-to-get-to places were her speciality. As a consequence, to bring to life her destinations, she'd used bad-tempered camels, stubborn donkeys, dangerous-looking vehicles driven by manic individuals and overcrowded ferries.

According to her editor, Glenn Shepherd, she might look as if a good puff of wind would blow her away but she had a hint of inner steel. She had to, to have coped with some of the situations she'd landed herself in.

She'd shrugged when he'd said this to her and had responded, 'Oh, I don't know. Sometimes looking and playing dumb works wonders.'

He'd grinned at her. 'What about the sheikh fellow who introduced you to all his wives with a view to you joining the clan? Or the Mexican bandit who wanted to marry you?'

'Ah, that required a bit of ingenuity. I actually had to steal his vehicle,' Holly had confessed. 'But I did have it returned to him. Glenn, I've been doing travel for a couple of years now—any chance of a change?'

'Thought you loved it?'

'I do, but I also want to spread my wings journalistically. I'd love to be given something I could *investigate* or someone I could get the definitive interview from.'

Glenn had sat forward. 'Holly, I'm not saying you're not capable of it, but you are only twenty-four; some kinds of—insight, I guess, take a bit longer than that to develop. It will come, but keep up the good work in the meantime. More and more people out there are getting to love your pieces. Also, re the definitive interview, we have a policy; any of our staff can try for one, so long as they pull it off ethically, and if it's good enough we'll publish it. But I must warn you, it has to be outstanding.'

'As in?'

'Mostly as in, well, surprise factor.' He'd shrugged. 'Brett Wyndham, for example.'

Holly had grimaced. 'That's like asking for the moon.'

Holly came back to the present and took one last look at herself. 'If you're sure,' she said to her mother, 'We're not terribly over-dressed?'

'We're not,' Sylvia said simply.

Holly saw that she was right when she took her place in the upmarket Milton restaurant that had been turned into a tropical greenhouse. She was amidst a noisy throng of very upmarket-looking guests. Almost without exception, the women were exquisitely groomed, expensively dressed and their jewellery flashed beneath the overhead lighting; many of them wore hats. Not only that, a lot of them seemed to know each other, so it was a convivial gathering helped along by the wine that started to flow. Recent cruises, skiing holidays and tropical islands featured in the snippets of conversation Holly heard around her, as well as the difficulties attached to finding really good housekeepers.

There were men present but they were rather outnumbered. One of them took his place beside Holly.

Goodness, gracious me! was Holly's first, startled reaction.

The man who sat down beside her was tall and beautifully proportioned; he was dark and satanic looking. He had a suppressed air of vitality combined with an arrogance that was repressed, but nevertheless you couldn't help but know it was there in the tilt of his head and the set of his mouth. All in all he made the little hairs on her arms stand up in a way that made her blink.

He was casually dressed in khaki trousers, a sports jacket and a navy-blue shirt. He looked out moodily over the assembled throng then concentrated on the first speaker of the day.

The patron of the shelter society introduced herself as Sue Murray. She was petite and dark, and clearly under some strain, as she stumbled a couple of times, then looked straight at the man beside Holly, drew a deep breath, and continued her speech smoothly. She gave a short résumé of the shelter society's activities and plans for the future, then she thanked everyone for coming. There was loud applause as she stepped down.

'Poor thing,' Sylvia whispered into Holly's ear. 'Her husband's been playing around. Darling, would you mind if I popped over to another table? I've just spied an old friend I haven't seen for ages. I'll be back when they start serving lunch.'

'Of course not,' Holly whispered back, and turned automatically to the man beside her as she unfolded her napkin. The seat on the other side of him was empty too, so they were like a little island in the throng. 'How do you do?'

'How do you do?' he replied coolly and studied all he could see of her, from her upswept hair, her pearls, the vee between her breasts exposed by her jacket and her slim waist. But it was worse than that. She got the distinct feeling he was viewing her without her clothes and with a view to assessing her potential as a partner in his bed.

She lowered her lashes swiftly as her blue eyes blazed at the sheer insolence of this unexpected appraisal, and at the inexplicable reaction it aroused in her. A wholly unexpected ripple of awareness touched her nerve ends.

Her lips parted on a stinging retort, but before she could frame it he smiled slightly, a lethally insolent twisting of his lips as if he was quite aware of his effect on her, and posed a question to her with an air of patent scepticism.

'Are you a great supporter of animal shelters?'

Holly looked taken aback for a moment but she recovered swiftly and said, 'No—not that I'm against them.' She shrugged. 'But that's not why I'm here.'

His eyes left her face briefly and she realized he was keeping tabs on the progress of Sue Murray as she moved from table to table introducing herself to everyone. When his gaze came back to her, he posed another question. 'Why *are* you here?'

'I came with my mother.'

A glint of amusement lit his dark eyes. 'That sounds as if it came from a list of excuses the Department of Transport publishes occasionally: "my mother told me to hurry up, that's why I was exceeding the speed limit".'

If she hadn't been so annoyed, if it hadn't been so apt, Holly would have seen the humour of this.

'Clever,' she said coldly. 'But I have to tell you, I'm already regretting it. And, for your further information, I don't approve of this kind of fund-raising.'

He lifted a lazy eyebrow. 'Strange, that. You look so very much the part.'

'What *part*?' she asked arctically.

He shrugged. 'The professional, serial socialite. The embodiment of conspicuous philanthropy in order to climb the social ladder.' He glanced at her left hand, which happened to be bare of rings. 'Maybe even in the market for a rich husband?' he added with soft but lethal irony.

Holly gasped, and gasped again, as his gaze flickered over her and came back to rest squarely on her décolletage; she had no doubt that he was mentally undressing her.

Then she clenched her teeth as it crossed her mind that she should have stuck to her guns. She should not be sitting there all dolled up to the nines, with her hair strangled up and starting to give her a headache, all to support a cause but giving off the wrong messages entirely. Obviously!

On the other hand, she thought swiftly, that did not give this man the right to insult her.

'If you'll forgive me for saying so,' she retorted, 'I think your manners are atrocious.'

'Oh. In what way?'

'How or why I'm here has nothing whatsoever to do with you and if you mentally undress me once more who knows what I might be prompted to do? I am,' she added, 'quite able to take care of myself, and I'm not wet behind the ears.'

'Fighting words,' he murmured. 'But there is this—'

'I know what you're going to say,' she broke in. 'It's

chemistry.' She looked at him scornfully. 'That is such an old, dead one! Even my Mexican bandit didn't use that one although, come to think of it, the sheikh did. Well, I think that's what he was saying.' She tipped her hand as if to say, 'you win some, you lose some'.

He blinked. 'Sounds as if you have an interesting life.'

'I do.'

'You're not making it all up?'

'No.' Holly folded her arms and waited.

'What?' he queried after a moment, with utterly false trepidation.

'I thought an apology might be appropriate.'

He said nothing, just gazed at her, and after a pensive moment on her part they were exchanging a long, telling look which came as quite a surprise to Holly. The luncheon and its environs receded and it was if there was only the two of them...

Whatever was happening for him, for Holly it became a drawing-in, not only visually but through her pores, of the essence of this man and the acknowledgement that his physical properties were extremely fine. He was not only tall, he was tanned, and he looked exceedingly fit, as if sitting at charity luncheons did not come naturally to him. His hands were long and well-shaped. His dark hair was crisp and short, and the lines and angles of his face were interesting but not easy to read.

In fact, she summarized to herself, there was something inherently dangerous but dynamically attractive about him that made you think of him having his hands on your body, his exciting, expert, mind-blowing way with you.

That's ridiculous, she told herself as a strange little thrill ran through her. *That's such a* girlish *fantasy!*

Nevertheless, it continued to do strange things to her.

It altered the rate of her breathing, for example. It caused a little pulse to beat rather wildly at the base of her throat so that her pearls jumped. To her amazement, it even caused her nipples to become sensitive and make the lace of her black bra feel almost intolerably scratchy.

Her lips parted, then she made a concerted attempt to gather her composure as his dark gaze raked her again, but he broke the spell.

He said very quietly, 'I don't know about the bandit or the sheikh, ma'am, but I can't help thinking chemistry is actually alive and well—between us.'

Holly came back to earth with a thud and rose to her feet. 'I'm leaving,' she said baldly.

He sat back and shrugged. 'Please don't on my account. I'll say no more. Anyway, what about your mother?' he queried with just a shadow of disbelief.

Holly looked around a little wildly. 'I'll take her with me. Yes!' And she strode away from the table.

'I'm sorry, I'm so sorry,' Holly said as she clutched the steering wheel and started to drive them home. Her mother still looked stunned. 'But he was—impossible, the man sitting next to me! Talk about making a pass!' she marvelled.

'Brett Wyndham made a pass at you?' Sylvia said in faint accents as she clutched the arm rest. 'Holly, slow down, darling!'

Holly did more, she stamped on the brakes then pulled off the road. 'Brett Wyndham,' she repeated incredulously. '*That* was Brett Wyndham?'

'Yes. Sue Murray's his sister. We can only assume that's why he's there. I told you, she's having husband troubles, and perhaps he's providing moral support or something like that. I've never seen him at such a function before, or any kind of function for that matter.'

Holly released the wheel and clutched her head, then she started shedding hairpins haphazardly into her lap. 'If only I'd known! But would I have done anything differently? He was exceedingly—he was— That's why he was watching her.'

'Who?'

'His sister. In between watching me,' Holly said bitterly. 'On the other hand, I could maybe have seen the funny side of it. I could have deflected him humorously and—who knows?'

'If I had the faintest idea what you were talking about I might be able to agree or disagree,' her mother said plaintively.

Holly turned to her then hugged her. 'I am sorry. On all counts. And don't mind me; it's just that an interview with Brett Wyndham could have been the real boost my career needs.'

CHAPTER TWO

A COUPLE of days later, Holly found she couldn't get out of the masked fancy-dress ball she'd agreed to attend with her mother, much as she would have loved to.

When she raised the matter, Sylvia pointed out that it would make the table numbers uneven, for one thing, and for another wasn't her costume inspired—especially for a girl called Holly?

'So, who are we going with?' Holly queried.

'Two married couples and a gentleman friend of mind, plus his son: a nice table of eight,' Sylvia said contentedly.

Holly had met the gentleman friend, a widower, but not the son. In answer to her query on that subject, she received the news that the son was only twenty-one but a very nice, mature boy. Holly digested this information with inward scepticism. 'Mature and twenty-one' in young men did not always go together, in her opinion, but then she consoled herself with the thought that her mother couldn't have any expectations of a twenty-one-year-old as in husband material for Holly, surely?

Still, she wasn't brimming with keenness to go—but she remembered how she'd probably embarrassed the life out of her mother a few days ago, and she decided to bite the bullet.

Unfortunately, the memory of the lunch brought Brett Wyndham back to mind and demonstrated to her that she didn't have an unequivocal stance on the memory. Yes, she'd been outraged at his approach at the time— who wouldn't have been? He'd accused her of being a serial socialite and a gold-digger.

Of course, there'd been an intrinsic undercurrent to that in his own fairly obvious distaste for the lunch and all it stood for. Why else would he challenge her motives for being there? But—another but—how did that fit in with his sister being the patron of the shelter society?

Ironic, however, was the fact that two things had chipped away at her absolute outrage, making it not quite so severe: the undoubted frisson he'd aroused in her being one. Put simply, it translated into the fact that he'd been the first man to excite her physically since, well, in quite a long time…

She looked into the distance and shivered before bringing herself back to the present and forcing herself to face the second factor that had slightly lessened her outrage. Had she mucked up a golden opportunity to get the interview that would have boosted her career?

Yes, she answered herself, well and truly mucked it up. But there was no way she would have done anything differently so she just had to live with it!

All the same, militant as she felt on the subject of Brett Wyndham on one hand, on the other she had an impulse, one that actually made her fingers itch—to look him up on the Internet.

She shook her head and fought it but it was a fight

she lost, and her fingers flew over the keys of her laptop, only to find that not a lot personal came to light. He was thirty-five, the oldest of three. There was a brother between him and his sister Sue, a brother who was getting married shortly. In fact, there was more about this brother Mark, his fiancée Aria and Sue Murray than there was about Brett Wyndham, so far as personal lives went.

She dug a bit further and established that the Wyndhams had been pioneers in the savannah country of Far North Queensland where they'd established their cattle stations. She learnt that Haywire, situated between Georgetown and Croydon, was the station they called home. And she learnt that the red-basalt soil in the area produced grass that cattle thrived upon—quite beside the point. Well, the treacherous little thought crept into her mind, not so much beside the point if she ever got to interview the man!

She also learnt that Brett Wyndham was a powerful figure in other ways. The empire was no longer based solely on pastoralism. He had mining interests in the area, marble from Chillagoe, zinc and transport companies. He employed a significant amount of people in these enterprises, and he was respected for his environmental views, as well as views on endangered species.

Then she turned up gold, from her point of view—a rather bitchy little article about one Natasha Hewson, who was described as extraordinarily beautiful and extremely talented. Apparently she ran an agency that specialized in organizing events and functions down to the last exquisite detail for the rich and famous. But, the article went on to say, if Natasha had hoped to be last in the long line of beautiful women Brett Wyndham had squired when they'd got engaged, her hopes had been dashed when they'd broken off the engagement recently…

Holly checked the date and saw that it was only nine months ago.

She sat back and tapped her teeth with the end of her pen. She had to admit that he'd got to her in a way that had reawakened her from a couple of years of mental and physical celibacy—but had she wanted to be reawakened? Not by a man who could have any woman he wanted, and had had a long line of them, she thought swiftly.

Mind you—she smiled a rueful smile—there was no hope of her getting an interview with him anyway, so it was best just to forget it all.

Brett Wyndham wondered how soon he'd be able to leave the ball. He'd come partnerless—well, he'd come with his sister. True to her word, she was looking stunning in a lavender crinoline, but otherwise apart from her tiny mask was quite recognizable as Sue Murray. Moreover she was putting a brave face on even if her heart was breaking and, whether it was his presence or not, no-one appeared to be making a laughing stock of her.

He watched her dance past—he'd left their table and was standing at the bar—and he found himself pondering the nature of love. Sue felt she shouldn't be able to love Brendan Murray now but was that all it took in matters of the heart? Dictating to yourself what you should or should not feel?

Which led him in turn to ponder his own love life. The nature of his life seemed to ensure that the women in it were only passing companions, but there had been no shortage of them. The problem was, he couldn't seem to drum up much enthusiasm for any of them.

Not only that, perhaps it was the inability of those partners to disguise their expectations that he was getting tired of, he reflected. Or the fact that none of them ever said 'no.' Well, one had quite recently, now he came to think of it. His lips twisted with amusement at the memory.

He shrugged and turned to watch the passing parade.

He'd come, courtesy of Mike Rafferty, as a masked Spanish aristocrat with a dark cropped jacket, dark, trousers, soft boots and white, frilled shirt, complete with scarlet cummerbund and black felt hat.

Dinner was over and the serious part of the evening under way—the serious dancing, that was. They were all there, strutting their stuff to the powerful beat of the music under the chandelier: the Cleopatras, the Marie Antoinettes, the belly dancers, the harem girls, the Lone Rangers, the Lawrences of Arabia, the three Elvises, a Joan of Arc and a Lady Godiva in a body stocking who looked as if she was regretting her choice of costume.

Some of them he recognized despite the masks and towering wigs. All of them, he reflected, bored him to tears.

He was just about to turn away when one girl he didn't recognize danced past in the arms of an eager pirate complete with eye patch, one gold earring and a stuffed macaw on his shoulder.

She was quite tall, very slim and dressed almost all in black. Something about her, probably her outfit, stirred something in his memory, but he couldn't pin it down.

'Who's she supposed to be?' he enquired of an elderly milkmaid standing beside him. He indicated the girl in black.

The milkmaid beamed. 'Isn't she perfect? So different. Of course, it's Holly Golightly—don't you remember? Audrey Hepburn in *Breakfast at Tiffany's*. That gorgeous black hat with the wide, downturned brim and the light, floaty hat-band; the earrings, the classic little black dress and gloves—even the alligator shoes. And to think of using her sunglasses as a mask!'

'Ah. Yes, she is rather perfect. You wouldn't happen to know who she is in real life?'

The milkmaid had no idea and Brett watched Holly Golightly dance past again.

She looked cool and detached, even slightly superior, but that could be because the pirate was having trouble containing his enthusiasm for her.

In fact, as he watched she detached herself from her partner as he attempted to maul her, swung on her heel and swept away towards the ballroom balcony with a hand to her hat.

The pirate looked so crestfallen, Brett could only assume he was either very young or very drunk.

Without giving it much thought, he took a fresh glass of champagne off the bar and followed the girl onto the balcony.

She was leaning against the balustrade, breathing deeply.

'Maybe this'll help to remove the taste of the pirate?' he suggested and offered the champagne to her.

Holly straightened and wondered if she was imagining things. She'd been rather darkly contemplating the fact that she'd been right about very young men such as the pirate who was the son of her mother's friend; he hadn't been able to keep his hands off her!

But could this tall, arrogant-looking Spaniard be who she thought he was? Could you ever forget Brett Wyndham's voice, or his athletic build? Or the pass he'd made at her? More importantly, did she want to be recognized? As a serious journalist, perhaps, but like this? As a *serial socialite…*?

In a lightning decision that she did not want to be recognized, she lowered her voice a notch and assumed a French accent. '*Merci*. I was of a mind to punch his parrot.'

Brett laughed then narrowed his eyes behind the mask. 'You sound as if you've just stepped out of France.'

'Not France, Tahiti.' It wasn't exactly a lie. She'd returned from her last travel assignment, Papeete, a bare week ago.

'So, a Tahitian Holly Golightly?'

'You may say so.' Holly sipped some champagne. 'What have we with you? An Aussie *señor*?'

He looked down at his attire. 'You could say so. Are you into horses, Miss Golightly?'

Holly gazed at him blankly.

'It *is* the kick-off to the Winter Racing Carnival, this ball,' he elaborated.

'Of course! But no, you could say not, although I

have done some riding in my time. Generally, though, on inferior beasts such as asses and camels.'

Brett's eyebrows shot up. 'Camels? In Tahiti? How come?'

'Not, naturally, Tahiti,' Holly denied regally. 'But I have a fondness for some out-of-the-way places you cannot get to by *other* means.' She gave the word "other" a tremendous French twist.

'So do I,' he murmured and frowned again as his masked gaze roamed over her.

Holly waited with some trepidation. Would he recognize her beneath the Holly Golightly outfit, the wide, downturned hat-brim and the French accent? She'd recognized him almost immediately, but that deep, mesmerizing voice would be hard to disguise. For that matter, so were those wide shoulders and lean hips.

Then it occurred to her that she was once again being summed up in that inimitable way of his.

The slender line of her neck, the outline of her figure beneath the little black dress, the smooth skin of her arms above her gloves, her trim ankles—they all received his critical assessment. And they all traitorously reacted accordingly, which was to say he might as well have been running his hands over her body.

'Actually,' she said airily—not a true reflection of her emotions as she was battling to stay cool and striving to take a humorous view of proceedings, 'You make a *trés* arrogant Spaniard.'

'I do?'

'*Oui.* Summing up perfectly strange women with a view to ownership is what I would call arrogant. Could it be that there is little difference between you and the pirate with the parrot, *monsieur*?'

'Ownership?' he queried.

'Of their bodies,' she explained. 'Tell me this was not so a moment ago?' She tilted her chin at him.

He pushed his hands into his pockets and shrugged. 'It's a failing most men succumb to. But unlike the pirate I would never attempt to maul you, Miss Golightly.'

He paused and allowed his dark, masked gaze to travel over her again. 'On the contrary, I would make your skin feel like warm silk and I would celebrate your lovely, slim body in a way that would be entirely satisfactory—for both of us.'

Holly stifled a tremor of utmost sensuousness that threatened to engulf her down the length of her body—at least stifled the outward appearance of it, by the narrowest of margins.

All the same, she went hot and cold and had to wonder how he did it. How did he engender a state of mind that could even have her wondering what it would be like to be Brett Wyndham's woman. How dared he?

Despite his arrogance, did that dark, swashbuckling presence do it to most women he came in contact with?

Her mind swooped on this point. Would it be a relief to think she was just one of a crowd when it came to Brett Wyndham? Or would it make it worse?

She came to her senses abruptly to find him studying her intently now and rather differently. 'You have a problem, *señor*?'

'No. Well, I just have the feeling I've met you before, Miss Golightly.'

Holly took the bit between her teeth and contrived a quizzical little smile. 'Many men have that problem. It is a very—how do you say it?—unoriginal approach.'

'You feel I'm making a pass at you?' he enquired lazily.

'I am convinced of it.' She presented him her half empty champagne glass. 'Thus, I will return to my party. *Au revoir.*'

But he said, 'Were you riding a camel when your sheikh propositioned you?'

Holly, in the act of sweeping inside, stopped as if shot.

'Or a donkey, when the Mexican approached you?' he added softly.

'You knew!' she accused.

'The accent and the outfit threw me for a while, but I'm not blind or deaf. Is it *all* made up? And, if so, why?'

Holly walked back to him and retrieved her champagne. 'I've got the feeling I might need this,' she said darkly and took a good sip. 'No, well, Tahiti was true—a bit. I've just come back so it seemed like a good idea to—' she gestured airily '—to…' But she couldn't think of a suitable way to cloak it.

'Help pull the wool over my eyes?' he suggested.

Holly choked slightly on a second sip of champagne but made a swift recovery. 'Why would I want to be recognized by you? All you ever do is query my motives, accuse me of appalling posturing and make passes at me!'

'You have to admit it all sounds highly unlikely,' he drawled. 'Are you here with your mother?'

Holly opened her mouth but closed it and stamped her foot. 'Don't you dare make fun of my mother! She—'

A flash of pale colour registered in her peripheral vision and she turned to see her mother coming out onto the balcony. Her mother was dressed as Eliza Doolittle at the races, complete with huge hat and parasol. 'We might as well both reprise Audrey Hepburn roles,' Sylvia had said upon presenting the idea to her daughter.

'Mum!' Holly said. 'What—'

But her mother interrupted her. 'There you are, darling! And I see you've met Mr Wyndham.' Sylvia turned to Brett. 'How do you do? I'm Sylvia Harding, Holly's mother—yes, her real name is Holly, that's why we thought of Holly Golightly!' Sylvia paused and took a very deep breath. 'But I feel sure there was some misunderstanding at the shelter lunch, and she didn't have the opportunity to tell you that she's a journalist and would love to interview you.'

There was dead silence on the balcony but Sylvia went on, apparently oblivious to the undercurrents. 'I also know she'd do a great job; she's not her father's daughter for nothing. He was Richard Harding, incidentally—perhaps you've heard of him?'

'Yes, I have. How do you do, Mrs Harding?' Brett said courteously.

'I'm fine, thank you. You may be wondering how I recognized you, but as soon as I saw you with Sue it clicked. She's such a lovely person, your sister. Well, I'll leave you two together.' She hesitated then walked back inside.

Holly let out a long breath then finished the champagne with a gulp. 'Don't say a word,' she warned Brett, once again presented him with her glass. 'I did not arrange that, and anyway I don't believe leopards change their spots, so I have no desire to interview you.'

'Leopards?' he queried gravely but she could see he was struggling not to laugh. 'On top of camels, asses, Mexicans and sheikhs?'

'Yes,' she said through her teeth. 'I believe they can be cunning, highly dangerous and thoroughly bad-minded into the bargain. If anyone should know that, you should.'

'I do,' he agreed. 'Uh—where is this analogy leading?'

'I have no faith in you *not* making any more passes at me, that's where.'

'I'd be demolished,' he said. 'But I'm pretty sure it isn't all one-sided.'

Another deadly little silence enveloped the balcony.

Holly opened her mouth but had to close it as no inspiration came to her. In all honesty, how could she deny the claim? On the other hand, every bit of good sense she possessed told her that to acknowledge it would be foolhardy in the extreme.

So, in the end, she did the only thing available to her: she swung on her heel and walked away from him.

'How was the ball?' Mike Rafferty enquired of his boss the next morning.

Brett lay back in his chair and appeared to meditate for a moment. 'Interesting,' he said at last.

'Well, that's got to be better than you expected,' Mike

replied and placed some papers on the desk. 'The lead up to the wedding,' he said simply.

Brett grimaced and pulled the details of Mark's pre-wedding festivities towards him. 'I just hope it's not a three-ring circus. Oh hell, another ball!'

'But this one's just a normal ball,' Mike pointed out.

Brett did not look mollified as he read on. 'A soirée, a beach barbecue, a trip to the reef—da-da, da-da.' Brett waved a hand. 'All right. I presume they've got someone in to organize it all properly?'

Mike hesitated and then coughed nervously.

Brett stared narrowly at him. 'Who? Not…? Not Natasha?'

'I'm afraid so.'

Brett swore.

'She is the best—at this kind of thing,' Mike offered.

'But I believe they had someone else to start with who made a real hash of things, so they called on Ms Hewson and she saved the day, apparently. She and Aria are friends,' he added.

'I see.' Brett drummed his fingers on the desk then looked to have made a decision. 'Mike, find out all you can about a girl called Holly Harding. She's Richard Harding's daughter—the well-known writer—and I believe she's a journalist herself. Do it now, please.'

Mike stared at his boss for a moment as he tried to tie this in with Mark Wyndham's wedding.

'What?' Brett queried.

'Nothing,' Mike said hastily. 'Just going.'

* * *

On Monday afternoon Glenn Shepherd called Holly into his office, and hugged her. 'You're such a clever girl,' he enthused. 'I might have known I was laying down the gauntlet to you when I mentioned his name, but how on earth did you pull it off? And why keep it such a secret?' He released her and went back behind his desk.

Holly, looking dazed and confused, sank into a chair across the desk. 'What are you talking about, Glenn?'

'Getting an interview with Brett Wyndham, of course. What else?'

Holly stared at him, transfixed, then she cleared her throat. 'I—wasn't aware that I had.'

Glenn gestured. 'Well, there are a few details he wants to sort out with you before he gives his final consent, so I made an appointment for you with him for five-thirty this afternoon.' He passed a slip of paper to her over the desk. 'If you've got anything on, cancel it. This could be your big break, Holly, and it won't do *us* any harm, either. Uh—there may be some travel involved.'

'Travel?'

'I'll let him tell you about it but of course we'd foot the bill where necessary.'

'Glenn...' Holly said.

But he interrupted her and stood up. 'Go get it, girl! And now I've got to run.'

At five-twenty that afternoon, Holly glanced at the piece of paper Glenn had given her and frowned. Southbank was a lovely precinct on the Brisbane river, opposite the tall towers of the CBD. It was made up of restaurants, a swimming lagoon and gardens set around the civic theatre and the art gallery. It was not exactly where she would have expected to conduct a business meeting with Brett Wyndham.

Then again, that was the last thing she'd expected to be doing this Monday afternoon, or any afternoon, so why quibble at the venue?

She parked her car, gathered her tote bag and for a moment wished she was dressed more formally. But that would have involved rushing home to change, and anyway, she didn't want him to think she'd gone to any trouble with her appearance on his behalf, did she?

No, she answered herself, *so why even think it*?

Because she might have felt more mature, or something like that, if she wasn't dressed as she usually was for work.

She looked down at her jeans, the pink singlet top she wore under a rather beloved jacket and her brown, short boots. This was the kind of clothes she felt comfortable in when she was traveling, as well as at work.

As for her hair, she'd left it to its own devices that morning and the result was a mass of untamed curls.

There could be little or no resemblance to the girl at the shelter lunch or Holly Golightly, she reasoned, which should be a good thing.

But, she also reasoned, really her clothes and hair were nothing compared to her absolute shock and disbelief at this move Brett Wyndham had made. What was behind it?

She shook her head, locked her car and went to find him.

It took a moment for Brett Wyndham to recognize Holly Harding. He noticed a tall girl in denims and a pink singlet with a leather tote hanging from her shoulder, wandering down the path from the car park. He noted that she looked completely natural, with no make-up, from her wild, fair curls to her boots, as well as looking young and leggy. Then it suddenly dawned on him who she was.

He saw her look around the restaurant terrace—their designated meeting place—and he raised a hand. He thought she hesitated briefly, then she came over.

He stood up and offered her a chair. 'Good day,' he murmured as they both sat down. 'Yet another incarnation of Holly Harding?'

'This is the real me,' Holly said dryly, and studied him briefly. He wore a black sweater, olive-canvas trousers and thick-soled black-leather shoes. His short, dark hair was ruffled; while he might have made a perfect Spanish aristocrat a few nights ago, today he looked tough, inscrutable and potentially dangerous.

'Would you like a drink?'

'Just a soft one, thank you. I never mix business with pleasure,' Holly replied.

He ordered a fruit juice for her and beer for himself, ignoring her rather pointed comment. 'If this is the real you,' he said, 'What makes you moonlight as a social butterfly?'

'My mother. Please don't make any smart remarks,' she warned, and explained the situation to him in a nutshell.

'Very commendable.' He paused as his beer was served, along with a silver dish of olives and a fruit-laden glass of juice topped by a pink parasol for Holly.

'But a bit trying at times,' Holly revealed, allowing

her hostilities to lapse for a moment. 'I think I would have preferred standing on a street corner with a collection box rather than that lunch, but perhaps I shouldn't say that in deference to your sister.' She eyed him curiously then stared out over the gardens towards the river. The sun was setting and the quality of light was warm and vivid.

He watched her thoughtfully. 'Each to his own method, but we seem to have a few things in common.'

'Not really,' Holly disagreed, going back to clearly hostile, and turned to look straight at him. 'Why have you done this?'

He countered with a question, 'Did you or did you not tell your mother you would love to interview me?'

'I…' Holly paused. 'I told her an interview with you could provide the boost my career needed. I told her that I'd had no idea who you were, but if there'd ever been any chance of an interview I'd blown it.'

'Only, being a mother, she didn't believe you,' he said wryly. 'Well, it *is* on, on certain conditions.'

'So I hear.' She glanced at him coolly, as if she was highly suspicious of his conditions—which she was. 'What are they?'

'I'm a bit pressed for time. I need to be in Cairns—Palm Cove, precisely. I have an important meeting. And I need to be out at Haywire the following day for a few days. It's the only free time I have before my brother gets married, and anyway—' he looked at her over the rim of his glass '—it will set the scene for you.'

'You—want me to come to Palm Cove and then on to this Haywire place with you?' she queried a little jaggedly.

He nodded. 'Not only am I pressed for time, but logistically it makes sense. The best way to get you to Haywire is for you to fly out there with me from Cairns.'

'Do I,' Holly gestured, 'actually have to see this Haywire place?'

'Yes.'

'Why?'

He sat back and shoved his hands into his pockets with a slight frown. 'That doesn't sound like a dedicated journalist. Why wouldn't you want to see it?'

'Mr Wyndham,' she said carefully, 'You have not only accused me of being a serial socialite and a gold-digger, you've mentally undressed me often enough to make me *seriously* wary of being stuck somewhere out beyond the black stump with you!'

Like lightning, a crooked grin creased his face which didn't impress Holly at all.

'I apologize,' he said then. 'I was—' he paused to consider '—not in a very good mood—not at the lunch, anyway. However, you'd be quite safe at Haywire. There's staff up there, and I'm not in the habit of forcing myself on unwilling women.'

Holly chewed her lip then said finally, 'What are the other conditions?'

'I mainly want to talk about the work I do—so nothing personal, unless it's ancient history. And I want to vet it before it gets published.'

Holly blinked several times, then she said frustratedly, 'Why me?'

He shrugged. 'Why not? Not only are you a journalist, but you're interesting.' He looked amused. 'I've never been walked-out on before, as you did at the lunch. I've never been told I was making a pass in a French accent. And I've *never* been accused of being as bad-minded as a leopard.'

Holly realized she'd been staring at him open-mouthed. She shut it hastily and watched him twirl his beer bottle in his long fingers before pouring the last of it into his glass.

'But what really decided me,' he continued, 'was your mother.'

'My mother?' Holly repeated in dazed tones. 'How come?'

'I thought what she did was quite brave. Maybe it's mistaken maternal faith—we'll see, I guess—but I liked her for it.'

Holly was seized by strong emotion and had to turn away to hide it as her eyes blazed. If it killed her, she would dearly love to prove to Brett Wyndham that her mother's faith in her was not *mistakenly maternal*, even if it meant spending some days with him at Palm Cove and beyond the black stump…

After all, there was bound to be staff at the station, and Palm Cove was highly civilized, wasn't it? It was not as if she'd be stranded in some jungle with him. It would actually be quite difficult to be stalked by him up there, as predator and prey, and she was no silly girl to be seduced by palm trees and mango daiquiris.

Was that all there was to it, however? Was simply to be in his company seductive? Was he just that kind of man? She couldn't deny he'd had a powerful effect on her a couple of times—without even trying too hard, she thought a little bitterly. But surely that was in *her* power to control? Well, if not control, ignore.

After all, was she not getting gold in return for a little self-discipline?

She opened her mouth, looked frustrated and said, 'You never give interviews. So I'm having a little difficulty with that.'

'I'm branching out in a new direction that I was going to publicize anyway. I've read some of your pieces, you have your father's touch and I thought you could do justice to it.'

Holly's lips parted and he could see the quickening of interest drowning the doubt and suspicion in her eyes. 'Am I allowed to know what it is?'

He shook his head. 'Not yet. But it's the very good reason for you to see Haywire.'

Holly looked unamused. 'I find you extremely— annoying at times,' she told him.

Brett Wyndham's lips twisted; he wondered what she'd say if he told her how annoyed he'd been when they'd first met. He'd been annoyed at the lunch; he'd arrived annoyed, then got further annoyed at finding himself feeling a niggle of attraction towards the kind of girl he'd castigated to himself so thoroughly. When she'd walked out, the niggle had become tinged with a grudging kind of admiration—that had also annoyed him.

Then her Holly Golightly hauteur had claimed his attention, and on discovering it was the same girl his annoyance had turned to intrigue. He was still intrigued by this version of Holly Harding—even more intrigued because he was quite sure he'd stirred some response in her...

Still, he reflected, these were improbable lengths to go to over a smattering of intrigue to do with a woman, particularly for him. But he had liked her fresh, slightly zany style in the pieces he'd read, he reminded himself, and he had even considered the possibility of offering her some publicity work for his new venture.

'So?' He lifted an eyebrow at her.

Holly meditated for a moment then replied quite candidly. 'I'd love to say no, because you've pressed a few wrong buttons with me, Mr Wyndham. But—' she flipped her hand '—you've also pressed a few right ones. My mother was an inspired one, in more ways than one.' She cast him a strange little look from beneath her lashes. 'Then there's my editor. How I would explain to him I've knocked back this opportunity, I can't even begin to think.'

She paused to take several breaths.

'There's more?' he queried with some irony.

'A bit more. You've got to be interesting—you've certainly captured the public's imagination—so, on a purely professional level, I can't turn it down.'

'Am I expected to be flattered?'

Holly searched his eyes and could just detect the wicked amusement in their dark depths. 'Yes,' she said baldly. 'I'm usually no pushover.'

'OK, take it as read that I'm flattered.' He stopped, flagged a passing waiter and ordered a bottle of champagne.

'Oh. No!' Holly protested. 'I didn't mean...'

'You don't think we should celebrate?' He looked

offended. 'I do. It's not every day I score a coup like this. Besides, I thought you liked champagne.'

'You're making fun of me,' she accused.

'Yes,' he agreed. 'Well, yes and no. You can be quite an impressive twenty-four-year-old. Thanks,' he said to the waiter who delivered the champagne and carefully poured two glasses.

He handed one to Holly and held up his own. 'Cheers!'

Holly reluctantly raised her glass to his. 'Cheers,' she echoed. 'But I'm only having one glass. On top of everything else, I'm driving.'

'That's fine,' he said idly.

'Isn't that a waste of champagne? Or are you going to drink it all?'

'No. I'm meeting someone else here shortly. She also likes champagne.'

Holly took a hurried gulp. 'Well, the sooner I get going the better.'

'No need to rush; she's my sister.'

Holly looked embarrassed. 'Oh. I thought…' She tailed off.

'You thought she was a girlfriend?'

'Yes. Sorry. Not that it matters to me one way or the other.'

'Naturally not,' he murmured.

She eyed him over her glass. 'You know, I can't quite make you out.'

He allowed his dark gaze to drift over her in a way that caused her skin to shiver of its own accord. She'd been inwardly congratulating herself on *not* having this happen to her during this encounter—an involuntary physical response to this man—but now it had.

'The same goes for me,' he said quietly. 'Can't quite make you out.'

Holly made an effort to rescue herself, to stop the flow of messages bombarding her senses. How could it happen like this? she wondered a little wildly. Out of the blue across a little glass-topped table on a terrace in the fading light of day.

But her rather tortured reflections were broken by a canine yelp, a squeal then howls of pain as, limping badly, a dog skittered across the terrace and disappeared into the shrubbery.

CHAPTER THREE

HOLLY jumped to her feet but Brett Wyndham was even quicker.

He plunged into the shrubbery, issuing a terse warning to her over his shoulder to be careful because the dog, in its pain, could bite.

The next few minutes were chaotic as Brett captured then subdued the terrified dog, a black-and-white border collie. How, Holly had no idea, but he did, and a lot of people milled around. None of them was its owner, or had any idea where it had come from, other than it must have got loose from somewhere and possibly got run over as it had crossed the road.

'OK.' Brett pulled his phone out and tossed it to Holly. 'Find the nearest vet surgery.' He pulled out his car keys and tossed them to her. 'And drive my car down here as close as you can get. It's the silver BMW.'

Holly grabbed her tote and did so, and ended up driving the four-wheel-drive so Brett could attend to the dog on the way to the surgery. He was staunching a deep cut on its leg with his handkerchief and she heard him say, 'You're going to be all right, mate.'

She found the surgery with the aid of the GPS and

helped carry the dog in. 'Is he really going to be all right?' she asked fearfully as they handed it over.

'I reckon so.' He scanned her briefly then looked more closely. 'You better sit down; you look a bit pale. I'm going in for a few minutes.' He turned to the receptionist, who was hovering. 'Could you get her a glass of water?'

'Of course. Sit down, ma'am.'

Holly was only too glad to do so. A mobile phone with an unfamiliar ring sounded in her tote. She blinked, remembered it must be Brett's phone and after a moment's hesitation answered it.

'Brett Wyndham's phone.'

'Where is he and who are you?' an irate female voice said down the line.

Holly explained and added, 'Can I give him a message?'

'Oh.' The voice sounded mollified. 'Yes, if you wouldn't mind. It's his sister, Sue. I'm waiting for him at Southbank, but I'm going out to dinner so I won't wait any longer. Could you tell him I'll catch up with him tomorrow?'

Ten minutes later Brett reappeared and held his hand out to Holly. 'Let's go. He's got a broken leg, as well as the cut, but he'll be fine. He's in good hands, and he's got a microchip so they'll be able to track down his owner.'

'Thank heavens.' She got to her feet.

'How are you?' he queried.

'OK.'

He studied her narrowly. 'You don't altogether look it.'

'I...I once lost a dog in an accident. He was also a border collie. I called him Oliver, because as a puppy he was always looking for more food. He was run over, but he died. It just took me back a bit.'

Brett released her hand and put an arm around her shoulder. He didn't say anything, but Holly discovered herself to be comforted. Comforted and then something else—acutely conscious of Brett Wyndham.

She breathed in his essence—pure man—and she felt the long, strong lines of his body. She was reminded of how quick and light on his feet he'd been, how he'd used the power of his personality and expertise to calm the dog—but above all how he'd impressed her on a mental level, and now on a physical one.

'Better?' he queried.

'Yes, thanks.'

They stepped out onto the pavement, but he stopped. It was almost dark. 'My sister,' he said with a grimace and reached for his phone, but it wasn't there.

Holly retrieved it from her bag and gave him the message.

'OK.' He steered her towards his car.

'If you drop me off at the parking lot...' Holly began.

He shook his head. 'You still look as if you could do with a drink.'

'No. Thanks, but no. Anyway, we left the restaurant without paying!'

He shrugged and opened the car door. 'They know me. In you get—and don't argue, Holly Golightly.'

Holly had no choice but to do as she was told, although she did say, '*My* car?'

'Mike will collect it.' He fired the engine.

'Who's Mike?'

'The miracle worker in my life.' He swung out into the traffic. 'The PA *par excellence*.'

Not much later, Holly was sitting on a mocha-colored leather settee in what was obviously a den. The walls were *café au lait*, priceless-looking scatter rugs dotted the parquet floor and wooden louvres framed the view of a dark sky but a tinsel-town view of the city lights.

Brett had poured her a brandy then she'd washed her face and hands and handed her car keys over to his PA. Brett had gone to take a shower.

She'd only taken a couple of sips but she was thinking deeply when he strolled back into the room. He'd changed into jeans and a shirt; his hair was towelled dry and spiky.

'Will you stay for dinner?' he queried as he poured his own brandy.

'No thank you,' Holly said automatically. 'You know, it's just struck me—this could look strange.'

'What could?' He sat down opposite her.

'Me flitting around with you.'

'In what respect?'

She glanced at him then looked away a little awkwardly. 'People might wonder if I've joined the long list of, well, perhaps not beautiful—I mean *they* were all probably stunning—but the long list of women you've squired around.'

'What long list is that?' he enquired in a deadpan kind of way that alerted her to the fact he was secretly laughing at her.

Holly went slightly pink but said airily, 'Just something I read somewhere. But, believe me, I have no ambition to do that. Unless...' she stopped, struck by a thought, and relaxed a bit. 'I'm not stunning enough or upmarket-looking enough to qualify? Don't answer that,' she said with a lightning smile. 'I'm just thinking aloud.' She sobered and contemplated her drink with a frown.

Does she have no idea of how unusually attractive she is? Brett Wyndham found himself wondering. *Maybe not*, he conceded. She certainly didn't appear to expect him to counter her claim that she wasn't stunning enough to qualify as someone he would "squire around".

On the other hand, she'd had to fight off a bandit and a sheikh, if she was to be believed, so...

He shrugged. 'I never bother with what people think.'

'You may be in a position not to bother—your reputation is already set,' she retorted. 'Mine is not.' Then she took a very deep breath. 'Please tell me why you're doing this.'

He rolled his glass in his hands then looked directly into her eyes. 'I'm intrigued. I can't believe you're not.' He paused. 'And I guess that's brought out the hunter instinct in me. At the same time, I *don't* ever force myself on unwilling women, if that's what's worrying you.'

Holly looked away. She paused and pressed her palms together tightly. 'And if I told you I don't have any interest in... Well, the thing is, I got my fingers pretty badly burnt once due to "chemistry". It's—it hasn't left me yet. I don't know if it ever will.'

He narrowed his eyes. 'Not the bandit or the sheikh, I gather?'

Holly waved her hand. 'Oh, no,' she said dismissively.

'I think you better tell me.'

She glanced at him from under her lashes, then smiled briefly. 'I don't think I should. It's supposed to be the other way round—you telling me stuff. And *you* have no intention of going into your private life.' She looked at him with some irony.

A silence lingered between them.

'So, should we just leave it there?' she suggested at last.

He stared at her pensively. 'Don't you want the interview now?'

'I thought you might have changed your mind.'

His lips twisted. 'Because I got my wrist slapped metaphorically? No, I haven't changed my mind.'

'But you won't—I mean—bring this up again?' she queried, her eyes dark and serious.

'Tell you what,' he drawled. '*I* won't say a word on the subject.'

Holly frowned. 'That sounds as if there's a trap there somewhere.'

'Sorry, it's the best I can come up with. So, are we on or off?'

She hesitated then put down her glass, stood up and walked over to the louvres that framed the city view. She was in two minds, she realized. She sensed an element of danger between her and Brett Wyndham, but she had to admit he'd been honest, whereas she hadn't—not entirely, anyway.

On the other hand, her career was vitally important to her. It had been her mainstay through some dark days.

She turned back to him. 'On. My journalistic instincts seem to have won the day,' she said ruefully. 'Can I go home now?'

'Of course.' He stood up, called for Mike Rafferty, and when he came asked him if he'd found Holly's car.

'Sure did,' Mike replied, and handed Holly the keys. 'It's parked downstairs, Miss Harding.'

'Thank you,' She hesitated then turned back to Brett Wyndham. 'Well, goodnight.'

'Goodnight, Holly,' he said casually, and turned away.

After he'd dined alone, Brett took his coffee to his study, where he intended to work on his next trip to Africa, only to find himself unable to concentrate.

The fact that it was a girl coming between him and his plans was unusual.

He swirled his coffee and lay back in his chair, Well, a change of direction in his life was on the cards; whilst he knew it was one he needed to make, would he ever be able to resist the call of the wild? Was that why he was unsettled?

It was a juggling act holding the reins of all the Wyndham enterprises based here and being away so frequently. Also, there was something niggling at him that he couldn't quite put his finger on, but he suspected it was the need to establish some roots.

In the meantime—in the short term, more accurately—a girl had come to his attention. A girl he wasn't at all sure about.

A girl who continued to hold him at arm's length, now with the claim that she'd had her fingers burnt due to "chemistry". How true was that? he wondered.

Could it all be part of a plan to hold his interest? He'd come across many a plan to hold his interest, he reflected dryly.

None of that changed the fact that she was attractive in a different kind of way—when did it ever? Good skin, beautiful eyes, clean, very slim lines; at times, sparkling intelligence and a cutting way with her repartee...

He smiled suddenly as he thought of her 'Holly Golightly from Tahiti' act.

He finished his coffee and contemplated another possibility. It was so long since any woman had said no to him he couldn't help but be intrigued. Especially as he could have sworn there'd been that edgy, sensual pull between them almost from the moment they'd first crossed swords.

Why, though, he wondered, had he gone to the lengths of dangling an interview before her?

Because she was likeable, kissable, different?

He drummed his fingers on the desk suddenly; or did he have in mind using her to deflect his ex-fiancée?

'I'm off to Cairns—well, Palm Cove—then the bush for a few days tomorrow,' Holly said to her mother that evening over a late dinner. She pushed away the remains of a tasty chicken casserole. 'You're not going to believe this, but I got the Brett Wyndham interview after all.'

Sylvia uttered a little cry of delight. 'Holly! That's

marvellous. I wasn't sure I did the right thing. I know you tried to gloss over it, but I wasn't sure whether you really approved.' Sylvia paused and frowned. 'But why do you have to go to Cairns?'

Holly made the swift decision to gloss over that bit and murmured something about Brett being short of time.

Sylvia mulled over this for a moment, then she said, 'He's very good-looking, isn't he? I mean he has a real presence, doesn't he?'

'I guess he does.'

'Holly,' Sylvia began, 'I know that awful thing that happened to you is not going to be easy to get over. Actually, you've been simply marvellous with the way—'

'Mum, don't,' Holly interrupted quietly.

'But there has to be the right man for you out there, darling,' Sylvia said passionately.

'There probably is, but it's not Brett Wyndham.'

'How can you be so sure?'

Holly moved the salt cellar to a different spot and sighed. 'It's just a feeling I have, Mum. For one thing, he's a billionaire, so he could have anyone and there's nothing so special about me. And, for me, I suppose it started with the way he behaved that day of the lunch. Then I read that he'd broken off his engagement to a girl who would have thought she was the last in a *long* line of women he'd escorted. And it seems,' she said bitterly, 'He's a master at getting his own way.'

'In view of all that,' Sylvia replied a shade tartly, 'I'm surprised you're going to Palm Cove and the bush.'

Holly shrugged. 'I once made the decision I wouldn't

be a victim, and what really helped me was my career. I can't knock back this opportunity to further it.'

Glenn Shepherd said to Holly the next morning, 'So it's all set up?'

'Yes. But there's no personal side to it, Glenn, other than "ancient history"—I guess that means how he grew up—and he wants to have final say. It's his work he wants to talk about, and some new project.'

'Even that's a scoop. So, you're off to Palm Cove and points west?'

Holly nodded then looked questioningly at her editor. 'How did you know that? I mean, so soon?'

'His PA has just been on the phone. They offered to pay for your flights; I knocked that back, but they will provide accommodation in Palm Cove—they own the resort, after all.'

Holly grimaced. 'I'd rather stay in a mud hut.'

'Holly, is there anything you're not telling me?' Glenn stared at her interrogatively.

'What do you mean?'

'I don't know.'

'No,' Holly replied. *'No.'*

'Enjoy yourself, then.'

Cairns, in Far North Queensland, was always a pleasure to visit, Holly reflected as she landed on a commercial flight and took the courtesy bus out of town to Palm Cove. With its mountainous backdrop, its beaches, its lush flora, bougainvillea, hibiscus in many colours, yellow allamanda everywhere and its warm, humid air, you got a delightful sense of the tropics.

It was also a touristy place—it was a stepping-off point for all the marvels of the Great Barrier Reef—but it wasn't brash. It was relaxed, yet still retained its solid country-town air.

Palm Cove, half an hour's drive north of Cairns, was exclusive.

Lovely resorts lined the road opposite the beach and there was a cosmopolitan air with open-air cafés and marvellous old melaleucas, or paper-bark trees, growing out of the pavements. There were upmarket restaurants and boutiques that would have made her mother's mouth water. The beach itself was a delight. Lined with cotton-woods, casuarinas and palms, it curved around a bay and overlooked Double Island and a smaller island she didn't know the name of. On a hot, still, autumn day, the water looked placid and immensely inviting. Whilst summer in the region might be a trial, autumn and winter—if you could call them that in the far north—were lovely.

The resort owned by the Wyndhams was built on colonial lines. It was spacious and cool and was right on the beach.

Holly unpacked her luggage in a pleasant room. It didn't take her long; she was used to travelling light and had evolved a simple wardrobe that nevertheless saw her through most eventualities. She'd resisted her mother's attempts to add to it.

She was contemplating going for a walk when she got a phone message: Mr Wyndham presented his compliments to Ms Harding; he had some time free and would like to see her in his suite in half an hour.

Ms Harding hesitated for a moment then agreed.

As she put the phone down, she felt a little trill of

annoyance at this high-handed invitation but immediately took herself to task. This was business, wasn't it?

She had a quick shower and put on jeans and a cotton blouse. But the humidity played havoc with her hair, so she decided to clip it back in order to control it.

That was when she found a surprise in her bag. Her mother had been unable to let her come to Palm Cove without some maternal input: she'd tucked in a little box of jewellery. Amongst the necklaces and bangles was a pair of very long, dangly bead-and-gilt earrings.

Holly stared at them then put them on.

Not bad, she decided, and tied her hair back.

Finally, with her feet in ballet pumps and her tote bag on her shoulder, she went to find Brett Wyndham's suite.

It was on the top floor of the resort with sweeping views of Palm Cove. Although the sun was setting in the west behind the resort, the waters of the cove reflected the time of day in a spectrum of lovely colours, apricot, lavender and lilac.

It was a moment before she took her eyes off the panorama after a waiter admitted her and ushered her into the lounge. Then she turned to the man himself, and got a surprise.

No casual clothes this time. Today he wore a grey suit and a blue-and-white-striped shirt. Today he looked extremely formal as he talked into his mobile phone.

Merely talking? Holly wondered. Or in the process of delivering an extremely cutting dressing-down as he stood half-turned away from her and fired words rather like bullets into the phone? Then he cut the connection, threw the phone down on a sofa in disgust and turned to her with his dark eyes blazing.

Holly swallowed in sudden fright and took a step backwards. 'Uh—hi!' she said uncertainly. 'Sorry, I didn't mean to interrupt. Maybe I'll just go until your temper has cooled a bit.' She turned away hurriedly.

He reached her in two strides and spun her back with his hands on her shoulders. 'Don't think you can walk out on me, Holly Harding.'

Holly stared up at him, going rigid and quite pale with anger. 'Let me *go*!'

Brett Wyndham paused, frowned down at her then let his hands drop to his side. 'I'm sorry,' he said quietly and went over to a drinks trolley. 'Here.' He brought her back a brandy.

'I don't—'

'Holly...' he warned.

'All I ever seem to do is drink either champagne or brandy in your presence,' she said frustratedly.

A faint smile twisted his lips. 'Sit down,' he said, and when she hesitated he added 'Let me explain. In certain circumstances I have a very short fuse.'

'So it would appear,' she agreed wholeheartedly.

He pulled off his jacket. 'Yes, well.' He gestured towards the phone. 'That was news that a breeding pair of black rhino—highly endangered now in Africa—has been injured in transit. I bought them from a zoo where they were patently *not* breeding due to stress, too small a habitat and so on.'

'Oh,' Holly said and sank into a chair, her imagination captured—so much so, she forgot her fright of a few minutes ago. 'Badly injured? In a road accident or what? A road accident,' she answered herself. 'That's why you were informing the person on the other end of the phone—' she glanced over at his mobile phone lying on the sofa opposite '—that he must have got his driving licence out of a cornflake packet. Amongst everything else you said.'

Brett Wyndham grinned fleetingly. 'Yes. But no, not badly injured. All the same, their numbers are shrinking at such an alarming rate, it's a terrifying thought, losing even two. And it only adds to their stress.'

'I see.' She frowned. 'Not that I see where I come into it. Are you trying to tell me that when your short fuse explodes anyone within range is liable to cop it?'

'It's been known to happen,' he agreed. 'However, there was a grain of truth in what I said. By the way, your hair looks nice. But I have an aversion to long, dangly earrings.'

Holly raised her eyebrows. 'Why?'

He said, 'A girl invited me home for dinner once. I arrived on time with a bunch of flowers and a bottle of wine. She opened the door. She had her hair all pulled back and all she wore were long dangly earrings, high heels and a G-string.'

Holly gasped.

'Exactly how I reacted,' he said gravely. 'Only I dropped the flowers as well.'

'What did you do then?' Holly was now laughing helplessly.

'I was younger,' he said reflectively. 'What did I do? I suggested to her that maybe she was putting the cart before the horse.'

'Oh no! What did she do?'

'She said that if all she'd achieved was to bring to mind a cart horse—not what I'd meant at all—she was wasting her time, and she slammed the door in my face. Of course, I've often wondered whether it didn't fall more into a "looking a gift horse in the mouth" scenario or "horses for courses".'

'Don't go on!' Holly held a hand to her side. 'You're making me laugh too much.'

'The worst part about it is I often find myself undressing women with long, dangly earrings to this day—only mentally, of course.'

'Oh, no!' Holly was still laughing as she removed her earrings. 'There. Am I safe?'

He took his tie off and unbuttoned his collar as he studied her—rather acutely—and nodded. 'Yes.' He paused and seemed to change his mind about something. 'OK. Shall we begin?'

Holly felt her heart jolt. 'The interview?'

'What else?' he queried a little dryly.

'Nothing! I mean, um, I didn't realize you wanted to start tonight—but I've made some notes that I brought with me,' she hastened to assure him and reached for her bag.

He sat down. 'Where do you want to start?'

She drew a notebook from her tote and a pen. She nibbled the end of the pen for a moment and a subtle change came over her.

She looked at Brett Wyndham meditatively, as if sizing him up, then said, 'Would you like to give me a brief background-history of the family? I have researched it, but you would have a much more personal view, and you may be able to pinpoint where the seeds of this passion you have for saving endangered-species came from.'

'Animals always fascinated me,' he said slowly. 'And growing up on a station gave me plenty of experience with domestic ones, as well as the more exotic wild ones—echidnas, wombats and so on. I also remember my grandmother; she was renowned as a bush vet, although she wasn't qualified as one. But she always had—' he paused to grin '—a houseful of baby wallabies she'd rescued, or so it seemed to me anyway. She used to hang them up in pillow slips as if they were still in their mother's pouch.'

'So how far back does the Wyndham association with Far North Queensland go...?'

An hour later, Brett glanced at his watch and Holly took the hint. She put her pen and notebook back into her tote, but she was satisfied with their progress. Brett had given her an insight into how the Wyndham fortune had been built, as well as a fascinating insight into life on cattle stations in the Cape York area in the early part of the twentieth century—gleaned, he told her, from his grandmother's stories and diaries. And he'd included a few immediate-family anecdotes.

'Thank you,' she said warmly. 'That was a really good beginning. It's always important to be able to set the scene.' She drained her brandy. 'And I'll try not to require any more medicinal brandy for our next session.'

He stood up and reached for his jacket. 'I'm sorry; I have a dinner to attend, but you're welcome to use the resort dining-room on us.'

Holly slung her bag on her shoulder. 'Oh no, but thank you. I was planning to wander down the waterfront and indulge in a thoroughly decadent hamburger at one of the cafés, then an early night. We are still flying to Haywire early tomorrow, I take it?'

'Yes. I plan to leave here at nine sharp. I'll pick you up at Reception.' He hesitated and frowned.

Holly studied him. 'Are you having second thoughts?' she queried.

'No. But you're good,' he said slowly. 'Especially for one so young.'

'Good?' She looked puzzled.

'You seem to have the art of putting a person at ease down to a fine art.'

'Thank you,' Holly murmured. 'Why do I get the feeling you don't altogether approve, though?' she added.

'Could you be imagining it?' he suggested with a sudden grin, and went on immediately, 'I am running late now; I'm sorry...'

'Going; I'm going!' Holly assured him and turned towards the door. 'See you tomorrow.'

But, even though he *was* running late, Brett Wyndham watched her retreating back until she disappeared. Then he walked out on to the terrace and stared at the moon and the river of silver light it was pouring onto the waters of the cove.

She'd been right, he reflected. He wasn't entirely approving of her skills as an interviewer. She did have an engaging, relaxing way with her. She did also have an undoubted enthusiasm for, and a lively curiosity about, his story and that of his family and its history. Not that he'd told her anything he hadn't wanted to tell her, nor did he have any intention of exposing the dark secret that lay behind him.

But was she capable of digging it out somehow?

Or, in other words, had he unwittingly put himself into a rather vulnerable situation because he'd under-estimated a leggy twenty-four-year old who intrigued him?

For some reason his thoughts moved on to the little scene that had played out when she'd first arrived in his suite, and how she'd reacted when he'd stopped her walking out. She'd been genuinely frightened and angry at the same time. She *had* told him she'd got her fingers burnt once and it was still with her. He had to believe that now. He also had to believe it had pulled him up short, the fact that he'd frightened her.

All the same—call it all off and send her home? Or deliberately shift the focus to the project he really wanted to publicize, as had been his original intention?

He shrugged and went out to dinner with his brother, his sister, his sister-in-law-to-be and several others. He was unaware that his ex-fiancée would be one of the party.

Holly had her hamburger, and was strolling along the beach side of the road opposite the fabulous restaurants of Palm Cove, when she stopped as Brett Wyndham caught her attention.

He was with a party of diners at an upmarket restaurant that opened onto the pavement and had an amazing old melaleuca tree growing in the middle of it. It was not only an upmarket restaurant, it was a pretty upmarket party of diners, she decided. One of the women was his sister, Sue Murray, looking lovely in turquoise silk with pearls in her ears and around her neck. Two of the other women were exceptionally sleek and gorgeously dressed, one a stunning redhead, the other with a river of smooth, straight blonde hair that Holly would have given her eye teeth for.

It looked to be a lively party as wine glasses glinted beneath the lights and a small army of waiters delivered a course.

After her initial summing-up of the party, Holly turned her attention back to Brett and felt that not so unexpected frisson run through her. She frowned. Was she getting used to the effect his dark good looks and tall physique had on her? She certainly wasn't as annoyed about it as she'd been only a few days ago.

But there was something else to worry about now, she acknowledged. Ever since she'd left his suite she'd been conscious of a sense of unease. *Was* she imagining it, or had he rather suddenly developed reservations about the interview?

No, it wasn't her imagination, she decided. Something had changed. Had she asked too many questions?

She shook her head and went back to watching Brett Wyndham, only to be troubled by yet another set of thoughts. How would she feel if he pulled out of the interview? How would she feel if she never saw him again?

Her eyes widened at the chill little pang that ran through her at the thought, leaving her in no doubt she would suffer a sense of loss, a sense of regret. If that was the case for her now, after only a few brief encounters, how dangerous could it be to get to know Brett Wyndham better?

CHAPTER FOUR

HOLLY decided to go for a swim as dawn broke over Palm Cove the next morning.

She put on her swimsuit, a pretty peasant blouse and a skimpy pair of shorts. She laid out the clothes she would wear after her swim and looked at her luggage, all neatly packed. The only thing that wasn't quite neat and tidy in her mind was, which way would she go when she left Palm Cove? Out to Haywire, or back to Brisbane?

She collected a towel from the pool area and walked through the quiet resort to the beach.

There was a sprinkling of early-morning walkers and swimmers and, even so early, a feel of the coming heat of the day on the air.

She hesitated then opted to go for a walk first.

Palm Cove—most of Far North Queensland, for that matter—didn't offer blinding white sand on its beaches, although its off-shore islands might. What you got instead was sand that resembled raw sugar but it was clean, and towards the waterline, firm.

What also impressed her was that from further down the beach you would not have known Palm Cove was there, thanks to the height limitations put on the buildings and the trees that lined the beach.

She strode out and reviewed her dilemma as she did so. If she did go back to Brisbane off her own bat—assuming she wasn't sent back, and she had the feeling it wasn't impossible for that to be on the cards—how would she handle it? She would have to confess to Glenn and her mother that she'd been unable to handle the Wyndham interview, and she would go back to travel reporting with a sense of relief.

If she did get sent back, though, she'd have to confess that she must have pressed some wrong buttons with Brett Wyndham.

In either case, she would not even contemplate the fact that at times Brett Wyndham fascinated her mentally and stirred her physically, probably more than any man had done. Well, she could tell herself that, anyway.

It would be true to say she was still on the horns of a dilemma when she got back to her towel. She shrugged frustratedly, dropped her top and shorts on it and waded into the water. It was heavenly, refreshing but not cold, calm, buoyant; when it was up to her knees, she dived in and swam out energetically.

After about ten minutes, she swam back to where she could stand and floated on her back, feeling rejuvenated—cleansed, even—as if she'd experienced a catharsis and could put the whole sorry business behind her one way or another.

'Morning, Holly.'

She sank, swallowed some water and came up spluttering. Brett Wyndham, with his dark hair plastered to his head, was standing a few feet away from her, his tanned shoulders smooth and wet.

'What are you doing here?' she demanded, somewhat indistinctly, through a fit of coughing.

He looked around. 'I thought it was a public beach.'

'Of course it is!' She felt for the bottom with her toes. 'I mean—it doesn't matter.'

'Have I done something to annoy you?' he queried gravely.

Holly lay back in the water and rippled it with her fingers. Then she sat up and flicked her gaze from the strong brown column of his throat, from his sleek outline, and eyed a line of opal-pale clouds above, then their reflection on the glassy surface of the sea. 'I thought it might be the other way round.'

He raised an eyebrow. 'Why?'

'I thought—I thought you were having second thoughts last night.'

She moved a few steps towards the beach, then something swirled in the water next to her; she jerked away and fell over with a cry of fright.

'Holly!' Brett plunged to her side and lifted her into his arms. 'What was it? Are you hurt?'

'I don't know what it was. I don't think I'm hurt, though. I just got a fright!'

'OK.' He carried her up the beach and put her down on her towel. 'Let's have a look.'

He could find no wound on her feet or legs and he looked patently relieved.

Holly sat up. 'What could it have been?'

'It could have been a stingray.'

She stared at him round-eyed. 'That could have been fatal!'

He smiled. 'Not necessarily, not in your feet and legs, but it can take a long time to heal.'

Holly allowed a long breath to escape. 'So, a serpent in paradise, you could say.'

'Mmm… Have you had breakfast?'

'No. Uh, no, but—'

'Come and have it with me.' He stood up.

Holly stared up at him. He wore a colourful pair of board shorts; as she'd always suspected, his physique was outstanding: not an ounce of excess weight and whipcord muscles. There was only one way to describe it: he was beautifully proportioned. Tall, lean, strong as well as dark, and pirate-like—altogether enough to set her pulses fluttering.

She swallowed and realized she was on the receiving end of his scrutiny. His dark gaze lingered on her legs, her waist and the curve of her breasts beneath the fine lycra of her costume, as well as the pulse beating at the base of her throat. She found herself feeling hot and cold as her nipples peaked visibly.

She jumped up. 'Thanks, but no thanks. I really…' She picked up her towel and flapped it vigorously. 'I really got the feeling last night that things had gone sour somehow, and it might be best if I just go back to Brisbane, so—'

'Holly.' He wrested the towel from her. 'Before you cover us completely with sand, if you still want to go after breakfast, fine. But I haven't told you about my new project yet—my plans to open a zoo.'

Holly went still and blinked at him. 'A zoo?' she repeated.

'Yes, I'm planning one along the lines of the Western

Plains zoo outside Dubbo, but up here on Haywire—that's why I wanted you to see it. I'm thinking of an adopt-an-animal scheme as a means of publicizing it, as well as the whole endangered-species issue.'

Her eyes widened. 'What a great idea! Tell me more.'

He shook his head. 'You have to come to breakfast if you want any more details.'

She clicked her tongue. 'You're extremely domineering, aren't you?'

He shrugged and handed her back her towel.

He ordered breakfast to be served on the terrace of his suite.

Holly sat outside waiting for it while he made and received some phone calls to do with the welfare of his rhinos, and she tried to work out a plan of action.

Nothing had occurred to her by the time breakfast arrived. It was a ceremonial delivery. There was champagne and orange juice; there was a gorgeous fruit-platter with some of the unusual fruits found in the area, like rambutans and star-fruit; there was yoghurt and cereal, a mushroom omelette for her and eggs and bacon for him.

The toast was wrapped in a linen napkin and there was a silver flask of coffee.

'Thank you, we'll help ourselves,' Brett murmured, and the team of waiters withdrew discreetly.

'I'll never eat all this,' Holly said ruefully.

'Eat as much or as little as you like. I usually start with the main course then work my way backwards, with the fruit topped with a little yoghurt—as dessert, you might say.'

'Really?' Holly eyed him with some intrigue. 'That's a novel approach.'

'Try it.'

'I will. By the way, how long would we stay at Haywire, assuming we go?'

He glanced at her. 'Two or three days.'

'You did mention your brother's wedding.'

He glanced at his watch to check the date. 'That's a week from today, here.'

'Here?'

'Uh-huh, but there are a few preliminaries in the form of balls, soirées, a reef trip et cetera.'

Holly had to smile. 'You don't sound impressed.'

'I'm not.' He shrugged. 'But he is my brother. OK—the zoo.' He started on his eggs and bacon, and gave her the broad outline of his plans for the zoo—the size of the paddocks he intended to create, the animals he wanted and some of the difficulties involved.

'Impressive,' she said. 'I think it's a marvellous idea. But...' She pushed away her plate and picked up a prickly purple rambutan, wondering at the same time how you were supposed to eat it. 'But I'm not sure I'm the right person to do this. What I mean is, I'm not sure *you* think I am.' She watched him keenly for a long moment.

He reached for the coffee pot, poured two cups and pushed one towards her. 'I do think you're right for it. I think you have fresh, innovative views.'

'But something changed last night,' she persisted quietly.

He looked out over the water and was silent for a time. *Yes, Holly Golightly*, he thought with an inward grimace, *some things did change last night—one you're not even aware of—but it's the reason I'm* not *putting you on the next plane down south.*

He clenched his fist as he thought of the dinner last night. His sister-in-law-to-be had decided she might be able to mend some fences, so she'd produced Natasha Hewson at the dinner with the disclaimer that the wedding next weekend was going to be all Nat's work of art, and they'd be bound to run into each other anyway.

So I'm back in the bloody position, he thought, gritting his teeth, *of using you, Ms Harding, to deflect my ex-fiancée*. Not that he had any expectations that the two would ever meet, because he intended to whisk her off to Haywire as planned this morning before she went back to Brisbane. But as soon as Nat knew he was travelling with a girl—and he had no doubt she would know it!—she might get the message.

Not exactly admirable behaviour, he mused rather grimly, *but needs must when the devil drives.*

'It occurred to me last night,' he said, switching his gaze suddenly back to Holly, 'That I might be going into areas I don't really want to go into—not any further, anyway.'

Holly looked puzzled for a moment and she opened her mouth to say that it had all been pretty harmless, surely? But she changed her mind at the last moment. It was, of course, his prerogative, but it raised a question mark in her mind.

'Um…' She hesitated and put the rambutan down.

'That's up to you. I'm happy to go along with whatever you want to talk about.'

'So.' His lips twisted. 'Are we on again?'

Holly looked down and felt a strong pull towards taking the safe path—the one that would get her away from the dangerous elements of this man. From the undoubted attraction she felt towards him—her fascination with the mystique behind him. But at the same time her feeling was that Brett Wyndham could not be a long=term prospect for her.

She thought briefly of the dinner party she'd witnessed last night and it struck her that, while the man himself embodied the kind of life she found fascinating, there had to be a dimension to his life that occupied another stratum—one she did not belong to—that of ultra-glamorous, gorgeously groomed, sleek and glossy women. Last night they'd all looked like models or film stars.

Should that not make her feel safe with him, however? The fact that she patently didn't look like a model or a film star…?

She shrugged at last. 'On. Again.'

They exchanged a long, probing glance until finally he said, 'I see. We're still in the same boat.'

She looked perplexed. 'Boat?'

'We can't quite make each other out.' He smiled, but a shade dryly. 'All right. Are you ready to fly out shortly?'

Holly hesitated momentarily, then nodded. She went away to change and collect her things.

As she changed into her jeans, a sunshine-yellow singlet top, her denim jacket and her boots, she stared at her image in the mirror a couple of times and realized she looked and felt tense, and didn't know how to deal with it.

Here she was about to step out into the wide blue yonder with a man she hardly knew—a man she'd clashed with but at the same time felt attracted to—and her emotions were, accordingly, in a bit of a tangle.

How was she going to revert to Holly Harding, journalist, on a very important mission?

She was still preoccupied with this question as she drove down the Bruce Highway with Brett Wyndham, between sugar cane fields, towards the city of Cairns in its circle of hills and the airport.

Brett piloted his own plane, she discovered later, still not quite able to believe what was happening to her. The plane was a trim little six-seater with a W on the tail.

She was still pinching herself metaphorically as the nose of the plane rose and the speeding runway fell away. She was also trying to decide how to handle things between them. Common sense told her a matter-of-fact approach was the only way to go, but even that wasn't going to be easy.

She waited until they reached their cruising altitude then asked him how long the flight would be.

He told her briefly.

'Can you talk?'

'Of course,' he replied.

'Could you give me a run-down on the country we're flying over and our destination?'

He did so. They were flying west over the old mining towns of the Tablelands towards volcanic country

famous for its lava tubes; then the great, grassy lands of
the savannah/gulf country, as in the Gulf of Carpentaria,
where their destination lay.

'Haywire?' she repeated with a grin. 'Where did it
get its name?

He grimaced. 'No-one seems to know.'

Holly glanced across at him. He looked thoroughly professional in a khaki bush-shirt and jeans, with
his headphones on and his beautiful hands checking
instruments.

Professional and withdrawn from her, she contemplated as her gaze was drawn to her own hands clasped
rather forlornly in her lap.

Who was she to quibble about 'professional and withdrawn' being the order of the day? It was what she'd
almost stipulated, wasn't it? The only problem was she
needed to get him to open up if she was going to get full
value out of this trip. But—big but—there was a fine
line between getting him to talk easily and naturally
from a professional point of view and not finding herself
loving his company at the same time.

She shook her head and realized he was watching
her.

She coloured a little.

'Some internal debate?' he suggested.

'You could say so. Where are we now?' She looked
out at the panorama of red sandy earth below them,
with its sage-green vegetation, at the undulations and
the space.

'About halfway between Georgetown and Croydon.
If you follow the Savannah Way it takes you on to
Normanton and Karumba, on the gulf. Over that way,'

he pointed, 'is Forsayth and Cobbold Gorge; it's quite amazing. And those are the Newcastle Ranges to the east, and the sandstone escarpment to the west.'

'It's very remote,' she said in awe. 'And empty.'

'Remote,' he agreed. 'Hot as hell in summer, but with quite a history, not only of cattle but gold rushes and gem fields. Georgetown has a gem museum and Croydon has a recreation of the life and times of the gold rush there.'

'They look so small, though—Georgetown and Croydon,' she ventured.

He shrugged. 'They are now. Last count, Georgetown had under three-hundred residents, but it's the heart of a huge shire, and they're both on the road to Karumba and the gulf, renowned for its fishing. With the army of grey nomads out and about these days, they get a lot of passing traffic.'

Holly grinned. 'Grey nomads' was the term given to retired Australians who travelled the continent in caravans or camper vans or just with tents. It could almost be said it was the national retiree-pastime.

Half an hour later they started to lose altitude and Brett pointed out the Haywire homestead. All Holly could see was a huddle of roofs and a grassy airstrip between white-painted wooden fences in a sea of scrub.

Then he spoke into his VHF radio, and over some static a female voice said she'd walked the strip and it was in good order.

'Romeo, coming in,' he responded.

Ten minutes later they made a slightly bumpy landing and rolled to a stop adjacent to the huddle of roofs Holly had seen from the air.

A girl and a dog came through the gate in the airstrip fence to meet them.

'Holly,' Brett said, 'This is Sarah. And this—' he bent down to pat the red cattle-dog who accepted his ministrations with every sign of ecstasy '—is Bella.'

'Welcome to Haywire, Holly,' Sarah said in a very English accent.

Holly blinked in surprise, and Brett and Sarah exchanged grins. 'Sarah is backpacking her way around the world,' Brett said. 'How long have you been with us now?' he asked the English girl.

'Three months. I can't seem to tear myself away!' Sarah said ruefully. 'Brett, since you're here, I'm a bit worried about one of the mares in the holding paddock— she's lame. Would you mind having a look at her? I could show Holly around a bit in the meantime.'

'Sure. I'll leave you to it.'

Haywire homestead was a revelation to Holly in as much as it wasn't a homestead at all in the accepted sense of the word. All the accommodation was in separate cabins set out on green lawns and inside a fence designed to keep wallabies, emus and other wildlife out, according to Sarah.

All the other facilities were under one huge roof: lounge area, dining area, a small library-cum-games room et cetera. But the unique thing was, there were no outside walls.

The floor was slate; there was a central stone-fireplace, and at intervals there were tubs of potted plants and artistically arranged pieces of dead wood, often draped with ferns.

There was a long refectory table, comfortable cane-loungers and steamer chairs; beyond the fence and lawn, looking away from the rest of the compound, there was a lake alive with birds, reeds and water lilies.

The whole area reminded Holly of a safari lodge, and she was most impressed.

'Just one thing, what do you do when it rains or blows a gale?' she asked Sarah ruefully.

'Hasn't happened to me yet,' Sarah replied. 'But there are roll-down blinds.' She pointed them out. 'And I believe they put up shutters if they get a cyclone. Otherwise it lets the air flow through when it's really hot. Here's the kitchen.'

The kitchen was not visible from the rest of the area; it was also open on one side, yet had all mod cons. There were, Holly learnt, several sources of power on Haywire: a generator for electricity and gas for the hot-water system. There were still some old-fashioned combustion stoves for heating water in case other means failed. And there was a satellite phone as well as a VHF radio for communications.

There was an above-ground swimming pool surrounded by emerald lawn and shaded by trees.

Sarah explained that she was actually a nurse, but she enjoyed cooking, she loved the outback and she loved horses, so a stint as a housekeeper at Haywire suited her down to the ground.

'Mind you, most often there's only me, Bella, the horses and a few stockmen here. We don't get to see the family that often. Actually, I'm surprised to see Brett. I thought he'd be down at Palm Cove with the rest of them.'

'We were—he was,' Holly said, and intercepted a curious little glance from Sarah. She found herself thinking, *I knew this would happen! Probably no passable woman is safe in Brett Wyndham's company without being thought of as his lover.* 'I'm actually working with him,' she added.

'So she is,' the man in question agreed as he strolled up to them.

They both turned.

'The mare has a stone bruise in her off-fore. I've relieved the pressure, but keep an eye on her or get Kane to,' he added to Sarah. 'Are they coming in tonight? Kane,' he said for Holly's benefit, 'Is station foreman, and he has two offsiders.'

Sarah shook her head. 'They've got a problem with a fence on the northern boundary. That's miles away, so they decided to camp out overnight.'

'OK, then it's just us. I'm going to take Holly for a drive; we'll be back before dark. Incidentally, what's for dinner?'

Sarah grinned her infectious grin. 'Would you believe? Roast beef!'

'Standard cattle-station joke—roast beef for dinner,' Brett said to Holly as they climbed into a sturdy, high-chassis four-wheel-drive utility vehicle. Holly had brought her camera.

She laughed, but said, 'Look, I'm really surprised at how few people you have working here. From memory you run ten-thousand head of cattle; that sounds like a huge herd to me, and Haywire covers thousands of square kilometers.' Holly said.

'That's because you probably don't know much about Brahman and Droughtmaster cattle.'

'I know nothing,' Holly confessed.

'Well—' he swung the wheel to avoid an anthill '—Brahmans come down from four Indian breeds; they were first imported here from the USA in 1933. Droughtmasters are a Brahman cross, developed here. They've all adapted particularly to this part of the world for a variety of reasons. They're heat-and-parasite resistant, they're mobile, good foragers and they can survive on poor grass in droughts. They have a highly developed digestive system that provides efficient feed-conversion.'

'They sound amazing.'

'There's more,' he said with a grin. 'The fact that they're resistant to or tolerant of parasites means they don't require chemical intervention, so they're clean and green,' he said humorously. 'The cows are good mothers; they produce plenty of milk and they have small calves, so birthing is usually easy, and they're renowned for protecting their calves. All of that—' he waved a hand '—means they require minimum management. In answer to your question, that's why we don't need an army of staff.'

Holly looked around at the now undulating countryside they were driving through. It was quite rocky, she noticed, and dotted with anthills as well as spindly trees and scrub. The grass was long and spiky.

'But this is only one of your stations, isn't it?' she said.

'Yes, we have two more, roughly in this area, and

one in the Northern Territory.' He drew up and pointed. 'There you are—Brahmans.'

Holly stared at the cream and mainly brown cattle with black points. They were gathered around a dam. They had big droopy ears, sloe eyes, dewlaps and medium humps. 'They look so neat and smooth.'

'It's that smooth coat and their highly developed sweat glands that help them cope with the heat.'

'Do they come in any other colours?'

'Yes, grey with black points, but we don't have any greys here on Haywire.'

'It's so interesting!' She took some pictures then folded her arms and watched the cattle intently.

Brett Wyndham watched her for a long moment.

In her yellow singlet top, her jeans and no-nonsense shoes, she didn't look at all out of place in the land-scape. In her enthusiasm, she looked even more apt for the setting; with her pale skin, that cloud of fair curls and no make-up, she was different and rather uniquely attractive.

He thought of her in her swimming costume only this morning: very slender, yes, but leggy with a kind of colt-ish grace that he'd found quite fascinating. Then again, in all her incarnations he'd found her fascinating...

He stirred and glanced at his watch. 'Seen enough?'

Holly turned her head and their gazes clashed for a moment. She felt her skin prickle as an unspoken com-munication seemed to flow between them, one of mutual awareness.

Then he looked away and switched on the engine, and the moment was broken, but the awareness of Brett

Wyndham didn't leave her as they bounced over the uneven terrain back to the compound.

Quite unaware that her thoughts echoed his thoughts, she remembered him all sleek and tall in the waters of Palm Cove that morning. She recalled how easily he'd picked her up in his arms and carried her up the beach. She shivered inwardly as she remembered the feel of her skin on his skin.

Brett parked the ute outside the compound fence and pointed out of his window. Holly followed the line of his finger and saw three emus treading with stately precision down the fenceline.

She breathed excitedly—not only in genuine interest, but because she was grateful to be relieved of her memories of the morning...

'It's already like a zoo here,' she told him.

They watched for a while, then got out, and he led the way to the cabin she'd been allotted.

'You've got half an hour before pre-dinner drinks. Would you like to freshen up?' he asked.

'Thanks,' she said gratefully.

'This is a guest cabin. By the way, there's plenty of hot water.'

'Lovely,' Holly murmured,

He turned away, but turned back. 'Oh, there should be a functioning torch in there—use it when you're walking around the compound at night. There could be frogs. Or snakes.'

'Frogs I can handle,' Holly said. 'Snakes I'm not too keen on, but I guess usual practice—make a bit of a noise as you move about so the ground vibrates and otherwise beat a hasty retreat?'

'Good thinking; they're not common,' he agreed.

'That's nice to hear,' Holly said with some humour.

'We *are*—almost—beyond the black stump.'

'Now you tell me,' she quipped, and closed herself into the cabin.

She immediately discovered that Haywire might be remote, and might resemble a safari camp in some respects, but its cabins were sturdy, beautifully appointed and had very modern bathrooms.

The double bed had a sumptuous thick-looking but light-as-air doona covered in an intricately embroidered cream-linen cover, with four matching pillows. It was also a four-poster bed. There were paintings on the dark-green walls and the carpet was the kind your feet sank into in a soft sea-green. There was a beautiful cedar chest, two armchairs and a delicate writing-desk with cabriole legs. The bedside lamps had porcelain bases and coral-pink linen shades.

The bathroom was a symphony of white tiles, black floor and shiny chrome taps. Lime-green and lemon-yellow was echoed not only in the towels and the robes that hung behind the door but in the cakes of soap and toiletries all provided in glass bottles, with an ornamental 'H' for Haywire entwined with a 'W' for Wyndham.

She took a hot shower and changed into a pair of clean jeans and a long-sleeved blue blouse that matched her eyes. She thought about wearing her heavy shoes as protection against any snakes on the loose, but decided her feet needed a change, and slipped them into her ballet pumps.

As usual she spent a few minutes grappling with her hair; she'd washed it, but in the end merely pushed her fingers through it and left it to its own devices. She'd discovered that very few people with curly hair actually appreciated it, whilst many who did not have it thought it would be marvellous to do so. She grimaced at her reflection as she recalled the agonies in her teens when she would have given her eye teeth to have straight smooth hair.

That Brett Wyndham didn't seem averse to it occurred to her—and, since she had five minutes to play with, she sat down in one of the armchairs and thought about him.

In particular she thought about that charged little moment out in the ute when their gazes had locked and she'd been so aware of everything about him. Not only that, but she'd sensed it was mutual. Where could it ever lead? she wondered. There was something about him she couldn't put her finger on. Yes, she'd decided he was a loner—it was pretty obvious he lived the kind of life that didn't go well with domestic ties—but was there something even more remote about him?

If so, did it come from his broken engagement to Natasha Hewson or did it go deeper than that?

She frowned as she suddenly remembered what he'd said this morning about going into areas he didn't want to go to. What could that be about? she wondered as she cast her mind over all the material she'd collected from him the previous evening. None of it had been especially riveting, mostly family history, history of the area and some anecdotes... *Hang on!*

She paused her thoughts as it struck her that those

few anecdotes from his formative years had included his brother Mark, his sister Sue, his mother, who was a doctor, and his grandparents but not one word about his father. Wasn't that a little strange?

She shook her head, more than ever conscious that Brett Wyndham was an enigma. She also had to concede that there was a spark of chemistry between them— more than a spark. She couldn't deny there were times when she loved his company, even though he'd so incensed her at the beginning, but she also couldn't deny her wariness.

Of course, some of that was to do with what had once happened to her, but who would wittingly fall in love with an enigmatic loner? She posed the question to herself.

CHAPTER FIVE

SHE didn't encounter any snakes or frogs on the way to dinner. In fact, Bella came to meet her as she opened her door and escorted her.

'You are a lovely dog,' she said to Bella as they arrived, then, 'Wow—this looks amazing!'

Oil lamps hung from the rafters, shedding soft light. The table was set with colourful, linen place mats, pewter and crystal, and a bowl of swamp lilies. There was a bottle of champagne in an ice bucket, and there was the tantalizing smell of roast beef in the air.

Brett had obviously showered too; his hair was damp and spiky and he'd changed into khaki trousers and a checked shirt. He looked devastatingly attractive, Holly thought privately.

'Champagne?' he invited, lifting the bottle by its neck and starting to ease the foil off.

'Yes, please.' Holly looked around. 'I must say this is amazingly civilized for beyond the black stump.'

'We do our best. Champagne, Sarah?' he called.

'No, thanks,' Sarah called back. 'I'm in the midst of dishing up; I'll have one later.'

'Has it always been like this—Haywire?' Holly

asked, and lifted her glass in a response to Brett's silent toast.

'More or less,' he replied and shrugged. 'Ever since I can remember, although the cabins have been renovated and more mod cons put in. But I never wanted to change *this*.' He gestured comprehensively.

'I'm so glad; it's magic,' Holly said enthusiastically.

Not a great deal later Holly said to Sarah, 'That was fantastic,' as she put her knife and fork together and pushed her plate away. 'Not only roast beef but Yorkshire pudding.'

'I am a Yorkshire lass,' Sarah revealed as she stood up and began clearing plates. 'There's fruit and cheese to come, and coffee.'

'Please, let me help,' Holly offered.

'No way! I am being paid to do this. You and Brett relax,' Sarah ordered.

Holly breathed a little frustratedly. She didn't really want to be left alone with Brett—well, she did and she didn't, she decided. But she felt tense about it; she felt jittery.

On the other hand, she didn't want to force herself on Sarah in the kitchen. Some cooks hated having their space invaded with offers of help.

She got up, but stood undecided beside her chair, and it seemed to show in her face.

She saw Brett watching her rather narrowly and wondered what he was thinking. Then she realized, as his dark gaze flicked up and down her figure, that he was thinking of her in a particular context—the awareness that continued to spring up between them—and she felt herself colour; she turned away, biting her lip.

He was the one who solved the problem. He said, 'I've got a few things to do, a few calls to make. Why don't you look through the albums? It might give you more background material.'

She turned back. 'Albums?'

He indicated the library area and some thick albums arranged on a teak table. A comfortable armchair stood beside the table and a lamp above it shed light.

'There are photos going way back; there are visitors' comments and press cuttings.'

'Oh, thank you! I will,' she said eagerly, but didn't miss the ironic little glance he cast her. In fact, it caused her to bridle as she stared back.

But he only shrugged and drew her attention to a drawer in the table that contained pens and paper, if she wanted to make notes.

'Thank you,' she said stiffly. Feeling foolish, which didn't sit well with her, she waved her hands and recommended that he go away and leave her alone.

'By all means, Miss Harding,' he said with soft sarcasm. 'By all means.'

Holly ground her teeth.

An hour later she looked up as he came back into the library area, then put her pen down and stretched.

'Finished?' he enquired.

'No. They're fascinating—I could go on for hours, but I won't. Thanks very much.' She closed the album she'd been working on and stood up. 'I think bed might be a good idea. I seem to have done an awful lot today,' she said with evident humour.

'I'll walk you to your cabin,' he murmured.

'I can walk myself.' But she paused, feeling recalcitrant and juvenile. What could happen between here and her cabin? 'OK. Thanks.'

They called goodnight to Sarah, who was watching a DVD, and set off. In the event, there were no snakes, but there was a flying fox. As Brett opened her cabin door and reached in to switch on the light, it swooped down on Holly.

It startled her so much she dropped her torch, gave a yelp and with an almighty shudder sought refuge in Brett's arms.

The creature flew into the cabin, then straight out again.

'It's only a flying fox,' he said, holding her close, though, and flipping off the light. 'It was the light.'

'Only a flying fox!' she repeated incredulously. 'Aren't they responsible for the Lyssa virus or the Hendra virus—or both?'

'It didn't actually touch you, Holly.' He passed a hand over her hair then closed the cabin door.

She shuddered again. 'Can you imagine it getting caught in my hair? Yuck!'

'Some people love them.'

'Not in their hair, I bet they don't. Look, I'm not keen on them; snakes, spiders, rats and frogs I can manage to stay sane about—flying foxes, not!'

He laughed down at her then bent his head to kiss her.

Holly was taken completely by surprise, but it felt

so good, she was immediately riveted and all her fears seemed to melt away.

Then some common sense prevailed and she drew away a little.

'We shouldn't be doing this,' she whispered.

'We've been wanting to do it all day,' he countered.

'I...' She swallowed. 'The thing is, I'm here to do a job and I really need to concentrate on that. So.' She managed to look up at him humorously. 'Thanks for being here, otherwise I could have really freaked out! But now I'll say goodnight.'

He released her promptly, although with a crooked little smile. 'All right. Don't switch the light on until you're closed in.' He turned away and left her.

Holly closed herself into the cabin and stood in the dark for a long moment with her hand to her mouth.

The next morning, after breakfast, he had a surprise for her.

She'd greeted him cautiously, but he'd been casual and friendly and they'd eaten breakfast companionably.

Then he recommended that she bring a hat and sunscreen, along with her camera, and meet him at the holding-paddock gate.

When she got there, there were two saddled horses tied to the fence.

'I'm sorry,' he said. 'I couldn't rustle up a camel or a donkey.'

Holly groaned. 'Thank heavens! But I have to tell you that, although I have ridden horses before, I'm not much of a rider—I usually get led.'

'No problem.' He produced a long rein out of his

saddle bag and attached it to one of the horses' bridles. 'Up you get.' He put his hands around her waist and lifted her into the saddle.

'Where are we going?'

He mounted his horse with ease and clicked his tongue. As they set off, he said, 'We're putting in a new dam; I want to see the progress. It's a pleasant ride.'

'You're not going to gallop or do anything that'll contribute to me falling off?' she queried as she clutched her reins and tried to adjust herself to the motion as they broke into a trot.

'Nope. Just relax. Are you always this nervous when you're on a job?'

'Often with good cause, believe me,' she said a shade tartly. 'I've even been known to get off and walk, but I do always get there in the end.'

Brett Wyndham grimaced.

'What?' she asked with conspicuous hauteur.

He laughed softly. 'I believe you. You're a stubborn one, Holly Golightly; that I don't doubt. OK. Let's see if we can enjoy this ride.'

An hour later they reached the dam sight, and to Holly's surprise she had enjoyed the ride. They'd stopped a couple of times, once on a rocky crest that had afforded them a sweeping view of the countryside, and once beside a salt lick.

Both times she'd dismounted and asked a lot of questions. By the time they reached the dam, she was confident enough of her horse not to need the leading rein, and she was genuinely charmed when Brett lit a small fire and boiled the billy he had in his saddle bag.

She reached into hers as instructed and withdrew some damper Sarah had baked to go with their tea.

'A real bush picnic,' she enthused as she sat on a rock and fanned herself with her hat. 'Oh—I can see a bulldozer over there. And a camp—but not a soul in sight!'

'Yes.' Brett squatted beside the fire and put a few more sticks on it. 'They usually work two weeks on, one week off. I wanted to check it all out on their off-week. Ready for your tea?' He poured boiling water onto a teabag in an enamel mug and handed it to her.

'Mmm…I'm looking forward to this. Thank you. But I don't see any cattle.'

'We rotate paddocks; this one's resting.'

'I see. How long…?'

But he interrupted her to give her all the information she was about to ask for about the paddocks, and more besides.

Holly had to laugh, although a little self-consciously, when he'd finished. 'Sorry, I'm asking too many questions, but it is interesting.'

He sent her a thoughtful look. She seemed to be completely unfazed by the heat and the flies; she seemed quite unaware that she had a dirty smudge on her face, or that her hands were grimy, that her hair was plastered to her head or that her shirt was streaked with sweat.

'You'd make a good countrywoman,' he said at last.

Holly tried the damper and pronounced it delicious. 'I'm insatiably curious,' she said. 'That's my problem.'

He looked thoughtful, but he didn't comment. When

they'd finished their tea, he put the fire out carefully, they mounted again and went to explore the dam workings.

Two hours later they cantered back into the holding paddock and Brett suggested a swim in the pool.

'Sounds heavenly,' Holly said in a heartfelt way, and went to change into her togs. She was on her way to the pool when it occurred to her that Sarah wasn't around, and that she hadn't been quite her cheerful self at breakfast. She hesitated then went to knock on her cabin door.

Sarah opened it eventually and was full of apologies. 'I'm sorry, I'll get stuck into lunch—I've just got a touch of sinus, but I've taken something. Makes me feel a bit sleepy, though.'

Holly studied the other girl's pale face and the dark rings under her eyes. 'Oh, no,' she said. 'You go back to bed. I can handle lunch!'

'I wouldn't dream of it,' Sarah replied, but her gaze fastened on something over Holly's shoulder. Holly turned round to see that Brett was standing behind her. Before Sarah got a chance to say anything, she explained the situation to him and finished by saying, 'I could make lunch easily.'

'Done,' Brett said with authority. 'You do as you're told, Sarah.'

'I should be better in time to make dinner,' Sarah said anxiously.

'We'll see about that,' her boss replied, and reached out to rumple Sarah's hair. 'Take it easy,' he advised her.

Sarah sighed and looked relieved.

* * *

In the event Holly made both lunch and dinner. They had a swim in the pool before lunch, then Brett poured them a gin and tonic each—a fitting aperitif for the middle of a hot day, he told her—while she made open cold roast beef sandwiches with hot English mustard and salad.

They took their drinks and lunch to a table beside the pool beneath a shady tree.

Holly had put her peasant blouse on over her togs but Brett had added nothing to his board shorts. Bella lay beside them, gently indicating that she'd be happy to clean up any scraps. The bush beyond the fence was shimmering in the heat and vibrating with insect life.

'How do you manage to leave this place so often?' Holly asked.

'Don't kid yourself,' Brett responded. 'You can feel isolated up here.'

'But you can drive out, can't you?'

'Sure, but it's a long way on a rough road.'

Holly sipped her drink. 'Do your sister and brother like it up here?'

'From time to time, but they don't really have cattle in their blood. Neither does Aria. She doesn't really enjoy roughing it.' He grimaced then elaborated. 'She's the girl Mark's marrying.'

'What's she like?'

Brett considered and gave Bella the last bit of his sandwich. 'Very beautiful. She has long blonde hair, a striking figure. She and Natasha make a good pair, come to think of it, although Nat's a redhead.' He paused. 'My ex-fiancée.'

Holly's mind fled back to the dinner party she'd

witnessed at Palm Cove. Unless there were two stunning redheads in his life, had the one she'd seen been his ex-fiancée? If so, did that mean they were still friends?

'No curiosity on that subject, Miss Harding?' he queried, a shade dryly.

Holly shrugged and looked away. 'I'm sure it's out of bounds, and besides, its none of my business.'

'True.' He looked reflective. 'Anyway, Aria is a biochemist and actually very nice, although something of a meddler.' He looked briefly heavenwards. 'But since Mark's a computer genius they have similar lifestyles in common.'

Holly looked around. 'So all this falls to you? I mean all the responsibility, the planning and so on.'

'Yes.' He sat back and crossed his hands behind his head.

'It must be quite a handful, combining it with your other work.'

'More or less what I've been thinking for a while now,' he agreed with a wry little smile. He sobered. 'But it's in my blood. Just as you inherited your father's writing gene, I must have inherited my f—' He stopped abruptly.

Holly waited but found she was holding her breath.

'Much as I don't care to admit it,' he said finally, 'I must have inherited my father's gene for cattle and the land.'

Holly released her breath slowly. Although the thought chased through her mind that she'd been right—there had been something between Brett and his father—she was mindful of his warning about going into things he didn't want go into.

'So it's something you really love,' she said instead. 'I can understand that.'

He looked at her penetratingly. 'You can?'

'I think so. It's probably unfair to say there are more challenges out here than in suburban life, but to me anyway these open spaces are not only exciting—' she looked up at the wide arc of blue, blue sky above '—they're liberating. I guess that's what motivated my father and may have come down to me.'

'You really mean that, don't you?' He sat up.

Holly nodded, then grimaced. 'Probably easy enough to say. So. What's on this afternoon?'

He eyed her, sitting so relaxed in her chair in her peasant blouse with its pretty embroidery, her legs long and bare and her hair curling madly.

What's on this afternoon? he repeated to himself. *What would you say, Miss Harding, if I told you I'd very much like to take you to bed? I'd love to strip your togs from your body and explore those slender lines and delicate curves. I'd like to touch you and make those pink lips part in surprise and pleasure, those blue eyes widen in wonder...*

It was a disturbance over the fence in the holding paddock that drew his attention away from Holly—saved by the bell, he thought dryly. He saw that his foreman, Kane, had arrived back from the fencing trip with his two offsiders.

But as his gaze came back to Holly, he saw that she was staring at him with her lips parted, her eyes wide—all in some perplexity.

His lips twisted. 'Why don't you relax? I've got some things to discuss with Kane. I may take him back to the dam to show him what I want done, so I could be tied up all afternoon.'

'Uh, all right,' Holly responded after a moment. 'I can do some work anyway.' She hesitated. 'If Sarah's still not well would you like me to cook dinner?'

'Thanks.' He stood up. 'That would be great.'

Holly withdrew her gaze from the physical splendour of Brett Wyndham in his board shorts. 'Um, do I cook for Kane and the others?'

'No. They'll cater for themselves in their quarters. See you later.' And he walked away.

Holly cleared up their lunch and retreated to her cabin, where she admitted to herself that she was somewhat bothered and bewildered. Or bewitched.

She lay down on the bed and stared at the ceiling, feeling like a star-struck teenager, she admitted as she pulled a pillow into her arms. So, what to do about it?

No answer presented itself and she fell asleep.

It was starting to cool down when she re-emerged, showered and once again changed in her blouse and jeans.

She checked on Sarah first and took her a pot of tea and a snack—all she wanted. She persuaded her to stay where she was, assuring her she was quite able to handle dinner.

A couple of hours later, with the oil lamps lit and the table set attractively again, Brett put down his knife and fork and said, 'You can cook. Another gene from your father?'

Holly's face dimpled into a smile as she glanced at the remains of the golden-brown lasagne she'd prepared, along with a fresh green salad and some warm rolls.

'No. The cooking gene comes from my mother, in case you thought I was all my father's doing.'

Brett lay back in his chair and studied her. He had also showered and had changed into a clean khaki shirt and beige chinos. 'What does come to mind...' He twirled his wine glass. 'Is the fact that you'd make someone a really handy wife.'

Holly looked put out, although there was glint of laughter in her eyes. 'That's not exactly a compliment, Mr Wyndham,' she said gravely.

'Sorry,' He grimaced. 'As well as a very attractive wife, of course.'

'That's a bit better!' Holly approved. 'But I don't think I'd make a good wife, actually.'

'Why not?'

She gathered their plates. 'Oh, I don't know.' She shrugged and stood up.

He rose too and told her to sit down. 'I'll do this.'

Holly sank back and watched him clear the table. He came back and topped up their wine glasses. 'Why not?' he asked again.

She looked at him and looked away. She stroked Bella's head. Somehow the dog must have gauged her inner distress with the subject, because Bella had risen and put her head on Holly's lap. Despite her inner distress, there was something else, something new. For the first time she wanted to explain why she was the way she was.

It was to do with this man, she thought. Because he moved her, whether she liked it or not...

She took a deep breath. 'A couple of years ago I fell madly in love,' she said quietly. 'What I didn't know was that he was a married man. And I only got to know it when his wife started stalking me.'

Brett stopped with his wine glass poised in his hand, then he slowly put it down. 'I'm sorry. *Seriously* stalking you?'

'I thought so. She wrote threatening letters, she threatened me over the phone, she turned up at work, she harassed my mother—she threw a brick through my car window once. It got to the stage where I was looking over my shoulder all the time, even scared to go out.'

'She sounds crazy,' he said.

Holly shrugged. 'I'll probably never know whether it was the cause or the effect of her husband's philandering, but it left me with several complexes. Strangely, although she scared me silly at times, I felt a streak of sympathy for *her*, whereas I could have killed her husband for putting me in that position. You could say I fell off cloud nine with a huge bump.'

She looked away and for a moment tears glittered in her eyes.

'Go on,' he murmured eventually.

'I couldn't believe I'd been so thoroughly taken in by him. I can only—I'd just lost my father, who meant the world to me, so I was depressed and so on when I met him.'

'He was still living with her?'

'No, he'd moved out, so I had no reason to suspect he was married. But I guess that's my number-one complex—a terrible lack of judgement on my part. Funnily enough, I'd never believed I was the kind of girl to be swept off her feet by a man.'

'Or vice versa—who does?'

Holly smiled bleakly. 'It doesn't help. Anyway, I'm very much on guard against that kind of thing happening to me again. And I'm terribly, terribly wary now of the maelstrom of emotions that can go with love and marriage.'

'Maybe she was a unhinged. Perhaps you struck a one-in-a-million situation?' he suggested.

'Or maybe she just felt herself to be a woman scorned. Maybe she felt she couldn't live without him; they had two children. Maybe she just felt desperate; I don't know,' Holly said.

'What happened to them?'

'He went back to her and they moved overseas.' Holly fiddled with her napkin then looked straight into his eyes.

'But for a few months I was in serious trouble. I felt so guilty, even though I hadn't known about her. I was a nervous wreck—I still sometimes break out into a sweat and think I'm being followed. But my mother finally persuaded me to get some counselling and that's when I realized only I could get myself out of it. So I plunged into my work and the harder, even the more dangerous it was, the better.'

'And now?'

Holly rubbed her hands together. 'For the most part, fine, but still terribly wary of men and love and marriage—and my own lack of judgement.'

'I see.' He finished his wine. 'I guess that explains your aversion to *chemistry*.'

Holly bit her lip. Of course, he was quite right. The only thing was, she hadn't had any problems with "chemistry" after that disastrous affair until *he* had come into her life. Well, she'd been perfectly capable of stonewalling it without feeling it herself, but that was not the case now.

She looked across at him. 'My mistrust of it, yes. But I can't say it hasn't happened.'

'Between us?'

'Yes,' she whispered. She gestured a little helplessly. 'But you—you're… This is business, *serious* business for me anyway. I need to get this interview right. If I don't, you'll can it or my editor will.' She said with sudden passion, 'I need to make it vibrant and compelling. I can't do that if I'm—distracted.'

He stared at her with his lips twitching.

'What?' she asked huskily.

'You are on the horns of a dilemma.'

'If you're going to laugh at me…'

'I'm not,' he interrupted. 'Although that did strike me as, well, probably the least of our problems.'

Holly felt herself blush. She said honestly, 'You're right. I don't know where that bit came from.'

'Come and see the moon.' He stood up, came round to her and held out his hand.

She looked up at him. 'Where did *that* come from?'

He smiled. 'The moon? It just struck me, it's full tonight. See?' He pointed out towards the east.

Holly gasped at the orange globe rising above the tree line. 'Oh! How beautiful.' She got up.

'Mmm…' He took her hand and led her out onto the lawn.

Holly was transfixed as the moon rose, and in the process lost some of its orange radiance and shrunk a bit. She shivered. Days out in the savannah might be hot, but the nights were very cold, and she hadn't put on her jumper.

Brett put his arms around her. She couldn't help herself, and she snuggled up to him.

'Maybe this says it all,' he murmured, and started to kiss her.

Her lips quivered, but it seemed to her that her senses would no longer be dictated by her mind. They clamoured for his touch; they were lit by the feel of him, tall and hard against her, and tantalized by the pure essence of man she was breathing in.

She loved the press of his fingers against her skin; she loved the way they explored the nape of her neck and behind her ears while he kept his other hand around her waist.

But a skerrick of common sense claimed her and she raised her hands to put them on his chest. 'We ought to stop and think,' she breathed. 'This could be very dangerous.'

He lifted his head. 'Why? It has nothing to do with anyone but us, and we couldn't be in more agreement at the moment if we tried.'

Holly made a strange little sound in her throat. He stared down at her mouth in the moonlight and started to kiss her again.

She was almost carried away with delight when he stopped and raised his head to listen.

She came out of her enchanted trance with a start as she too heard footsteps. 'Sarah,' she breathed. 'I'd forgotten about her. She must be feeling a bit better—hungry, maybe!'

'We'll go to your…'

'No! I need to go and see if she's OK.' Holly stood on tiptoe and kissed him swiftly. 'Thanks for listening.' She sped off back towards the house.

Brett said something unrepeatable under his breath then looked down to see Bella sitting beside him. 'Come to sympathize, old girl? Well, what would you say if I told you that Holly Harding could be the right one for me? She's taken to Haywire as if she was born to it; she could be running the place, but of course it's not only that. She's becoming more and more desirable. But do I want a wife? It's hard to put down roots without one. How good would I be with a wife, though?

CHAPTER SIX

THERE was a triple knock on Holly's door before sunrise the next morning.

She'd been hovering on the edge of wakefulness for a while and she jerked upright, scrambled out of bed and went to open the door. 'What? Who? Why?' she breathed. 'Has something happened?'

'No.' It was Brett dressed in jeans and a jacket. 'Come and see the sunrise.'

'But I'm not even dressed!'

'Throw some warm clothes on, then; we haven't got much time.'

She hesitated then shrugged. 'OK.'

Ten minutes later she joined him in the ute.

She'd thrown on some slouchy trousers and a jacket and she was finger-plaiting her hair. They bumped over some rough ground for a few minutes then came to a lip in the ground, as far as she could see in the headlights.

Brett pulled up and switched the ute off. 'Won't be long now. Come and sit on the bonnet.'

Holly did as she was bid, and slowly the rim of the horizon started to lighten. As it did the chill breeze that had seen her wrap her arms around herself dropped.

With gathering speed, the darkness faded and she was looking down a long valley; all the colours of the landscape—the burnt umber and olive greens, the forest greens and splashes of amber—started to come alive as the sun reached the horizon.

It was so beautiful in the crystal-clear cool air, and alive in every little detail. She found she was holding her breath as she watched a wedge-tail eagle planing the thermals. Then as the sun climbed higher, that particular vividness of early dawn faded a little, and she sighed wistfully.

'Thank you for that,' she whispered, as if she was afraid of breaking the spell by talking aloud.

He merely nodded and got off the bonnet, but only to reach into the ute for a thermos flask and two cups.

The coffee he poured from the flask was full-bodied and aromatic. 'I thought you might be cross with me for dragging you out of bed.'

'No. Well...' Holly grinned. 'That may have been my first tiny reaction.' She sipped her coffee and sniffed appreciatively. 'Smells so good!'

He climbed back onto the bonnet. 'So you slept well?'

'I did. I...' She hesitated and thought of the tussle she'd had with herself before she'd been able to fall asleep. 'I did decide I needed to apologize.'

He raised an eyebrow at her. 'What for?'

Holly chewed her lip. 'This is not that easy to say but I seem to have developed the habit of—kissing you—and, uh, sloping off.'

'You have,' he agreed after a moment.

Holly looked slightly put out.

'What did you expect me to say?' He drained his coffee and put his cup down.

'I didn't expect you to agree quite so readily. And there are reasons for it, of course.'

'Of course,' he echoed. 'Such as, we just can't seem to help ourselves? That's what promotes it in the first place, at least.'

Holly wrapped her hands around her mug and was considering her reply when he went on, 'Then you get cold feet.'

'Well, I do! Why wouldn't I?'

He tilted her chin, observed the indignation in her eyes and smiled slightly. 'I could be going too fast. Should we just be friends for today?' He released her chin and put his arm around her shoulders.

Holly opened her mouth to ask him *what* he was going too fast towards, but she decided against it. She diagnosed one good reason for that: it felt so good to have his arm around her, and to contemplate a friendly day ahead, she didn't feel like debating anything.

'What else will we do today?' she enquired.

'I'm flying to Croydon for a meeting, cattle stuff. If you'd like to come, you could visit the old gold-rush museum and we could fly onto Karumba for lunch. Karumba is on the Gulf of Carpentaria.'

'Sounds great. I think I'd like that very much.'

She did.

She pottered around Croydon while he was in his meeting, she marvelled at the size of the Norman River from the air and she enjoyed a seafood basket on a thick, green lawn beneath shady trees. The Sunset Tavern at

Karumba Point sat on the mouth of the Norman River and overlooked the shimmering waters of the gulf.

'It must be magic at sunset,' she said idly.

'It is. Pity we can't stay, but I've got another meeting this afternoon at Haywire.' He stretched his legs out and clasped his hands behind his head.

'Never mind. It's been beautiful.'

He looked across at her. 'You're easy to please.'

'I don't think it's that. It *has* been great.' She pushed away her empty seafood-basket. 'So were the prawns.'

He laughed. 'Karumba is the headquarters of the gulf prawning-industry—they should be!'

Holly patted her stomach and sat back. That was when she noticed a couple of young women seated at a table nearby and how they were watching Brett with obvious fascination.

She grimaced mentally and felt some sympathy for them. Whether they knew who he was or not, *she* did. Thinking about him in his cargo pants and black sweat-shirt, with his ruffled dark hair and that eagle intensity at times in his dark eyes, and with his tall, streamlined physique, she had no difficulty picturing him engaging in dangerous exploits like shooting tranquilizer darts out of helicopters or parachuting into jungles.

Worse than that, she herself had not been immune from the effect of Brett Wyndham, although it had been designated a 'friendly' day. His hands on her waist when he'd lifted her down from the plane had sent shivers through her. Walking side by side with him had done the same.

Even doing those mundane things—not to mention laughing, chatting and sometimes being teased by him, channelled an awareness of him through her pores, both physical and mental.

I love him, she thought suddenly. *I love being with him. I love his height and his strength, his hands; I love breathing in his essence. But how can that be? It's only been a few days...*

She looked up suddenly to see him eyeing her with a question in his eyes.

'Sorry,' she murmured, going faintly pink. 'Did you say something?'

'Only—ready to go?'

'Oh. Yes. Whenever you are.'

'Something wrong?' His dark eyes scanned her intently.

'No,' she said slowly—but thought, *I don't know; I just don't know...*

Back at Haywire that afternoon, she took herself to task and forbade any more deep thinking on the subject of Brett Wyndham—in relation to her personally, that was. She went to work on her notes while Brett had his next meeting. She didn't ask what his business was, but two planes landed on the strip and he was closeted with the passengers for several hours.

She worked in her cabin, going over all the material she'd gathered, including the zoo details, and putting it into order.

She paused once; she was conscious of a lack, a hole in her story about Brett Wyndham, and realized it was the lack of any detail about his father. But there was another lack, she felt, brought on by her vision of him out at Karumba performing dangerous deeds. So far she had no details about his life as a vet in far-off exotic lands, and she would need that.

She made some notes then paused again and frowned. It occurred to her that if she were asked whether she could capture the essence of Brett Wyndham she would have to say no. There *was* something missing. But what made her think that? Some invisible barrier in him, drawn fairly and squarely so you couldn't cross it. The way just occasionally, when he was talking about his life, she sensed that he retreated and you knew without doubt you'd come to a no-go zone.

She realized she'd put it down to him being a genuine loner, but now she couldn't help wondering if there was more to it.

She shook her head as she wondered if it was her imagination. Then she put her pen down as she heard the noise of aircraft engines, and the two visiting planes taking off. Bella scratched on her door. She let her in and noticed a note attached to her collar with her name on it.

'Why, Bella,' she murmured. 'You clever girl!'

She smoothed the note open and digested the gist of it: a couple of the visitors had decided to stay overnight and would be picked up the following morning. Would Holly care to have dinner with them in about an hour?

Holly sent Bella back with an acceptance penned to the note. Then she went to find Sarah and offer her help, but Sarah was quite restored and wouldn't hear of it. So Holly showered and changed, this time into slim burgundy trousers and a pale-grey jumper over a white blouse.

* * *

It was a pleasant evening.

The two visitors were a couple from a neighbouring station and they proved to be good, lively company. It wasn't until ten-thirty that Holly excused herself and Brett walked her to her cabin.

'Had a nice day?' he enquired when they got there.

Holly turned to him impulsively. 'I've had a *lovely* day!'

'That's good. Ready to fly back to Cairns tomorrow?'

Holly grimaced. 'Yes, if not willing. But thanks for everything.' She glanced back towards the homestead where his guests were still sitting. 'You better get back. Goodnight.'

'Goodnight,' he echoed, but with an ironic little smile.

'I know what you're thinking,' she said, then could have shot herself.

'You do?' He raised an eyebrow at her.

She clicked her tongue in some exasperation and soldiered on. 'You're thinking *I'm* thinking that I've been saved by the bell!'

'Something like that,' he agreed. 'That the presence of visitors will prevent me from kissing you goodnight? But, since I've been on my best behaviour all day, and since it really has nothing to do with anyone else, you're wrong.'

And he put his hands around her waist, drew her into him and kissed her deeply.

Holly came up for air with her pulses hammering and her whole body thrilling to his touch, to the feel of him against her.

He put her away from him gently and smoothed the collar of her blouse. 'Don't put the light on until you're closed inside,' he advised. 'Goodnight.' And he turned away.

It took ages for Holly to fall asleep that night as she examined and re-examined her feelings; as she wondered about his, was conscious of a thrilling little sense of excitement. How could she have grown so close to him in such a short time? she asked herself. It was like a miracle, for her. But it wasn't only the physical attraction—although that was overwhelming enough—it was the powerful pull of his personality. It was as if he'd taken centre-stage in her life and she had no idea how to go on with that lynchpin removed...

Where would it all lead?

There was no opportunity for any personal interaction the next morning. The two guests were picked up after breakfast and then Brett and Kane were called to the home paddock for a colt with colic.

Holly watched the proceedings from the paddock fence as Brett worked to keep the horse on its feet whilst Kane prepared a drench. Once again she could see how good Brett was with animals as he soothed and walked the stricken horse and then administered the drench.

He came out of the paddock wearing khaki overalls, with sweat running down his face, and asked her if she was ready to leave. She nodded, said her goodbyes to Sarah and Bella and looked around. 'Bye, Haywire,' she murmured. 'You're quite a place.'

She hadn't realized that Brett was watching her thoughtfully while she'd said her goodbyes.

When they were alone, finally in the air, they didn't have much to say to each other at all, at first—until Brett made a detour and flew low over the ground to point out to her where he planned to locate the zoo.

'There's water.' He indicated several dams. 'There's good ground cover, but of course we'll have to feed by hand, so we'll establish several feed-stations.'

'There are no roads,' she said slowly.

'Not yet, and no fences, but that'll all come.'

'Are you planning to make it a tourist attraction?' she queried. 'I don't know if it's what you have in mind, but I read somewhere about a zoo that offered a camping ground as well. If you're thinking of an adopt-an-animal scheme, people might be interested in seeing their animals in the flesh, so to speak.'

He glanced at her. 'Good thinking.'

'It's a huge project.'

'Yes,' he agreed. 'But it needs to be done—I feel, anyway. OK.' The little plane lifted its nose and climbed. 'Back to the mundane—well, back to Cairns, anyway, and the wedding.'

But fate had other ideas for them. Not long after they reached their cruising altitude, the plane seemed to stutter, and Brett swore.

'What?' Holly asked with her heart in her mouth.

'I don't know,' he replied tersely as he scanned gauges and checked instruments. 'But it could be a blocked fuel-line. Listen, I'm going to bring her down.' He scanned the horizon now. 'Over there, as best I can.'

Her eyes nearly fell out on stalks. 'Over there'

appeared to be a dry river-bed. 'But we're in the middle of nowhere!'

'Better than what might be the alternative. I'm also going to put out all the appropriate distress signals and hope to get a response before we go down. Holly, just do exactly as I say and buckle in tightly. If anything happens to me, once we're on the ground get out as fast as you can in case the fuel tanks go up.'

She swallowed convulsively several times as he spoke into his radio and the plane lost altitude and stuttered again.

Expecting to nose-dive out of the sky any moment— not that she knew anything about the mechanics of fly- ing—she had to admire his absolute concentration and the way he nursed the little plane down.

'All right, now duck your head and hold on tight,' he ordered. 'I'm bringing her in.'

Holly did just that as well as send up some urgent prayers for help, through the next terrifying, never- ending minutes.

They landed and hopped over the uneven sandy ground, slewing and skidding madly until they finally came to a halt with the nose about a metre from a huge gum-tree on the bank. A cloud of birds rose from the tree.

It had been like being in a dry washing-machine, for Holly. She'd been buffeted and bruised even within the confine of her seat belt. Her limbs had reacted like she'd been a rag doll being shaken, but all of a sudden everything was still and there was an unearthly quiet. Even the birds had stopped squawking.

She stared at the gum tree, so close, so solid, and

swallowed. Then she switched her gaze to Brett. He was slumped over the half steering-wheel with a bleeding gash on his forehead. After a frozen moment of panic for Holly, he lifted his head, shook it groggily and was galvanized into action.

'Out,' he ordered. 'It only takes some fuel to drip onto a hot pipe and we'll be incinerated.'

With an almost Herculean effort, he managed to open his door and climb out. He turned immediately and reached for Holly, manhandled her out of her seat and down onto the ground, where he took her hand and dragged her away from the plane.

They were both panting with exertion by the time he judged them far enough away to be safe; running through the sand of the riverbed had been almost impossible. Holly sank to her knees, then her bottom, her face scarlet, her chest heaving. Brett did the same.

They waited for a good half-hour in the shimmering heat of the river bed but the plane didn't explode. He told her he was going back to it to salvage whatever he could. He also told her to stay put.

'No,' she said raggedly. 'I can help.'

'Holly.' He looked down at her with blood running down his face. 'Please do as you're told, damn it!'

'No.' She reared up on her knees. 'I can help,' she repeated. 'And you can't stop me. Besides, you're bleeding—you could have concussion—'

'It's nothing,' he broke in impatiently.

'I'm coming. In fact, I'm going.' She got painfully to her feet and started staggering through the sand.

He swore quite viciously, then followed her.

Between them they managed to get their bags and two

blankets out of the plane. Brett also found a spare water-bottle strapped to a small drinking-fountain with a tube of plastic cups. He took out not only the spare bottle but the fountain itself. Then he discovered a few cardboard cartons with Haywire stencilled on their sides.

'I was probably meant to deliver these, but no-one mentioned it.'

'What's in them?' Holly breathed.

'No idea. Maybe soap powder—maybe not. We'll take them,' he said.

He also checked the radio, but it was dead, and the satellite phone was smashed. Just as he left the plane for the last time, the starboard wheel-strut collapsed suddenly, tilting it to an unnatural angle and crumpling the starboard wing into the ground.

They froze and waited with bated breath but nothing more happened.

'When is it completely safe?' she asked shakily.

He put an arm round her shoulder. 'If it was going to happen, it would probably have happened by now.' He put his other arm around her. 'Holly.' He stopped and put his other arm round her. 'How are you?'

She tried to break free but he held her closer, and it was only then that she realized she was shaking like a leaf and not quite in control of herself. 'I—I'm sorry,' she stammered. 'It's reaction, I guess. But I'll be fine; just give a me a few moments.'

'Of course.' He held her very close and stroked her hair until she stopped shaking.

'How do you feel now?'

It was a few hours later and the sun was starting to slip

away. The constraint that had had them in its grip earlier in the day had melted away under the circumstances.

'Oh, fine,' Holly responded. 'Thank you. You?'

They'd made themselves as comfortable as possible in the creek bed not far from the plane. Brett was leaning back against a smooth rock. There was a tree growing out from the bank, giving them shade. They'd pegged out in the sand a bright-orange plastic sheet with a V on it, which they'd got from the plane, where it would be most visible from the air.

He grimaced. 'I've got a headache that would kill a cow.' He touched his fingers gingerly to the cut on his forehead that Holly had cleaned as well as she'd been able to.

The packages for Haywire had proved a godsend. They contained packets of biscuits, some self-opening tins of luncheon ham, packets of dates and raisins, six tins of sardines, six tubes of condensed milk and one cardboard carton of white wine.

An odd mixture, he'd commented when they'd broken them out, but at least it was not soap powder, so they wouldn't starve.

She'd agreed ruefully.

They'd also found a small axe and a gas firelighter.

Now, as she watched the sun slipping away, she said, 'It looks as if we'll have to spend the night here.'

'Yes.' He shrugged. 'I doubt if it will be more than a night. But it takes time to co-ordinate a search and hard to do in the dark.'

She looked around and shivered. 'It's a big country.'

He studied her dirty, rather tense face. 'Come here.'

She hesitated then crawled over and leant back beside him. He put an arm round her.

'I'm really worried about my mother,' she said. 'She'll be devastated when she hears this news.'

'Yes.' He said nothing more for a long moment, then, 'You do realize you have me at your mercy, don't you, Holly?' He brushed his lips against her hair.

'Well, I certainly wouldn't take advantage of you with a headache, if that's what you mean,' she returned with some humour.

'Pity about that,' he drawled, then relented as she looked at him incredulously. 'What I meant was, we could talk—fill in the gaps, go on with the interview.'

'Now? But I'm not at all organized.'

'I wouldn't have thought it would take a girl who handled a crash-landing in the middle of nowhere with aplomb long to organize herself.'

'It wasn't all aplomb.'

'Believe me, one little attack of the shakes is very close to aplomb.'

She considered. 'Well, I've got a good memory, so I'll rely on that. Oh!' She put a hand to her mouth. 'My laptop. I didn't even think to check if it got smashed. But hang on…' She fumbled in one of her pockets and with a cry of triumph produced a flash key. 'Safe and sound.'

'You back everything up on that and keep it on your person at all times?' he guessed.

She nodded vigorously. 'Bitter, if not to say heartbreaking experience has taught me that. OK. Uh, I was thinking only yesterday that we haven't touched on any of your exploits to do with saving endangered species. I'm sure readers would find that riveting. And do you have a favourite animal?'

He thought for a while. 'Yes—giraffe. There's nothing like seeing them cross a plain with that rocking-horse rhythm, or staring down at you from above the crown of a tree. I'm very keen on giraffe—or Twiga, which is their Swahili name.'

She chuckled and led him on to talk about some of the successes he'd had as an endangered-species expert. Then their talk turned general until he asked her about her childhood.

She told him about her adventures with her father and couldn't prevent the love and admiration she'd felt for her father shining through. 'I miss him every day of my life. Is your father alive—?' She stopped and bit her lip.

'No.'

'Your mother?'

'No.'

'I'm sorry,' she said.

'You don't need to be sorry on my father's account,' he said dryly.

Holly took an unexpected breath and wondered if he would enlarge on what she was pretty sure was the thorny subject of his father. But he said no more, and she regretted the fact that they had somehow lost their sense of easy camaraderie, so she took another tack.

'How *do* you combine your lifestyle—travelling the world and so on—with running a grazing empire? And it's more than that, isn't it? You've branched out into mining, transport, even a shipping line for live-cattle exports amongst other things. Or does it all run itself?'

She felt a jolt of laughter run through him and breathed a secret little sigh of relief.

'No, it doesn't.'

'They say you're a billionaire,' she observed. 'They say you're responsible for tripling the family fortune.'

He shrugged. 'I told you, in some ways I'm a quintessential cattle man. It's in my blood, so some of it comes naturally. I'm also very attached to this country.' He looked around. 'And I did set out to prove something to myself—that when I took over I'd never allow the empire to go backwards.' He paused, pushed himself upright and looked down at her. 'Do you realize you have a dirty face?' He touched the tip of her nose.

Holly grimaced as she thought, *subject closed*. She said, 'If you had any idea how battered as well as dirty I *feel*.' She looked around. 'There wouldn't be any pools in this river bed, do you think?'

'There could be. There could be tributaries with some water in them, it was a fairly good wet season, but there'll also be crocs.'

'Croc... Crocodiles?' she stammered.

'Uh-huh. Mostly fresh-water ones, usually safe, but enough to give you a fright. And it's not completely unknown for the odd salt-water croc to find its way up here. They are not safe.'

'I see. OK,' she said judiciously. 'I'm happy to stay dirty.'

He frowned. 'You also said battered, but you told me you were fine earlier. Where...?'

She held up a hand. 'I am fine. Just a bit shook up. It's

also starting to get cold—that might be making me feel my age,' she said humorously. 'Don't old cowboys feel every mended bone when there's a chill in the air?'

'I don't know.' He looked rueful. 'But we should make some preparations. I don't want to light a fire— the breeze is blowing towards the plane now—so our best bet is to wear as much of our clothing as we can.'

Holly had inspected their bags earlier. Hers had mostly contained clothes, his had yielded a few useful items other than clothes: a serious penknife with all sorts of attachments, a small but powerful pair of binoculars, a compass and a torch. And they both had wind cheaters fortunately, for later when the temperature dropped.

'All right.' She got up. 'But I do have to go on a little walkabout. I'll add some clothes at the same time. I presume if I'm not close to water I'm safe?'

'Relatively,' he replied. 'But don't go far, and stamp around a bit. There could be snakes.'

Holly swore under her breath.

When she returned, he'd laid out a meal. He'd cut up one of the tinned hams and, together with biscuits, dates and raisins, he'd set it all out on two pieces of cardboard roughly shaped as plates. And he'd poured two plastic cups of wine.

He handed her his pocket knife and said he was happy to use his fingers.

They ate companionably in the last of the daylight, then the dark. He told her about some of the safaris he'd been on and the electronic-tagging system he'd been involved with that tracked animals.

She got so involved in his stories, she might have

been in Africa or Asia with him, experiencing the triumphs and the disasters he'd encountered.

He also poured them a second, then a third, cup of wine.

'This will send me to sleep,' she murmured. 'Or make me drunk, as well as give me a hangover.'

She didn't see the acute little glance he beamed her way.

'I doubt the hangover bit,' he said. 'It's very light, but it might be an idea to get settled now. How about we scoop some sand about to make a bit of a hollow and something to rest our heads on?'

'OK. You hold the torch and I'll—'

'No. *You* hold the torch and I'll—'

'But I can—'

'For once in your life, just do as you're told, Holly Harding!'

She subsided, then chuckled suddenly.

'I probably look quite amusing,' he said as he scooped sand. 'But you don't have to laugh.'

'I'm not laughing at you,' she told him.

'Who, then?'

She waved a hand. 'It just seems a very long way from society weddings, balls and so on— Oh!' She put a hand to her mouth. 'When was your first pre-wedding party?'

'Tomorrow. Nothing we can do about it,' he said with a grimace.

'Perhaps they'll cancel it because you haven't turned up?'

'Perhaps. Not that I would wish it on them—having

to cancel it—but the more concerned people are about us, the sooner they'll start organizing a search.'

'Of course,' she said eagerly, then sat back again. 'What was I saying? Yes, it's actually rather lovely. Look at the stars,' she marveled, and hiccupped. 'Told you,' she added.

'Listen, take the torch if you need another bathroom call—don't go too far—and then let's go to bed, Miss Harding.'

'Roger wilco, Mr Wyndham!'

When she came back, he'd lined the hollow that he'd scooped with the cardboard of the cartons and the paper the foodstuffs had been wrapped in. As they settled themselves, he draped the rest of their clothes over them, then the two blankets.

She slept for about three hours, curled up beside him with his arm protectively over her.

Then she woke, and it wasn't so lovely any more. It was freezing. At first she had no idea where she was, then there was something large moving around on the edge of the creek bed.

She moved convulsively and backed into Brett's arms with a squeak of fear.

'Shh,' he murmured and flicked on the torch. 'It's only a kangaroo. I've been watching it for a bit. It's just curious. Kangaroos aren't renowned for attacking and eating people.'

'I k-know that,' Holly stammered. 'It must have been all the tales of Africa you told me. I feel terrible.' She added.

'What's wrong?' he queried with a hint of surprise.

'Stiff and sore. Everything's aching. How about you?'

'I'm too damn cold to feel a thing. Come closer,' he ordered, and as she turned around with difficulty he gathered her into his arms. 'It's all the result of bouncing around in the plane, performing heavy tasks and sleeping on a river bed.'

'I suppose so. Mmm…at least that's a bit warmer. Do you mind if I really burrow in?'

'Why should I mind?' He stroked her back. 'In the light of hypothermia, it's the only thing to do. Just relax if you can.' He pulled the thin blankets from the plane more securely over her.

She was too grateful to protest, and gradually the protection of both blankets plus his body brought her some warmth, and her aching muscles unknotted a little.

She wasn't aware of the moment things changed—the moment when it wasn't only warmth and comfort she was seeking, or receiving, but something different. It came about so subtly it seemed entirely natural, a natural progression towards a greater closeness that claimed them both at the same time.

His hands slipped beneath her clothes as their mouths touched and he teased her lips apart. She moved her hands and slid them beneath his windcheater, responding to his kiss as she hugged him. From then on she forgot the cold and the discomfort of the river bed; she was lost to all good sense, she was to think later.

But, at the time, it was magic. She remembered something he'd said to her at the masked ball about celebrating her lovely, slim body to both their satisfactions. It wasn't quite like that—they were too hampered by clothes, covers and freezing night-air for that—but he gave her an intimation of what it would be like if they were together on a bed, or anywhere smooth and soft.

He transported her mentally to an oasis of delight where her skin would feel like warm silk—as he'd also promised. Even in the rough environment of a dry river-bed he managed to ignite her senses to a fever pitch as he kissed and caressed her, as he touched her intimately and made her tremble with longing, need and rapture.

She had her own sensory perceptions. She drew her fingers through the rough dark hair on his chest; she laid her cheek then her lips on the smooth skin of his shoulder, before returning her mouth to his to be kissed deeply again. And again.

She cupped her hand down the side of his face; she moved against the hard planes of his body. She was provocative, pressing her breasts against him and tracing the long, strong muscles of his back.

She was alight with desire for Brett Wyndham, she thought, when she could think. Alight, moving like a warm silken flame he couldn't resist in his arms.

How much further things would have got out of hand between them, she was never to know as a belligerent bellow split the chilly air.

They both jumped convulsively then scrambled to their feet, rearranging their clothes as best they could as Brett also searched for the torch. When he found it, it was to illuminate a mob of wild-looking cattle, some with huge horns, advancing down the creek bed towards them.

'Bloody hell!' Brett swore. 'Stay behind me,' he ordered. He reached up and tore a spindly limb from a tree growing out of the bank. 'They're probably as surprised as we are.'

With threatening moves, and a lot of yelling and whistling, he dispersed the mob eventually—but only after they'd got uncomfortably close. Then they took to their heels as if of one mind and thundered back the way they'd come, causing a minor sandstorm and leaving them both coughing and spluttering, sweating and covered in sand.

'Just goes to show, you don't have to go to Africa for wildlife excitement,' he said wryly.

'You have quite a way with cattle!'

'That was more luck than anything.'

Holly frowned. 'They didn't look like Brahmans.'

'They weren't, that's why I was a bit lucky. They were cleanskins, in case you didn't notice.'

'Cleanskins?'

'Yes. Rogue cattle that have evaded mustering and branding and therefore are not trained to it. Independent thinkers, in other words. Throwbacks to earlier breeds.'

'Oh.'

'Yep.' He dragged a hand through his hair and put the torch on the ground. 'Where were we?'

CHAPTER SEVEN

THEY stared at each in the torchlight then started to laugh.

In fact, Holly almost cried, she laughed so hard; he put his arms around her.

'I know, I know, but one day I will make love to you with no interruptions,' he said into her hair.

Holly sobered and rested against him.

'Look,' he added. 'You can just see the horizon. A new day.'

'How long will it take them to come?' she asked.

'No idea, but just in case we have to spend another night we'll need to get organized.'

Holly sat up. 'Another night?'

'That's the worst-case scenario,' he said. 'The best is that they know we're missing and they know roughly the area. So they'll keep looking until they find us.'

But full daylight brought another challenge: rain and low cloud.

'I thought this was supposed to be the dry season,' Holly quipped as a shower swept up the river bed.

They'd moved all their gear under tree-cover on the bank as best they could as soon as the clouds had rolled over. They were sitting under the cover of the plastic V-sheet Brett had hooked up from some branches.

'It is. Doesn't mean to say we can't get the odd shower. You know...' He stared out at the rain drumming down on the river bed, then looked at her. 'If you cared to take your clothes off, it might be quite refreshing.'

Holly looked startled. 'Do you mean skinny-dip?'

He shrugged. 'Why not? It's our only chance of getting clean for a while.'

Holly drew a deep breath and closed her eyes. 'Clean,' she repeated with deep longing. Her eyes flew open and she jumped up and started shedding clothes.

Brett blinked, not only at the fact that she did it but at the speed she did it. A rueful little smile twisted his lips as she stopped short at her underwear—a lacy peach-pink bra with matching bikini briefs.

'That's as far as I'm going to go,' she told him, and climbed down the bank to run out into the rain with something like a war cry.

He had to laugh as he watched her prancing around for a moment, then he stood up to shed his clothes down to his boxer shorts and climbed down the bank to join her.

It was a heavy, soaking shower but it didn't last that long. As it petered out, Holly—now more subdued—said in a heartfelt way as her wet hair clung to her head and face, her body pale and sleek with moisture, 'That was divine!'

She ran her hands up and down her arms and licked the raindrops from her lips.

'Yes, although I didn't expect you to do this.' He

grinned down at her and flicked some strands of wet hair off her face.

'I suspect most girls would have done the same if they'd been through what we have. Now, if only I had a towel…'

As she spoke, thunder rumbled overhead and a fork of lightning appeared to spear into the river bed not far from them.

Holly jumped convulsively and flew into Brett's arms. He picked her up and carried her swiftly to their makeshift shelter.

'Th-that was so close,' she stammered.

'Mmm…I don't think it'll last long; it's just a freak storm.' But he held her very close as more thunder rumbled.

'Lightning,' she said huskily, 'Is right up there with flying foxes for me. It's funny; there are a whole heap of things I can be quite cool about.'

'Mexican bandits and sheikhs?'

'Yep—well, relatively cool. But lightning—' she shivered '—I don't like.'

'Just as well I'm here, then,' he murmured and bent his head to kiss her.

'This—this is terrible,' Holly gasped, many lovely minutes later.

'What's so terrible?' He drew his hands down her body and skimmed her hips beneath the elastic of her briefs.

They were lying together beneath the protection of the plastic sheet in each other's arms on one of the blankets. They were damp but not cold—definitely not cold…

'How did I get to the stage of not being able to keep my hands off you?'

He laughed softly. 'For the record, I'm in the same boat.'

'But it's been so *fast*. There's got to be so much we don't know about each other.'

'It's *how* you get to know people that matters.'

'Maybe,' she conceded. 'I guess it helps, but there's an awful lot I don't know about you.'

He opened his mouth, appeared to change his mind and then said, 'Such as?'

Holly went to sit up but he pulled her back into his arms.

'In fact, you know more about me than most people,' he growled into her ear.

'But, for example—' She hesitated suddenly aware that she was about to tread on sacred ground, from an interviewer's perspective. But surely she was more than that now? 'I know you were engaged and that it didn't work out, but I don't know why. And I sense some—I don't know—darkness.'

She felt him go still for a moment, then his arms fell away and he sat up and stared through the dripping view to the river bed.

Holly sat up too after a couple of minutes, during which he was quite silent.

'Have I offended you?' she ventured hesitantly. 'I didn't mean to.'

He turned his head and looked down at her. Her pink bra had a smudge of mud on it, but he could see the outline of her high, pointed breasts clearly. Her waist was tiny, tiny enough to span with his hands, but her hips were delicately curved and positively peachy.

He rubbed his jaw. 'No.' He smiled suddenly and ironically. 'Are you open to a suggestion?'

'What is it?' she asked uncertainly.

'That we put some clothes on? Just in case a rescuer arrives.'

Holly stared at him, convinced she'd crossed a forbidden barrier, then she looked down at herself and took a sharp little breath. She scrambled up. 'Definitely!'

The thunder storm moved away pretty quickly as Brett had predicted, and there was no more rain, but the low cloud-cover remained.

'That's got to make it harder for them to find us,' she said as they ate a very light lunch, with a view to preserving their limited supplies. They'd also rationed the water, but Brett had found some shallow rock pools with fresh water in them for future use.

By mid-afternoon the cloud cover had cleared and they heard two planes fly over—not directly overhead, but fairly close.

They said nothing during the tense wait both times, just exchanged wry little looks when the bush around them returned to silence.

Brett returned to the plane and, after crawling in with some difficulty, spent some time working on the radios but to no avail.

By four o'clock they were sitting back against their rock in the shade when he put his arm around her. Without any conscious thought, she leant her cheek against his shoulder.

'There is an option to consider now,' he said. 'We could walk out.'

'Is that a viable option?' she queried.

'It's not what I'd prefer to do. At least we're visible here—the plane is, anyway. I do have a rough idea of where we are, though, and where this river leads. But it's a long walk—maybe a couple of days.'

'What's at the end of it?'

'A cattle station near the head waters. We'd have to travel light, more or less food and water only. We'd really have to eke out the food, but it could be done.'

'What if someone spots the plane but we're not there?'

'We'd leave a note, but anyway they'd automatically assume we've followed the river bed. You see—' He paused and glanced at her, as if he wasn't quite sure whether to go on, then said, 'I didn't mention this yesterday but there's the possibility that none of our signals or radio calls were picked up. That means our position won't be known except very roughly, and we did make a detour.'

'Ah,' she said on a long-drawn-out breath. 'Well, then, I guess it makes sense to take things into our own hands. At least,' she added rather intensely, 'We'd be doing something!'

'My thoughts entirely.'

'And if we take the V-sheet with us we can always wave it if anyone flies overhead.'

'Good thinking,' he said, and kissed her on the top of her head. 'But listen, it could mean a very cold night. He sat up. 'Unless I make a sled of some kind so we could take a bit more with us—a blanket, at least. Come to that,' he said as if he was thinking aloud, 'once we're well away from the plane, we could make a fire. I had thought of doing that this afternoon, but well away from the plane.'

'Send up smoke signals, you mean?' she asked humorously.

'Something like that,' he replied with a grin. 'But everything's still damp. Tomorrow it may have dried out if we get no more rain. Uh, I have to warn you, though—this river bed could have rapids in it that would mean rock climbing, now its mostly dry, so it could be a very arduous walk.'

'And there could be wild cattle, there could be dingoes, heaven alone knows what,' she said with a delicious little shiver of anticipation of adventure.

His eyebrows shot up, then he laughed down at her. 'You're a real character—you're actually looking forward to it.'

'I was never one for sitting around! Perhaps we should have gone today,' she added seriously.

'No. It'll have done us the world of good to have a lay day after all the trauma of yesterday. But an early night'll be a good idea. Should we put it to the vote?'

'Aye aye, skipper—I vote yes.'

'OK. We'll get to work before the light runs out so we can leave at the crack of dawn tomorrow morning.'

It was just that, barely light, when they set off the next morning.

They'd finished all their preparations the afternoon before and spent a companionable night. Holly was at least buoyed up by the prospect of some action rather than sitting around waiting for what might not come. The more she thought about the vast, empty terrain surrounding them, the more she realized it could be like looking for a needle in a haystack.

Brett used the axe to make two long poles from tree branches and, using a variety of clothes, they constructed a light but sturdy sled for carrying stuff. Holly wrought two back-packs out of long-sleeved shirts.

Between them they smoothed an area of sand in the middle of the creek bed, helped by its dampness, and in big letters they wrote WALKED UPSTREAM, with several arrows pointing in the direction they would take. Then they lined the scores the letters had made in the sand with small rocks to make them more lasting and visible.

Brett also wrote a note and left it in the plane. He pointed out that the heavy shower of earlier had been a blessing for another reason, apart from allowing them to clean up a bit—it would also provide rock pools of fresh water along the way.

Not surprisingly—after a light supper of sardines on biscuits, and half a tube each of condensed milk for energy plus one cup of water each—they had little trouble falling asleep. Even the cold hadn't bothered Holly as much as it had the night before. Being curled up in Brett's arms gave her a lovely feeling of security.

She did wonder, briefly, where all the passion that had consumed them last night had gone, and concluded that either she had touched a nerve he hadn't wanted to be touched although he'd been perfectly normal during the day—or the physical exertion they'd expended had simply worn them out too much even to think of it.

She was to discover soon enough that being tired was no guard against anything…

It was a long, arduous day.

They walked in the cool of the morning, they slept beneath some leafy cover through the midday heat and they walked again in the afternoon.

It was fairly easy going, as far as sand could be easy, and they encountered no rocks they had to climb over.

They did see some pools of water and a couple of times they saw freshwater crocodiles slither into them.

She marvelled at Brett's strength and tirelessness as he towed the sled with a belt around his waist, as well as carrying a backpack.

As for herself, she sang songs to keep herself going when she would have loved to lie down and die. And she thought a lot as she trudged along, thoughts she'd never entertained before, about mortality and how, when you least expected it, swiftly, you could be snuffed out. It was delayed reaction to the plane crash, probably, but nonetheless to be taken seriously. It was about seizing the day or, instead of looking for perfection in every thing you undertook, letting the way life panned out have some say in the matter.

Brett took a lot of the credit for keeping her going. Every now and then he made her stop and he massaged her shoulders and back, or he told her jokes to make her laugh. He'd insisted on adding her backpack to the sled when she was battling.

Fortunately they both had hats in their luggage and Holly had a tube of factor thirty-plus sunscreen with which they'd liberally anointed themselves. This proved to be a mixed blessing, causing the sand to stick to them.

But there were some marvels to observe along the way: some black cockatoos with red tail feathers sailed overhead, with their signature lazy flight and far-away calls. They also saw a huge flock of pink-and-grey galahs and a family of rock wallabies.

Otherwise, the hot, still bush all around them was untenanted, even by wild cattle. Again they heard plane engines a couple of times but, the same as the day before, the planes were nowhere near enough to see them.

Then, just as they were about to call it a day, they got a wonderful surprise: the river bed wound round a corner and opened into a lagoon, a lovely body of water full of reeds, water lilies and bird life and edged with spiky, fruit-laden pandanus palms.

'Is it a mirage?' Holly gasped.

Brett took her hand. 'No, it's real.'

'Thank heavens! But is it full of crocodiles?'

'We'll see. Look.' He pointed. 'There's a little bay and a rock ledge with a beach above it. There's even a bit of a shelter. Good spot to spend the night.'

Holly burst into tears, but also into speech. 'These are tears of joy,' she wept, and laughed at the same time. 'This is just so—so beautiful!'

He hugged her. 'I know. I know. Incidentally, you've been fantastic.'

The shelter was rough-hewn out of logs, closed on three sides with a bark roof. There was evidence of occupation, a burnt ring of sand within a circle of rocks outside, and a couple of empty cans that had obviously been used to boil water over a fire.

'We can't be too far away from somewhere!' Holly enthused as she slipped her backpack off with a sigh of relief. Then she sat down, and took her boots off and wiggled her toes with another huge sigh, this time pure pleasure.

'No,' Brett agreed as he cast around, looking at the ground inside and outside the shelter. 'But there's no sign of— Ah, yes, there is.' He squatted down and outlined something in the sand with his fingers. 'A hoof print. Who ever uses this place comes by horse.'

'A horse, a horse, my kingdom for a horse!' Holly carolled. 'Or a camel. Or a donkey!'

Brett laughed.

'So who do you think uses it?' she enquired.

'A boundary rider—a mustering team, maybe.' He stood up. 'Whoever, we could be closer to the homestead than I thought.'

'That is music to my ears. Now, if only I wasn't covered in a repulsive mixture of sweat, sand and sunscreen, I'd be happy.'

'There's an easy remedy for that.' As he spoke Brett pulled off his shirt. 'I'm going for a swim.' He stripped off to his boxer shorts again and jogged down to the beach.

'But...' Holly temporized, thinking inevitably of crocodiles.

'This is fresh water,' he called back to her after he'd scooped a handful up and tasted it. 'And this,' he added as he waded in up to his waist, sending a variety of birds flying, 'is an old Aboriginal remedy for crocs.'

He started to beat the water with his palms. 'Frightens them off. Come in, Holly. I'm here anyway.'

She hesitated only a moment longer, then started shedding her clothes down to her underwear. Today she was wearing a denim-blue bra and matching briefs. She went into the water at a run in case her courage gave out to find it was divine, cool and refreshing, cleansing, incredibly therapeutic.

They played around in it for over half an hour then came out to the chilly air; it was close to sunset.

'Use whatever you can to dry off properly,' he recommended. 'We can always dry clothes tomorrow in the sun.' They'd only brought one change of clothes each.

'What if it rains again?'

'I doubt it will.' He towelled himself vigorously with a T-shirt and looked around. 'You know what they say— red sky at night, shepherd's delight.'

'Oh.' She looked around; the feathery clouds in the sky, a bit like a huge ostrich-feather fan or a group of foxtails, turned to orange as she watched.

'Anyway, I'm going to build a fire, so we can dry things beside it as well as keep warm. But get dressed and warm in the meantime.' He hung his shirt on a nail in the shelter wall and pulled on jeans and his second T-shirt. He was just about to turn away when he kicked his toe on something sharp protruding from the sandy floor.

He knelt down and, using his long fingers, unearthed a metal box. It wasn't locked, and what it contained made him say with absolute reverence, 'Holy mackerel! Look at this.'

Holly was now dressed in a pair of long cotton

trousers and her long-sleeved blue blouse. She bent down and looked over his shoulder. 'Oh my,' she breathed. 'Coffee! Tea! And a plate and a cup. I could kill for a cup of tea or coffee; don't mind which. But what's the other thing?' She frowned.

'This.' He lifted the red plastic spool out of the box. 'Is like gold. It's a fishing reel, complete with lure.' He showed her the curved silvery metal plate with a three-pronged hook on it. 'And sinker. I wondered if there'd be fish in the lagoon; there usually are.' He stood up. 'I was thinking I could kill for a beef steak, but a grilled fish would do nicely. All right, I'm going to collect firewood, you're going to fish.'

'Uno problemo—I have never used one of those things.'

'I'll show you how. Just watch.' He walked to the rocky ledge above the lagoon and unwound about a metre of the fishing line from the reel with the lure on the end. Holding the reel facing outward in one hand, he swung the lure on the line round several times then released it towards the water. The fishing line on the reel sang out as it followed suit, and she heard the lure plop into the water.

'Now what?' she asked keenly.

'Hold the line—you can put the reel down—and when you feel a tug on the line give it a jerk and pull the line in. Try.' He wound the line back onto the reel and handed it to her.

It took Holly several goes—the first time she hooked the lure into a tree—but finally she got it right and was left in charge in the last of the daylight as Brett went to collect firewood.

Her ecstatic shout when she felt the first tug on the line and pulled in a fish set all the water birds squawking in protest. Getting it off the line was her next test. Brett had to show her how to wrap one of her socks around the fish so she could hold it with one hand and wiggle the hook out of its mouth with the other. By the time he'd collected a big pile of wood and was setting the fire, she'd caught six very edible fish.

Brett had a go but caught none.

The first thing they did when the fire was going was boil water in one of the tins and make a cup of coffee, which they shared. Then, using a grid he'd found under one of the rocks around the fire area, Brett grilled the fish, which he'd cleaned with his penknife.

They shared the plate and ate the fish with their fingers.

'I don't know why,' Holly said, 'But this is the best fish I've ever tasted.'

'Could be a couple of reasons.' He glanced at her in the light of the blazing fire, but she didn't see the wicked little glint in his eye. 'After two days of ham and sardines on biscuits, anything would taste good.'

Holly pouted. 'That's one, what's the other?'

'I'm a good, inventive cook.'

'All you did was put them on a grid.'

'That's *not* all,' he countered. 'I had that part of the fire going to perfection so it wouldn't burn them, dry them out or leave them raw.'

'But I caught them!'

'So that makes them very superior fish?'

'Yes,' she said with hauteur, then giggled. 'You wouldn't be a little miffed because you *didn't* catch any?'

He looked offended. 'No. What makes you say that?'

She shrugged, still smiling. 'Just that I can't help feeling very proud of the achievement.' She paused and sobered. 'If I wasn't so worried about my mother, I'd really be enjoying all this.'

'We may be able to end her suspense sooner than we thought—end everyone's.'

'I hope so,' Holly said fervently. 'And she is an eternal optimist.'

She was sitting with her knees drawn up and her arms around them. He was stretched on the sand with his head on his elbow. Because of the fire they were not rugged up to the nines, and Holly had arranged the V sheet in the shelter for them to lie on, with the one blanket they'd brought covering them.

Brett thought to himself, as he watched her in her light trousers and blue shirt, with her bare feet and the fire gilding her riotous hair, that she had never looked more desirable.

Was it because she'd coped so well? he wondered. Had that added to his attraction to her? But was he going to be able to overcome her wariness? She might tell him she couldn't keep her hands off him, but he knew that deep down she was still wary, still burnt by her previous experience.

And he thought about *his* wariness—about the discovery he'd made about himself that he hated and feared, and made him wonder if he was a fit mate for any woman.

It was, of course, the thing Holly had sensed in him, the thing she couldn't put her finger on—the thing he had never wanted to admit to himself. But what was between them wasn't the same thing that had happened to him before, was it?

This was a powerful attraction, yes, but it was also affection. Yes, it was sweet, but it was also sane and sensible because she would fit into his lifestyle so completely...

Then he realized she was returning his regard, her deep-blue eyes very serious, as were the young, lovely curves of her face.

A slight frown came to his face, because he had no idea what she was thinking. Was she thinking about her mother? He got the feeling she was not.

'Holly?'

She looked around, as if unwilling for him to see what was in her eyes. She looked at the fire, at the darkened lagoon beyond, at the moon rising above them and the pale smoke of the fire wreathing against the dark blue of the sky. 'I think I'm running out of steam,' she said at last. 'I feel terribly weary.'

'I'm not surprised,' he said after a moment, and stood up. 'Come to bed. But have a cup of water first; I don't want you to dehydrate.'

'Are you coming to bed?' she asked.

'Shortly. I'm going to get more wood so we can keep the fire going as long as possible. Goodnight.' He held his hand out to her.

She took it and got to her feet. 'I— Thank you.'

'What for?'

'All you've done today, and tonight. The swim, the fish, the fire; that's all been magic.'

He frowned. 'You're not afraid we won't get out of this, are you?'

She shrugged. 'No. What will be, will be.'

He stared down at her intently for a moment then kissed her lightly. 'Sweet dreams, Holly Harding.' He turned away.

Holly woke from a deep, dreamless sleep at two o'clock. There was just enough light from the glowing embers of the fire for her to see her watch, but her movement woke Brett. She was resting in his arms.

'Sorry,' she whispered.

'Doesn't matter,' he mumbled.

It was nowhere near as cold as it had been the two previous nights, even though the fire had died down. The heat of it must be trapped within the shelter, she thought.

She went still as Brett pulled her closer into his arms and his mouth rested on her cheek. Her senses started to stir, started to clamour for his touch, for his kiss. But had he gone back to sleep?

Her lips parted and his mouth covered hers; no, he hadn't. But he hesitated, and Holly suddenly knew she couldn't bear it if he withdrew.

She put her hand on his cheek and arched her body against him, and found herself kissing his strong, tanned throat. He made a husky sound and then his hands moved on her body and she rejoiced inwardly, knowing they were claimed by the same need and desire.

Once again they fumbled with their clothes as best they could, but the rhythm of rapture made light work of it. She put her arms above her head and let his hands travel all the way down her, then gasped as they came back to her breasts.

She lay quietly, quivering in his arms, and allowed him to tantalize her almost unbearably as those fingers sought her most secret places. Then she wound her arms around him and kissed him as if her life depended on it.

He accepted the invitation to claim her completely in a way that brought them both intense and exquisite pleasure.

They were still moving to that pleasure as they slowly came back to earth, then they separated at last but stayed within each other's arms.

'We didn't say a word,' he murmured, and kissed her.

'It didn't seem necessary,' she answered. 'Did it?'

'No, but—' He broke off and lifted a hand to stroke her hair.

'I wanted to say something earlier,' she told him. 'When we were sitting by the fire—I wanted to say I didn't think I could do it.'

He raised his head and frowned down at her. 'Holly...'

'No.' She touched her fingers to his lips. 'Let me finish. I wanted to say I didn't think I could lie on this V-sheet without wanting to be held, kissed and made love to.'

He sat up abruptly.

'Not after everything,' she went on. 'Because you

were incredible—not only in all you did today, but in the way you kept me going.'

'Holly…'

She broke in again. 'I'm just happy to be with you tonight. It—it just seemed to be so fitting and right for the moment, and sometimes I think you need to *live* for the moment. But you don't have to worry about the future.'

He sank back beside her and pulled her into his arms again. 'I'm not worried about it. I'm looking forward to it. When will you marry me?'

CHAPTER EIGHT

HOLLY gasped, then evaded his arms and sat up urgently. 'That's exactly what I *don't* want you to feel you have to do!'

He propped his head on his elbow and looked up at her with a glint in his eyes she couldn't decipher. 'You've had time to work that out?' he queried.

She bit her lip. 'Obviously, otherwise it wouldn't have come to mind.'

He grimaced. 'But why not?' He lifted a hand and touched his fingers to her nipples.

Holly shivered but forced herself to concentrate. 'How could you suddenly want to marry me? I'm sure you don't ask every girl you sleep with to do that.'

He looked briefly amused. 'No. But it's not so sudden. It's been on my mind since you came to Haywire. Look, you asked me how I juggled things earlier: the truth is I'm at a bit of a crossroads. I'm getting tired of all the juggling I have to do. I'm thinking of coming home on a fairly permanent basis. That's what prompted the zoo idea—it's a way I can carry on my work and be here at the same time.'

Holly turned her head. 'Won't that be an awful wrench for you?'

'Sometimes,' he said slowly and pulled her back against him. 'And I'll probably always take off now and then; I won't be able to help myself. But it's time to put down some roots. The thing is—' He paused. 'I've had trouble really coming to grips with the idea—not the zoo, but putting down roots. Because I've had no-one to do it with. But now there's you.'

Holly tried to think. 'I'm—I don't know what to say. Please tell me, are you serious?'

'Deadly serious.'

She stirred against him. 'Brett, could I be—and I ask *this* seriously—a bit of a novelty for you?'

She felt him shrug. 'A wonderful novelty,' he agreed. 'But we also have a lot in common. You fitted into Haywire almost as if you'd been born to it.' He threaded his fingers through hers. 'Could you see yourself living there? Us living there?'

It occurred to Holly that she could. It was a lifestyle that encompassed all the things she loved: far away, exciting, different and still a challenge at times. And with a huge challenge coming up, if he went ahead with his plans for the zoo.

What about her career, though?

She could always freelance, she thought.

She even found herself contemplating a serious journalistic career focusing on the cause that was so dear to his heart and was becoming more and more fascinating to her.

Of course, there was the other factor: she was conscious of his body against hers and the sheer delight, the strength and warmth, it could bring her. Not only that, it was as if she'd found the centre of her universe in him.

She moved abruptly. 'I... Brett, could this not be love but something more—convenient?'

'It didn't feel convenient a little while ago. Did it for you?'

She shivered again as she relived their passion. 'No,' she whispered, shaken to her core.

'And there's this,' he went on very quietly. 'How easy would it be for you to get up and walk away from me?' He smiled ironically. 'Assuming it was possible anyway and we weren't marooned in an oasis in a bloody river-bed.'

She had to smile but it faded swiftly as she battled with how to answer him. 'I...' She stopped as tears suddenly beaded her lashes.

'Don't cry,' he said very quietly. 'It would be hell for me too.'

'The last thing I would want to feel is that you're sorry for me.' She sniffed.

'I'm not. But I do feel as if I want to look out for you.'

'That could be the same thing,' she objected.

'No. It means I care about you.'

Holly sniffed again. 'Do I have to make a decision right now?'

'Why not? We're never going to get as good an opportunity to think clearly.'

She frowned. 'What—how do you mean?'

'No outside influences at all.'

She swallowed in sudden fear. 'What if we don't get rescued or we don't find the station?'

His lips twisted. 'Perhaps the perfect solution. We could do a "me Tarzan, you Jane" routine. No, only joking. We will get rescued.' He pushed aside the layer of cover and took her in his arms. 'Believe me,' he added, and kissed her gently.

Holly felt herself melting within, and when he lifted his head she laid her cheek on his shoulder.

'Is that a yes?' he queried.

She hesitated. 'I don't know yet. I just don't know.'

He grimaced but said, 'Never mind. I'll ask you again every hour on the hour until our rescuers arrive or we arrive somewhere. Go back to sleep.' He looked at his watch over her head. 'We've got a couple of hours before dawn. Comfy?'

'Yes,' she breathed. 'Oh, yes.'

Five minutes later she was fast asleep, although Brett stayed awake for a while and contemplated this turn of events. Surely she wasn't planning to walk away from him now? he theorized.

It wasn't dawn that woke them; they slept well past it, in fact.

It was the sound of a man clearing his throat and saying, 'Excuse me, but were you two in a airplane crash?'

CHAPTER NINE

THEY both shot up. Holly immediately grabbed the blanket and pulled it up as she realized what a state of disarray she was in.

Not only was there a tanned, wiry little man with bowed legs and a big hat looking in on them, but two horses were looking over his shoulders with pricked ears and what appeared to be deep interest.

Even Brett was lost for words.

The man said, 'Don't mean to disturb anything, but if you are from the plane there's a hell of a hue and cry going on over you. Tell you what, I'll just take a little walk while you get—organized.' He wheeled his horses around and walked away.

Holly and Brett turned to each other simultaneously and went into each other's arms.

'I told you we'd get out of this,' he said as he hugged and kissed her.

'You did, you did!' she said ecstatically. 'And I offered my kingdom for a horse—I can't believe this! Where on earth did he come from?'

In the event, their saviour was a boundary rider for the station they were making for, and he was quite happy to wait while they had a swim. Fully clothed and decorous, they changed into their other set of clothing. He even made them a cup of coffee while he waited.

While they drank coffee, he explained how he'd heard the news of the loss of the plane just before setting out from the homestead on a routine inspection, and how he'd promised to keep his eyes open.

'Didn't see nothing, though,' he added. 'But last night I smelt smoke on the breeze and the breeze was coming from this direction, so I thought I'd take a look and see.'

'Is this your camp?' Brett asked.

'Sure is,' the man, Tommy, replied proudly. 'I put the shelter up, and they call it Tommy's Hut.'

'Well, your fishing gear was a lifesaver, Tommy. So was the rest of it. How far are we from the homestead?'

Tommy chewed a stalk of grass reflectively. 'Bout a three-hour ride, considering there's three of us and only two horses. Won't be able to make much time. You and the missus can share a horse.'

'Any family in residence at the homestead?' Brett enquired.

'Nope, just a manager. The place has gone up for sale, actually—family quarrels over money, I hear, so they need to cash it in. But they got radios and phones to get word out you're OK, and to rustle up a plane to get you back to Cairns.'

'Great.'

'Goodbye,' Holly said softly half an hour later when the camp had been tidied up and most of their gear stowed in the shelter.

She was perched in front of Brett on a tall brown horse.

'Talking to me?' he enquired.

'No. I'm farewelling a lovely spot, a place that was a bit of a lifesaver and a bit of a revelation.' She turned for a last look at the lagoon, the water lilies, the birds and the palms. 'An oasis.'

'Yes,' he agreed. 'And more.' But he didn't elaborate.

It was late that afternoon when they flew back into Cairns. A plane similar to the one they'd crashed in had retrieved them from the cattle station, where they'd taken fond farewells of their rescuer and his horses.

They hadn't had any time alone together at all.

What Holly hadn't expected, or even thought about, was that there would be an army of press waiting behind a barrier to greet them. She blinked somewhat dazedly into the flashlights as she stepped down onto the runway in the general-aviation section of the airport. Then she made out a face she knew in the crowd and, with a little cry, she ran forward and into her mother's arms.

A day later, Holly was still at Palm Cove.

Her mother had gone home and Holly had been in two minds as to whether she should go back to Brisbane too. She'd seen little of Brett, who'd been tied up with air-crash investigators and all sorts of authorities. She herself had kept a very low profile.

In fact, after she'd said farewell to her mother, she'd gone for a walk along the beach and felt like pinching herself. Had she dreamt that Brett Wyndham had asked her to marry him? Had she dreamt up a magic oasis that had become a place of even greater pleasure? No, she knew she hadn't dreamt that. She still had some marks on her body to prove it.

But was she a journalist with an interview to complete, or what?

'Remember me?'

She jumped as Brett ranged up alongside her. 'Oh. Hi! Yes, although I was wondering if I'd ever see you again.'

He took her hand and swung her to face him. He wore a loose, blue cotton shirt and khaki shorts; his feet were bare.

'I'm sorry.' He bent his head and kissed her lightly. 'Can you remind me the next time I'm tempted to crash-land a plane that the amount of paperwork involved is just not worth it? And it's not finished yet!'

Holly giggled. 'All right.'

'Incidentally, I sent a helicopter out to the crash site and Tommy's Hut. They brought all our stuff back.'

'Good. Although my mother brought me some clothes.' She looked down at the long floral skirt she wore with a lime T-shirt.

'Would she have brought anything appropriate for a ball?'

Holly stiffened.

'It's tonight,' he said. 'Please come as my partner. And to the wedding tomorrow evening.'

'No. Thank you, but no. I—'

'Holly, sit down. Look, there's a handy palm-tree here.'

'Brett' She tried to pull away, but he wouldn't let

her, and finally they sank down and leant back against the tree.

'You're looking a little dazed,' he said. 'And I can't blame you—'

'Yes, well, if I didn't dream it,' she interrupted, 'please don't ask me to marry you again, because at the moment I am— I don't know if I'm on my head or my heels.'

He stared down at her. 'You didn't dream it,' he said with a glimmer of a smile in his eyes. 'Although I won't ask—not immediately, anyway.' He sobered. 'But this ball is a way for us to be together tonight, because I can't get out of it and I'm having withdrawal symptoms. How about you?'

Holly drew her knees up, put her arms around them and rested her chin on them in a bid to hide the powerful tremor that had run through her.

'Holly?' He said her name very quietly.

She turned her head and laid her cheek on her knees. 'Yes. Yes, I am. I'm missing you.'

'Then?'

She sighed and looked out to sea. 'All right. Do you have to go off somewhere now?'

'Not for at least half an hour,' he said. 'What would you like to do?'

'In half an hour?' She smiled. 'Well, talk, I guess.'

He stretched out his legs as she sat up, and he put his arm around her. 'Did I tell you how fantastic you were?'

Holly made her preparations for the ball in a state of mind that could have been termed 'a quandary'.

On one hand, she wanted to be with Brett rather desperately but, on the other, did she want to be with him under the scrutiny of his family and doubtless a whole host of people?

Not only a host but probably a high-profile host.

It was in line with this thought that she followed an impulse and booked into a beauty parlour when she normally wouldn't have. The impulse was not only prompted by a need to hold her own in an upmarket throng; her nails were broken and ragged and her hair resembled a dry bird's-nest despite having washed it.

So she had a manicure and a deep-conditioning hair treatment, as well as a mini-facial. She came out of the parlour feeling a bit better about the ball and definitely better about her hair and nails.

Next decision was what to wear. For once in her life she was tempted to shop, then she remembered that her mother had brought one of her favourite dresses, one that was the essence of simplicity but which she always felt good in.

It was black, a simple long shift in a clinging silk jersey with a scoop neck and no sleeves. With it she wore a necklace made of many strands of fine black silk threaded with loops and whorls of seed pearls and tiny shells. It was the necklace that really made the dress, and the shoes. They were not strappy sandals but a pair of low court-shoes in silver patent with diagonal fine black stripes. Her mother had even packed the bag that went with the outfit, a small patent-leather purse that matched the shoes.

How had her mother known she would need these items? Holly wondered suddenly. Then she recalled with a smile that Sylvia never went anywhere without being fully prepared for any eventuality. It struck her suddenly—had her mother guessed that there was something between her only daughter and Brett Wyndham?

It probably was not such an unusual conclusion to come to since they'd been forced into each other's company for the last three days, not to mention the days that had gone before, and Sylvia could be pretty intuitive.

She shrugged and started to put on a light make-up.

Brett came to collect her from her room an hour early, and took her breath away in a dinner suit.

'You look lovely,' he said and took her hand.

'So do you,' she answered with a glint of mischief in her deep-blue eyes.

'Lovely?'

'In your own way.' She studied his tall figure in the beautifully tailored black suit. 'Distinguished. Dangerous.'

His eyebrows shot up 'Dangerous?'

'Dangerously attractive. Did I ever tell you that you were rather stunning as a Spanish nobleman?'

'No.' He grinned down at her. 'You were far too busy impersonating a French Holly Golightly and spinning me yarns about asses and camels.'

Holly gurgled with laughter. Somehow the ice was broken between them, which was to say, somehow she felt a lot better about going to this ball with him.

'I'm early,' he said as they walked away from her room, 'Because Sue is having pre-ball drinks in her suite. I'll be able to introduce you to her, as well as

Mark and Aria. Incidentally.' He paused. 'My ex-fiancée will be at the ball, and she could be at Sue's drinks. I don't think I told you she's in charge of all the wedding festivities.'

Holly missed a step.

He stopped beside her. 'She's a friend of Aria's, and she's the best at this kind of thing. It's been over between us for some time now.'

Nine months; it shot through Holly's mind. *It's not that long, is it?*

But she said nothing, although some of her feel-good mood about the ball ebbed a little as she thought of being confronted by Natasha Hewson.

She need not have worried, she soon discovered. Her presence both at Sue's drinks and the ball was that of a celebrity—the girl who'd survived the plane crash with Brett but kept a very low profile since.

Mark and Aria were warmly friendly, so was Sue Murray. And so was Natasha Hewson. She *was* the same redhead Holly had seen dining the night before they'd flown to Haywire.

She was also extremely beautiful, tall and exotic in a bouffant shocking-pink gown.

Holly did have a momentary vision of Natasha and Brett as a couple and thought they would have been absolutely eye-catching. But Natasha appeared to be happily in the tow of a handsome man, and Holly could detect no barely hidden undercurrents between her and Brett. Which was probably why what did eventuate later in the evening came as such a shock to Holly.

In the meantime, she started to enjoy herself.

The resort ballroom faced the beach and the cove

through wide glass windows, so the view was almost unimpeded. Due to a trick of the evening light, you felt as if you could lean across the cove and touch Double Island and its little brother.

Dinner was superb, a celebration of "reef and beef" that included the wonderful seafood found in the waters off the coast. Not only was dinner superb but the company beneath the chandeliers and around the exquisitely set tables was too.

Cooktown orchids decorated the tables, and the women's gowns, in contrast to the men in dark dinner-suits, brought almost every colour of the spectrum to the scene: primrose, topaz, camellia pink, sapphire, violet, oyster, claret and many more. Not only the colour, but there was every style and texture: there were silks, satins, taffetas, there were diaphanous voiles encrusted with sequins that flashed under the lights. There were skin-tight gowns, strapless ones, ruched and frilled ones. As it happened, there was only one plain-black one...

She and Brett dined at a table for eight that included his sister Sue as well as the bridal couple, Mark and Aria. Natasha Hewson was on the other side of the room.

After dinner, Brett invited her to dance.

'You know,' he said as she moved into his arms, 'You've done it again.'

She shot a startled look at him.

'You stole the show as Holly Golightly; you've done it here.'

Holly blinked, then shook her head. 'Oh, no.'

'Believe me, yes.' He pulled her close. 'Do you dance as well as you do everything else, Miss Golightly?'

She lowered her voice a notch. 'Possibly better than I ride, monsieur.'

He laughed and dropped a kiss on her hair.

Neither of them noticed that Natasha Hewson was watching them as Brett swung Holly extravagantly to the music. When they came back together, lightly and expertly, they danced in silence for a few minutes.

They really were well matched, but it wasn't only a rhythmic experience, Holly thought. It was a sensuous one too. She was aware not only of her steps but that she felt slim, vital and willowy.

As his dark gaze ran down her body, a frisson ran through her because she knew he was visualizing her breasts and hips beneath the black material. Nor could she help the same thing happening to her, being aware of his grace and strength beneath his dinner suit.

But as the moment threatened to engulf her in more specific fantasizing, the music came to an end. They came together but he didn't lead her off the floor.

He said instead with his arms loosely around her, no sign of humour in his dark eyes, 'Have you made up your mind, Holly?'

She took a breath. 'I— Brett, this isn't the time or place—'

'All right.' He broke in and took her hand. 'Let's do something about that.' And he led her off the floor, through a set of glass doors, out onto the lawn and behind a row of trees. There was no-one around. 'How about this?'

She took a frustrated little breath. Not only was there no-one for them to see, there was no-one to see them. 'Brett.' She paused, then took hold. 'All right, I've been thinking really seriously about it. It seems to make good sense.'

'There has to be more to it than that now.'

'Well, yes,' she conceded. 'I don't know how reliable that is, though.' She paused, then she said urgently, 'Please, could you give me a little longer? It's a huge step for me…' She trailed off a little desperately.

He said after a long moment, 'Only if I'm allowed to do this?' He took her into his arms.

'Do what?' she breathed.

'Kiss you.'

'Well…'

But he did the deed anyway. As she stood in the protective circle of his arms afterwards, she was trembling with desire and conscious of the need to say *yes, I'll marry you, I'll marry you…*

Some tiny molecule of resistance held her back. Something along the lines of *he always gets his own way* managed to slip above her other feelings. 'Will you?' she whispered. 'Give me a little more time?'

Something she couldn't decipher passed through his eyes, then his lips twisted. 'All right. So long as you stay by my side. The wedding's tomorrow evening—will you come?'

Holly hesitated.

'Or do I have to make all the concessions?' he asked rather dryly.

Holly shook her head. 'I'll come. But in the meantime perhaps we should get back in case people imagine all sorts of things?'

'Such as, I've made off with you and seduced you?'

He looked briefly amused. 'If it wasn't for Mark and Aria that's just what I'd like to do.'

Holly gazed at him and thought for a moment that, despite his dinner suit, he looked dark and pirate-like and quite capable of spiriting her off to a place of seduction. She shivered slightly.

'Cold?' He looked surprised.

'No. But I do need to visit the bathroom. I don't want to look…' She stopped.

'Thoroughly kissed,' he suggested with a definitely pirate-like smile. 'Believe me, it suits you.'

He took her hand and led her back inside.

Holly went to find the facilities. The only person she encountered as she crossed the foyer, other than staff, was Natasha Hewson in her beautiful bouffant shocking-pink gown that should have clashed with her hair but didn't. They stopped, facing each other.

'The bathroom is that a-way,' Natasha said, indicating the direction she'd come from.

'Thank you,' Holly replied, then paused a little helplessly.

'Do you think you'll hold him?' Natasha asked. 'Do you think you'll be the one he'll give up his jungles and his endangered species for? Or were you planning to join him? Don't,' she warned, 'be fooled by *this* Brett Wyndham.'

Holly couldn't help herself. 'What do you mean?'

'Not many of us are immune from that charisma—the good company, the man who makes you tremble, makes you laugh and want to die for him. But he's really a loner. He reminds me of one of the tigers he's trying to save: secretive, thrives on isolation and challenges, clever, dangerous.'

Holly blinked several times. 'Natasha,' she said then, 'Do you have any hopes of getting him back?'

Natasha Hewson shrugged her sleek, bare, beautiful shoulders. 'One day he'll realize that even tigers need a tigress. And that will be *me*.' She blew Holly an insolent kiss as she walked past her.

Fortunately, Holly found herself alone in the bathroom. Fortunately, because as she stared at herself in the mirror she could see how shell shocked she looked as she rinsed her hands.

It was printed in her eyes; it came from the fact that, whether wittingly or not, Natasha had pinpointed the core of her concerns about Brett.

Was he a loner who would never change? He himself had told her he'd probably always take off for the call of the wild. Would she ever get to know what that darkness she sensed in him was about? Would she be a convenient, handy wife who would give him roots, a family perhaps, but never be a soul mate?

She took a painful breath; that wasn't the only cause of her shell shock, intensely disturbing as it was. No, there was also the fact that it wasn't over between Brett and Natasha—it certainly wasn't over for Natasha—and that brought back terrible memories for Holly. Memories of being stalked by a bitter woman pushed almost over the edge.

I can't do it, she thought, and felt suddenly panic-stricken. *I have to get away—but how?*

She finally gathered enough composure to leave the

bathroom to find Brett waiting for her in the foyer. A rather grim, serious-looking Brett.

'Holly,' he said immediately. 'I've just had a call redirected to my phone because they couldn't raise you. Your mother—' he hesitated '—has been taken to hospital. She's going to be all right; it could be an angina attack, but they feel they have it under control. She's asking for you.' He put his arms around her. 'I'm sorry.'

'Oh!' Holly's eyes dilated. 'I've got to get down to her. Oh, it's late—there may not be flights. What will I do?' She stared up at him, agonized.

'Relax. It's all organized?'

'Organized? How?'

'The company jet is here in Cairns on standby. It's picking up some special wedding-guests in Brisbane tomorrow. It was due to fly out early tomorrow morning, but there's no reason for it not to leave now.'

'Thank you,' Holly breathed. 'I don't know how to thank you enough.'

'You don't have to. Look, I'd come with you—'

'No,' she interrupted. 'It's the wedding tomorrow. You need to be here for them.'

'I'll be down the day after. Promise me one thing.' He cupped her face. 'Don't go away from me, Holly Harding.'

She made a gesture to indicate that she wouldn't, but she did.

She wrote him a note while she was winging her way through the dark sky back to Brisbane and her mother. She told him she believed she'd never get to know him well enough to marry him. She told him she'd come to know that Natasha hadn't got over him, and maybe never would, and how that would always make her feel uneasy.

She bit the end of her pen and wondered how to point out that, if things hadn't been resolved completely for Natasha, perhaps they hadn't been for him either. But she decided against it. She asked him to please not seek her out because she wouldn't be changing her mind.

Then she wondered how to end her note so he wouldn't guess that her heart was breaking. Finally she wrote, *thanks for some wonderful experiences, and so long! It's been good to know you…*

She sealed it in an envelope and asked the stewardess to make sure it was delivered to Brett when the plane returned to Cairns.

Then she sat with tears rolling down her cheeks, feeling colder and lonelier than she'd ever felt in her life. How could she have grown so close to him in such a short time? she wondered. It was as if he'd taken centre-stage in her life and she had no idea how to go on with that lynchpin removed.

But it wouldn't have worked, she told herself; it couldn't have worked.

CHAPTER TEN

SEVERAL weeks later, Holly brushed another set of tears from her cheeks and wondered when she'd stop crying whenever she thought of Brett Wyndham.

What brought him to mind this early morning was the fact that she was walking down a beach on North Stradbroke island when she came across a fisherman casting into the surf.

North Stradbroke, along with South Stradbroke and Moreton islands, formed a protective barrier that created Moreton Bay. On the other side of the bay lay the waterside suburbs of Brisbane and the mouth of the Brisbane River. It was a big bay littered with sandbanks and studded with islands, and huge container ships threaded their way through the marked channels to the port of Brisbane. Holly was on the ocean side of North Stradbroke, affectionately known as 'Straddie' to the locals, where the surf pounded the beaches and where there was always salty spray in the air, and the call of seagulls. It was where her mother owned a holiday house, at Point Lookout.

Sylvia had recovered from what had turned out to be a chest infection rather than angina.

Holly had been coming to Point Lookout ever since

she could remember for school holidays, long weekends and annual vacations. Her father had loved it. The house was perched on a hillside with wonderful views of the ocean, Flat Rock and Moreton Island across the narrow South Passage bar.

She'd come over on the vehicle ferry in her car and some mornings she drove back to Dunwich on the bay side of the island. She had a fondness for Dunwich and for a particular coffee shop that served marvellous cakes and pastries, as well as selling fruit and vegetables.

There was also a second-hand shop, an Aladdin's cave of room after room of 'tat,' from jewellery to clothes, china to books and everything in between. Outside there were bird baths, garden gnomes and logs of treated woods. You could lose yourself for hours in it.

She loved wandering through the Dunwich cemetery, beneath huge old tress with the thick turf beneath her feet, reading the inscriptions on the graves that went back to the first settlers to come to Brisbane in the eighteen hundreds. She loved wandering down to the One Mile Anchorage where the passenger ferries came in and all sorts of boats rode at anchor.

Point Lookout might be upmarket these days, but Dunwich was actually an old mining town—although the only evidence of that was the huge trucks that rumbled through the little town laden with mineral sands mined on uninhabited parts of the island.

This overcast, chilly morning she'd decided not to drive across the island but take herself for a long, long walk along the beach. Her thoughts had been preoccupied with how she'd managed to persuade her mother that she needed some time on her own, although Sylvia rang her daily.

Of course, the reason she'd declared a need for peace and privacy and an inspirational setting was so she could write the Brett Wyndham interview.

Although she herself had heard nothing from Brett, to her amazement her editor Glenn had let her know that he'd been in touch and had given the go-ahead for her to write the piece, although he would still have the final say.

Why had he done that? she'd asked herself a hundred times. She could only assume he'd decided not to go back on his word in the interests of her career.

The magazine had given her two weeks' leave after the plane crash and she'd tacked on to that the two weeks' leave she was overdue. She had a week to go before she was due back at work, but she hadn't written a word. A fog seemed to descend on her brain every time she thought about it. She'd spoken to Glenn and explained the difficulty she was having.

'So if you're holding a slot for it, Glenn, I may not be able to reach the deadline—I'm sorry.'

'Holly.' Glenn had said down the line to her. 'You don't walk away from a plane crash and three days of wondering if you're going to survive without some mental repercussions. Don't force it; I'm not holding any slot for it. If it comes, when it comes, we'll see.'

Holly had opened her mouth to ask him if he'd heard from Brett again, but she'd shut it resolutely. Brett Wyndham needed to be a closed book for her now, but she'd clicked her tongue exasperatedly as soon as the thought had crossed her mind. How could he be a closed book when she had this interview to write?

Why hadn't she just admitted to Glenn she couldn't do it? Perhaps she could hand her notes to someone else—but so much of it was still in her head...

On the other hand, why couldn't she grit her teeth and get herself over him?

You did it once before, she reminded herself. *Yes, but I came to hate and despise* that *person,* she answered herself. *I could never hate Brett...*

If she'd had any doubts about that, they were quashed as she walked down the beach and saw a man fishing. She stopped to watch. She saw the tug on his line and the way he jerked the rod back to set the hook in the fish's mouth, just as Brett had shown her, although she'd only had a reel. She watched him wind the line in and saw the silver tailor with a forked tail on the end of it.

She took a distressed breath and turned away as she was transported back to the lagoon in the savannah country, with its reeds, water lilies and all its birds, where she'd swum and caught fish; where she'd sat over a fire; where she and Brett Wyndham had made love without saying a word.

Wave after wave of desolation crashed through her like the surf on the beach as she acknowledged what she'd been trying to deny to herself: that he would always be with her. He would always be on the back roads of her mind. There would always be a part of her that would be cold and lonely without him.

How it had happened to her in such a short time, she still didn't fully understand. She knew there were things about him she didn't know, areas perhaps no-one, no woman, would ever know. But it changed not one whit the fact that she loved him.

She knew that somehow he'd helped her overcome her fear of men and relationships. And she knew something else—that it wasn't her old fears that had affected her so badly that evening at Palm Cove when confronted by Natasha, it was her dreadful sense of loss because she'd come to know that it could never work for them.

She didn't notice that it had started to rain and that the fisherman had packed up and gone home after glancing uncertainly in her direction a couple of times. She ignored the fact that she was soaking wet, so consumed was she by a sea of sadness.

Then, at last, she turned towards the road and started to trudge home.

There was a strange car parked outside the house.

Well, not so strange, she realized as her eyes widened. It was a car she'd actually driven—a silver BMW X5—and as she came to a dead stop Brett got out of it. Brett, looking impossibly tall in charcoal jeans and a black rain-jacket.

They simply stared at each other, then he cleared his throat. 'Holly, you're soaked. Can we go in?'

She came to life, reached into her pocket for her key then stopped. 'Why… Why have you come?'

'I need to talk to you. You didn't think I'd leave it all up in the air like that, did you?'

'I don't think there's any more to say.'

'Yes, there is.' He closed the gap between them and took the key from her. 'And you need to get warm and dry before you get pneumonia. What have you been doing?'

'Walking. Just walking.'

He took her hand and propelled her down the path to the front door, where he fitted the key and opened the door. With gentle pressure on her shoulders, he manoeuvred her inside.

The front door opened straight into an open-plan living, dining and kitchen area. The floors were polished boards, the furnishings comfortable but kept to a minimum. The view was spectacular even on a day like today as showers scudded across the land and seascapes.

'Holly.' He turned her round to face him. 'Holly, go and have a shower. I'll make us a hot drink in the meantime.'

She licked her lips.

He frowned. 'Are you all right?'

She swallowed and made a huge effort to recover from the shell shock of his presence. 'Yes. Fine. Oh.' She looked down at herself. 'I'm dripping! I'll go.' And she fled away from him towards the bedroom end of the house.

He followed her progress with another frown, then turned away and walked into the kitchen area.

Twenty-minutes later Holly reappeared, wearing a silky dressing gown tied at the waist.

She'd hastily dried her hair and, because it looked extremely wild, she'd woven it into a thick, loose plait.

'I hope you don't have anything against plaits,' she said brightly as she reappeared. 'There was *nothing* else to do with it. Ah.' She looked at the steaming mugs on the kitchen counter and inhaled. 'Coffee. Thank you.

Just what I need. Do bring yours into the lounge; we might as well be comfortable.' She took her mug over to an armchair.

He followed suit and sat down opposite. 'You seem to have made a bit of a recovery.'

She grimaced. 'I wasn't expecting you, although I had been thinking of you. I guess I got a bit of a surprise. How did you find me?'

'I persuaded your mother to tell me where you were.'

Holly's lips parted in surprise, which he noted with a faint, dry little smile.

Holly sat back. 'I'm surprised she didn't ring me.'

'You have been out for quite a while,' he pointed out.

Holly sipped some coffee. 'So, why have you come?' she asked quietly. 'You don't have to explain to me why you've gone back to Natasha. I understand.'

'I haven't.'

'Then you should.'

'No.' He put his mug down on a side table. 'And I need to tell you why.'

'Shouldn't you be telling her?'

'I have. Holly, will you just listen to me?' he said with a bleak sort of weariness that was quite uncharacteristic.

'Sorry,' she said on a breath of surprise. 'I'm sorry.'

He beat a little tattoo on the arm of his chair with his fingers. 'This is not generally known outside the family, but my father had a very violent temper.'

Her lips parted. 'I wondered—I mean, I sensed

there was something about your father…' She couldn't go on.

'You were right. I hated him. I hit him once when he and my mother were arguing. She, and I, were usually the ones he took his temper out on. I can't say she was blameless.' He stopped and sighed. 'She should have got out, but it was as if there was this life-long feud going on between them that neither of them could let go of.'

'Why you, though?' Holly whispered. 'I mean you, as opposed to your brother and sister?'

He shrugged. 'Oldest son—maybe he saw me as a threat. I don't know. I do know he never stopped putting me down and I swore that when I took over I would never look back.

'I haven't. Things are in far better shape than they ever were when he was at the helm. But I guess I have to credit him with my interest in animals.'

Holly blinked. 'How so?'

'It was a world I could retreat into when things got impossible—my dogs, my horse and more and more anything on four legs. But the real irony is, much as I hated him, I'm not so unlike him.'

Holly stared at him, struck speechless.

'I also have a temper at times. I also got into a relationship that was—explosive.'

'Natasha,' Holly breathed, her eyes huge.

He nodded and rubbed his jaw. 'Once the first gloss wore off, we argued over the little things, we fought over the big things. We drove each other crazy, but she didn't see it that way. Every grand reunion we had seemed to reassure her that while it might be tempestuous between us—perhaps that even added a little spice to it for her—it was going to endure.

'I don't think she had any idea that I was really alarmed at the way I felt at times. I couldn't tell her. I couldn't put it into words, but I knew I had to get out. Whereas she thought that the fact we were so good in bed was going to compensate for the rest of it. But I could see myself looking down a tunnel at something that closely resembled my parents' marriage.'

'So—so you walked away?'

'Yes, I walked away. I broke it off. I told her— All I told her was that I wasn't cut out for marriage; I was a loner.' He shook his head. 'It was what I preferred to believe rather than admit the truth to myself. I hated the thought that there was any way I could resemble my father. Now, looking back, I can see it was always there. That's why I prided myself on being on the outside in my affairs with women, never deeply, crucially involved. Until Nat managed to break through.'

Holly put a hand to her mouth. 'Have you told her now?'

'Yes.'

'What happened?'

'She didn't believe me at first, but I had some other insights that I tried to explain. Such as—' he paused '—how egos get involved in these matters. How we were two naturally competitive people with a penchant for getting our own way, and we always would be. But that real hole in the gut and the heart, that sense of loss for someone who is not there for you, hadn't touched us. Not that kind of love.'

He got up and walked over to the windows.

Holly stared at his back and the lines of tension in his body.

'She understood that?' she queried huskily.

'I don't know. It made her stop and think. But it clarified things for me. We were never right for each other.' He said it sombrely but intensely.

'How can you be sure?'

He turned at last. 'Because that hole in the gut and heart slammed into me when I got your note.'

Holly's mouth fell open.

'That sense of loss and love almost crippled me, because I knew you were right to go away from me.'

'Brett,' Holly whispered. 'In light of all this, and the fact that you did ask me to marry you…'

'Let me finish,' he broke in. 'I asked you to marry me out of respect, affection, admiration—the way you seemed to fit into my life. But I told myself it wasn't a grand passion. I told myself I was safe from that, *you* were safe from that. Now I know I was wrong.

'I feel more passionate about you than I've ever felt in my life. It wasn't until you left I realized I'd got my grand passions mixed up. But the problem is that whilst how we are—you and I—is different from anything that went before, I keep wondering if my father will come out somehow and that scares me. Scares me far more than it did with Nat.'

She found it hard to speak as her heart beat heavily somewhere up near her throat. 'What—what are you saying?' she asked jaggedly.

His shoulders slumped and he took an uneven breath. Then he said harshly, 'It's best if we say goodbye now, but I had to explain.'

Holly stumbled to her feet with her thoughts flying in all directions. Then, out of nowhere, her epiphany from the plane crash came back to her: her conviction that she should really put her past behind her and live for the future. Plus the belief that had come to her this morning—that this man meant more than anything in the world to her.

She clenched her fists. 'Brett, she *was* the wrong one for you. Just as your parents were probably wrong for each other. But you've dug into your psyche and exposed the roots of it all—that means you *can* cope with it. It also means you could never be a carbon copy of your father. Anyway, you aren't. I know.'

'Holly.' He walked over to her and touched his fingers lightly to her face. 'You're very sweet, but you don't know what can happen—although you should have an inkling of it. I did lose my temper with you once, and frightened you into the bargain.'

Holly looked backwards in her mind's eye and shrugged. 'It wasn't at me, in the first place. It was at some driver who got his licence out of a cornflake packet. And you made amends almost immediately. Right from then you've always protected me,' she said tremulously.

He looked away from her and a nerve beat in his jaw.

'And there's something I do know,' she continued barely audibly. 'I'd trust you with my life, Brett Wyndham. I believe in you with all my heart. You can walk away from me now, but I'll always believe in you, and I'll always carry you in my heart.' Tears slid down her cheeks but she didn't notice them.

He hesitated, then brushed her cheeks with his thumbs. 'It'll go; it'll pass.'

'No, it won't.'

'We haven't known each other that long.'

'That was my line,' she said huskily, and smiled faintly through her tears. 'Yours was, "it's how you get to know people that matters".'

'Holly,' he said on a tortured breath, then swept her into his arms.   He held her closely, not speaking, and little by little she began to feel the terrible tension in him receding. He said, 'I had to warn you.'

'I'm glad you did because I always knew there was something buried really deep within you that I didn't understand. Now we both know we can cope with it together.' She hesitated. Although it was no longer a primary concern for her, she had some sympathy and had to ask the question: 'How is Natasha?'

'She's decided to open a branch of her agency in London. She told me it was over for her, whatever the rights and the wrongs of it were.' He smiled slightly. 'Whatever else, she's not one to wallow.'

Holly rested against him and sniffed.

He tilted her chin so he could look into her eyes. 'Tears? For Nat?' he queried.

Holly considered denying it, but found she couldn't. 'I've held some not altogether complimentary opinions of Natasha Hewson,' she confessed. 'But I'd like to wish her well.'

'Me too,' he murmured. 'You know, you don't have to worry about her—in any other context.'

Holly nodded. 'I've got over that. It was silly to go

through life waiting for it to happen again. Anyway, compared to losing you, it just seemed to fade away.'

'Do you really mean that?'

She looked deep into his eyes and breathed. 'Yes.'

'Sure?' A glint of humour suddenly lurked in his dark eyes and she felt her heart starting to beat faster.

'Yes. Why?'

'You were the one who accused me of being thoroughly bad-minded. Like a leopard,' he added for complete clarification.

'Ah.' She controlled the smile that wanted to curve her lips. 'You were the one who kept making verbal passes at me, not to mention mentally undressing me in the most awkward circumstances!'

'In that respect, I have to warn you I'm unlikely to change my spots—and definitely not in the immediate future,' he told her gravely.

She relented and laughed softly. 'I actually like the sound of that. And there's something I can bring to it that'll be unique for us.'

He raised his eyebrows questioningly.

'A bed.' Her eyes danced. 'A real bed. Not a river bed. No sand, no plastic V-sheet or cardboard bedding, no wild cattle to frighten the life out of me...'

He stopped her quite simply by kissing her. Then he lifted his head and looked into her eyes. 'Since you were the one to bring it up, could you lead me to it before I expire with desire?'

She took his hand. 'Come.'

It was not only a bed, it was a double bed, with a beautiful silk coverlet in the colours of the sea and sky on a clear day. Beneath the cover, the linen was starched and white.

'This is almost too much luxury,' he remarked as he pulled the cover down and laid her on the sheets.

'I know. Despite the sand and everything, I have some wonderful memories of a certain lagoon and Tommy's Hut, as well as—'

'I bought it,' he interrupted.

'As well as— You *what*?' Holly sat up, wide-eyed and incredulous.

'I bought the station.'

'Brett,' she breathed. 'Why?'

'Why do you think?' He looked down at her. 'Because of its memories of us, and you.'

'I— I…' There were tears in her eyes as she slipped her arms around his neck. 'I had no idea you were so romantic.'

'Neither did I. Would you like it as a wedding present?'

'I—I'm speechless. Are you serious?'

He nodded and kissed her. He laid her back against the sheets again and leant over her. 'We can go back on our anniversaries.'

'That would be lovely; thank you,' she whispered. 'Oh, Brett, I don't know what more to say.'

He smiled into her eyes and started to unzip her tracksuit top. 'We don't have to say anything. I seem to recall it working pretty well for us like that.'

'So do I. OK; my lips are sealed…'

But of course they weren't, as he took his time about undressing her. Then, when they were naked and

celebrating each other's bodies, he took her to the edge
several times, only to retreat and sculpt her breasts and
hips with his lips and hands. She had to open her lips, not
only to kiss him and his body, but to tell him that—much
as she'd loved their love-making in Tommy's Hut—the
freedom from clothes and the comfort they were experiencing now were adding a dimension to it that was
mind-blowing; it drew a joyous response from her.

She moved in a way that obviously tantalized him.
She grew bolder and touched him in a way that drew a
growling little response from him.

Desire snaked through her from head to toe, but at
times she felt as light as air and more wonderful than
she'd ever felt in her life.

Then the rhythm changed and what he did to her was
so intense, she was wracked with pleasure and begging
for the only release she wanted.

'Now?' he breathed.

'Please, now,' she gasped, and they moved on together
as one until he brought her to the shuddering peak of
sensation he shared.

She was breathless and speechless as those waves of
climax subsided slowly and they clung to each other.
Finally they were still and he loosened his arms around
her.

She took his hand and put it against her cheek. 'I love
you,' she said huskily.

'I love you,' he answered. 'I always will.'

Later, when they were snuggled up together on the sofa
sipping champagne and watching the afternoon sky

clear up, she said rather ruefully, 'How is my mother? Did you see her or speak to her on the phone?'

'I went to see her. We have one thing in common, your mother and I.'

'What's that?'

'We'd both probably die for you.'

'You don't have to do that, either of you.' Holly wiped a couple of tears from her eyes. 'Just be friends.'

'We will. If you can convince her you're happy. You see, she told me that, if I hurt you again, I'd have her to contend with.'

Holly gasped. 'I didn't know she knew. She never said a word.'

'I actually always admired your mother,' he informed her.

Holly chuckled, then was struck by a thought. 'How did the wedding go?' she asked.

'The wedding was very nice—had I been in the mood to appreciate it.' He looked rueful.

'You...?' She hesitated.

'I felt like cutting my throat.' He played with a strand of her hair. 'But there was a positive note. Sue met someone at the wedding. She's very taken with him, and I get the feeling he could be the right one for her. Uh, talking of weddings...?'

'Yes. Let's,' Holly said contentedly, but hid the sudden sparkle of mischief in her eyes. 'I'm not into balls and barbecues, but I did think perhaps we could hire an island in the South Pacific? We'd need one with accommodation for, say, at least a hundred guests—and we could have fire walkers and luaus—'

'There's not much difference,' he broke in ominously, 'Between a beach barbecue and a luau.'

'Well, there is. Roast suckling-pigs on spits. We could all wear leis and dance those fabulous Polynesian dances to drums.'

'Holly, stop!' he commanded.

But she'd stopped anyway, because she couldn't stop laughing. 'If you could see your face,' she teased. 'Look, I'd be happy to marry you in a mud hut with a herd of giraffe as guests.'

He kissed her. 'You're a witch, you know. But we won't go to those lengths. Something small and simple?'

'Done! When?'

'A month from today?'

She looked at him innocently. 'Why do we have to wait so long?'

'Just in case you want to change your mind.'

'Brett.' All laughter fled. 'I won't,' she promised. 'I won't.'

'Darling,' Sylvia said a month later, 'Are you very sure about this?'

'Mum.' Holly put her bouquet down and pulled her mother to sit down beside her on her bed.

Sylvia looked beautiful in a cornflower-blue silk suit with a cartwheel hat and lilies of the valley pinned to her bodice.

Holly, on the other hand, was all in white, an exquisite lace dress over a taffeta slip with a heart-shaped bodice, long-sleeves and slim skirt.

Her hair was loose, although suggestions had been

made that it should be put up or pulled back—suggestions she declined with a secret little smile in her eyes.

Her full veil fell from a sparkling coronet and her bouquet was made up of six just-unfurled roses, each a different subtle colour from cream through to salmon.

'Mum,' she said again. 'I know you're—I know you've got reservations about Brett. But you did send him to me because, you told me, you thought only I could decide what to do.'

'I know. And I did think that; I still do.' Sylvia heaved a sigh. 'It's just that sometimes people don't change, however much they want to.'

'That was what Brett was afraid of,' Holly said quietly. 'And he may never have, if he didn't have someone who really believed in him as I do. And you know what Dad always used to say?' Holly went on. 'If you really believe in something, you have to go for it, otherwise you're denying that belief.'

'That's true. Well, my darling, I hope you'll be as happy as I was with your father, even though we were like chalk and cheese,' Sylvia said.

They both laughed. 'I will, I will.' Holly kissed her mother.

The wedding was small but very beautiful.

The homestead without walls at Haywire was decorated with greenery and magnificent flowers, all flown in that morning along with the bouquets.

A small altar had been contrived at the library desk, where Holly had made notes on her first visit to Haywire, and a red carpet led to it.

A feast was laid out on tables covered in heirloom damask cloths that Sue had inherited from her grandmother; each table was decorated with orchids in silver pots.

Mark and Aria were there, looking bronzed and exuberant after their prolonged and exotic honeymoon. Sue Murray was there with her new man, looking like a new person.

Glenn Shepherd was there, quite resigned to the fact that he'd lost the Brett Wyndham interview, as well as his travel writer extraordinaire, although the magazine would be the first to break the news of the zoo. He and Holly had also discussed the possibility of her freelancing for the magazine.

Sarah was still in residence, so she was there as well as well as Kane, the station foreman, and some of the staff from the other stations. And there were friends of both Holly and Brett as well as Sylvia, of course.

Even Bella had been invited, and she wore a silver horseshoe attached to her collar.

There was a covey of small planes on the airstrip and they'd stay there for the night.

The ceremony itself was short but moving—mainly, as many noted after the event, because of the palpable emotion between the bride and groom.

They all sat down to the luncheon; the champagne flowed, and it moved on to become a party.

In fact the only ones to leave were Brett and Holly. They took off on their honeymoon to a destination so secret, not even Holly knew where she was going—although she soon had an inkling.

It was a short flight and one that still brought back

some hair-raising memories, despite her having flown it with Brett several times since their plane had crashed. But, by the time they landed at the station Brett had bought for her as a wedding present, she'd long since been in no doubt as to where they were going.

This time they didn't ride the distance between the homestead and Tommy's Hut on a horse, they drove in a powerful, tough four-wheel-drive and reached their destination before sunset.

And there were other changes. Someone had been there before them. Someone had chopped the firewood and piled it up handily. Someone had provided camp chairs and a blow-up mattress. Someone had left an esky with champagne and foodstuffs in it.

All the same, Holly looked around with tears in her eyes, at the water lilies, the birds and the palms. 'I never, never thought I'd come back. Thank you.' She went into his arms.

'Did you like your wedding?' he enquired, holding her close.

'I loved it. How about you?'

'Same. Well,' he said after kissing her thoroughly, with a sudden little wicked glint in his eye, 'how about a swim, then a fish? We have two reels now, and I'm determined to out-fish you.'

Holly lifted her head from his shoulder. 'Oh! We'll see about that!'

But later, much later, when the fire had died down and they were lying in each other's arms, all forms of competitiveness had left them and they were awash with a lovely form of contentment.

'By the way,' he said, 'I thought two nights here, then

a trip to Africa. Or anywhere on earth you'd like to go, Mrs Wyndham.'

Holly breathed happily. 'I wondered when the mud hut and a herd of giraffe were going to make an appearance in my life!'

CHAPTER ELEVEN

Two years later they were sitting on a beach watching the moon rise and holding hands.

But this beach wasn't in the middle of nowhere; it was Palm Cove, and they'd come down from Haywire for a very important appointment.

It was a magic evening. The moon hung in the sky like a silver Christmas bauble. The sea was a slightly darker blue than the sky, apart from its ribbon of reflected moonlight, and you felt as if you could reach out and touch Double Island again.

It had been a magic two years since she'd married Brett Wyndham, Holly thought. Busy, productive and fulfilling.

His zoo was no longer a dream, it was a reality, and she'd taken part in a lot of the planning and the doing of it. Haywire was now very much home to her, although they spent time in Brisbane and they travelled extensively.

Yes, she conceded, there'd been some ups and downs—and she'd decided it was not possible to go through a marriage without them—but if anything they were growing ever closer.

And she felt confident that Brett had got over his fears that he was going down the path his father had trod.

Curiously, or perhaps not so curiously, it was her mother who'd put it into words only a few days ago.

When Holly had rung her full of delighted suspicions, Sylvia had said, 'You were right, darling—about Brett and believing in him.'

'You can tell now?' Holly had queried.

'Of course. Would you be so happy otherwise?'

'No.'

Now on the beach at Palm Cove, after an appointment in Cairns with a gynaecologist that had confirmed her pregnancy, Holly patted her stomach and said a little anxiously, 'Are you really thrilled at this news?'

'Of course.' He released her hand and put his arm round her shoulders. 'Why wouldn't I be? I like kids, and our kids will be special.'

She smiled, but it faded. 'But it means—it does mean we'll be tied down a bit. You see, I've got the feeling I'm going to be a pretty hands-on mother, and that will cut down on travelling and so on.'

'Holly.' Brett put his hands on her shoulders and turned her to face him. 'When will you accept that it's where *you* are that counts for me? Nothing else.'

And he stared down into the deep blue of her eyes with complete concentration in his own.

'Still? I mean, it hasn't worn off a bit or…?'

'Still. Always,' he said very quietly. 'Don't doubt it, Holly.'

She breathed deeply and went into his arms.

˚MILLS & BOON®

Why not subscribe?
Never miss a title and save money too!

Here's what's available to you if you join the
exclusive **Mills & Boon Book Club** today:

✦ *Titles up to a month ahead of the shops*
✦ *Amazing discounts*
✦ *Free P&P*
✦ *Earn Bonus Book points that can be redeemed
   against other titles and gifts*
✦ *Choose from monthly or pre-paid plans*

Still want more?
Well, if you join today we'll even give you
50% OFF your first parcel!

So visit **www.millsandboon.co.uk/subs**
or call **Customer Relations on 020 8288 2888**
to be a part of this exclusive Book Club!

MILLS & BOON®

Why shop at millsandboon.co.uk?

Each year, thousands of romance readers find their perfect read at millsandboon.co.uk. That's because we're passionate about bringing you the very best romantic fiction. Here are some of the advantages of shopping at www.millsandboon.co.uk:

* **Get new books first**—you'll be able to buy your favourite books one month before they hit the shops

* **Get exclusive discounts**—you'll also be able to buy our specially created monthly collections, with up to 50% off the RRP

* **Find your favourite authors**—latest news, interviews and new releases for all your favourite authors and series on our website, plus ideas for what to try next

* **Join in**—once you've bought your favourite books, don't forget to register with us to rate, review and join in the discussions

Visit **www.millsandboon.co.uk**
for all this and more today!